Grass
IN THE
Wind

Grass
IN THE
Wind

SARA SMITH BEATTIE

www.ivyhousebooks.com

PUBLISHED BY IVY HOUSE PUBLISHING GROUP
5122 Bur Oak Circle, Raleigh, North Carolina 27612
United States of America
919-782-0281
www.ivyhousebooks.com

ISBN 1-57197-360-5
Library of Congress Control Number: 2002114521

Printed in the United States of America

For my husband, Chester Sanford Beattie

Special thanks to Elizabeth Dempster
and
My sister, Bethel J. Smith

Contents

Organization of Characters

SLAVEHOLDERS

I. William and Mary Pettigrew
    a. Owners of the slave plantation that became Smyrna
    b. Their slaves: Bessie, Tessa, Nate, Scully, and Ben
    c. Mary manumitted these slaves in 1858
    d. Freed slaves formed Smyrna in 1859

II. Karl and Mary Eliza Au Bignon
    a. Owners of Margrace Plantation
    b. Their slaves: Liza, Enoch, Amos, Noah, and Nicodemus
    c. Plantation overseer, Bernard (Brute) O'Brien

FAMILIES

I. Mary Hutchinson married to William Pettigrew
    a. No children

II. Mary Eliza Calhoun married to Karl Au Bignon
    a. One daughter, Dolly

III. Bessie Pettigrew married to Enoch Au Bignon
    a. Bessie changed their names to Epps
    b. A baby given to them is named Webster

IV. Tessa Pettigrew married Nate Pettigrew
    a. One son, Ozell

V. Tallaquah married Moonstar (black Indians)
    a. Two children, Tai and Skelly
    b. Tallaquah raised Tom Biggers, son of an Indian chief

★Slaves were given the slaveholders' last names for identification purposes.

Noah gave Webster the once-over and remarked, "From the way you be lookin', they did good by you. You need to stick with the folks that brung you up, stuck bread in your mouth, and took care of you when you be sick. They be your real folks. *Ain't no need huntin' for grass in the wind.*"

Prologue

They brought her in leg irons late one summer day, forced her into a shed and locked it. She was a giant of a woman, over six feet tall, muscular, with a huge head and jet-black skin. Her large, angry brown eyes radiated a ferocity that Bessie and Tessa had never witnessed before.

Bessie and Tessa were teenage slave girls belonging to William Pettigrew. The two girls cowered behind the shed until the mean-eyed men went away, then they sneaked over to a tiny window in the shed and looked in. The massive defiant woman was struggling to break free of her chains.

It wasn't long before Pettigrew came back to the shed with his whip, a cat-o-nine-tails. "Get over here," he yelled and snapped the whip in the air. "From now on, you'll answer to Minnie!"

In a proud voice the woman responded, "My name is Smyrna. It was my mother's name, my mother's mother's name, and my name. I will be called Smyrna."

"How dare you defy me!" An angry Pettigrew shouted and raised his whip and brought it down on her back. Smyrna lunged at him and with both fists brought them down so hard on Pettigrew's head that she knocked him unconscious.

Then she dropped to the floor, took the chain key from Pettigrew's pocket, and unlocked the chains that held her legs. She took aim at the door, crashed through it, ran toward the river, and plunged in.

Bessie and Tessa had witnessed this and waited until they thought that Smyrna had made good her escape before going to the house to get help for their master.

Ben and Scully, two men slaves that Pettigrew owned, came and carried him to his house and put him to bed. The next morning with his head bandaged, Pettigrew, with several slavehunters, and his slaves searched for Smyrna, but they never found any trace of her. Pettigrew believed that she had drowned in the river.

Bessie and Tessa knew Smyrna had escaped because they had found her footprints deep in the marsh grass on the other side of the river. Not wanting her to be captured, the girls walked in Smyrna's footprints and disguised them as their own.

Smyrna

So begins the story of how the free black settlement of Smyrna, deep in the rolling hills of North Carolina near the Virginia border, came into existence, taking its name from its eponymous heroine. The story recounts the origins of a free black settlement and describes the lives of the freed blacks who made Smyrna their community, their Canaan, and ultimately focuses on Webster Two-Hawks, his mysterious birth, his coming of age, and his attempt to seek out his true racial heritage.

Smyrna lay in a gentle valley in the shadow of the Bushy Mountains. This string of low-lying, tree-covered mountains stretched down the valley to the mouth of the Nebo River. The river was called "Nebo" after a long-dead Peedee Indian chief whose people still lived in the hills above the valley. The Nebo, lazy and muddy, snaked its way through the valley, then meandered northwest, cutting through some high, red bluffs dotted with caves caused by erosion. The river narrowed as it flowed through the bluffs where a wooden train trestle spanned it to an isolated island called Scroggs, where a mental asylum was built.

Beyond these bluffs the Nebo forked. One branch flowed south and emptied its water into the Big Tom Tom River. The smaller branch flowed east around the town of Cowpens. Cowpens was the county seat and the largest town in the valley. It was also the railhead of the Western North Carolina and the Southern Virginia railroad lines.

꙳

But Smyrna had not always been a free settlement. It had once been a slave plantation owned by William Pettigrew, five miles north of Cowpens.

Will Pettigrew was one of four slaveholders in the Nebo Valley. After his first wife had died, he decided to marry again. His cousin, Efe, who lived in Charlton, the village that nestled high up in the Bushy Mountains, told Will about the new schoolteacher in the village. Her name was Mary Hutchinson.

In 1853, Mary's mother and father, who were missionaries, settled in Charlton. There, they established a church and a one-room school for poor white children who lived in the mountains. Mary, along with her mother, taught at the school.

Using his cousin Efe's information, Will sought out the new school-teacher, and in spite of Mary's plain looks and shyness, he was taken by her—perhaps because he was a virile man and needed a woman in his bed at night. After a brief courtship, he asked Mary to marry him.

Reverend Hutchinson, Mary's father, was against the marriage. Will was a slaveholder and Hutchinson was a man of the cloth. He told Will that slavery was wrong in the eyes of God, so if he wanted to marry his daughter he'd have to manumit his slaves. Will refused.

Against her father's advice and her mother's pleadings, Mary accepted Will's offer of marriage, because she feared she'd not get a husband. She believed herself to be unattractive, and she didn't want to be a spinster. Even though Will was years older than Mary, she was happy to have a husband.

On the first day of July 1855, Mary became Pettigrew's wife and traveled with him to his plantation in the Nebo Valley.

Will's house was a plain white two-story building with a large front porch. It sat atop a hill that overlooked the Nebo River. Wildflowers grew in the front yard, and in back of the house stood two stately maple trees with a clothesline stretched between them. To the right of the clothesline was the smokehouse where meats from hogs, sheep, and cattle were kept. A large vegetable garden extended back from the smokehouse to a fruit orchard of peaches, apples, and pear trees. Beyond the orchard were Will's farmlands. Farther away from the house was an oversized barn and a chicken shed. Down closer to the river were two crude log cabins where the slaves lived; the two women in one and the three men in the other.

Although Will's home was not at all what Mary had expected, a large mansion like other slaveholders in the valley, she quickly settled in at the plantation.

A week after her marriage, Mary told Will that she wanted to start a school for the children who lived in the valley. She was surprised at his answer.

"I want a wife, not a schoolteacher," was Will's gruff reply.

Will Pettigrew owned five slaves. The three men were named Nate, Scully, and Ben, and the two teenage girls were Bessie and Tessa. Although the slaves worked hard in his fields, Will worked alongside them. He refused to hire an overseer, saying overseers were lazy and he'd not waste his money on them.

Because Will was always working, he and Mary seldom had company. Only after they had attended church services did Mary get to see and speak with other women.

One Sunday after church, the minister's wife invited Mary to join her Women's Christian Club. The club met once a month in Cowpens, and the minister's wife believed that Mary, having been a schoolteacher, had much to offer the group. Mary was so excited because she would have an opportunity to meet and socialize with other women in the valley. When she told Will about the invitation, he said he'd not have his wife socializing with a bunch of sharp-tongued women.

Despairing and feeling lonely, Mary was seen talking to herself, and soon the women of the valley began whispering that Mary was cursed with "the" sickness. This sickness meant she was mentally unsound.

But Mary wasn't mentally unsound; she was suffering from a deep depression brought on by loneliness and isolation because Will was cold, demanding, and unresponsive to her needs.

Mary had observed the laughing and talking of Bessie and Tessa as they worked together doing chores and decided to join in their conversation and to help them with their work.

At first the girls tried to discourage her. "Miz Mary," Bessie said. "You ain't got to help me and Tessa. We can do this little ole work."

"But I want to," Mary answered.

After awhile the girls just accepted her presence, and soon the three were laughing and talking as they worked together.

Mary made sure that Will never saw her helping with the work. She knew he'd forbid her to fraternize with his slaves. So, whenever he was around, she kept her distance from the girls.

Mary soon grew fond of Bessie and Tessa and secretly began teaching them reading and writing. Each day after all the work was done, she and the girls would slip upstairs to her bedroom for lessons. Mary would go to her closet, open a large brown box, and take out books, paper, and pencils that she had brought with her. Then with the girls sitting on the floor by the two bedroom windows, the lessons would begin.

Teaching energized Mary because it engaged her mind. There had been times after her marriage that she thought marrying Will had been a terrible mistake. He seldom talked with her, and when she tried at night to hold a conversation he'd just sit silently in his big, leather chair and smoke his pipe. During these times, Mary believed that Will only wanted her to share his bed at night.

June in the Nebo Valley was the fruit canning season. Each day, Bessie and Tessa picked large baskets of fruit from the orchard and brought them back to the kitchen where they peeled, sliced, and cut peaches, apples, and pears into chunks. Then they'd put the fruit into pots with sugar and water and set the pots boiling on an iron stove. After the fruit had cooled, they filled glass jar after jar.

The heat from those hot summer days in the valley and the stove's fire made it almost unbearable in the kitchen, and the girls would be soaked with sweat down to their waists.

In early August the canning ritual slowly came to an end. On the last day of the canning, Mary decided to give the girls and herself a reward. She'd teach a reading lesson.

Upstairs in Mary's bedroom, Bessie and Tessa plunked down on the floor near the open windows to take advantage of an occasional breeze. Mary went to get the reading books and dictionaries. She kept all of her teaching materials in a brown box inside her closet on the floor.

That August day was so hot that the earth seemed to be on fire. Will, who had been riding through his wheat fields to see if the wheat was ripe enough to harvest, headed home for a drink of his cool water that he kept in his root cellar.

The root cellar's door was right under Mary's bedroom windows, and as Will yanked opened the cellar door he heard Bessie and Tessa giggling. The sound came from Mary's bedroom. Will thought, What were they doing up there in his bedroom? He had spoken several times to Mary about being too easy with them. Well, they had now overstepped their bounds and needed to be taken in hand.

With his riding whip in hand, Will rushed into the house, up the stairs, and burst into the bedroom. His eyes flashing with anger, he shouted at the girls, "What the hell are you doing in here?"

The surprised girls dropped the dictionary that they were using and cowered in the corner near the bed. Then Will saw a stack of books on the floor and turned to see Mary closing her closet door. Angrily, he snatched up the books from the floor, and hurled them out the window. Then he stormed over to Mary, shoved her aside, opened the closet door, and grabbed up her precious box of teaching materials.

Upon seeing him with her materials, Mary took hold of his arm and began pleading, "Oh Will, please don't take my box!"

Will jerked free of her and yelled to the cowering girls, "Git out to the garden and pick them ripe peas!"

As the two girls ran out the bedroom door and down the stairs, they heard Will shout, "I've a mind to take my whip to you, woman! I warned you before about teaching. You disobeyed me!"

After that incident, Mary never again taught the girls, nor did she join in their conversations again. She fell into a deep depression because Will had destroyed all of her teaching materials. She sat for hours in her bedroom with the shades pulled down. In vain, Bessie had tried to coax Mary from the bedroom but to no avail, and it wasn't until one September morning that she realized the depths of Mary's despair. Bessie had gone to the smokehouse to get some meat to cook for dinner. When she opened the door, a flood of sunlight lit up the dark, dank, windowless smokehouse. What she saw caused her great fear.

There in a corner was Mary sitting in the sawdust on the floor, clad in her nightgown. Tears were streaming down her face. She had looped a rope over her head and around her neck.

Bessie flung down her pan and rushed to her. On her knees, she cried anxiously, "Miz Mary, what you be doin'?"

When the terrified Bessie carefully slipped the rope from around Mary's neck, she collapsed into Bessie's arms, sobbing uncontrollably.

"There, there," Bessie said tenderly, cradling Mary's frail body. "You goin' be fine, Miz Mary. You goin' be just fine."

With her apron, Bessie dried Mary's eyes and began humming a tune that Mary had taught her and Tessa. They often sang the tune with Mary before she taught each lesson, to remind them to strive for God's Kingdom.

> "I got shoes, you got shoes
> All God's chillun got shoes;
> When I get to Heaven, gonna put on my shoes;
> I'm gonna walk all over God's Heaven,
> Heaven, Heaven;
> Ever'body's talking 'bout Heaven
> I'm a-goin' to Heaven;
> Heaven, Heaven;
> I'm gonna walk all over God's Heaven."

The singing calmed Mary, but Bessie knew by the worried look on Mary's face that she didn't want Will to find out what she had tried to do.

"Tell you what, Miz Mary," Bessie whispered softly. "You and me goin' keep this our secret. I ain't even goin' tell Tessa."

Bessie had been gone well over an hour when Tessa went looking for her. It was getting near noontime, and Will Pettigrew would be coming home for his noontime meal. He'd not tolerate his food being late.

Tessa opened the door of the rank-smelling smokehouse and found Bessie sitting on the smokehouse floor with Mary in her arms.

Upon seeing the two women together, Tessa asked suspiciously. "What you two be doin'?"

"Help me git Miz Mary up to her bed," Bessie quickly replied. "She be sick."

"We best git that meat on the stove," Tessa replied. "Mr. Will be coming soon, and you know what he'll do if he ain't got no hot dinner waiting."

"Never mind Mr. Will," Bessie shot back. "Miz Mary need lookin' after."

The two girls helped the limp Mary upstairs to her bedroom, took off her clothes, and put her to bed.

They had just finished cooking the noonday dinner when Will came home, and before he sat down to eat, Bessie told him about Mary. "Miz Mary don't feel good, so Tessa and me put her in her bed."

Bessie waited for Will to ask her some questions about Mary, but he didn't. He just sat down at the table and ate his dinner in silence. When he had finished eating, he left the house and went back to the field without going upstairs to see his wife.

It took weeks of patience and tender care from Bessie and Tessa before Mary recovered from her deep depression. She never did explain to Bessie why she tried to kill herself.

Israel Coffin owned a large slave plantation far up the Nebo Valley. But as Israel grew older, he began preaching to the people of the valley that he was God's prophet and God had bid him to warn the people to free the slaves or God would destroy the land.

Coffin's sons tried to stop him from preaching around the countryside, but Israel refused to listen to them. They perceived that their father had become mentally deranged and committed him to the mental asylum on Scroggs Island.

Coffin made good his escape from the asylum one August morning by hiding in a fishing boat. A fisherman had brought fresh fish to sell to the hospital. By chance a hospital attendant had taken Coffin for a walk on the hospital's grounds the morning that the fisherman came.

The fisherman asked Coffin's attendant if he'd show him where the kitchen was. The attendant left Israel and walked with the fisherman around the side of the hospital and pointed out the building where the kitchen was located.

As soon as the attendant was out of sight, Coffin, wearing pajamas and a heavy, black coat draped over his shoulders, ran through the shrubbery down toward the river with his Bible in hand. Upon seeing the fisherman's boat tied up at the hospital's dock, he leaped onto it and crawled under a pile of rope and burlap fish bags.

When the attendant came back, Coffin was gone.

"Israel! Israel!" he called as he searched for him. Since Coffin had run away from the attendant many times, the attendant was not alarmed and was confident he'd find him because he knew all of Coffin's hiding places on the hospital grounds.

While the attendant was searching for Israel, the fisherman came back to his boat and sailed down the river to Cowpens where he docked.

Israel lay under the pile of hot stinking sacks until it was dark, then he sneaked off the boat. The first building up from the dock was the courthouse. Being weary and tired, he fell asleep under a tulip tree that stood near the courthouse steps.

The next morning, Coffin was awakened when he heard voices. Two men were talking as they walked toward the courthouse. Coffin sprang up from his sleep, grabbed his Bible, and climbed up the stone steps to the courthouse door and blocked the men's way.

"Repent! Repent!" he screamed at them.

"Repent, you sinners, you sons of iniquity!"

Coffin pointed a shaking finger at the two men and screamed even louder, "Repent! Do God's bidding or burn in hell's fire!"

The men were startled at the strange-looking man, smelling of fish, who was wearing a heavy black coat in the hot August weather. He was six feet tall, gaunt, with a long white beard and gray matted hair that hung to his stooped shoulders. A sleeve was missing from his coat and underneath it he wore striped pajamas. His shoes were on the wrong feet and the shoelaces were untied, hanging down the sides of his shoes.

The Bible he held in his trembling hands had torn pages dangling out its sides and part of the black cover had been ripped off.

"Repent! Repent!" Coffin yelled again at the men in a bombastic voice. "God's wrath is coming to destroy you wicked people!"

He then flung off the heavy black coat and screamed at the men. "Slavery is against God's will!"

Then he began chanting and waving his arms about. "There will be fire in the mountains! In the valleys! The ground will be soaked with blood! There will be wails and lamentations in the land! Death everywhere!"

With sweeping gestures of his ragged Bible and his wild eyes flashing as sweat rolled down his wrinkled brow, Coffin leaned toward the two men who had stopped in their tracks. A crowd of people had now gathered to find out what was going on.

"I am God's prophet!" Coffin yelled and thumped on his Bible. "He sent me to warn you before it's too late!"

Then Coffin became enraged. "Fields burning! Homes will go up in fire! Men dying! Obey God! Free the slaves or burn in hell! Free the slaves! Free the slaves! Free the slaves!"

Among the crowd who had stopped to listen were Will and Mary Pettigrew. Will had brought Mary with him that morning for the first time since her illness. He had come to Cowpens to talk with his lawyer, Jordan Graham, about buying another slave.

Coffin ranted on. "Obey God!" Then his ragged Bible fell from his hands when he raised both arms skyward. It rolled down the steps and into the crowd at Mary's feet.

With eyes closed and arms raised to the heavens, Israel began singing off-key.

"Onward Christian Soldiers marching on to war!

With the cross of Jesus, going on before!"

Some people in the crowd began laughing when they heard his creaking voice.

Israel stopped singing. "Laugh if you will, heathens! They laughed at Noah and the apostle Paul." He pointed a gnarled finger at one man. "You won't be laughing when the hell comes!"

Mary stooped down and picked up the battered Bible, and she tugged at Will's coat sleeve, whispering in an agitated voice. "You must stop the people from laughing at God's prophet!"

"Graham's waiting for me," Will said, and took the Bible from Mary's hands and threw it on the ground. Then he clasped Mary's arm and led her away from the crowd.

Mary protested and tried to pick up the Bible, but Will's grip was too strong for her to pull away from him.

Days after Mary had heard Coffin's words, she kept remembering them. She just knew that something dreadful was going to happen if the slaves were not freed. Each day, Mary became more and more agitated and then depressed because of the feelings of dread overcoming her. It was as if she were failing into a deep, black, bottomless pit, and she could neither eat nor sleep at night.

Will had noticed that Mary was not eating. He had also noticed the black circles around her sad eyes and asked her what was wrong with her. At first, Mary refused to say what was bothering her because she was afraid of angering him. She still remembered how angry he had become when she suggested that he manumit Bessie and Tessa.

But by November, Mary's fears were looming up inside her like big black thunderclouds, and her pain became so great that she ventured to speak to Will about freeing his slaves.

Mary broached the subject after supper one night. Will had settled comfortably in his big leather chair smoking his pipe, and she sat in a chair across from him with her knitting basket.

"Whatever happened to the prophet?" Mary asked softly.

"Who?" Will asked, leaning toward her because he had become hard of hearing.

"The prophet," Mary repeated. Only this time she spoke louder.

Will frowned. "You mean that ole fool who was ranting and raving on the courthouse steps?"

Mary nodded her head.

"The sheriff hauled him off back to the asylum where he belongs, the ole fool." He puffed on his pipe some more, then spoke sternly to Mary. "He's not a prophet."

Mary knitted on in silence before replying, "God often chooses the least among his people to do his bidding. Maybe we ought to heed the prophet's word."

Will jerked his pipe from his mouth and roared at Mary. "Turn my slaves loose? Never!" He glared at her for a moment, then said, "You're getting sick again!"

Without looking up from her knitting, Mary answered. "We must obey God, Will, or something terrible will happen to us."

Will jumped up from his chair and glared down at Mary. Breathing hard, he replied in a threatening voice, "If you ever speak of that ole fool again, I'll put you where he is! Now, go upstairs to bed."

Mary quietly tucked her knitting needles into the ball of yarn, put the basket onto a table, and left the room. Will then settled back down into his big leather chair and continued smoking.

In December of that year, Will went duck hunting down by the Nebo River. There, he slipped and fell into the icy water trying to retrieve a duck he had shot. Soaked to his skin and chilled to his bones, he struggled for several hours to get home.

When he did reach his home, Mary quickly helped him get out of his wet clothes and into his bed. She piled on two heavy quilts because Will couldn't stop shaking. "I'll fix you one of my hot drinks," Mary told him after he was tucked in.

"No," Will said weakly. He didn't trust Mary's concoction of green pine needles and dried bunchgrass roots that she often made a tea from and drank. He believed the stuff to be dangerous and had caused her sickness.

"I'll be fine as soon as I'm warmed up," Will told Mary. "Just let me sleep."

During the night, Will's chills grew worse, and he began coughing violently and having choking spasms. Mary decided he needed some of her remedy.

She quickly went down to the slave quarters and called Bessie and Tessa to come to the house. By the time the girls reached the house, Mary had already lit a fire in the stove, crushed the weeds into the big iron kettle, and set it on the stove to boil. It didn't take long for the foul-smelling weeds to boil. Mary then poured some of the liquid into a cup and went upstairs to Will's bed.

Will refused to drink Mary's tea, and when she tried to force the drink into him he'd spit it out. After several tries, Mary gave up and had Bessie and Tessa keep putting hot, damp towels onto Will's forehead to try and break his fever.

By morning, Will had become delirious, and Mary sent Nate to Cowpens for Dr. Whisanant. An hour passed before Nate returned with the doctor. After the doctor had examined Will, he told Mary that Will had pneumonia. Two days later, Will died.

Mary was convinced that Will's death was caused by him not heeding Coffin's warning. For disobeying Him, God has struck Will down.

A week after Will's burial, a grieving Mary sent for Jordan Graham, Will's lawyer. As she sat on a sofa between her mother and father, she told Graham that she had decided to manumit her slaves.

Puzzled by Mary's decision, Graham asked, "Why?"

"It is the will of God."

"What will you do with all this land if you don't have slaves to work it?" Graham asked.

"My land will be used to form a community for freed slaves," Mary replied. "They can come here, build their homes, have their families, and farm the land."

"Mrs. Pettigrew," Graham warned, "I strongly advise you against this. Your plantation is one of the finest in the valley. Why not sell it?"

With her hands folded across her lap and a look of piety, Mary replied emphatically, "I must obey God."

"But Mrs. Pettigrew," Graham insisted, "Will and I were boys together, and I knew Lillie, his first wife. Why, he'd turn over in his grave if he knew you planned to free his slaves and use his land for a free slave community."

Mary's reply was swift. "Mr. Graham, Will is in his grave because he did not obey God. Now, if you cannot not do as I ask, I will hire another lawyer to do so."

Holding his daughter's hand firmly, Reverend Hutchinson reiterated Mary's decision. "You must do as my daughter tells you. Her slaves must be given their freedom!"

Graham realized that no amount of talking would dissuade Mary from her decision. So, he went back to his office in Cowpens and drew up the papers that manumitted Bessie and Tessa, Nate, Scully, and Ben.

When Graham returned with the papers of manumission several days later, Mary's father, Reverend Hutchinson, asked Bessie, Tessa, Ben, Scully, and Nate to come to the house.

There, on a Sunday morning, December 14, 1858, five years after Mary Hutchinson had married Will Pettigrew, her father, Reverend Hutchinson, read to Bessie, Tessa, Ben, Scully, and Nate their documents of manumission.

When Reverend Hutchinson had finished reading, he prayed a prayer of thanksgiving. Then he said, "You're now free men and women!

He told them that, if they chose, they could continue to live there, because Mary's plantation would be used as a free black community open to all free men and women.

Upon getting their freedom, the first thing the five former slaves did was to name their settlement. They called it Smyrna, in honor of the woman who had refused to be a slave.

Margrace

Margrace was the largest and richest slave plantation in the Nebo Valley. It had been passed down through the Calhoun family for two generations, and it now belonged to a third-generation Calhoun, Mary Eliza. Margrace had been named for the first owner's two daughters, Margaret and Grace.

Mary Eliza was married to Karl Au Bignon, a crude, foul-mouthed man with a vicious temper. Not only was he cruel and coarse, but he also was known for his underhanded dealings.

Karl came up the hard way, working with his father, a Frenchman, who came to the Nebo Valley from South Carolina looking for cheap land. All his father could afford to buy was ten acres of unwanted scrubland that bordered on the rich farmland of the Margrace Plantation. There, he eked out a living with his wife and son. When Karl was nine, his mother died from poverty and hard work, and fifteen years later his father died too. Karl was now twenty-four years old and alone.

In the fall of 1854, Karl Au Bignon by chance met Mary Eliza Calhoun, daughter of Richard Calhoun, owner of Margrace Plantation. Mary Eliza had a withered leg caused by a paralysis when she was an infant, and she was six before she learned to walk. When she did, she limped.

Most of Mary Eliza's years had been spent indoors because she was frail and sickly. Her skin had taken on a pallid look, and her dark, brown hair was limp and hung lifeless down to her shoulders. Although Mary Eliza was not a beauty, she was kind and gentle.

By eighteen, Mary Eliza had never dated because her mother and father were overprotective and viewed all young suitors with distrust. "The men will just be after your money," they told her.

Because she couldn't have a beau like the other girls in the valley, Mary Eliza had become unhappy. To cheer her up, Liza, her slave nanny, taught her how to drive a horse and buggy, and the two often went for long rides on the dirt roads that encircled the large plantation.

In early October, the valley always appeared like a fantasy land. From the bottomlands to the tops of the Bushy Mountains, there was a confusion of leaf colors: flaming reds, golden yellows, and bright orange. This was the time of year that Mary Eliza liked best and when she was happiest.

One October morning, Mary Eliza wanted to go riding in the woods. Liza told her to wait until after she had served her mother and father breakfast. The Calhouns were late risers and often slept until noon. Mary Eliza didn't want to wait that long because the woods were quieter and prettier in the early morning.

She knew her parents would forbid her to drive the horse and buggy alone, so before they had gotten out of bed, she slipped out of the house, went to the barn, and hitched up her horse to the buggy. She knew the men who worked on the plantation could not stop her because they had gone to work in the fields before sunrise to start the haying.

After Mary Eliza had hitched her horse to the buggy, she led it quietly out of the barn and down to the road. Then she climbed into the buggy and drove off onto a seldom-used dirt road.

As she neared a reed pond on the plantation, there was a loud gunshot. A large flock of gray geese that were swimming on the pond took flight, squawking and flapping their wings. Frightened by the noise, the horse suddenly began racing wildly down the bumpy road.

Mary Eliza was flung back onto the buggy's seat, and the reins were jerked out of her hands and went flopping and snapping about the horse's rump. She panicked. She had always relied upon Liza, but Liza wasn't there and she was all alone with a runaway animal.

Karl Au Bignon, who was secretly hunting on Margrace property, had fired at the geese from some nearby bushes on the roadside and was getting ready to retrieve a dead goose that he had shot.

Suddenly, he heard screams and the pounding of hooves. He stood up from his crouched position and saw a runaway horse racing toward the clump of bushes where he was hiding, He felt he'd surely be killed.

Minutes before the beast crashed into Karl, he leaped out of the way, then jumped astride the horse's back and, grabbing hold of its bridle, yanked back hard. The panic-stricken horse reared up onto its hind legs, causing a cloud of dust and dead leaves.

Foaming at the mouth, the snorting animal was stopped. The buggy went swerving into a ditch and landed on its side, as the back wheels twirled and spun round and around.

Karl quickly dismounted and rushed over to see if anyone was hurt inside the buggy. He looked in and saw Mary Eliza screaming and crying hysterically. She was slammed against one side of the buggy's seat, her hair and clothes in disarray.

"It's all right now, Miss," Karl said, trying to calm the young girl. "I stopped the rascal."

It took a few minutes before Mary Eliza could calm herself. Then she wiped her eyes with a portion of her dress and looked at the stranger. "I believe you saved my life, Mr. . . . ."

"Au Bignon, ma'am. Karl Au Bignon."

When Mary Eliza saw the man looking down at her withered leg, she quickly pulled her dress down to cover it. Although the man's clothes were dirty, his blonde hair unkempt, and he smelled musty, she didn't want him to see her affliction.

"I'm ever so grateful, Mr. Au Bignon," she said, righting herself on the buggy seat. With her hand she smoothed down her hair.

Karl gazed at her intensely for a moment, then asked, "Ain't you Mr. Calhoun's daughter?"

Mary Eliza smiled weakly and nodded her head.

"I'd better drive you home." Karl promptly announced.

Before Mary Eliza could refuse him, he righted the buggy and climbed in. She slid over on the seat as he took up the reins and snapped them hard. The horse trotted off up the dirt road back toward the Calhoun house.

The Calhouns lived in an elegant white mansion. It could be seen for miles, because of its six big, red-brick chimneys crowned with black chimney pots. The house had a wide veranda where wisteria vines had climbed onto the lace railing that wrapped around the house from the front door to the kitchen door. Several French windows opened out to the veranda. Two huge, white, sculptured columns that held up a balcony on the second floor were on each side of a massive oak door that was the house's entrance.

Inside the house, the floors were made of pecan wood, and a wide stairway curved gracefully up to the second-floor bedrooms and to a family sitting room. In the family sitting room, two more French windows reaching from floor to ceiling opened onto a balcony directly above the veranda below. These windows served as a breezeway on hot summer nights.

Downstairs, the parlor extended along a wall to the beautifully satin-draped French windows, where a manicured lawn with dogwoods and crepe myrtle trees surrounded by large beds of flowers and ferns were seen. Oak-paneled doors opened from the parlor into a large dining room where a crystal chandelier hung directly over a mahogany table that seated twelve. The walls and ceiling of the dining room were painted with a mural of a gentle landscape of streams, waterfowl, and grazing animals.

The mansion had twenty rooms where four house slaves worked. Two women cooked, cleaned, and did the washing and ironing. Liza was a nanny to Mary Eliza. A male slave called Amos was the groundskeeper, and Calhoun's five other male slaves labored in his fields, planting, cultivating, and harvesting his crops.

When Karl and Mary Eliza reached the mansion, he drove the buggy up the graveled driveway and stopped the horse at the front door.

Mary Eliza leaned her head out the buggy window and called, "Liza!"

In a few minutes, a tall black woman wearing a white apron came out of the house.

When she saw the buggy parked in front of the house, she went to it.

"Where you been, child?" she asked as she looked inside the buggy. Then she saw Karl sitting there holding onto the reins. "Who is this man?"

"Liza, this is Mr. Karl Au Bignon," Mary Eliza said proudly. "He drove me home."

"I kin see that," Liza frowned. "Well, let me hep you out so I kin take the horse to the barn."

Before Liza could get to Mary Eliza, Karl jumped out of the buggy and rushed around to where Mary Eliza sat. He nudged Liza aside with an elbow and said, "You take care of the horse. I'll help Miss Calhoun out of the buggy."

"Well, I be," Liza said aloud as she stood watching disapprovingly the brazen man with a musty odor helping Mary Eliza up the steps to the front door.

"Come in," Mary Eliza told Karl. "I want you to meet Mama and Poppa." And she led the way into the parlor and pointed toward a long, pink, velvet sofa in front of three French windows. "You can sit there. I'll go get Mama and Poppa."

In spite of the fact that Mary Eliza was wearing a long dress, she struggled not to walk lopsided. She didn't want the young man to notice her limp.

In a few minutes, Mary Eliza returned with a middle-aged woman wearing a pink dress with a wide, white collar. Her gray hair was pulled back and twisted in a tight ball that made her face look pinched and drawn. Following the woman was a short, overweight, white-haired man with a bulbous nose and beady eyes.

Without a greeting, the woman sat down on a flowered winged-back chair and the man sat in another. Both chairs faced the velvet sofa where Karl was sitting.

Standing behind a white satin-covered chair, Mary Eliza said dramatically, "Mama, Poppa, this is Karl Au Bignon. He saved my life this morning!"

Mrs. Calhoun clutched at her heart, revealing a large diamond ring on her middle finger. "He what?" she gasped.

"Saved my life!"

Sounding annoyed, Mr. Calhoun asked, "Now, why was he saving your life, Mary Eliza?"

"The horse starting running away, Poppa, and Karl stopped him!"

"Oh, dear," Mrs. Calhoun said. "Where was Liza?"

"I went by myself," Mary Eliza said proudly. "I was going along fine until someone shot off a gun. That frightened my horse."

Calhoun's face turned a beet red. "It was that poacher again shooting my birds! If I ever catch him shooting on my land, I'll make it too hot for him! I won't have worthless folks stealing from me!"

"Mary Eliza," her mother reprimanded, "how many times have I told you not to go riding without Liza? I shudder to think what could have happened to you!"

Calhoun reached over and patted his wife's hand. "Now, now, stop your fretting, Mrs. Calhoun. Mary Eliza knows how to handle a horse."

Calhoun had immediately taken a dim view of the rough and crude-looking man in his house and wanted the filthy rascal to be on his way. Struggling mightily, he pulled himself up from his chair and waddled toward the entrance's door.

Mrs. Calhoun started to speak but was interrupted by husband.

"Now Mrs. Calhoun, I'll do the talking," he said and turned his attention to Karl. "Mrs. Calhoun and me thank you, Au Bignon, for assisting our daughter. You can get on back to your work, now." He opened the door.

"Poppa," Mary Eliza quickly said, "we must offer our guest some refreshment."

"Refreshment?"

"Yes, Poppa, refreshment," Mary Eliza insisted. "We mustn't forget our manners."

Calhoun frowned as Mary Eliza waited anxiously. "Oh yes, refreshment," he mumbled and reluctantly closed the door.

Although wanting Karl to leave immediately, Calhoun remembered his proper southern upbringing. Hospitality was always offered to a guest. "Liza," he called.

The same woman that Karl had pushed aside at the buggy came to the living room.

"Bring us some blackberry wine and sweet breads, Liza," Calhoun told the woman.

Liza rolled her large eyes at Karl and very slowly left the room. She later returned with a large platter of cookies and cakes and set it on a serving table near Mrs. Calhoun.

On this serving table were four small plates made of fine china and four cut crystal glasses that sparkled like diamonds.

Liza went back to the kitchen and later returned with a pitcher of blackberry wine and poured some into three crystal glasses. She gave Karl another nasty look as she went off to the kitchen.

"Mama and Poppa," Mary Eliza said, smiling at Karl and sipping her wine. "You should have seen how Karl stopped my horse! Why, if he hadn't come along, no telling what would have happened to me!"

"We're ever so grateful to you, Au Bignon," Mrs. Calhoun replied dryly through tight lips. "Our little daughter means the world to us."

Karl leaned his dirty head back against the pink velvet sofa and flexed his muscles and smiled at Mary Eliza. "I'm strong as a bull," he said. "A pretty girl like you should have a strong man to look after her."

Calhoun's bushy eyebrows furrowed together in a ferocious frown. "Our Mary Eliza is well-protected, Au Bignon."

Mary Eliza knew from the way her father looked and tone of his voice that he disliked Karl and was afraid that if the conversation continued he'd tell Karl. So, she quickly scrambled up, took the platter of sweet breads over to Karl, and offered him some.

Karl reached in with dirty hands and grabbed a handful of sweet breads, and before Mary Eliza had served her parents, Karl had gobbled down the small cakes. When she offered him more sweet breads, he grabbed up another handful of the crumbly cookies and stuffed them in his mouth and began chewing loudly. He drank the glass of blackberry wine in two gulps and burped loudly.

This behavior was more than Calhoun could take. With determination, he waddled to the entrance hall again and opened the massive oak door. "We'll say good-day to you, Au Bignon," he announced.

As Karl stood up, the cookie crumbs on his shirt spilled onto the pecan floor. Ignoring the crunchy crumbs, he stepped on them as he went to the door. At the opened door, he paused and winked his eye at Mary Eliza who had followed him there. "I'll see you again, Miss Calhoun."

Karl Au Bignon had never seen nor had he ever been in such lavish surroundings. The morning he left the Calhoun mansion, he swore to himself that one day he'd live the way they did. And his only hope of escaping his poverty was to marry into money. And Mary Eliza had it.

Karl knew he'd have to lay his plans carefully, so he began watching every day for Mary Eliza's buggy. One day he saw it coming. He quickly ran up on the roadside and began cutting grass with a scythe. As the buggy neared, he jumped out into the middle of the road waving for Mary Eliza to stop.

"There's Karl in the road," Mary Eliza cried excitedly to Liza who held the reins. "I think he wants a word with me. Stop when you get to him."

But Liza aimed the horse and buggy right at Karl and nearly ran him down. He had to leap off the road into a ditch.

"Why didn't you stop?" Mary Eliza cried as she looked forlornly out the buggy window back down the road.

"Stop for what?" Liza asked.

"For Karl. He was standing right there in the road."

"I ain't see'd him," Liza replied innocently. "Mary Eliza, how many times do I need to tell you? My eyes be bad."

Try as hard as they might, the Calhouns couldn't keep Mary Eliza from seeing Karl. Mary Eliza knew she'd never get the chance as long as Liza was driving the buggy. She began slipping away from Liza to drive the buggy alone.

She'd tell Liza she wanted to rest in her room. There, she'd wait until Liza was busy with other chores. Then she'd sneak out of the house, hitch her horse to the buggy, and drive off.

She'd drive the buggy to a secluded part of the woods where Karl would be waiting. He'd climb inside and the two would sit and talk. Each time Karl came to the buggy, he'd sit closer and closer to Mary Eliza. He knew she liked being close to him because she never moved away.

One morning Karl greeted Mary Eliza with a bunch of Queen Anne's lace, wildflowers that he had picked from the roadside.

"Why you giving me flowers?" Mary Eliza asked coyly.

Karl kissed her hand, then cuddled her in his strong arms, "'Cause you are a sweet little thing."

Then he kissed Mary Eliza hard on her lips, so hard that it took her breath away. This was the first time she'd ever been kissed by a man, and she liked it.

"How about me being your boyfriend?" Karl whispered in her ear. "I can come around your house to see you. Then we won't have to meet in a buggy."

Mary Eliza drew back from him. Even though she wanted ever so badly to have Karl for her boyfriend, she knew she couldn't invite him to her house, not just yet.

Karl read her thoughts. "I'll come around your house as if I'm visiting the family. After your ma and pa get use to me coming, then you'll tell them I'm your boyfriend."

Mary Eliza agreed to Karl's plan.

The very next Sunday afternoon Karl came to visit. Just as the Calhouns were having their Sunday tea in the parlor, Liza came and announced that Karl Au Bignon was at the door.

"Karl Au Bignon? Who's he?" Calhoun asked Liza.

"Poppa," Mary Eliza said anxiously, "Karl saved my life. You remember?"

"Well, what's he after? Money?" He waved his hand at Liza to dismiss Karl. "Tell him we're busy."

"I'll go, Liza," Mary Eliza quickly said. She pushed past Liza and went to the door and invited Karl in. Karl followed Mary Eliza back to the parlor. He was dressed in a checkered woolen suit that was too small for him and a faded cotton shirt that was thin from wear, and his blonde hair was parted in the middle and held down by Vaseline. He wore heavy black boots and no socks.

The sight of Karl standing in his parlor infuriated Calhoun. He considered him poor white trash. Why was he coming to visit his family, and on Sunday? They had nothing in common with him. Hadn't he thanked this man for saving Mary Eliza? What more did he want?

Without speaking to Karl, Calhoun heaved himself up from his winged chair to leave the parlor. "Liza," he snapped as he waddled by her, "bring my tea and cakes to the dining room table."

Liza brought him a plate of sweet breads and a pot of tea. Calhoun sat there alone eating, and every now and then he'd glance angrily toward the parlor.

Mrs. Calhoun tried to act cordial toward Karl, but she knew her husband was angry and she needed to get rid of the man.

"We must rush off, Mr. Au Bignon," she said sweetly and stood up. "The family is expected to pay respects to the sick."

When Mary Eliza tried to intercede, Mrs. Calhoun quickly admonished her. "Mary Eliza, mind your manners."

When Mary Eliza tried to walk Karl to the door, Mrs. Calhoun barred her with an outstretched hand. "Liza will see you out," she told Karl.

Mrs. Calhoun then went to join her husband in the dining room. Mary Eliza felt so despondent at her mother's intervention that instead of going to the dining room, she went upstairs to be alone.

"How come that ole Karl fella keep coming here?" Calhoun asked his wife as he sat chewing his fifth sweet cake.

"I think he's hoping to court Mary Eliza," Mrs. Calhoun answered and poured herself a cup of tea.

Calhoun banged his fist down so hard on the table it caused Mrs. Calhoun's tea to splash out of her cup. "He's what?" he yelled and began coughing violently choking on the cake he was chewing. Mrs. Calhoun banged him on his back until he managed to swallow the cookie.

When his windpipe was clear, Calhoun told Mrs. Calhoun angrily, "I'll put a stop to this!" Then he struggled up from the table and went to the stairway. In a booming voice he called up the stairs. "Mary Eliza, come down here! Now!"

It took a few minutes before Mary Eliza came to the dining room. Her father ordered her to sit down.

After she was seated, he began pacing back and forth in the room as if he were thinking. All this time Mary Eliza sat meekly with hands folded across her lap looking down at the floor. Mrs. Calhoun, with arched brows, sipped tea.

Finally, after what seemed like an eternity to Mary Eliza, her father began talking.

"That ole Karl fella is up to no good, Mary Eliza. He's not in our class, and I won't allow you to keep company with him!"

He wagged his stubby finger at Mary Eliza. "You must remember that you are a Calhoun! And we Calhouns are FIRST-CLASS people! We only keep company with first-class people. Tell him to stay away! Do you hear me?"

"Yes, Poppa," Mary Eliza replied meekly.

"Now, have your tea and sweet bread."

"Yes, Poppa."

In spite of her father's orders, Mary Eliza was determined to have Karl for a boyfriend. She wasn't going to let her parents ruin her chance for happiness. When she saw Karl the next day, she told him she needed more time to convince her parents to let him keep company with her.

The two devised a plan. Whenever he saw the Calhouns drive by his shack in their buggy, he was to come to the house and see Mary Eliza.

Karl kept a lookout for the Calhouns' buggy, and in a few days he saw them go by. He then ran through the woods, and up through the cow pasture, past the barn, and to their house.

This was the beginning of a torrid, secret romance between Mary Eliza and Karl. He visited her three to four times a week. She first entertained him in the upstairs family room because she didn't want to meet in the downstairs parlor.

Liza warned her against what she was doing, but Mary Eliza begged Liza to keep her secret. "Please don't tell Mama and Poppa!"

One afternoon when Liza saw Karl slipping out of Mary Eliza's bedroom, she grew frightened. What if the Calhouns found out what Mary Eliza was doing and she had not told them about it? She'd surely be whipped.

After Karl had run down the stairs and out the door, Liza confronted Mary Eliza in the hall. "Honey," Liza counseled, "it ain't nice to have a man visit you in your sleepin' place."

"It's because Mama and Poppa will never let me court like the other girls in the county do!"

"Honey," Liza assured her. "They goin' let you court jest as soon as the right fella come along. But you got to keep Karl out of your sleepin' place."

"No, they won't! Poppa won't ever let me marry!" she wailed. "He thinks I'm too sickly!" Mary Eliza ran back into her bedroom and fell across her bed crying.

Liza followed her into the bedroom, and through her tears Mary Eliza cried, "I just want to be a woman and have a husband and babies! If Poppa runs Karl off I won't ever find another man! I'll be doomed to be an old maid like Auntie Edna! I don't want to be like her, alone and growing a mustache!"

"You mustn't talk mean about your pa's sister. She's real good to you. Ain't she bought you them fine dresses at Christmas?"

Mary Eliza sobbed. "I want more than fine dresses!"

Liza sat down on the bed and reached out with her big arms and hugged Mary Eliza. "Honey, stop all this cryin'. You ain't goin' be no old maid! One day a fine youn' man goin' come and take you off to the preacher."

"I don't want another man! I want Karl!" She pointed at her withered leg. "He doesn't care about my leg. He says it's not how you look but what you have in your heart. Liza, please don't tell on me!"

Although Liza disliked Karl immensely, she promised that day to keep Mary Eliza's secret. Deep in her heart she believed the big, strapping, yellow-haired man, with hard eyes and an "ugly attitude toward her," to be evil. But if he made Mary Eliza happy, it was all right with her. Heaven knows the child was very unhappy. She had been made fun of and called a cripple behind her back.

Liza understood why the Calhouns were overprotective of Mary Eliza. They were afraid she'd get hurt. But couldn't they see that Mary Eliza just wanted to be normal? She wanted to take company with boys and go to parties like the other girls in the county without being kept on a leash.

Two months after Mary Eliza met Karl, their courtship turned to intimacy. They'd make love in her bedroom every time he came calling.

One day the Calhouns came back earlier than expected. Just as their buggy turned into the driveway, Calhoun saw Karl walking briskly out the kitchen door and toward the orchards. Calhoun yelled to him, but before he could stop his buggy Karl had disappeared through the trees.

Calhoun angrily jumped out of the buggy, leaving his wife and striding up to his house. Inside, he yelled, "Mary Eliza, come down here!"

When Mary Eliza came downstairs, her father confronted her in an angry voice. "Was that poor white trash visiting you?"

Big tears welled up in Mary Eliza's eyes, and without answering her father, she fled limping back upstairs and into her bedroom and locked the door.

Calhoun went puffing after her. "How dare you have that white trash in my house without my knowledge!"

Calhoun pounded on her locked bedroom door. "Mary Eliza, you come on out here! You've got some explaining to do!"

By now, Mrs. Calhoun had scrambled out of the buggy and rushed into the house. She heard her husband yelling and banging on an upstairs door.

Quickly, she took the stairs. "What on earth is going on?" she asked anxiously when she saw her husband standing in the hallway banging on Mary Eliza's bedroom door.

"Mary Eliza's been seeing that poor white trash!" he bellowed. "I want her to tell me why she disobeyed my orders."

"Mr. Calhoun, stop yelling at her," Mrs. Calhoun said calmly. "You'll frighten the poor child to death."

"Well, you get her out!" the angry Calhoun demanded. "Now!"

In a sweet voice, Mrs. Calhoun called to her daughter. "Now, baby, you come on out and talk to Mama."

"NO!" Mary Eliza screamed. "If you don't go away, I'll jump out the window! I mean it."

Mrs. Calhoun clapped her hand over her mouth to muffle a cry, then turned to her husband. "We must wait until she's calm."

But Calhoun kept up his banging until Mrs. Calhoun stopped him. "We don't want Mary Eliza doing something foolish," she whispered. "She's such a sensitive child. We'll talk to her later. Let's go on back down-stairs."

As they were leaving, Mrs. Calhoun called softly, "You come on down when you are ready, baby. Poppa and I will be in the parlor."

As soon as Calhoun was downstairs, he yelled for Liza. If anyone in the house knew what was going on, it was Liza. The woman had a nose for gossip. She was always listening at bedroom doors, the parlor and while she worked in the kitchen. He didn't like her doing that, but whenever he tried to admonish her, Mrs. Calhoun would just say, "Liza's old. She means no harm."

When Liza came to the parlor, Calhoun said sternly, "Liza, I want the truth! Has that ole Karl fella been coming to my house when I've been away?"

"Why, Master Calhoun," Liza answered in a surprised voice. "I minds my own business and my business ain't to spy on Miz Mary Eliza. Why you'd be ever so mad if you thought I wuz."

Calhoun gave her a skeptical look. He believed Liza knew more than what she was owning up to, but for now he'd let it go. He waved her off. "Get on back to your work."

Mrs. Calhoun was so afraid of what Mary Eliza might do that she convinced her husband not to speak of the matter again. She believed that whatever attraction Mary Eliza had for Karl Au Bignon would soon go away. But it didn't.

A week after Calhoun had suspected Karl was coming to his house during his absence, Karl showed up at the front door.

"I came to see Miss Mary Eliza," he announced to Liza, who had opened the door.

Liza knew she'd better not get Mary Eliza because Mr. Calhoun was there, so she gathered her courage and spoke to Karl in a mean voice, "Master Calhoun ain't wantin' you comin' 'round heah."

Karl sneered at Liza, then in a harsh voice snapped, "Do as I say, nigger! Go get Miss Mary Eliza!"

Seething at Karl for calling her a nigger, Liza thought she'd fix him. Instead of telling Mary Eliza he was there, she went directly to the parlor where Calhoun was reading his paper.

"Master Calhoun, that ole stinkin' Karl fella is heah and he wants to see Miz Mary Eliza. I don' told him he ain't wanted 'round heah, but he ain't listenin'."

Calhoun slammed down his paper and scrambled up off his easy chair, "We'll see about that!"

He stormed off to the front door and faced Karl. "How dare you come to my home demanding to see my daughter, white trash!" He yelled in an angry voice. "If you don't stay away from my premises, I'll get my men to string you up!"

Smirking, Karl answered Calhoun. "Me and Mary Eliza have decided to get married, Mr. Calhoun."

Calhoun stood there for a moment dumbfounded, frozen in place, not believing what he'd heard. Then he bellowed, "Liza, bring me my pistol!"

Liza, who had followed Calhoun to the door, was looking over his shoulder. She had already gotten the pistol and four bullets and put them in her apron pocket. Quickly, she handed the gun over Calhoun's shoulder to him.

By now, Mrs. Calhoun had come to the door and, seeing her husband with the pistol, cried, "Honey, what are you going to do with that gun?"

"I aim to shoot this skunk right here and now!"

"Skunk? I don't smell a skunk!" Mrs. Calhoun said, standing tiptoed trying to see beyond Liza, who was blocking her view.

"It's this human skunk, Karl!"

"You mean Au Bignon?"

"That's the skunk! You know what this skunk just said, Mama?"

Wide-eyed, Mrs. Calhoun squeezed by Liza to look out the door.

"He wants to marry our little Mary Eliza," Calhoun snapped. "Now, I'm going to deal with this trash!"

He yelled back to Liza. "Liza, get me some bullets!" She quickly reached over Mrs. Calhoun's shoulder and handed him two of the bullets she had in her apron pocket.

Poor Mrs. Calhoun began waving frantically for Karl to leave. "Leave!" she cried. "Run!"

"Not 'til I see Mary Eliza," Karl answered defiantly. "I come to see her and I mean to before I go."

"You won't see a thing when I'm finished with you," the red-faced Calhoun shouted and began ramming the bullets into his pistol.

"Oh, please, honey, you just can't shoot him!" Mrs. Calhoun begged. "Just run him off!"

"The hell I can't," Calhoun snorted. "The best way to get rid of trash is to stamp it out! Kill it!"

"Poppa! Don't hurt Karl!" came Mary Eliza's frantic, shrill voice. She had come downstairs when she heard the yelling and screaming. She pushed her mother and Liza aside and tried to grab the gun away from her father.

Weeping profusely, she struggled with her father. "I'm pregnant, Poppa!"

Mrs. Calhoun let out a little gasp, clutched at her heart, staggered backward into the hall, and fell against a table.

Calhoun stood staring at his daughter as though he didn't believe her. Then he twirled around and yelled at Karl. "You nasty lowdown bastard! You done raped my little girl!"

"No!" Mary Eliza screamed. "We love each other, Poppa! Please don't shoot Karl!"

Picking herself up off the floor, Mrs. Calhoun cried, "Liza, get hold of that gun!"

Liza pretended not to hear Mrs. Calhoun. She so wanted Karl to get his buttocks full of lead!

"Die, trash!" Calhoun shouted and aimed his pistol at Karl.

When Karl saw Calhoun pointing the gun at him, he knew he'd underestimated the man. Calhoun had turned into a madman, and this was no time to stick around. He started running across the lawn.

"He be gittin' away, Master," Liza yelled as the fleeing Karl ran around the side of the house. "You gots to go after him!" Liza shouted and shoved Calhoun down the steps and into the yard.

As he tumbled almost to the ground, the heavy Calhoun gingerly held the pistol away from his head until he got his balance. Then he went after Karl, who had now raced through the flower beds, down through the vegetable garden, and on toward the cow pasture.

Huffing and puffing, Calhoun ambled through the flower bed, down through the vegetable garden, and on toward the cow pasture. Following at his heels was Liza, who was holding two bullets in her hand.

Just as Karl jumped the fence to the cow pasture, Calhoun, who was some distance away, raised his pistol and fired. The bullet missed its mark.

When Calhoun reached the fence, he couldn't climb over it, but Liza did.

"Give me the pistol!" she shouted from the other side. "I'll git him!"

The winded Calhoun could barely raise the pistol up to the top of the fence. Liza snatched it from his hand, rammed in two bullets, then chased after the fleeing Karl, firing the pistol as she ran. Both bullets hit close to Karl's heels, kicking up dust and weeds as he dashed into the cover of the woods.

Liza stood for a moment, looking off wistfully toward the woods. She felt disappointed she had missed the mean bastard. Then she let out a peal of laughter. This would teach the trash not to mess with her again.

Liza rested for a few minutes at the woods' edge, then walked slowly back to the fence. There, crumpled on the ground gasping for breath, was Calhoun.

Frightened, Liza ran toward the house calling, "Miz Calhoun, come quick! Somethin' done happened to Master!"

She then ran back to Calhoun and, struggling with his great bulk, was able to get him to his feet just as Mrs. Calhoun came running with Amos. Amos and Liza helped Calhoun to the house and upstairs to his bed.

"Ride into Cowpens and get Doctor Patterson," Mrs. Calhoun told Amos.

Then she tried to comfort her husband. "You mustn't upset yourself like this. You know what Doctor Patterson told you. You're not a well man."

It took Amos less than an hour to return with Doctor Patterson. After examining Calhoun, the doctor prescribed complete bed rest and Calhoun was to stop eating sweets because he needed to reduce his weight.

Liza went looking for Mary Eliza. She found her sitting alone in the parlor sobbing. "Come on, child, I'll help you to your room."

Half-stumbling and weeping, Mary Eliza, leaning on Liza, groped her way upstairs to her room. She fell across her bed and sobbed uncontrollably.

"Honey," Liza said quietly, as she sat on the bed stroking the girl's hair. "Your pa's goin' to be fine."

Mary Eliza looked at Liza with her tear-stained face, "I'm not crying for Poppa. I'm crying for Karl," she confessed.

"It ain't lack the sky be fallin'," Liza snapped. "He ain't no nice man, Miz Mary Eliza. He be mean."

Speaking between snatches of sobs, Mary Eliza replied. "He's not mean, Liza. He's just firm. I want him for my husband!" And she dissolved into tears again.

With Liza holding her in her arms, Mary Eliza blurted out again. "I'm going to have Karl's baby!"

Liza wasn't surprised that Mary Eliza was pregnant, because she knew what Karl and Mary Eliza had been doing in the bedroom.

"Honey," Liza whispered in her ear. "I kin take care of that ole baby. I jest give you some of my special drink, and poof!" She snapped her fingers. "Baby be gone jest lack that!"

Mary Eliza struggled out of Liza's arms and cried even harder. She told Liza to leave her room and refused to eat her supper that night.

The next morning when Mrs. Calhoun saw Liza carrying a breakfast tray up to Mary Eliza, she told Liza she'd take the food to her daughter's bedroom.

"You didn't eat supper last night," Mrs. Calhoun said cheerfully as she entered the room, "so, I brought you some breakfast. Hot oatmeal sprinkled with sugar and milk. Now, come on. Sit up and eat." She plumped up two feather pillows behind the girl's back as she sat up and took the tray.

When Mary Eliza had finished eating the oatmeal, Mrs. Calhoun first looked out the bedroom door to see if Liza was listening there. When she didn't see Liza in the hallway, she closed the door and came back to the bed and sat on it.

Lowering her voice she whispered. "Now, Mary Eliza, you do know how long our family has been in Cowpens?"

Mary Eliza nodded.

Mrs. Calhoun reached over and brushed back a lock of Mary Eliza's stringy brown hair that was hanging close to the empty cereal bowl. "We Calhouns are the most important family in these parts. Now, don't that just make you feel proud?" She smiled at her daughter.

Again, Mary Eliza nodded her head in agreement with her mother.

"You know we can't have a blemish on the Calhoun name."

Mrs. Calhoun then moved closer to Mary Eliza and lowered her voice even more. "I spoke with Doc Patterson yesterday when he came to the house to see your father, and I told him he must get rid of that baby you are carrying. He agreed to do it. But you must never tell anyone. Not even Liza. It'll be our secret: you, your father, Doctor Patterson, and me."

A look of horror came over Mary Eliza's pale face. "I won't! I won't!" she screamed. "If Doctor Patterson takes away my baby, I'll kill myself!"

"Mary Eliza," Mrs. Calhoun responded trying to quiet her. "Stop shouting! You'll do no such thing! Calhouns never killed themselves!"

"Then you'd better not try and take away my baby!"

"It's all been settled, so you just calm yourself."

"Go away! Go away, now!" Mary Eliza screamed and covered her head with a pillow.

Whenever Mrs. Calhoun tried to touch her she'd yell as loudly as she could. No amount of coaxing and pleading from her mother changed Mary Eliza's mind. She was not going to give up her baby.

That afternoon when Mrs. Calhoun talked with her husband, she told him that Mary Eliza wouldn't have an abortion and if they forced her she'd tell everyone in the county about it. Their good name would be ruined and Doctor Patterson would be in a lot of trouble. Performing an abortion was not only against good Christian principles, but against the law.

Although Calhoun wanted desperately to have the sheriff run Karl off, he also wanted to protect the Calhoun name. He couldn't allow his daughter to have a baby out of wedlock. If so, his family would be ostracized by the other important people in Cowpens, and he couldn't let that happen. So, reluctantly, Calhoun gave his consent for Karl and Mary Eliza to marry.

At the wedding reception, the guests were appalled at Karl's crude behavior and his personal grooming. He was totally devoid of good manners, used profanity, and made rude jokes. Many of the guests wondered how Mary Eliza came to court this man. Not only was he dirt poor, but he also was mean-spirited in the way he acted toward the servants. Some guests believed that Mary Eliza's chances of getting married were slim, but to Karl? Why would the Calhouns allow their daughter to marry a man who was so far beneath them?

The people in Cowpens County didn't have to wait long for an answer. Six months after the wedding, Mary Eliza gave birth to a baby girl. She named her Dolly, after her favorite grandmother.

After Dolly's birth, the county was soon rife with gossip about Mary Eliza being pregnant before she had said her wedding vows. The friends in the Calhouns' social circle thought that the Calhouns had not kept a proper watch over their daughter. No wonder they let her marry Karl. Getting pregnant before marriage was a disgrace for upstanding, God-fearing Christian people.

Soon, many of the Calhouns' friends refused to have anything more to do with them because of the gossip about Mary Eliza. The Calhouns were devastated by the way their friends had turned their backs on them. Even at church, the Calhouns were shunned by friends whom they had known and socialized with since childhood.

The shunning was too much for Mr. Calhoun's weak heart. One year after the wedding, he had a massive heart attack and died.

Mrs. Calhoun grieved for him over a year. Always wearing black, she now seldom left her bedroom, even took her meals there.

One morning Liza found her dead in her bed. Liza believed that Mrs. Calhoun died from a broken heart because of Mary Eliza's choice of a husband, who had caused the Calhouns to become social outcasts in the county that their families had lived in for a hundred years.

Although Margrace had been passed on to Mary Eliza, Karl now took over running it. He told Mary Eliza that she didn't have the stamina to run a plantation because it took a strong hand to handle slaves. Whatever Karl did was all right with Mary Eliza because she now had what she wanted—a husband and a baby. She couldn't have been happier.

Mary Eliza inherited all of the Calhouns' holdings but their will specifically stated that Karl Au Bignon was to get nothing, and their will couldn't be broken.

Karl hired an overseer, named Bernard "Brute" O'Brien to help him with the slaves. Karl had wanted to make Liza a field hand or to sell her, but Mary Eliza wouldn't hear of it. She needed Liza in the house to take care of her, and since Karl knew Mary Eliza held the purse strings he dared not cross her. She meant to have Liza at her side because she was the only friend she had and she loved her dearly.

Karl disliked Liza intensely. He believed she filled his wife's head with mean things about him, and he hadn't forgotten the shooting episode and how he had to run for his life. He longed to punish her for it, but whenever he spoke to Liza harshly, Mary Eliza would quickly tell him angrily not to bother Liza. He knew she meant it, so he kept his distance from Liza.

Karl, along with his ruthless overseer, Brute, drove the slaves on Margrace Plantation mercilessly.

Brute, being a sadistic man, derived great pleasure from working the slaves from sunup until sundown. They were given little food and little time off, and he used the whip often. The work from the slaves' labor soon made Mary Eliza very rich. She was far richer now than her parents or her grandparents had ever been.

Twelve years after Karl and Mary Eliza had married, Will Pettigrew, whose plantation was down the road from Margrace, died, and his wife Mary had manumitted Will's slaves and turned the plantation into a free settlement.

Karl was furious. "The woman's a fool!" He told the other slaveholders in the Nebo Valley, "If she wasn't a white woman, I'd take her out and horsewhip her!"

Karl said Mary's act would cause trouble for the white people in the valley by establishing what he called a "nigger heaven." He tried to organize the other slaveholders to ride with him over to Smyrna and clean out the niggers.

Although the slaveholders disliked what Mary Pettigrew had done, they disliked Karl even more and did not take him up on his offer.

Bessie Meets Enoch

Before she was freed Bessie had met Enoch, a slave from Margrace Plantation. It was late July 1857, when Will Pettigrew's wheat crop was ripe and he had wanted it harvested before the rains came in August. He had hired three men from Margrace Plantation to help out. Au Bignon often hired out his slaves to work for money.

Enoch and two other men were sent to help bring in Pettigrew's wheat crop. Bessie and Tessa, the two teenaged slave girls owned by Pettigrew, had also been sent to the wheat fields to work. The girls tied the freshly cut wheat into small bundles so that it could be stacked into shocks to dry. This work was difficult for them because the wheat stems were sharp and often cut their fingers, and they were also tormented by the vicious bites of wheat bugs. These tiny insects' bites caused itching and a rash. The big bonnets that covered most of the girls' faces and their long-sleeved dresses were little help against these bugs.

Some men that day were using scythes to cut the wheat down while others tied and stacked it. Enoch was stacking wheat alongside the girls.

All morning he had been watching Bessie, and he liked what he saw: heavy hips and big breasts. In Enoch's mind, women like Bessie made great lovers, and since his primary interest in women was to make love, Enoch wanted to get to know Bessie.

He began stacking wheat close to where the two girls were working. Soon he started a conversation with Bessie. "You sho' looks good to me, baby," Enoch said from the corner of his mouth. "What they call you?" He glanced around to see where Brute, Au Bignon's overseer, was.

Brute was sitting upon a big chestnut horse where he could see all Au Bignon's slaves. His shotgun laid across his hefty lap, and a bullwhip dangled from his hand. Whenever he saw one of the men talking or not working as hard as he thought they should, he'd crack his whip in the air just to remind them that he was watching and he meant business.

"Go on, shet up your mouth," Bessie replied coyly to Enoch.

"I ain't knowed what to call you," Enoch insisted.

"Bessie."

"That be a right pritty name," he flashed a toothy grin at Bessie. "I'm Enoch."

"I know that," Bessie replied as she stood holding a handful of wheat, smiling up at the huge black man with dark, penetrating eyes.

Enoch reached over and slowly slid the wheat stems from Bessie's hand. Then he quickly tied it, flipped the bundle up into the air, and caught it in his big hands.

"Who done told you my name, baby?" he asked and handed the bundle to Bessie.

"Ain't nobody. I been hearin' it all mornin'."

Enoch inched closer to Bessie and lowered his voice. "You gots a man, baby?"

Bessie giggled. "Why you wantin' to know?"

"How 'bout me bein' your man?" Enoch asked. "I sho' know how to make a gal feel good."

Bessie giggled again. "You best shet up your mouth and go on away from me."

"I done ask you a question, baby. I wants to be your man."

Bessie couldn't answer because she was too flattered. This was the first time a man had paid any attention to her. The men on Pettigrew's plantation always flirted with Tessa, who was petite and had big brown eyes.

Bessie, on the other hand, was rotund and unattractive, and whenever the men did pay attention to her, it was to get her to mend their clothes or bake them a sweet potato pie.

Enoch's attentiveness made Bessie feel good, and when he purposely brushed up against her breasts it awakened feelings inside of her that she had never felt.

Brushing up against Bessie's breasts caused Enoch to have an erection, and he quickly put his hand over his crotch. After this happened, he knew he had to see Bessie again but under more favorable conditions.

"How 'bout me slippin' over your house late tonight?" he whispered.

When Bessie's eyes said yes, he acknowledged it. "Jest listen for my scratches on the door."

Enoch then chuckled and winked at her. "You sho' goin' be glad I come, baby."

Then Enoch saw Brute looking in his direction. He quickly called to Sully, another man who was cutting wheat just ahead of him. "Give me that cuttin' blade! I'll show you how to cut wheat." He rushed up to him, took the scythe, and began furiously cutting down wheat.

Bessie was so excited that she could hardly wait to tell Tessa what Enoch had in mind. She waited until they were getting a drink of water from a water bucket that was put under a tree at the field's edge.

After Bessie had taken a drink from the dipper, she said matter-of-fact-ly, "Enoch goin' be comin' over tonight and spendin' some time with me. I'm goin' need the cabin for myself."

Tessa, who had just taken a dipper of water from the bucket, stopped drinking and stared at the smiling Bessie. "You be crazy?" she snapped. "You jest see'd this big, ole, ugly man for the first time. You don' know nothin' bout him." She took a long sip of water. "He gots them funny eyes that I don't trust. He be trouble if you ask me."

"Tessa," Bessie replied sternly and took the dipper from her. "I ain't askin' you. I likes him and I mean to have him for my man."

Tessa frowned at Bessie. "I ain't givin' up my bed for the likes of him!"

Bessie became annoyed at her friend. She had never called Nate, Tessa's man, ugly and crazy. Hadn't she always given up the cabin when

Nate came calling at night? She'd leave the cabin and go down to the riverbank and wait until she saw Nate slip out when it was near daylight. Now, she had found a man and wanted some privacy, and Tessa didn't want to give it to her.

Bessie kicked over the bucket of water and stood glaring at her friend. "You listen to me, Tessa. If you don't let me have the cabin tonight, you can forgit 'bout me leavin' for you again. You heah me?"

Tessa didn't respond. She was staring down at the cool water that was trickling into the ground. Now, they didn't have any water to drink while they worked in the hot field.

Tessa loved Bessie as a sister and wanted her to have a man, but this Enoch? Why couldn't it be someone else?

That night after work, Bessie took the big, tin tub that they kept in a corner of the cabin, filled it with water, and took a bath. Then she rubbed on some lilac-smelling talcum powder that Mrs. Pettigrew had given her when she was cleaning her bedroom one day. Mrs. Pettigrew didn't like the smell. She had to bang the can hard against a chair to get out the last of the powder. Tessa had been using it when she knew Nate was coming to the cabin, and most of it was gone.

After her bath, Bessie dressed in the pink flannel gown Mrs. Pettigrew had thrown away in the spring. Bessie had found it in the rag box, mended it, washed it, and kept the gown for herself. She combed her thick hair and then down sat in their wire-bottomed chair with its rag cushion and waited.

Since they only had one chair, Tessa sat on their bed and looked on disapprovingly. She believed that Bessie was making a mistake getting involved with Enoch, but she could see that Bessie had made up her mind and there was nothing she could do.

"I'll leave when he gits here," she finally said and got into the bed and pulled the spread up over her head. She didn't want Bessie to see how annoyed she was.

It was nearing midnight when Tessa woke up and saw Bessie still sitting in the chair near the fireplace in the dim lamplight waiting for Enoch. The lamp was nearly out of kerosene, and its light fluttered and flickered as it was dying out.

"Aw, Bessie," Tessa yawned, "blow out the lamp and git in the bed. That rascal ain't comin'."

Bessie sat looking dejectedly down at her folded hands on her lap. "Guess you be right all the time," she said softly. "Enoch ain't meant what he said 'bout wantin' to be my man."

"I'd like to beat his tail," Tessa said angrily as she sat up in bed. "If ever I see him again, I'm goin' knock him upside his big, ugly head!"

Bessie didn't reply. She just blew out the lamp and crawled into the bed. She was glad that the cabin was dark, so Tessa couldn't see the tears in her eyes.

About two hours after Bessie had gone to bed, Tessa was awakened by a scratching sound on the door.

"Bessie, let me in," a voice said. "It be me, Enoch."

Tessa was furious. She could hear Bessie snoring softly, and she meant not to wake her. So she turned over and tried to go back to sleep, but Enoch was persistent. He kept scratching on the door and calling softly.

Finally, Tessa could take no more of Enoch's scratching. Quietly she slipped out of the bed and tiptoed to the door and jerked it open.

"What you doin' comin' 'round heah at this time of night?" she demanded.

"Somethin' come up," Enoch replied unapologetically as he looked past her into the cabin trying to see where Bessie was.

"Well, ain't nobody wantin' to see you at this hour."

"I ain't wantin' to see you," Enoch snapped at Tessa, who kept blocking his view. "Now, you jest git on outta the way. I come to see Bessie." He tried to push past her.

But Tessa refused to give ground. "I ain't knowed 'bout this."

"You ain't gots to know. I done 'cided I'm goin' be Bessie's man."

"I'll take a stick to your tail," Tessa said and grabbed up a big stick that they kept at the edge of the door to chase raccoons away when they came around the cabin at night looking for food. "If you don't git, I'm goin' lay this stick upside your head, you big fool!"

All the loud angry words outside the cabin had awakened Bessie. When she heard Enoch's voice, she quickly climbed out of bed and came to the door. There was Tessa standing with the big stick in her hand facing Enoch.

"Tessa," Bessie said, "put that stick down. Let Enoch in the house."

Tessa was dumbfounded at Bessie. Enoch had embarrassed her by keeping her waiting all night, and now he shows up near daylight and she's allowing him to come in?

"Well, I be!" Tessa said indignantly and threw the stick down and stepped back inside the cabin, grabbed up her shawl, and went out the door nearly knocking Enoch over. She was so angry that she had to give up her bed for him. Although Bessie had done this many times for her, that was different. She and Nate were in love.

That night was the beginning of Bessie's romance with Enoch. He only visited her occasionally, because he had affairs with other women and Bessie knew about it. She often heard Nate, Ben, and Scully joking about Enoch servicing all the slave women in Cowpens County. Even though Bessie was hurt by all this talk, it didn't matter to her. She had fallen in love with Enoch.

Bessie wanted to marry Enoch, but there was little hope of them ever becoming husband and wife. Will Pettigrew was against slave marriages and so was Karl Au Bignon, who didn't mind the women having babies because that meant he'd own another slave—but never marriage.

"Slaves getting married puts the wrong ideas into their heads," Au Bignon would say. "Next thing they'll be trying to run away."

Bessie often brought up marriage to Enoch at the times he visited her.

"You be crazy, woman," Enoch would say. "How I'm goin' marry you? I ain't never goin' marry 'less I'm a free man. Then I takes me a woman."

"Would you marry me if we was free?"

"You always bringin' up marry," Enoch replied. "I ain't free and you ain't free, so why we be talkin' 'bout it?"

"One of these days," Bessie remarked, "you goin' be free and I'm goin' be free, then we goin' git married and have a house full of babies.

Dolly

Karl and Mary Eliza Au Bignon lavished their love and attention on their daughter Dolly. Not only was Dolly spoiled, but she also had a terrible temper and was disliked by other children in the Nebo Valley because of her ugly behavior.

Even at eight years old, Dolly bragged incessantly to her playmates about how rich she was and that she could have anything she wanted.

When she was sixteen, Dolly told her parents that she wanted a coming-out party, and it had to be the biggest and most extravagant party that the valley had ever seen. Mary Eliza was reluctant to do so for fear of further alienating the girls in the county, but Karl set about getting ready for his daughter's sixteenth birthday.

For the entire month of April, the women who worked in the house were busy preparing for Dolly's party that was to be held in May. They baked pies, cakes, custards, puddings, and all kinds of sweet breads. In the oven, they roasted legs of lamb, ducks, and chickens. Spicy sausages, livermush, and minced barbecue were made and put into big pots and stored in the smokehouse.

Two days before the party, the men dug a huge pit near the barn and made a fire in it. When the fire pit was ready, they hung a freshly killed pig onto a spit to roast. The roasting pig was turned constantly as Amos, who was the house slave, brushed on a special sauce he had concocted from secret herbs, tomatoes, and a seasoning made from dried sage, salt, pepper, and ground onions and garlic.

Inside, the large house was made ready. Karl barked orders to his slaves who were painting the walls. The white paint had to be perfectly applied, and Karl was a hard man to please.

Mary Eliza supervised the women, who sewed new curtains and drapes for the windows. New bedspreads and bureau scarves were also made. Every floor was scrubbed and polished until it was shining as if it were new. Large pots of blooming petunias of many colors were set about the house on tables and the landings on the stairway.

Au Bignon ordered the outside of the house painted, and the road that led up to the house was regraveled. Even the barns were given bright new coats of red paint.

During all this activity, Dolly sat pouting in the porch swing because she didn't like the dust that the men were causing from digging holes to plant new shrubbery and trimming the hedges. She hated this red dust because it was sure to give her a rash. How was she to become the belle of her ball if she had pimples on her face? When she yelled to her mother to stop the men from making dust, Mary Eliza tried to explain to her that to plant the shrubs the men had to dig holes and digging holes caused dust.

"Darling, why don't you go inside until the planting is finished?" Mary Eliza said sweetly and tried to take Dolly's hand.

"No!" Dolly answered, jerking her hand away. "I want to sit in the swing!"

Exasperated, Mary Eliza called Liza, "Come and help me!"

Liza, who now was crippled with arthritis, came out to the porch. She frowned at Dolly. "Child, you goin' give your Mama a bad spell if you don't quit actin' up."

"Liza, you shut up!" Dolly screamed at her.

"Well, I guess there ain't nothin' to do but let you git them pimples! Come on, Miz Mary Eliza," Liza said. "You best go on back in the house before you git yo'self sick and have to take to your bed. Ain't nothin' you kin do 'bout this child." Liza held the door open for Mary Eliza, who obeyed her.

"Lord, I'd like to once smack that child's ass real hard," Liza mumbled to herself when she was alone. "She jest lack her ole hateful Pappy."

Liza despised Dolly because of the way she treated her mother. In Liza's mind, God didn't like ugliness and Dolly had more than her share of it. One of these days, she believed, Dolly was going to get what she deserved.

Dolly's sixteenth birthday party was to be held on the first Sunday in May. After breakfast that morning, Liza and Mary Eliza began getting Dolly dressed. As usual, she was in an ugly mood, and she fussed and complained all through her dressing. Nothing pleased Dolly. Everything Liza and her mother did for her she criticized. She now hated the very expensive white party gown made with yards of voile and lace with a tight lace-up bodice even though she picked it out herself.

Dolly was a hefty girl, and when her mother suggested another gown that would give her a more slender figure, she had a temper tantrum. "If I don't get what I want, I'll not wear anything!" Dolly screamed at her mother.

Mrs. Calhoun, Mary Eliza's mother, had given her a pearl necklace on her sixteenth birthday. All this time she had kept it in a safe in her closet since her mother's death. Now, she wanted her daughter, Dolly, to wear the pearls at her sixteenth birthday.

When Mary Eliza brought the necklace and tried to fasten it around Dolly's neck, she began screaming. "I want to wear your diamond necklace!" She then snatched the necklace off her neck and threw it onto the bed.

Liza, who was waiting with a pair of black shiny shoes, looked at Dolly with disdain. "You goin' wear these new shoes?" she asked and dropped the shoes down on the floor in front of the girl.

"Don't be a fool," Dolly snapped. "Of course I am. Didn't I pick them out?"

"You done picked out all this other stuff and now you won't wear it," Liza replied.

"Mama! Mama!" Dolly screamed. "Make Liza go away!"

"Liza," Mary Eliza whispered, "go downstairs and let the guests in."

Liza sucked her tooth. "That suits me jest fine! I jest git these ole bones outta the way. This be Sunday, my day of rest, and all I kin heah is complainin'."

At eleven o'clock, Karl came into the parlor wearing a new white linen suit he had bought in Cowpens the Saturday before. He seemed to be stuffed into it because he couldn't button the coat over his bloated stomach. When he saw Liza coming down the stairs, he snapped, "Why ain't you upstairs helping Miss Dolly get dressed?"

"She ain't wantin' me," Liza replied.

"Well, get in the kitchen and help out! We got folks coming!" He strutted around the parlor like a peacock making sure everything was to his liking.

"They sho' ain't goin' have no good time," Lisa mumbled as she went off to the kitchen. "It be best they stay home."

The party was to start at twelve, an hour after the Sunday church services had let out. The guests were to come from church to Margrace and eat dinner.

Every rich family in the county had been invited, but by twelve o'clock, only two families had arrived; a Mr. Sift, the bank president where Karl kept his money, and his wife, and a Mr. Gitney, who owned the feed and fertilizer store, and his spinster daughter Eva.

When it was twelve-fifteen, Mary Eliza believed that all the guests had arrived because the people in Cowpens were always prompt. She told Dolly that it was time for them to go downstairs and greet the guests.

Dolly refused. "Let them wait! I want them to be mad because I made them wait!"

"Honey," Mary Eliza replied softly, "you don't want your friends to be mad at you."

"Yes I do! I hate them all!" Dolly said and stomped over to the window, folded her arms and stood pouting.

The four guests along with Karl sat waiting silently in the parlor. It was now one o'clock. Where were the other guests? Where was Dolly?

Every now and then, Mr. Sift looked at his watch and then at Karl, who sat with an arrogant look on his face watching the door. He was growing angry that the other guests hadn't arrived. What was the matter with these folks? Didn't they know that being late would displease his daughter?

At one-fifteen, Dolly finally decided to come downstairs. With a smirk on her face and her mother following close behind her, she slowly descended the stairs. Hanging around her neck was her mother's diamond necklace, and setting high upon a mountain of hair was a tiara woven with red roses. Her puffy white gown made from yards and yards of voile filled each step as she made her way down looking like a walking haystack.

Dolly fully expected to see the parlor crowded with jealous, envious young women and handsome men looking up at her as she came down. But when she reached the bottom step, she saw only four elderly persons along with her father waiting to greet her.

Ignoring them, Dolly looked beyond the parlor expecting to see the crowd, but saw only empty chairs. She was stunned. Where was everybody? Only Liza was standing near the dining room entrance with a white towel over her arm.

Mary Eliza looked devastated when she saw the empty parlor. She couldn't imagine how Dolly was going to take this. Having a house full of guests meant so much to Dolly. She had bragged about it for weeks and how she planned to ignore all the girls and spend time only with the boys.

"Mama, they didn't come to my party!" she cried disbelievingly. "They didn't come to my party!"

Dolly then became enraged, screaming hysterically as she shoved her mother out of her way and bolted back up the stairs.

Karl, taking two steps at a time, went after Dolly.

Liza rushed over to Mary Eliza when she saw her leaning against the stair railing silently crying. She felt so hurt that the people Dolly had invited were so cruel as not to come to her sixteenth birthday party!

"Now, Miz Mary Eliza, you just stop your cryin'," Liza said and put an arm around Mary Eliza's waist. "We don't care if them ole folks ain't come."

Wiping her eyes with her lace handkerchief, Mary Eliza then tried to apologize to the four dumbfounded guests who didn't know what to make of this scene.

"We must have given the rest of Dolly's guests the wrong date," she said softly. "I am so sorry to have caused you this inconvenience, especially on Sunday."

"It's quite all right," Mr. Sift said. "We all make mistakes. Perhaps we'd better go." He and the other guests walked toward the door. "Say good-bye to Dolly and wish her a happy birthday."

Upstairs in a fit of anger and hurt, Dolly kicked off her black patent leather shoes and flung them across her bedroom just as Karl was entering. She snatched off the tiara, flung it on the floor, and stomped on it. Then she began throwing and breaking everything she could get her hands on.

"Dolly," Karl commanded. "You stop this. We don't care if them poorass folks didn't come! I didn't want them in my house anyway. Let's go downstairs and eat our food without them!"

Dolly turned on him like a viper. "It's all your fault!" she screamed at her father. "I'm going to get even with you! You'll see!"

She ran out of her bedroom, down the stairs, and out through the kitchen door. Running barefooted, she dashed across the lawn and down the graveled road. Her white party gown was dragging in the dirt, and pieces were being torn off by the rocks. Out across a newly plowed field she ran, headed toward the Nebo River. Close behind Dolly came her father, calling to her. His yelling caught the attention of three slave men who were seining for catfish in the Nebo.

With their pant legs rolled up, they were dragging an old burlap sack through the brackish river shallows. It was Sunday, and Enoch, Noah, and Nicodemus and the rest of Au Bignon's field slaves were given time to rest.

The men saw Dolly running headlong toward them. Waving his arms frantically, Au Bignon yelled to them. "Don't let Miss Dolly go into the river!"

The men dropped their seine and with Noah leading the way rushed out to where Dolly was wading out into the water. Noah caught hold of her arms and held her firmly as she struggled to break free.

Without hesitation, Karl, in his fancy white suit, rushed into the river and waded out to his screaming daughter. He shoved Noah head-over-heels backwards into the water and put his arms around Dolly.

"Honey," he said trying to console her, "them ole stuck-up gals ain't worth this! You come on back home with your daddy."

When Dolly began fighting and scratching at Karl, he lifted her up as dirty river water poured from her gown, put her across his shoulder, waded out of the river, and headed back to the house.

As the three men watched them go, Noah remarked, "What that liddle gal need is a good man."

"You best not say that loud," Enoch warned. "Ole man Karl have Brute on your ass with a whip!"

"Ain't I be right?" Noah said to Nicodemus. "That gal need a good man at night."

Nicodemus gave a knowing look at the soaking wet Noah, then said, "If we goin' git a mess of fish for supper we best git to it." The three men then went back to seining.

Not for Sale

Bessie, Tessa, and Nate settled down in Smyrna, but Sully and Ben left for places unknown and never returned. Mrs. Pettigrew's mother and father came to live with her in the big house on the hill.

Soon the word was out that Smyrna was a place where free blacks could live, work, and raise their families, and the freed blacks who had been scattered throughout Cowpens County came there to live.

Three years after it had been established, Smyrna had become a thriving settlement. The new settlers wanted to change the name to Canaan but Bessie, Tessa, and Nate held firm. They had named their community Smyrna, and Smyrna it would stay.

The people built their houses on each side of a broad dirt road that had once been Will Pettigrew's wheat field. Most houses had four rooms, tin roofs, and large stone chimneys. People often joked that these were shotgun houses, because if you fired a gun through the front door of the house, the bullet would go straight through it and out the back.

As some people in Smyrna grew prosperous they added another story to their homes, glass windowpanes, and front porches. They also planted shade trees in their front yards.

Around the side of the houses were gardens, fruit trees, and grape arbors. In back of the gardens were sheds for their cows and horses, chicken coops, and pigpens. A meandering creek that had branched off from the

Nebo and some woods divided the village. On the east side, where most of the people settled, their homes were whitewashed and had flowers planted in the front yards and picket fences built around them. Up beyond the eroded creek's west bank in a grove of scrub pines were clusters of ramshackle shacks with filthy surroundings. People who lived on this side of the creek were believed to be the lowlifes—root-workers and devil worshipers.

Many black families in Smyrna were entrepreneurs. They set up shops and did tailoring, millinery, and shoemaking. There were shops for potters, furniture-makers, carpenters, and goldsmiths. The blacksmith had his shop at the edge of the settlement.

Soon, the land around Smyrna was dotted with small farms where black farmers planted wheat, corn, peas, sweet potatoes, and turnips.

Above the valley were some dense woods to the north of the river. This area was called Indian Woods because a small band of Peedee Indians lived there.

The Indians stayed to themselves, but it was whispered that they had often given refuge to many runaway slaves from the Deep South and had helped them go north. It was also whispered that there were "Black Indians," part Indian and part black, also living in Indian Woods.

In 1859, Aunt Cindy, a midwife from Cowpens, came to Smyrna and set up her business. Because she was getting on in years, she needed an assistant. She hired Bessie and taught her midwifery. Aunt Cindy had grown feeble and so was unable to take care of herself. Bessie moved in with her, and a year after that Aunt Cindy died. Bessie now was the only midwife in the county. She decided to save all her earnings and buy Enoch's freedom.

It wasn't until the spring of 1860 that Bessie thought she had saved enough money for Enoch's freedom. On a night in early April when Enoch had slipped off Margrace Plantation to visit Bessie, she told him the good news.

Enoch was unimpressed. "You be wastin' your time, woman," he told her. "Ole Bignon ain't goin' sell you my papers. I works too hard for him."

"Ain't you wantin' to be free, Enoch?" Bessie asked as she put a big apple pie into the oven. She always cooked Enoch a pie no matter how late he arrived. She believed that cooking Enoch's favorite food bonded him to her.

"I wants to be free, woman!" Enoch replied gruffly. "I ain't lackin' no man beatin' on my tail and makin' me work hard and ain't givin' me enough to eat! But I done knowed that it ain't no use for me thinkin' that, so I jest gits it outta my head!"

"Well, we see 'bout that," Bessie replied haughtily as she bent down and opened the oven to see if the pie was browning.

When she stood up she reached into her apron pocket, pulled out a roll of dollars tied with a piece of string, and shook the bills in front of Enoch's eyes. "You put the greenbacks in front of ole Bignon's eyes and he be takin' 'em!"

At first, Enoch just stared at the money, then he sucked his teeth. "Ole Bignon ain't needin' greenbacks. Only way he lets me go is when his house come tumblin' down." He leaned back against the chair with a secret grin on his face, tapping his fingers on the table.

Slowly, Bessie dropped her money back into her apron pocket. She seemed perplexed. "What you mean by 'his house come tumblin' down'?"

Enoch gave her a sly smile as if he knew something was going to happen to the Au Bignons. "That pie be ready?" He sniffed the air. "It be stinkin' good."

Bessie took the browned pie from the oven and cut a huge steaming wedge of it, put it on a plate, and handed it to Enoch. "You wait 'til that pie cools," she warned.

Enoch sat looking impatiently at the plate. Then he began blowing hard on the pie to cool it.

"You ain't told me 'bout ole Bignon's house comin' down," Bessie said and sat down beside him at the table.

"I ain't goin' say," Enoch said as he tried to bite into the hot pie, but quickly put it back on the plate. "I KNOW me some stuff, sho' as I be eatin' this piece of pie." He grinned broadly at Bessie.

"Tell me 'bout Au Bignons' house comin' down," the curious Bessie insisted.

"It be fallin' down, Bessie," Enoch said with confidence. "Time ain't ripe to do talkin'. For now, my lips be sealed."

🌿

Mary Pettigrew, although frail, still lived in her big house at the edge of Smyrna. She had hired Tessa to take care of her house and cook the meals and Nate to take care of her grounds. She now spent most of her time reading the Bible.

The morning after Enoch's visit, Bessie went to Mrs. Pettigrew's house to tell Tessa her plan. As Tessa was preparing Mrs. Pettigrew's breakfast, Bessie came into the kitchen through the back door.

"What you doin' here so early?" Tessa cried when she saw Bessie and greeted her with a big hug.

"I come to tell you my secret!"

"Secret?" she said, looking at Bessie's stomach.

Bessie giggled. "Aw, it ain't what you be thankin'."

Tessa sighed and put the oatmeal pot on the stove. "All I know is Enoch be a busy man."

Then Bessie said excitedly, "I'm goin' to buy Enoch his freedom!" She took her roll of dollar bills from her pocket and waved it at Tessa. "I done save enough for it! Just thank, I'm goin' be married like you and Nate! I'm so happy!"

Tessa stopped stirring the pot of oatmeal on the stove and glared at Bessie. This news angered her. It was only a few days before that Nate told her Enoch was slipping off at night from Margrace and having a rendezvous with a free black woman over in Cowpens. He had met him on the path in the woods.

Nate laughed as he told his wife. "Now, don't you go puttin' that pea in Bessie's ear. I ain't wantin' to git Enoch in trouble."

"Enoch's a dirty dog!" Tessa replied. "But if you ain't wantin' me to tell Bessie, ain't no skin off my nose."

Hearing Bessie talk about buying Enoch's freedom not only angered Tessa, but pained her as well. Enoch didn't deserve Bessie. He'd make a fool of her once he got free because he'd be after every woman he'd see.

Bessie put her arms around her friend's waist and squeezed her hard. "Ain't I somethin'? I'm goin' git me a husband!"

"Why you want to spend your hard-got money on Enoch?" Tessa finally asked as she pulled away from the smiling Bessie.

Bessie walked over and sat down at the table, took off her bonnet, and laid it on the kitchen table. "The years keeps on rollin' by, and I wants Enoch in my bed all night."

"Ain't he in your bed evertime he come over?"

Bessie frowned. "I wants me a husband in my bed, not a slave! On Sundays I wants to walk with Enoch on my arm to church." She then got up from the chair and strutted around in the kitchen showing Tessa how she and Enoch should be walking.

"I wants to cook him his Sunday dinners and look after him when he gits sick. I needs him to love me every night and hold me to him."

"You be askin' a lot from Enoch," Tessa replied skeptically. "You sho' he gon' do all them things?"

"I know he will!" Bessie exclaimed. Then she looked real worried. "I don't want Enoch sneakin' off anymore to see me at night. It be too scary! Ole Bignon goin' find out, and he beat the skin off Enoch if he be caught!"

"Au Bignon be a mean bastard all right," Tessa concurred. "But that ain't stoppin' Enoch from doin' what he wants to do once ole Bignon be sleepin'."

Bessie walked over to the stove and put both her arms on Tessie's shoulders. "Now," she said solemnly, "I wants you to go to Miz Pettigrew and ask her to go to Au Bignon and buy Enoch for me. The reason I'm askin' Miz Pettigrew to do this is I ain't a good talker and, to tell the truth, I hate that ole man. I'd spit in his eye if I was to speak to him!"

Tessa drew back, shaking her head. "Why you askin' me to do this, Bessie?"

"'Cause you work for Miz Pettigrew. You see her every day."

Tessa quickly began stirring the oatmeal pot and then pushed it to the back of the stove. "I ain't goin' git mixed up in this."

Bessie looked hurt. "Why? You my best friend, lack a sister to me. Why you don't want to git mixed up in this?"

Tessa walked over to the kitchen cabinet and got a cup and poured herself a cup of coffee from a coffeepot. She motioned to Bessie as if to ask her if she wanted a cup.

Bessie shook her head. "Why?" she asked again.

Tessa took a sip of coffee, then said, "I'll tell you why. I don't much care for Enoch. I don't think you ought to spend your money on him. There is plenty of mens in Smyrna who'd love to be a husband to a hardworkin' woman like you!"

Bessie jumped up from the chair, grabbed up her bonnet, and jammed it on her head. Then she wagged her finger in Tessa's face. "Let me tell you somethin'! You ain't decidin' who I'm goin' marry. I ain't decided for you! If you ain't wantin' to speak to Pettigrew, then I will!"

Then without another word, she stormed out the kitchen door, slamming it hard, and left the speechless Tessa standing with a cup of coffee in her hand.

The next day Bessie went back to the Pettigrew house, only this time she had come to see Mrs. Pettigrew. When Tessa opened the front door, Bessie snapped, "I ain't come to talk to you. I come to see Miz Pettigrew." She stormed past her and went to the parlor where Mrs. Pettigrew was sitting by the window reading the Bible. Bessie knew Mrs. Pettigrew held strong convictions about marriage and believed a man and a woman were ordained by God for the purpose of rearing children. She knew this because she had once eavesdropped on her conversation to Will about her desires to have children. Will told her not to trouble herself because she was too frail to bear children.

Without wasting any time, Bessie told her why she had come. "Mrs. Pettigrew, I done found me a man and I wants to marry him. Now, the man I wants to marry is on Margrace Plantation. I wants to buy his freedom and I wants you to go to Mr. Au Bignon and get his papers."

Mary closed her Bible and paused for a moment. "I'm not sure I can do this, Bessie. You see I'm not well and. . . ."

"Miz Pettigrew," Bessie quickly interrupted, "I ain't wantin' to have children without a husband and. . . ."

"Oh!" Mary gasped and clutched at her heart, and before Bessie could finish speaking she interrupted. "Bessie, you cannot bear a child without the benefit of a husband! It's against God's will!"

Bessie suddenly realized that Mrs. Pettigrew had assumed she was pregnant. Well, there was no need to tell her differently if this would convince her to intercede. She motioned for Bessie to come closer to her. When Bessie came to her, Mrs. Pettigrew began. "Bessie, for God's good grace, I will go see Mary Eliza for you. She's a God-fearing woman. You must now pray to God to forgive your sin!" She wiped her eyes with a lace handkerchief and then motioned for Bessie to leave.

Bessie left the house feeling pleased with herself. If Tessa had gone to talk to Mrs. Pettigrew, she probably wouldn't have agreed to see Mr. Au Bignon.

The day after Mary Pettigrew's conversation with Bessie, she had Nate drive her in her buggy to Margrace Plantation. It didn't take long for them to reach the Margrace plantation, the huge, white mansion set back from the road. Its green lawn was dotted with flowering trees and shrubs in full bloom. Surrounding the velvety green lawn was a black iron fence about six feet high with a locked gate. With Mrs. Pettigrew at his side, Nate turned the horse into the graveled lane that led up to the locked iron gate. As they waited in the buggy at the gate, a large brown hound raced down off the veranda to the gate and began barking furiously.

They could see Au Bignon sitting at a white wicker table on the veranda eating his breakfast. When he heard the hound barking, he yelled in a booming voice, "Amos. Mind that dog!"

In minutes a barefooted black man hurried out of the house and down to the gate, calling to the dog. "Shep! Git on back to the porch!"

As the man came near, the dog quickly cowered, then trotted back up onto the veranda and laid down at Au Bignon's feet.

"Mornin'," Amos said. "Shep be a good dawg. He jest lacks to make a racket."

"Good morning," Mary and Nate replied.

Then Mrs. Pettigrew squinted her eyes and leaned her head out the buggy window. "I believe you're Amos. You made boots for my husband Will."

"Yes, ma'am," Amos concurred. "I 'member Mr. Will. He be a good man."

"Yes. He was," Mary replied, agreeing with Amos. "Mr. Pettigrew has passed on now."

"Yes, ma'am. I done heer'd he now gone."

Amos quickly unlocked the big shiny lock with a key and pulled opened the heavy iron gate. Nate drove the horse and buggy up to the veranda. Amos followed and helped Mary out of the buggy. Then Nate drove the horse and buggy around to the back where he tied the reins to a hitching post and waited.

Mary, all dressed in black, came slowly to the steps. "Good morning, Mr. Au Bignon, and God be with you."

"God be with me?" Au Bignon asked in an astonished voice and broke out into boisterous laughter. "God's long forgotten my name, Mrs. Pettigrew."

He turned and called back into the house, "Amos! Bring me some more fried chicken! Hot!"

Without getting up to help Mrs. Pettigrew, he motioned with his hand for her to come up on the veranda.

It took Mary some time before she climbed the steps to the veranda to sit down in one of the white wicker chairs.

Wiping his fingers on a towel that was on the table, Au Bignon said, "Mrs. Au Bignon and Dolly are visiting her cousins over in Cowpens." He frowned, "I don't much like Cowpens. A lot of fools in that town."

"I went there when my late husband was alive," Mary told him.

Au Bignon looked at Mary disapprovingly. "I heard about you listening to that ole Coffin fella."

"Prophet Coffin was quite an inspiration, a real religious man," was Mary's reply.

"Last I heard they had him chained up on Scroggs Island."

"God will free him," Mary replied confidently.

Karl grunted, then called back again toward the kitchen. "When you're going to bring me my chicken, Amos? I don't have all day."

Later, Amos came out to the porch with a plate of hot chicken. "I had to fry some mo'," he said quietly and set the plate on the wicker table.

Au Bignon reached into the plate, took a chicken leg, and began eating it. Amos poured him some more black coffee from the coffeepot that had been sitting on the table. Karl then drank some of the black coffee from the cup, belched, and wiped his mouth on the towel.

"Amos can't cook worth a damn!" he said to Mary. "He can make shoes, but he can't fry good chicken." He sighed. "I make do with him since I've had to get all my hands in the fields. It's planting time."

Au Bignon looked out at a field in the distance, green with new corn sprouts coming up from the ground. "I like eating where I can see my field hands work. Mrs. Au Bignon don't like me eating on the front porch, so this will be our secret." He winked at Mary.

Mary took exception to his winking at her and she also resented his poor manners, but she had not come to see him. She had come to see his wife, believing that Mary Eliza was a kind and sensitive woman who would be willing to let Enoch go so he could take care of his fatherly duties.

"I was hoping to speak to Mrs. Mary Eliza this morning," Mary said as she sat with folded hands across her lap.

"You can speak to me, Mrs. Pettigrew," Karl said gruffly. "My wife and I don't keep secrets from each other."

"But I really wanted to talk to her. When will she return home?"

Karl frowned as he rubbed his chin thoughtfully. "Can't say. When she visits her folks, she stays quite a long time. Sometimes they stay a week, a month, a couple of months."

"Then I guess I'd better tell you, because I don't believe there is a lot of time," Mary replied thoughtfully. "I came to speak to her about a business matter, Mr. Au Bignon."

"What kind of business?"

Mary was silent for a few minutes, then said, "About buying one of your slaves."

Au Bignon had reached over and was taking another piece of chicken from the plate, but he dropped it. He shifted his bulk in his chair to where he could look directly at Mary. "My niggers ain't for sale."

He leaned his body closer toward Mary and glared at her. "It's nigger-lovers like you who are spoiling things for us landowners. That's why we got all this news of war going around. Can't folks get it into their heads that we need our slaves? If we don't have slaves, who the hell do they think is going to work the fields and bring in the crops?"

"Mr. Au Bignon, I am a woman of God," was Mary's reply. "And it's wrong to hold another person against his will. God will punish you if you disobey him!"

When Au Bignon tried to interrupt, she silenced him by putting up her hand. "I also believe that Mary Eliza is also a woman of God, and she knows that it's not right to hold another human being in bondage. Haven't you heard about the children of Israel? Haven't you heard how God delivered them from the wicked Pharaoh? If you haven't, I know Mary Eliza has."

Au Bignon heaved his six-foot frame up off his chair. "Mrs. Pettigrew, I don't give a damn about the children of Israel! Mary Eliza will do what I tell her to do! Amos!" he yelled. "Bring around that buggy!"

Amos, who had been eavesdropping at the door, quickly went and told Nate to bring the buggy to Mary. He felt a pang of sadness as he watched Mrs. Pettigrew drive off because he had thought that she had been talking about buying him his freedom. After all, he knew she had manumitted her slaves.

The minute Bessie saw the buggy coming back from Margrace, she ran up the hill to the house to hear the good news. When Mrs. Pettigrew reported the news, Bessie was inconsolable. Mrs. Pettigrew was also inconsolable because of the sin she thought Bessie had committed. She told Bessie to begin a prayer vigil and ask God's forgiveness.

Bessie prayed constantly to God but not for forgiveness that she was pregnant. She wanted God to help free the man she loved.

"Lord, I ain't never asked you for nothin'," she prayed. "Even when the yoke of slavery was 'round my neck! I'd say to myself, 'This be your will, Lord. When you gits tired of me bein' in bondage, you goin' set me free! And I jest kept on waitin' on you to act and you did! Now, I'm askin' you, Lord, to let Enoch go! Lack you did the children of Israel!'"

It had been several weeks since Tessa had heard about Bessie's bad news. Although she was pleased that Au Bignon wouldn't sell Enoch, she had become worried about her friend. Tessa went to see her, not knowing what to expect from Bessie.

When Tessa reached Bessie's house, she rushed in without knocking and put her arms around the startled Bessie. "I'm real sorry about your bad news," she said, trying to sound sincere.

Upon seeing her best friend, Bessie began sobbing uncontrollably in Tessa's arms.

"Bessie, Bessie," Tessa said, trying to console her. "It ain't like Enoch died. You gots to git hold of yourself. Women in the valley givin' birth need you to help them through it. They countin' on you."

Bessie thumped on her chest with her fist. "I can't help them women when I'm carryin' this big ole burden in my heart! I goin' bust wide open one of these days!"

"No, you ain't," Tessa said reassuringly and wiped Bessie's eyes with her apron. "Now, you just come and set down and stop your cryin' and listen to me."

Tessa led her over to a big armchair and helped Bessie sit down and then she sat down. "On Sunday, you and me goin' git dressed up in our finery and Nate's goin' take us to church over in Cowpens. Nate said he heer'd that big ole colored church is stuff full of good-lookin' mens on Sundays! They be lookin at you and givin' you the eye. Next thang you know, you done hooked one!"

Bessie buried her face in her hands. After a few minutes, she said sadly, "I know you tryin' to help me, Tessa, but I ain't never goin' git over Enoch. You see, Enoch ain't carin' how I look. I ain't pritty like you, but it don't matter to him. He likes me jest the way I am. He always whisper in my ear when we be together at night, 'Woman, you suits me real fine!' Tessa, you jest don't know what he be like!"

Tessa knew what Enoch was like, a cheat and a liar, but she didn't have the heart to tell Bessie. All she could do was try to comfort her.

It was now June, a month after Bessie had tried to buy Enoch's freedom, and since that time he had not come once to her house. She complained bitterly to Tessa that Au Bignon must have had Brute punish Enoch because she had wanted to buy his freedom, and now Enoch was afraid to sneak off at night to see her.

However, Tessa knew differently, because Nate had seen Enoch many nights with a woman drinking whiskey in the woods near Smyrna.

Once Nate asked Enoch how he was able to sneak off the plantation at night. Enoch laughed and said he just waited until Brute went on one of his binges and got drunk from drinking homebrew whiskey. Then he'd listen at the window until he heard Brute snoring, and he knew it was safe for him to go.

"I goes anywheres I wants to," Enoch bragged to Nate. "Only thang is, I gots to come back 'fore sunrise."

"Why then?" Nate asked.

"No matter how drunk ole Brute gits, he always wake up 'fore sunrise. He jest lack a rooster. He know when that ole sun be comin' up."

Jumpin' the Broom

A month had passed since Bessie tried to buy Enoch's freedom. In that time, he had not come to see her. Bessie had grown despondent because she now believed she might never see Enoch again. She had prayed, cried, and prayed some more, but God had not answered her prayers. Enoch was lost to her.

When Tessa saw her friend in such a state, she tried to cheer her up by telling her it was planting time and Enoch was too tired to sneak out at night.

"That ain't it," Bessie said positively. "Ole Au Bignon gittin' ready to sell Enoch, and it's all 'cause of me!"

How Tessa wanted to tell her about Enoch's escapades, but she dared not. She had promised Nate that she wouldn't, and she had to keep her word.

On the night Enoch finally came again, Bessie was ironing one of her white dresses. Being a midwife, she never knew when she'd be called, and she was expected to wear a white dress during the delivery. As she stood sadly pushing a flat iron back and forth across her heavily starched white dress, her thoughts drifted off to Enoch and how much she loved him. She had opened the door because her tiny kitchen had become hot from the stove's heat.

Enoch always moved quietly and cautiously, and because Bessie's back was to the door, she didn't hear or see him arrive.

He stuck his head inside her door and yelled in a loud, booming voice, "You still be wantin' to jump the broom, woman?"

Bessie was so startled that she dropped the hot iron onto the floor, and as she jumped around, she saw Enoch standing in her doorway grinning.

"Enoch!" cried the excited Bessie, and she ran to him and put her arms around his waist and hugged him tightly.

In a firm voice Enoch said, "You best pick up that smoothin' iron, woman, or you be done burnt down your house."

She rushed over, picked up the iron, and set it on the stove. Then she came back to Enoch and put her arms around his waist again. "Enoch, baby, where you been all this time? Ole Au Bignon been keepin' you from me?"

Enoch puckered up his lips and replied poutingly, "I kin come and go as I please now, woman."

Bessie looked frightened, and she quickly loosened her arms from around his waist. "You been sold?"

"No, woman. I'm a free man!"

"You been set free?"

"Sho' is. Ole Au Bignon done give me my freedom! Tonight!" He proudly reached into his pants pocket and handed her a paper. "Read it! It's goin' say, 'Enoch be free'!"

Bessie quickly took the paper and went over to her lamp on the kitchen table and lit it. Straining hard to read the words, she said in disbelief, "This paper say you is free!"

Then she began jumping up and down, clapping her hands and half crying. "Oh, Enoch! God done answered my prayers! I been prayin' for God to set you free ever since I tried to buy your freedom. You 'member that?"

"Yeah, yeah," Enoch replied sullenly. "I knows all 'bout that. Nate done told me a hundred times."

Bessie kept on talking as if she were a preacher. "There been times when I almost give up hope, but that little ole voice inside me kept on sayin', 'Hold on, Bessie!'"

Enoch seemed to tire of her babbling. "You ain't answered me, woman I axed you if you wants to jump the broom with me?"

Bessie hugged him again and then buried her head against his strong chest. "Enoch, you knows I wants to marry you. You is the only man I ever loved!"

They stood in close embrace for a few minutes, then Bessie stepped back and gazed at Enoch for a minute. Then she asked, "How come ole Au Bignon set you free?"

"Thangs happen, woman."

"Au Bignon turned Miz Pettigrew down when she tried to buy you last month. He turnt her down jest like that!" Bessie snapped her fingers. "Now, why this month he done freed you? Enoch, that ole man be up to no good."

"You got somethin' to eat?"

Bessie quickly forgot about her question to Enoch and lovingly took his hand and led him to a chair at her table. "Now, you jest put your feets under my table."

Enoch sat down at the table, and Bessie went to the kitchen stove and took down her heavy iron frying pan that was hanging on a nail over the stove. She dug into a can of white lard and put a spoonful of it into the pan to melt. "I'm goin' make you some fried chicken and hot biscuits!"

Bessie put some flour on a plate, took three pieces of raw chicken from a damp cloth that she kept in a tin bucket, and quickly floured them. Then she placed the chicken into the hot grease. While the chicken was frying, she mixed flour and milk into a dough, rolled out the dough, cut out some biscuit, and put the bread into the oven.

"That cookin' chicken sho' smell good," Enoch said. "I ain't ate no fried chicken since the last time I was heah."

Bessie gave him a questioning look. "It's been over a month."

"Yeah," Enoch replied. "Sho' been a long time. Too long to git a piece of fried chicken."

When the food was ready, Bessie put it on the table. Enoch's eyes lit up when he smelled the aroma of fried chicken and hot biscuits. Before Bessie even had a chance to sit down, he began eating ravenously.

As Enoch was eating his third and last piece of chicken, Bessie inquired again. "How come Au Bignon set you free?"

Enoch kept on chewing.

"You ain't said 'bout Au Bignon's house fallin' down," Bessie insisted. "What you mean?"

"Woman, will you let me eat? I be starved!"

Bessie frowned. "I need some answers, Enoch. You can't mess 'round with that ole man."

Enoch licked his fingers and looked up at her. "I done struck me a bargain with him. It be so secret that nobody but me and Miz Au Bignon know about."

"Must be some kind of a secret!" Bessie retorted. "Au Bignon ain't known for lettin' his slaves go free. No siree! He'd rather see them dead than free."

"This secret be 'tween me, you, Miz Au Bignon, and the ole man."

"Now, wait a minute, Enoch," Bessie said. "I don't know nothin' 'bout no secret! I ain't in no secret if I don't know what it is!"

"Woman, this 'tween me and my Maker," Enoch replied, chewing loudly as he looked up at the ceiling. "My lips be closed. So you can jest quit askin'."

Bessie shoved her chair back from the table. "If you don't tell me why Au Bignon's house is fallin' down, I ain't goin' be in your secret!"

Enoch took her hands into his hands. "You love me, woman?"

"You know I do," Bessie replied and inched her chair closer to Enoch.

"Then you gots to be in this secret, or I ain't goin' be no free man! Tell you what, tonight, when we is in bed all snuggled up together, I'll tell you the secret."

Bessie giggled. "You like apple pie, Enoch? I can pop one in the stove. It's still hot."

"Woman, I loves apple pie!"

Bessie sat at the table and watched Enoch eat the apple pie. She had some more questions to ask him, but decided to wait until he had finished the pie. From the way he was eating, that wouldn't be long.

The Baby

Enoch and Bessie had been married only a month when they bought five acres of land down near the river in a grove of trees and had a four-room house built. The house consisted of four rooms: a parlor, two bedrooms, and a kitchen. Each room had a window, and there was a front door and a back door. The house also had a large front porch where Bessie had hung a swing.

And tongues were wagging in Smyrna. How did Enoch get his freedom without paying for it? Where did he and Bessie get money to buy five acres of land and to build a house? True, Bessie worked hard, but she hadn't delivered that many babies in the valley. Besides, a midwife didn't make that much money.

Bessie refused to talk about her good fortune. When Tessa inquired, she told her, "It's none of your business where me an' Enoch got our money. Quit meddlin'!"

"Enoch be into sneaky business," Tessa told Nate the evening after she had asked Bessie where she and Enoch had gotten money to buy land and build a house.

"Maybe Au Bignon done sent him to Smyrna to see if we be keepin' runaways," Nate replied as he sat waiting for his wife to put his supper on the table. "From now on, I'll mind what I say and do 'round Enoch."

"Ain't nobody hidin' slaves in Smyrna," Tessa replied. She filled Nate's bowl with pinto beans and set it on the table near a plate of hot cornbread.

"I know that and you know that," Nate said, dipping his spoon into his bowl of beans. He ate a spoonful of beans, then continued to talk. "It be jest like Enoch to make up somethin' to tell Au Bignon for all that money he done give him. Next thang we know ole Brute be sneakin' 'round our house." He ate some more beans, then said, "Ever'body in Smyrna is jumpy now with all that talk of war."

"Aw, quit talkin' 'bout war. It's jest talk and that's all," Tessa remarked and went over to a cradle she kept in the kitchen and looked in it.

"Oh, you little rascal," she said lovingly to her sleeping baby in the cradle. "Mama goin' let you sleep."

Tessa had given birth to a baby boy nine months before and had named him Ozell. When she was cooking in the kitchen, she'd bring the cradle in so she could watch him. Ozell loved crawling and getting into things in the kitchen.

During the days after getting Mrs. Pettigrew's noonday meal, Tessa would bundle up Ozell and go visit Bessie in her new home. She loved sitting with Bessie on her cool front porch, waving to everyone who went by on the road.

Bessie knew all the gossip in the community because the women she helped in childbirth confided in her. Then she'd tell Tessa, who loved hearing gossip.

Bessie would rock Ozell in her rocker until he'd fall asleep, then she'd lay him on her big feather bed and put puffy pillows around him to keep him from falling off the bed onto the floor. She envied Tessa because she too wanted to be a mother.

"Me and Enoch keeps on tryin' to git us a baby," Bessie told her friend as they sat one day on her porch sipping mint water, trying to keep cool in the hot July weather. "Enoch told me last night that if I don't git a baby soon, I be gittin' too old."

"Enoch's a fool," Tessa snapped, taking a sip of her mint water. "If he stops drankin' likker, he could give you a baby. That ole likker got him stopped up."

Bessie sighed heavily. "Enoch likes the bottle."

"Make him stop! Put your foot down," Tessa demanded.

"It ain't that easy with Enoch."

Just then Ozell, who had been sleeping, woke up and began crying. Tessa went and brought him back to the porch. She held the baby on her lap and began nursing him.

"When you goin' wean that boy?" Bessie asked. "He old enough."

"I know," Tessa sighed. "I can't see why you want a baby. Babies is trouble!"

"Me and Enoch got this nice house here. It jest seems a shame for us to be here all by ourselves."

Bessie rubbed her stomach looking at Tessa. "You know somethin'? If I can't get me a baby in my belly, I'm goin' see if I can get one from some woman who don't want hers."

Tessa stopped nursing her baby. "I ain't never heard of a woman not wantin' her baby. Ain't natural!"

"Tessa, you ain't knowed nothin'. Lots of women don't want their babies, black women and white women alike."

"I ain't heard of that." Tessa wiped her baby's mouth with her apron. "You done had enough," she said to her son.

Shaking a finger ruefully at Tessa, Bessie continued. "You don't know the half of it. I see lots of stuff other women don't see, bein' I'm a midwife. I knowed lots of women who would jest as soon give their babies away as they would a rabbit! They don't want to be bothered sucklin' a baby. It gets in their way for doin' other things." She winked at her friend.

"God help their souls," Tessa replied, rocking Ozell in her arms.

"You know something?" Bessie said. "Next time some woman say 'You kin have this baby,' I'm goin' take it."

Tessa stopped rocking her baby. "You best talk that over with Enoch."

Bessie bristled. "I ain't gots to talk nothin' over with Enoch! He do as I say!"

"If Enoch be wantin' a baby, he be done give you one," was Tessa's reply. "He ain't wantin' to wipe no baby's shitty ass."

"Enoch ain't got to do no ass-wipin'. If I gets me a baby, I'll take care of that."

Tessa looked quizzically at her friend. "You sho' you can't have a baby?"

"If I could get me a baby, I'd do so."

"Well, all I kin say is I got enough trouble with my own young'un. I sho' ain't wantin' to raise up somebody else's. I say if they git 'em, raise 'em! Don't go givin' 'em away. Children ain't like dogs you kin give away if you don't like 'em! God give you a baby it's your duty to raise that baby. I ain't got no use for peoples who give away a child!"

"Tessa, you don't know what peoples be up against when they give away their child. I ain't goin' do no judgin'. I let God do that." Bessie stood up and looked up at the slowly sinking sun in the sky. "You best git on back to Miz Pettigrew's. It's almost time for her supper."

"Yeah," Tessa concurred. "That ole woman is skin and bones, but she eats like a mule." She cuddled her baby in her arms, walked down off the porch, and headed out to the road.

A few days later when Tessa went to visit Bessie she wasn't at home. Every day for a week, Tessa went to Bessie's house but she was still not there. Soon, she grew worried about her friend.

Late one afternoon after visiting Bessie's house, Tessa saw Enoch staggering down the road. When he reached her, she knew he'd been drinking because he reeked of whiskey.

She disliked Enoch with a passion. She believed he had taken advantage of Bessie by marrying her. He never loved her. All he wanted was a woman to cook, wash, and put bread on the table for him to eat, while he caroused with low-life women. Now, he had a cushy life at Bessie's expense. No wonder Bessie wanted a child to look after! She certainly didn't get much love from Enoch, the scoundrel.

"Where's Bessie?" Tessa inquired.

"Bessie bin called away," Enoch replied as he reeled back and forth trying to keep his balance.

"What for?"

"Some woman up in the hills givin' birth. Bessie went up there to help her out."

Tessa eyed Enoch for a moment. He was lying. She could tell. She knew of no black people living up that way. True, there had been whispers about some people living up in the hills who called themselves black Indians, but no one knew for sure.

"Enoch, ain't no black folks living up in them hills." She walked closer to Enoch, put her hands on her hips, and gave him a mean look. "You is a lyin' low-down rascal! You know Bessie ain't up in no hills, 'cause ain't no black folks up there!"

"Tessa," Enoch snapped. "You ain't knowed where all black folks live. Plenty black folks livin' 'round here you ain't heer'd 'bout."

"What's their names?" Tessa yelled right into Enoch's face.

Enoch glared at her and stepped backwards. "I ain't said. Now, I ain't gots no more time talkin' to you."

"Just tell me names of the folks Bessie is helpin', and you ain't gots to talk to me."

"Tessa, you is a woman who lacks to poke your big ole nose in folks' matters. I ain't gots to tell you nothin'."

Enoch then staggered off down the road talking to himself, leaving the angry Tessa standing there glaring at his back.

A week later, Nate saw Enoch. Enoch told Nate that Bessie was home and she had brought a baby home with her when she returned from her midwife job. Nate rushed to Mrs. Pettigrew's house. He found Tessa washing clothes in the backyard.

"You ain't gone 'lieve this!" He called breathlessly to Tessa who was hanging a wet sheet on the clothesline. "I jest saw Enoch, and he said Bessie brought home a baby last night!"

Tessa stopped. "He say what?"

"That Bessie got a baby!"

"Here, finish hangin' out this sheet," she said and handed Nate four clothespins. Then she rushed into the kitchen, put on her bonnet, picked up Ozell from his cradle, and started for Bessie's house.

Bessie was sitting on the porch with the baby wrapped in a light blanket rocking back and forth in her big rocking chair. She smiled broadly when she saw Tessa coming.

As soon as Tessa started up the path to the porch, Bessie called to her, "God done answered my prayers, again!"

Breathing hard from hurrying and carrying her baby, Tessa could hardly reply, "I ain't b'lieved . . . my ears . . . when Nate . . . give me the news!"

She struggled up the porch steps to the smiling Bessie. After catching her breath for a few minutes, she finally said, "Let me see this baby."

Slowly, Bessie unwrapped the blanket so she could see her baby. It was a boy who had honey-brown skin, straight black hair, and bluish-green eyes.

A startled look came over Tessa's face as she stared down at the baby, then looked at Bessie. "This ain't no black baby!" she announced.

"No," Bessie replied calmly. "He be Indian and white."

"He be what?"

"He white and Indian."

Sounding concerned, Tessa quickly said, "Bessie, you ain't got no business with a white child! You got to give him back!"

"I ain't goin' do no such thing!" Bessie cried and held the baby close to her breasts. "This baby is mine!"

"Bessie, these white folks be after you 'fore sundown if they find out what you just told me."

"Ain't nobody else goin' know but you, me, and Enoch. I ain't goin' tell. Enoch ain't goin' tell. Is you goin' tell?"

When Tessa saw how her friend was clutching the baby, she didn't want to provoke an argument, so she said, "Ozell is sleepin'. I'm goin' lay him on your bed." Bessie nodded.

When Tessa returned, she sat down in a chair next to Bessie's rocker and remained silent as Bessie quietly rocked her baby.

Finally, she spoke. "You know I ain't goin' give away your secret. But other peoples goin' start askin' you questions. What you goin' tell them?"

Bessie kept on rocking her baby. "If anybody ask," she replied, "I tell them he be all Indian. Some Indians look white, you know."

Tessa saw how contented Bessie looked and decided not to ask any more questions about who the baby was.

"How'd you git him?"

"Well, a couple weeks ago, a white man come to the house," Bessie began. "It was late at night and Enoch and me was sleepin'. I woke up when I heard a rappin' at the door. It scared me! So, I tippy-toe up, got my gun from behind the door, and jerked it opened!"

"What was it?" Tessa asked anxiously.

"This ole, grizzly white man was standing there!"

"Well, what did he do?"

"He threwed up his hands when he see'd my gun."

Tessa pulled up her chair closer to Bessie to make sure she didn't miss anything. "And . . ."

Annoyed at her interruptions, Bessie retorted, "Will you let me tell the story!"

Tessa grew quiet and Bessie continued her story. "I say, 'What you want, white man?'"

"He say, 'My little wife is havin' a baby. Kin you come? . . .'"

"I say, 'Where you live?' and he pointed back up toward the hills."

Tessa couldn't resist another question because this story was getting a bit confusing to her. "How did this ole white man know you was a midwife?"

Bessie frowned deeply and Tessa grew silent. "He told me some white folks who live over in the valley told him I was a midwife. Since I'm a Christian, I couldn't turn that ole man away, 'specially since his wife was in need. So I wakes up Enoch and tells him I had to go help that man's wife. He say, 'Bessie if you gots to go, you gots to go!'"

"Sounds like Enoch." Tessa retorted. "He ain't gittin' his big butt up to go out at night."

"Tessa, Enoch can't birth no baby. I help with the birthin'." Bessie then held the baby up and patted its buttocks.

"Ain't you scared to go with a white man at night? You ain't knowed who he is? What if he be a paddyroller jest waitin' to grab you? Next thang you knowed, you be a slave again."

"I knowed in my heart that he ain't no slave catcher. I could see it in his eyes that he needed me bad! God done sent that man to me!"

"Well, go on and tell your story," Tessa said impatiently.

Bessie went on telling the story with relish. "I get my bag, my shawl, and I jumped on his hoss behind him. We rode most of the night. It was near daybreak when we get to his place."

"Where was his place?"

"It be a shack back up in them hills."

Bessie paused. "I sho' was glad to get there. I tell you, Tessa, my butt was tired! We go in the house and I see this little slip of a gal layin' there on a bunch of rags in a bed."

"What kind of gal?"

"She be Indian," Bessie answered. "I could tell by her long black hair and brown skin. Oh, that child was gripped in pain!"

"You don't say!" Tessa exclaimed, trying hard to sound as if she believed Bessie.

"She was. That child needed help real bad. I throwed off my shawl and got right to work. It took her and me all night to get this child birthed!"

"How come you stayed up there so long with her after the baby got heah?"

"If I ain't stayed with that child, she'd be gone from this world and so would this sweet baby."

Tessa reached over and patted Bessie on her shoulder. "I was real worried about you. Thought that rascal Enoch did somethin' to you."

"I'm a Christian woman," Bessie replied sweetly. "God looks after his sheep." Then she gazed at Tessa. "Why you think Enoch goin' hurt me? Enoch know who wear the pants in this house!"

Tessa turned her attention to the baby again. "How come them folks give you their baby?"

"Now, I done told you that God sent that man to me. This ole white man was takin' this gal back to the Indian country over the mountains. He ain't wantin' to take no baby with him."

Bessie thought for a moment. "He be some kind of a hunter. You know, he catchin' thangs outta the water. Now, you know a baby ain't got no business near cold water! So, he gives this sweet baby to me! I told him I'd be a good momma to him. And I will." She kept smiling down at the baby.

The story Bessie told was hard for Tessa to believe, and she hoped Bessie would not tell this story to other people. She didn't know where Bessie had gotten that baby, but it certainly wasn't from an old white man and an Indian girl.

Tessa, however, was determined not to question Bessie's story. "How you goin' feed this baby? You ain't got no milk."

"I ain't been a midwife for nothin'," Bessie replied. "I heat up some of my cow's milk and then I spoon it into the baby's mouth. It takes awhile for him to git it all down, but I feed all that milk to him. In a little while he goin' be big and fat!"

"Let me hold the little rascal," Tessa said, and took the baby from Bessie. She tickled the baby under his chin. He smiled and began waving his arms about, making gurgling sounds.

Tessa cooed at the baby, then asked, "Ain't that Indian gal wantin' to keep her baby?"

"Child, that gal do what that ole man say."

"What you goin' name him, little Enoch?"

Bessie sucked her tooth and frowned. "I'm goin' name my baby Webster!" She seemed so pleased at the sound of the name that she said it several times. "Don't that name make chills run down your back?" With resolve, Bessie stated, "I'm giving my baby a white folks' name."

"Why you want to do that?" Tessa asked. "Ain't black folks names' good enough?"

"Black folks names all be slave names! Some ole slave master done give you the name. Slaves sometime were called any ole thing if the master didn't like them. You remember how ole man Pettigrew tried to take away Smyrna's name?

Tessa nodded in agreement as Bessie went on talking. "You and me gots good names. I guess ole Pettigrew was too dumb to think of something else."

"He wasn't too bad," Tessa said.

"He ain't freed us," Bessie snapped and took her baby from Tessa and began running her finger up and down the baby's cheek, admiring him lovingly. "Since my baby ain't no slave, I give him a free name."

"What you mean a free name?"

"Tessa, white folks ain't been no slaves."

"All names be the same, Bessie. They jest lets you know when to come."

Bessie wagged her finger at Tessa. "Now, that's where you be wrong. A name tells you who you is. And the right kind of name lets you know how much you be worth. White folks' names don't beat you down. You take them slavery names, they kin really pull you down!" She demonstrated by raising an arm up over her head and slowly letting her hand and her head bend forward toward the floor.

When Tessa stopped laughing, she said, "Bessie, you makin' too much 'bout a name. When Ozell was born, I jest named him the first thing that popped in my mind."

"That's what I'm talkin' 'bout," Bessie admonished her. "You jest can't call a baby anythin' that pop in your head! You need to take time and think 'bout a name. Think what it's goin' to mean to your baby. Is he goin' be proud of the name you give him? Is he goin' be 'shamed by the name? You got to think about that! It's a good thing that the name Ozell popped in your mind, cause it ain't a slave name." She looked down proudly at her baby. "My baby's got a smart name."

"What did you say you goin' call him?" Tessa asked.

"Webster!"

"Well, how you know your baby is goin' like the name Webster?"

"You know how I know?" Bessie said and stopped rocking. "Cause a real smart man was named Webster. And my boy goin' be jest like him." She paused for a moment in thought. "You 'member when Miz Pettigrew was teachin' me and you to read?"

"Sure do," Tessa answered and frowned. "I ain't never goin' forgit how hard that was. It was the hardest thang I ever did, and I've done lots of hard things."

"We learnt, didn't we?" Bessie put in.

"What's that got to do with the name you give your baby?"

"You 'member that big ole book Miz Pettigrew made us use when we wanted to know what a word was?"

Shaking her head vigorously, Tessa replied. "I try to forgit everthin' 'bout learnin' to read."

"The man who wrote that book was named Webster. Now you can't get no smarter than him. He done wrote the book!"

Bessie patted the baby on his buttocks again. "My boy is goin' be real smart. Just lack that man." She looked toward the kitchen. "Tessa, go put the coffeepot on."

Dutifully, Tessa went to the kitchen and set the coffeepot on the stove that was still warm from the morning's breakfast. She waited for the coffee to heat and then returned with two cups of hot coffee.

"How come you don't give him a Indian name?" she asked, carefully handing the hot coffee to Bessie. "You say he be part Indian."

"'Cause I don't know nothin' 'bout no Indian name. All I know is white folks' names and slaverytime names."

"He goin' have part of a slaverytime name anyway."

"How you figure that?"

"Ain't Enoch got Au Bignon's last name? Ain't he called Enoch Au Bignon?"

"I'm way ahead of you Tessa. I done got rid of Enoch's slaverytime name and my slaverytime name. From now on our last name is goin' be Epps."

"Where you git that last name? From that ole smart book?"

"Tessa, I ain't got to tell you all my business." Bessie took a sip of her coffee.

Then the two women began chatting happily while drinking hot coffee.

Amos

The Christmas after Bessie had gotten her baby, the people in Smyrna heard that Dolly Au Bignon, Karl and Mary Eliza's daughter, was dead. The community was shocked. How could a young girl die when she hadn't been sick? Although Dolly had had every comfort, she was a very unhappy girl. But being unhappy couldn't have caused her to die, they reasoned. Perhaps she died by her own hand? Maybe she drowned herself, some people said. She was always threatening to do so.

But all this talk was rumor because the Au Bignons knew how to keep secrets, and Dolly's death remained a mystery.

Karl and Mary Eliza Au Bignon were devastated. Six months after Dolly was buried, Margrace Plantation and its slaves were sold and the Au Bignons moved into Cowpens.

Thaddeus Green, a rich white man in Cowpens, bought Margrace and Au Bignon's slaves. Within a year he secretly sold the plantation to Eben Dobbs, a farmer whose land bordered Margrace. Dobbs was a secret member of the antislavery movement and allowed his slaves to buy their own freedom by hiring them to work the plantation for him.

A year before Margrace was sold, Caleb Johnson, a strange little white man with a big, long beard, came to Smyrna and opened a country store at the edge of town near the forest that stretched away toward the hills and the mountains beyond.

His store was built of rough-hewn wood and was meant to serve all the people in the valley. It had a wide front porch, and Caleb put three benches on it where customers could sit and talk. Upstairs over the store was a room where Johnson lived. In the middle of the store was a huge pot-bellied stove that kept the store warm in winter. In the basement where he kept all his supplies was another small, windowless room.

The store was well-stocked with sugar, coffee, crackers, penny candy, snuff, chewing and pipe tobacco, and hard-to-get canned goods. There were barrels of nails, screws, and clothespins. Two wooden buckets of strong cheeses sat on the wooden counter along with dry goods of shirts, overalls, cloth, thread, and sewing equipment. On the back walls hung farm tools: hoes, rakes, scythes, hammers, bridles, and horse collars.

Caleb was a man of few words who kept to himself. The black folks whispered that he belonged to an antislavery movement, but no one knew for sure.

Once a month he took his wagon and went over to Cowpens to the big stores and bought new supplies. In Cowpens he heard about Amos and how well he made shoes. Amos had bought his freedom from Dobbs by working for him on Margrace Plantation. He was now struggling to get enough money to open up his own shop.

Caleb needed a shoemaker for his store and offered Amos a space in his store to make shoes. Since Amos was having such a hard time in Cowpens, he accepted Caleb's offer and came to Smyrna. Amos rented the small, windowless room from Caleb in the basement of his store.

Johnson sold goods to the people of Smyrna as well as to the white people who lived in the surrounding valley. When his customers didn't have money to pay for their supplies, he'd put the amount of the goods on a bill and they'd pay him later.

Amos liked working for Caleb. "He be fair," Amos would say. "He pay you a day's wages for a day's work, and he ain't stuck up like the white folks in Cowpens. Caleb treat you like a man."

Amos often visited with Bessie and Enoch because he had known Enoch from their days on the Margrace Plantation. The two men would sit together drinking, talking about the times when they were slaves, what they did to survive the harsh treatment meted out to them by Au Bignon and his overseer, Brute.

"There wuz never no let-up," Amos told Bessie one day when he was eating dinner with her and Enoch. "That ole whip was always lashin' out on your back and your butt."

"Yep," Enoch added. "That's how come I drinks. When I drinks I forgit them ole hard times." He poured himself another drink from a bottle he had set down on the floor near his chair at the table.

"You drinks cause you likes the taste of likker," Bessie fired back at him.

"That too," Enoch replied and took another swallow of whiskey from his bottle.

Then he offered the bottle across the table to Amos, who refused. "I done had enough. Too much of that stuff will addle my brains."

When Amos was visiting Enoch and Bessie, he loved taking care of Webster. He'd rock him in his cradle and sing him songs. His singing caused the baby to smile and wave his arms about.

"You sho' is a pritty baby," Amos would say, taking Webster from his cradle and bouncing him on his knee. "You goin' give the pritty liddle gals a fit when you gits a man!"

One Sunday afternoon when Amos came to visit, Bessie wasn't at home. She had left the care of the baby to Enoch. Enoch began talking to Amos about his favorite subjects, women and drinking whiskey. When Webster began crying, Enoch ignored him. After a few minutes of the baby's crying, Amos took Webster from his cradle and began rocking him.

This irritated Enoch because Amos was paying attention to the baby and not to what he was talking about. "That baby cry all the time if he ain't settin' up on Bessie's lap," Enoch told Amos. "She done spoilt him real bad!"

"Aw, Enoch, you be jealous of your own baby," Amos replied. "Bessie loves this baby. That's why she hold him all the time. Quit fussin'."

"I ain't fussin', Amos. I'm tellin' the truth. That baby ain't goin' grow up to be nothin'! He wants his way all the time. When he gits a little older, I'm goin' let him know he ain't the boss in this house. I'm goin' take my hand to his tail!"

"You best not touch this baby, Enoch," Amos warned. "Bessie will take her big ole washin' stick to your butt."

"Bessie ain't goin' know."

Amos laughed. "Enoch, you ain't got no sense. You think this baby ain't goin' learn to talk? My 'vice to you is keep your hands off Webster."

Enoch just sucked his tooth, then reached for his whiskey bottle.

Reverend Dewey Dye

War! By March 1861, the Civil War rumors were now widespread in many parts of the South. In July, after the battle of Bull Run and the men of Smyrna had heard the outcome, many young black men rushed up to Fort Belton on the Nebo River to enlist in the Union Army. They were refused enlistment and told to return home. Some did. Others made their way farther north to join the abolitionists.

However, most white farmers who lived near the Bushy Mountains were not like the fire-eaters of the Deep South, the people who owned slaves. These white farmers owned no slaves. Most were sharecroppers struggling to eke out a living. Many were as badly off as some blacks, so they had little enthusiasm for fighting a rich man's war.

On one raw November night, Amos brought the tall, handsome black man to Bessie and Enoch's house. He stood well over six feet, sporting a goatee, and had a mouthful of gold teeth. Reverend Dye, as Amos had called him, was wearing a black swallowtail coat, starched white shirt, bow tie, and black leather shoes covered with gray spats.

Amos told them that Dye was a preacher and had known Caleb Johnson, the storekeeper, back in Virginia. Johnson had encouraged him to come and settle in Smyrna. Dye was rooming with Amos and was looking for a building to use for his church. Amos had shown him the old cottage that Bessie owned down near the river, and Dye thought the old house was just what he needed.

"I'm a man of God," Dewey spoke slowly and deliberately as the four sat in the lamplight around the kitchen table that evening. "I'm here to save sinners! I need a church."

Bessie was sitting at the head of the table. She clapped her hands, giving a knowing look at Enoch, and replied, "Praise the Lord for that news! We all need to git closer to God in these terrible times!"

Enoch, who was sitting to the left of Dye, frowned deeply. The idea of a church being so close didn't appeal to him at all. Bessie would have him there every time the church doors opened. Besides, Dewey wasn't Enoch's idea of a preacher; too flashy with his fancy clothes and gold teeth.

"Why don't you go on up the road apiece and build a new church?" Enoch said, pointing his finger as if to show the man the direction he meant. "'Sides, that ole house be close to the river and is knee deep in weeds. Them ole bugs eat you up in there when it gits hot!"

"Aw, Enoch," Amos put in, "that be jest the right place on hot summer nights. Ole river help keeps you cool durin' revival meetin'."

"Shet up, Amos!" Enoch snapped. "You ain't got no religion!"

"Plan on gittin' it," Amos replied good-naturedly. "That be better than some folks I be knowin'." And he gave Enoch a sharp look.

"Now, now," Reverend Dye said in a calm voice with his hands outspread in a peacemaking way. "I ain't here to start a riff. If Miss Bessie don't want to sell, I'll just have to go on over to Cowpens."

"No, you won't," Bessie quickly said. "That ole house is mine! I bought it from Miz Pettigrew after I was free. Now, bein' I'm a woman who done found God, I'm goin' let you use it for your church. I ain't wantin' no money for God's house!"

Reverend Dye then pushed back his chair from the table, stood up, and smiled down at Bessie. "God will bless you for this. Brother Amos, we best be going and let these people eat their supper."

As Amos pushed away from the table, Enoch whispered to him. "I'm goin' git you for this!"

Within a week, Reverend Dye had gone out to Cowpens, bought a wagon load of lumber, and hauled it down to the old house. Soon hammering and sawing were heard coming from the building.

Soon all of Smyrna was abuzz with anticipation of the coming church. But after a few days, the hammering ceased and several weeks went by and the church hadn't opened. Some people, along with Bessie, began to express skepticism about the preacher. He had stopped working at the church and was either seen riding to Cowpens or rowing a small boat up the Nebo River toward the huge army fort that stood on the high bluffs that overlooked the river.

Early one morning when Bessie had gone down to the river to fish, she saw a small boat bobbing up and down a good distance from her. Then a man rowed over near the riverbank and tied the boat to a sapling. He then climbed out.

Bessie couldn't discern who the man was, but saw that he was carrying a package. He hurried into the tall, thick reeds behind the church. In a few minutes the man appeared again, quickly got into the boat and rowed up the river and out of sight.

Bessie strained to see who was rowing the boat, but the boat was quickly swallowed up in the thick fog. What had the man done with the package? Had he left it in the church? If so, why?

Bessie stood there perplexed. Then it came to her. That man looked like Reverend Dye. He must have hidden the package in the church. Could what Enoch believed be true—that Dewey Dye was a robber?

"Why you say that, Enoch?" Bessie had questioned him on the night he'd told her that.

"'Cause he gots a pocketful of money. You tell me where he done got it. He ain't got no job, and he always sneakin' out of Smyrna for long stretches of time. What's he be doin' whilst he gone? Bessie, that man gots shifty eyes jest lack a robber!"

"Enoch, you be crazy!" Bessie had answered. "Reverend Dye is a man of God, so you best hold your tongue! Folks in Smyrna ain't goin' stand for you talkin' 'bout a man God done called. Next thing you know you be tarred and feathered!"

Maybe Dye was hiding his share of money, Bessie reasoned, as she stood there watching. What better place to hide money but in a church? No one would ever think to look there.

Finally, curiosity got the better of Bessie, so she walked through the reeds that had grown up around the church to its front door. To her surprise, the church door was padlocked with a big rusty lock. Try as hard as she might, she could not pull the lock off the door.

After not being able to get into the church, Bessie went back to her fishing. She, however, felt troubled by what she had seen. Had she allowed her house to be used by robbers? Well, she needed answers and the one person who could give her answers was Amos. He had brought this man to her house.

Bessie gathered up her empty straw basket, wrapped her fishing line around her fishing pole, and took the path from the riverbank that led past Caleb's store where Amos and the Reverend Dye were living.

When Bessie neared the store, she heard Amos calling to his chickens as he fed them in a pen behind the store. Upon seeing Bessie coming out of the woods, Amos stopped his feeding and set down his basket of corn .

"Well I be darned," Amos teased. "You been fishin' agin and you come by heah to give me a fish for my breakfast?"

"Fish ain't bitin' this mornin'," Bessie said.

Amos picked up his basket and beckoned to Bessie. "Come on in. I jest set my coffee to boil. I smells it."

Inside the store Bessie plonked herself down on a barrel turned upside-down and waited until Amos gave her a cup of his strong black coffee before she spoke.

"Where's Reverend Dye?" Bessie inquired.

"He went off some place. Ain't come back," Amos answered nonchalantly.

"I thought he'd be workin' down at the church," Bessie stated, sounding a bit suspicious.

"Why you say that?" Amos asked.

"I say that 'cause I want to know when is he goin' open the church for services?" Bessie replied and sipped some of the hot coffee.

Amos walked from the stove to his workbench that was near the back of the store. With his coffee cup in one hand, he sat down and reached under the bench for a pair of unfinished shoes. Holding them up as if he were inspecting them, he said, "I been workin' on these shoes for two days. Looks lack I ain't never goin' git through with 'em."

Bessie followed him back to his workbench and sat down on another barrel. "When did you say the church goin' be ready?"

"Ain't heer'd," Amos replied as he stuck a tack into his mouth and held it with his teeth while adjusting the shoe's sole. Then he took the tack from his mouth and hammered it into the shoe.

"Dye's been hammerin' and nailin' for a mighty long time," Bessie told Amos. "Seems he ought to be done."

"Takes a lon' time to fix that ole house. It be fallin' down."

Bessie jumped up off the barrel nearly spilling her coffee. "It wasn't fallin' down when Reverend Dye wanted it. You said so yourself!" she snapped indignantly.

Amos stopped hammering on the shoe. "Why you gittin' so upset, Bessie?"

"Cause we need worshipin' to start. Folks is waitin'."

"Y'all kin worship. Ain't nobody keepin' you from it."

"Where?"

"Where you want to."

"Well, I want to worship in my church!" Bessie shouted. "Why in the world do you think I let him have my house!"

"Church ain't ready, Bessie," Amos said calmly. "So stop hollerin'. You goin' wake up Caleb."

Bessie wagged her finger in Amos' face. then shouted again. "I don't care if I wake up the dead! If Reverend Dye stayed in Smyrna and stopped sneakin' off, the church would be finished! Where he be goin' and stayin' away so long? You answer me that!"

When Amos didn't answer, Bessie grew furious. She stomped over to the stair steps that led down to Amos' room and yelled. "Dewey Dye, is you down there? You git up heah! I got things to say to you!"

"Reverend Dye left out of heah last night," Amos said. "He ain't come back."

Bessie turned and faced Amos. "Where he gone?"

"When you next see him, you kin ask him," Amos replied. He stopped hammering, stood up from the bench, stretched his arms, and rubbed on one hip. "My ole bones git real stiff settin' on this hard bench. I gots to walk 'round some." Then he said to Bessie, "Who takin' care of Webster?"

"Enoch," she snapped.

"Then you best git on home."

Bessie gathered up her fishing gear and without saying good-bye stormed out of the store.

The day after Bessie had had her encounter with Amos, Tessa came to visit. She had Ozell wrapped up in a big blanket from head to toe trying to keep out the cold November wind.

"I just had to get away from Miz Pettigrew," she told Bessie as she came through the door. "That ole woman is gittin' crazier and crazier!"

"You must be gittin' crazy to come out in this cold carryin' that big ole boy," Bessie replied as she quickly shut the front door. "Put Ozell over in my bed with Webster. He ain't woke up yet."

Tessa tucked her sleeping baby under the covers next to the sleeping Webster in Bessie's big feather bed. "Where's ole Enoch?" she inquired.

"In the back bedroom sleepin'. He ain't feelin' too good this mornin', so he sleepin' back there."

"Bet he's drunk and you ain't lettin' him sleep with you," Tessa mumbled under her breath.

The two women then drew their chairs up close to the fireplace, trying to stay warm from the raw November weather.

"Somethin' sneaky is goin' on at that church," Bessie said as she poked into the fireplace, trying to perk up the dying blaze. A few sparks flew up from the burning green log, causing her to jump backward against her chair trying to avoid the sparks.

"Why you say that?" Tessa asked and pushed back from the now crackling blaze.

Bessie propped the poker against the fireplace and sat down. "I say that 'cause it ain't opened for worshipin'. Now, I ask you, why would you want a church if you was a preacher and don't aim to preach in it?"

"I can't answer that," was Tessa's reply.

"Tessa, that so-called preacher been had that church for the longest time and he ain't preached in it. It's almost Christmas!"

"Why you call Rev. Dye a so-called preacher? Bessie, he's a man of God and you got to be careful 'bout the man God calls."

Bessie frowned deeply at her, then answered. "He's a so-called preacher 'cause he ain't done no preachin'! A real preacher can't wait to spread the Word of God! No! All Dye been doin' is slippin' in and out of Smyrna, stayin' long spells at a time, and he come back with a pocketful of money. It be wartime and folks around here real hard up, but not him! Where he git all his money?" Bessie wagged a fat finger in Tessa's face. "Now, you answer me that!"

At first, Tessa didn't want to answer because she remembered when Bessie wouldn't tell her where she and Enoch had gotten their money to build her house and to buy land before they got Webster.

Finally Tessa said, "People don't like talkin' 'bout their money. They keeps it a secret." When she saw Bessie frowning at her, she quickly added, "Why don't you ask Amos? He brought the reverend to you, didn't he? He ought to know 'bout the church."

"I did," Bessie snapped. "He wouldn't say. Started talkin' 'bout his ole bones."

Bessie pulled her chair closer to Tessa and lowered her voice. "I tell you, somethin' strange is goin' on down at that church and I ain't quite figgered it out yet."

Tessa leaned closer, eager to hear some gossip. "You don't say!"

"I do say. Now, I think the good reverend is hidin' out in Smyrna under a guise of bein' a preacher. He ain't no preacher, 'cause if he be one, he'd be after all these sinners here." She shook her head resolutely. "He be into somethin' and it ain't preachin'!"

Tessa's eyes grew wide. "What you think he be in?"

Bessie pulled her chair even closer and talked through clenched teeth. "Maybe he be what Enoch said, a robber!"

"No!" Tessa cried and drew back.

Ignoring her outcry, Bessie went on. "Yistiddy, I went early to the river to catch a mess of fish. Whilst I was there I see'd a man climb out of a boat and go over to the church. I couldn't make out who he was, but he had this bundle under his arm, and went to the church. After awhile he comes back with no bundle, gits into that boat, and row away!"

"Well?" Tessa asked, not fully understanding what Bessie was trying to tell her.

"Well, what did he do with that bundle? And what was in it?" Bessie questioned Tessa, who just sat there with a quizzical look on her face.

Bessie then shoved her chair back from the fireplace and stood up, grabbed her heavy shawl, and wrapped it around her shoulders. "You and me is goin' down there and look in that church," she announced to Tessa. "I aim to find out what is in that bundle."

"But what 'bout the boys?" Tessa asked.

Without answering Tessa, Bessie went to the back bedroom door and opened it. "Enoch," she called. "You keep an eye on Webster and Ozell. They sleepin' in my bed. Tessa and me got to go out." She waited for Enoch to answer. When he didn't, she went into the bedroom and shook the sleeping Enoch hard. "Did you hear what I say?"

Enoch just grunted and turned his back and covered his head with the blanket. Bessie jerked back the blanket and slapped him hard on his buttocks. "I asked you a question!"

"I done heer'd you, Bessie," Enoch whined and pulled the blanket back over himself. "Now, leave me sleep. I ain't feelin' good."

"You be feelin' real bad if somethin' happen to them babies!"

"Ain't nothin' goin' happen, Bessie." He yawned and stretched his arms. "I keeps a eye on them."

Bessie came out of the bedroom and nodded to Tessa, "He'll keep his eye on the boys."

Just as she started for the outside door Bessie grabbed up the fire poker.

"What you need the poker for?" Tessa asked.

"'Cause there's a big ole lock on the door, and we kin break the lock with this poker! Come on!"

In a frightened voice, Tessa said, "We jest can't break into a church, Bessie. You talkin' 'bout God's house!"

In a belligerent voice, Bessie yelled, "It's my house! I only lent it to God!"

Without another word, Tessa snatched her shawl from the back of the chair where she had been sitting and followed Bessie out the door, around to the back of her house where the woods began.

The two women rushed down a path strewn with damp moldy leaves through leafless trees that stood stark against a gray sky. The raw November wind caused them to hunch forward as they made their way toward the Nebo River.

Soon they saw a sad-looking cottage leaning to one side toward a big chestnut tree in a grove of straggly trees a short distance from the river. The reeds to the right of the cottage had been trampled down by the people of Smyrna to make an opening down to the water where they launched their boats. Around the cottage's sides were tall, thick, brown reeds that were bent forward from the force of the wind.

When the women came to the church's door, Bessie, with iron poker in hand, attacked the rusty lock. Tessa waded through the damp reeds around to the back of the church where she saw an old window on one side of the big rock chimney that was slightly open. Standing on her tip-toes, she tried to reach it but couldn't, so she called to Bessie.

Since Bessie was making little headway opening the lock, she came to see what Tessa wanted.

"Look," Tessa pointed to the window. "Remember that ole window we used to climb out of at night?"

"I had forgotten about it," Bessie said and handed her the poker. Then, using both hands, she shoved the window wide enough for her to crawl through it and into the church. Then she pulled Tessa up through the opened window.

Inside, the two women stood staring around at the disarray inside the church.

"What's he been doin'?" Bessie finally asked in an unbelieving voice as she surveyed an unfinished pulpit and the many broken floorboards that needed nailing down.

"Guess he was makin' them benches," Tessa replied, pointing toward several wood benches near the door. Then she asked. "What we be lookin' for?"

Bessie gave her a little shove. "Go look under them benches. Maybe you'll find ole Dye's wad of bills."

Tessa giggled. "Any money I finds is mine!"

Pushing through cobwebs, the two women began their search of the church, looking under old buckets, pieces of planks, and some old broken chairs and debris scattered about in the room. All of a sudden, Tessa tripped and went sprawling onto the floor, landing with a big thud. Bessie turned when she heard the noise and saw Tessa lying on the floor.

"I tripped on somethin'," Tessa said as she picked herself up off the floor. She saw that her foot had been caught on a slightly raised floor plank and there seemed to be something stuffed underneath it.

Tessa reached under the floorboard and yanked out a brown package. Believing the package to be money, she didn't tell Bessie what she had found. If money was in the package she meant to keep it. Her hands trembled a bit and her heart beat a little faster as she slowly untied the string and unwrapped the brown paper.

Tessa fully expected to see money. But to her surprise, inside the package were handwritten notes, old maps, newspaper clippings, and all kinds of strange drawings. Not knowing what to make of the papers, she called Bessie.

In the dim light of the musty-smelling room, the two puzzled women inspected the package.

"What is all this? Is it bank robbin' stuff?" Tessa asked.

"This ain't 'bout no bank robbin' stuff," Bessie remarked solemnly as she read some of the newspaper clippings. "These papers be 'bout the war! Dye be mixed up in war stuff!"

The two women sat silently for a few minutes on a bench in the little church. Then Bessie spoke, "I wonder if he be workin' to help free the slaves?"

"He got to be on our side." Tessa added, "He a black man and all black folks want to free the slave."

Bessie patted Tessa's hand. "You don't know that and I don't know that. Enoch told me that a man told him that there be black folks who own black folks."

Tessa shook her head and replied, "I don't believe that."

"I ain't said that was true," Bessie remarked. "These be spy papers, and we best put them back where you found them and keep our lips sealed!"

Carefully, Bessie wrapped the package and tied it with the string, then put it back under the floorboard and hammered the loose nails down with her poker.

After they had climbed back out the window, Bessie pulled it down tight.

"Why hide them papers in the church?" Tessa asked as the two walked back up the path.

"Who gon' be lookin' in a church for spy papers? You know what could happen if them papers be found in your house?" Bessie asked. "You be locked up in jail over in Cowpens jest like that!" She snapped her fingers. "So we keeps quiet, real quiet!"

To Arms, All

In the year 1864, the Civil War was raging in South Carolina. People in Smyrna had grown worried about their community. Here they were, a free black community, near a few slave plantations. Might they be attacked? They had heard about the battle for Fort Wagner and the massacre at Fort Pillow. Some people believed that Northern soldiers might bring the fighting to the Cowpens area even though there were fewer than five slave plantations there. If this happened, Smyrna could be left in ruins.

Late one June night as Amos lay sleeping in his basement room, he was awakened by a noise coming from outside Caleb Johnson's store. It sounded like footsteps. So, believing that it was Reverend Dye returning from one of his many trips, Amos went back to sleep, but not for long.

He was awakened a second time by low, mumbling voices. Thinking again that it was Reverend Dye, Amos waited for him to come in. When he didn't, Amos crept up the stairs and peeked out an open store window. There on the porch were two dark figures. One was pouring something from a can all around the porch. It smelled like kerosene. The dark figures were setting fire to the store.

Amos tiptoed over and grabbed the loaded shotgun that he always kept under his workbench. Then he quietly slipped back over to the opened window, stuck the gun barrel through it, and fired. The shots zinged over one figure's head and slammed into a big oak tree that stood near the store, breaking off a limb.

Yelping like frightened dogs, the shadowy figures leaped off the porch and fled around to the back of the store and into the woods. Amos ran to the store's corner and fired another shot at them.

The loud gunshots hadn't awakened Caleb, who was a heavy sleeper, so Amos ran back into the store, up the narrow stairs to his bedroom, and banged on his door. "Caleb!" he shouted, "Wake up!"

It took a few minutes before Caleb stuck his head out of the bedroom door. "What's the matter, Amos?"

"They tryin' to set us on fire!"

"Fire? Who?" Caleb asked, groggy with sleep.

"Them peoples I jest fired at. They done come in heah and. . . ."

"Amos," Caleb said as he adjusted his nightcap that was hanging off the side of his head, "slow down."

Caleb went back into his bedroom, lit a lamp, and came back. "Let's go down to the store."

Amos told Johnson what he had heard and smelled as they descended the stairs to the main part of the store. Caleb with the lamp in hand and Amos with his shotgun went out to the porch to inspect. There they found a rusty can lying on its side leaking kerosene and some dropped matches that were strewn about on the store's porch when the figures leaped into the yard.

"I told you they wuz tryin' to burn us up!" Amos said as he righted the can.

"You're right," Caleb replied. "I guess somebody found out what Dewey's been doing."

"Naw," Amos put in, "ain't nobody in Smyrna know what he be up to. I ain't even told my best friend, Enoch." He shook his head. "Nope, ain't a soul know 'bout Dewey. Nope. The folks all think he be a preacherman."

Caleb sighed. "You think they'll come back?"

"Naw, they ain't goin' try and jump on us agin. They be scared of ole Betsy." Amos patted his shotgun fondly.

Caleb sighed deeply then went back into the store and up the stairs to his bedroom. Amos sat down in a chair near the window with his shotgun across his lap and kept watch.

By the next afternoon everyone in Smyrna knew about the attempted arson. Some believed that fighting was surely now coming to Smyrna. They had heard rumors of entire towns being set afire, and this was just the beginning.

Bessie was sitting on the porch rocking Webster to sleep when Enoch came home early one evening. He had spent the whole day at Caleb's store. At the store people of Smyrna learned news about the war because Caleb went once a week to Cowpens to buy a newspaper and hear talk of battles, generals, and how things were going on both sides, the North and the South.

Enoch sat down on the steps to tell Bessie the war news. "If them ole Yankees ever come to Cowpens, they gits their tails whipped!" Enoch bragged. "They be runnin' lack dawgs!" He jumped off the steps and ran around the yard trying to show Bessie how the soldiers would run. Then he laughed and laughed.

Bessie was not amused. She got up from the rocker, holding five-year-old Webster in her arms. "Enoch Epps, you is the biggest fool I ever see'd! Why you laughin'? Don't you know the Yankees be on our side? Don't you know the Yankees tryin' to free black folks?"

Enoch came back and sat down on the steps and wiped his sweaty face on his shirtsleeve. "I be laughin' 'cause it be funny. So, don't you be hollerin' at me, woman."

"You is a fool! Here I'm holdin' our baby in my arms wantin' a better life for him than we got now, and you talkin' 'bout whippin' the Yankees' tail. Them Yankees goin' help make it better for Webster."

Enoch sprang up from the steps. "Aw, Webster be all you thank 'bout! It be 'Webster this,' and 'Webster that.' We be better off not havin' that ole baby!"

"The only thing you care 'bout, Enoch Epps, is your likker bottle!"

"I ain't tellin' you no more news," Enoch said, and strode off around the house, mumbling to himself and leaving Bessie standing holding Webster.

A few days later, Amos came and told Bessie that Reverend Dye was going to hold a meeting in the church on Sunday and he was letting all the people in Smyrna know about it.

Bessie was surprised to hear this news. Quickly, she took Webster by the hand and headed for Mrs. Pettigrew's house where Tessa worked. After she had left Webster to play in the yard with Ozell, she waited in the kitchen for Tessa's freshly baked cake to cool.

Bessie told her what Amos had said, then added, "That church still ain't finished. I been keepin' my eye on it. Every now and then I slip down there and look in the window. The inside still looks the same."

Tessa cut a piece of her cake, put it on a plate, and handed it to Bessie. "Nate said that yesterday when he was down by the river he saw Amos and Reverend Dye sweepin' out the church and puttin' some benches in place." She stopped talking for a minutes. "You think that bundle is still there?"

Bessie took a bite of the cake and savored its taste for a few moments. Then said, "Naw, that bundle been long gone." She took another bite of cake. "Tessa, this is the best cake you ever cooked!"

Tessa smiled approvingly toward Bessie. "I'm gittin' there." She waited a moment, then said, "You goin' to the meetin'?"

"I ain't missin' that for the world," Bessie replied.

The old house was packed with people on that hot, sultry July Sunday. It seemed that everybody in Smyrna was stuffed inside the church. Bessie and Enoch along with Tessa and Nate were sitting on the first bench directly in front of a makeshift pulpit.

After the congregation had waited for a full half-hour, Reverend Dye came in. He looked a bit haggard, his clothes disheveled, and he was carrying a brown satchel. He proceeded to the pulpit, put down the satchel, and raised one hand to the congregation for quiet.

When the people stopped talking, he began speaking. "I have been riding all night to get here and I am real tired." He hesitated for a moment, then rubbed his hands over his tired face and began again speaking at a slow, deliberate rate. "This will be my first and last time that I will speak to you in Smyrna."

A hushed quiet fell over the congregation. Reverend Dye then stepped down from the pulpit and stood facing the people. He stood silently for a few minutes, then said in a strong voice, "I am not a preacherman." He waited for the congregation's reaction. When there was only silence, he continued. "But in a way, I spread the gospel, the gospel against slavery! I spread the gospel against holding my brothers and sisters in bondage against their wills!"

The congregation began whispering in disbelief. Not only were they taken aback by learning that Dewey Dye was not a minister, but that he was brave enough to openly be telling them what he was doing. He was risking his life by admitting to the people of Smyrna that he was an abolitionist.

"Now, you people here in Smyrna are free, but that's not enough! Right down in this valley some of our people are still enslaved!" He paused and angrily said, "All our people must be free! Not one must be held in bondage!"

Then Dewey Dye began slowly pacing back and forth in front of the large congregation, who sat watching silently in the hot little church.

Finally, Nate stood up and asked, "How we goin' do that? How we goin' free our folks?"

"We join the Union Army!" Dewey's voice boomed.

Enoch frowned. "You be crazy!" he yelled. "We done tried that. Them white folks ain't lettin' black folks fight with them!"

"Brother Enoch," Dewey responded, "right now down in Charleston a group of our young menfolks are getting on a steamboat and heading north. From Boston to Philadelphia to way down in Louisiana, young black men are joining the Union Army in droves to fight for freedom!"

"So, we be marchin' up and down shootin' a big ole rifle," Nate said.

Dewey hesitated, then replied, "Yes, maybe. But what the army now needs most are men to drive wagons, haul supplies, put up tents, dig trenches, bury the dead and . . ."

"That be slaverytime work!" Enoch interrupted. "I ain't doin' no more slaverytime work! I did enough of that stuff! If that's what I gots to do, I ain't join' no army! Let them white folks do that! They start this war, so let 'em finish it!"

He jumped up off his seat and angrily stomped out of the church to catcalls and yells from the congregation saying that Enoch was a coward and a no-good.

It took some time before the angry people were calmed. When they were finally quieted, Dewey opened his brown satchel and drew out a flyer. In a loud, clear voice, he read:

"TO ALL COLORED MEN OF NORTH CAROLINA

"An offer to all able-bodied and brave men who are willing to fight for their freedom and who are willing to enlist in the service of the United States.

"FIVE HUNDRED DOLLARS AND RATIONS for every man will be paid when mustered out of the army. Every man will be able to secure a comfortable home for himself and his family. Help restore to home and freedom brothers, sisters, fathers, and mothers who in past years were torn from them by cruel traders and sold far south.

"FIGHT FOR FREEDOM!"

"Men," Dye said in an emotional voice, "you can join the fight! But let your conscience be your guide!"

After saying that, Dewey quickly buckled his satchel and walked out of the church leaving the people behind in a great uproar.

Nate stayed behind at the church to talk with some other men, so Bessie and Tessa walked toward their homes together.

"That ain't the same papers we found in that bundle," Bessie said. "He keepin' them other papers in his satchel."

"Them papers nailed up in the church," Tessa replied.

"No they ain't. I went back to the church a day ago, took me a hammer and jerked up the plank. That bundle be gone! Dye got it!"

"I wonder what he goin' do with them?" Tessa said.

"I wonder too," Bessie answered. "I really wonder about this Dewey Dye."

Most men in Smyrna had been eager to fight in the Civil War. Upon hearing the news of the first battle at Bull Run Creek where the Union soldiers were thrashed by the Confederate soldiers, a group of black men left Smyrna and rowed up the Nebo River to Fort Belton to volunteer for duty, but they were rebuffed. The white colonel in charge of the Union fort told the men to go back home. Blacks couldn't join the army.

Now, after four years of fighting, the army was willing to accept black soldiers. Was it because the Union was losing? Was it because white soldiers were deserting? True, Dewey Dye's flyer said they could enlist and that they would be paid, but could he be trusted? Hadn't he been masquerading around Smyrna as a minister?

The men agreed that night in the church that if the Union army wanted them to enlist, it would have to come to Smyrna and ask them.

A week after Dye had disappeared from Smyrna, Amos was fishing on the Nebo. He noticed in the distance some horses eating grass on the other side of the river. Quietly, he rowed his boat to the other side and crawled out of it. Moving in a crouch so as not to reveal himself, he sneaked toward the horses. As he drew closer, he heard voices. A group of soldiers were resting near the river. The men were wearing blue, so Amos knew they weren't Confederate soldiers.

Amos crept back to his boat and rowed with all his might back to the other shore. He tied up his boat to the dock and hurried up the path to the country store. Breathlessly, he yelled as he opened the store's door. "They here! They here!"

Caleb, who had just returned from Cowpens, was taking inventory of the products he had purchased. "Who's here?" he asked, sounding annoyed that Amos had interrupted him while he was doing this important work.

"Yankee soldiers!" Amos cried, nearly out of breath. "They camped over on the other side of the river!"

Caleb quickly stopped what he was doing, pulled off his bib apron that he wore while working in the store, and followed Amos out of the store down the path toward the river. When they reached the riverbank, they stood looking across the river.

Pointing north, Amos said, "They over there."

Straining his eyes, he tried to see the soldiers. Caleb said, "I don't see anything."

"Musta rode off," Amos replied anxiously. "I know what they want."

Caleb continued to look across the river, then replied, "We'll find out when they get here."

Amos, however, didn't wait for the soldiers to come. He knew the soldiers were coming to enlist Smyrna men in the Union Army. So, instead of going back to work he went door-to-door, spreading the word that the soldiers were coming to enlist men in the army.

Soon, every household in Smyrna knew about the soldiers on the other side of the Nebo.

Within an hour, the men of Smyrna began gathering at Caleb's country store to await the arrival of the soldiers. Many were dressed in Union uniforms their wives had sewn for them and were carrying their belongings in carpetbags.

Amos had managed to squeeze into his old Union uniform that he had made for himself three years before when he and a group of men made the trip up the river to Fort Belton.

The men of Smyrna, dressed in their uniforms, were now ready to offer their services again to the Union Army.

All day long the men waited anxiously and far into the night, but no soldiers came.

At first light, Amos along with some other men hurried down to the river to see if the soldiers were there. They had gone.

Disappointed again, the men went back to their homes, took off their uniforms, and went back to work.

"I knowed them soldiers ain't comin'," Enoch bragged to Bessie the next morning at breakfast. "They done turnt the black folks down agin."

"Maybe Amos had it wrong," Bessie said. "Maybe the soldiers ain't lookin' for fightin' men. Maybe they be goin' 'round lookin' for slaves to tell them 'bout the 'Great Paper.'"

"What paper?" Enoch inquired.

Bessie shook a fork at her husband. "I swear, Enoch, you ain't been keepin' up with the war news! You spend most of your time up at that store and you don't hear nothin'! It's lack your ears be blocked up!"

Enoch banged his fork down in his plate of food. "Bessie, is you goin' tell me 'bout this heah paper?"

"Well, this paper is called 'Eman . . . ci . . . pa . . . Eman-ci . . . paten Pro . . .' Aw, I can't say it! Anyway, ole man Lincoln done wrote this paper. He done freed the slaves! That's what the Great Paper say."

Enoch glared over at Bessie. "If that be true, how come they keeps on shootin' at each other? How come ole Dye try to git us fightin'?"

"'Cause some of these white folks ain't listenin'. That's why!" She paused. "I bet them soldiers moved on 'cause there ain't no more slaves 'round here. They done run off! Amos say ever slave plantation is shut down tight. Even Margrace."

"Ole man Dobbs pay them folks to work his land, but they done run off still. How come?"

"Enoch, workin' on Margrace Plantation kept them folks thinkin' 'bout the hard time when they was slaves. Folks ain't wantin' to think 'bout them times, so they jest go on some place else."

Bessie got up from the table and went over to the stove. "You want some more eggs?"

Enoch nodded his head and handed Bessie his plate. She scraped the rest of the scrambled eggs off the platter onto his plate and gave it back to him. Then she poured herself another cup of coffee and sat back down at the table.

"You know somethin', Enoch, that paper do a great thing settin' black folks free."

Enoch ate the last of his eggs, then replied, "This ole paper ain't set me free. I sets myself free. I use my ole black head. I cuts me a deal! Lots of black folks ain't wait for no paper. They done freed themselfs. And 'nother thang, Bessie," he waved his fork at her. "Them ole soldiers ain't gone. They be hidin'. I bet they be sneakin' back heah in the night stealin' us mens. From now on, I be sleepin' under my bed!"

Bessie frowned. "That's foolishness. The army don't steal men and make them fight."

"Oh, yes they do!" Enoch said emphatically. "A fella over in Cowpens told me his brother, who wuz a free man, was stole right out of his bed in the dead of night! Yankee soldiers busted down his door, jerked him out of bed, tore up his free papers, and took him away to the war!"

Shaking her head in disbelief, Bessie replied. "Them ole soldiers was fightin' for the slaveholders."

"No they ain't. They wuz wearin' blue!"

"Well, why didn't this black man jest go on and help fight?"

Enoch grew angry at Bessie. "Cause he ain't wantin' to. And I ain't wantin' to. So, I sleeps under my bed come night. And you, Bessie, best seal your lips!"

Even though the Union soldiers never came to Smyrna, Enoch slept under his bed until April 1865, when word came that the Civil War had ended.

Double Oaks

Jesse Hustellar had inherited Double Oaks, a large slave plantation, five miles from Cowpens near Smyrna. When the Civil War broke out, Jesse's father was afraid his son might be killed, so he secretly slipped Jesse out of Cowpens to his relatives in northern Missouri. There Jesse stayed until the war was over.

When Jesse returned to Double Oaks, it was in ruins. His father was dead, the slaves were gone, and there was no money because his father had used his money to help finance the Confederacy.

Many people, both black and white, were now destitute. Whole families, with all their possessions piled high on rickety wagons, roamed the countryside looking for land to farm and a house to occupy. Hustellar decided to allow farmers to live and work on his land in exchange for a large share of the crops they raised. He rented to ten families.

Within a few years, Double Oaks was restored to its former glory. The proud mansion sat high on a hill overlooking Smyrna. The home commanded a view of the rolling green hills that ran up to the wooded crowns of Bushy Mountains. An oak tree had been planted near the steps of the house's wide veranda that provided shade during the sultry Carolina summers. A grassy lawn dotted with rosebud trees and white dogwoods stretched down from the house to a dirt road. Oak trees had been planted on each side of this road. These trees were massive and their crowns had met, forming a green tunnel that led up to the house—thus the name Double Oaks.

Behind the house, a woodland reached down to the river, and hidden in these woods of maple, oak, and ancient wild cherry trees were the former slave quarters. Crude one-room log cabins now stood empty, rotting away from weather and time.

Bob Kelley, his wife Massie, and their sixteen-year-old daughter, Ellen, were squatters in one of these huts. Bob was an alcoholic and refused to work. Massie and Ellen spent most of their time looking for food. They gleaned wheat fields and turnip and potato patches, fished in the river, and when they couldn't find food, they'd beg.

One September morning they came into Smyrna and knocked at Bessie Epps' door. When Bessie opened her door, she saw a pinched-faced white woman with stringy, dull hair, and thin as a rail, carrying on her arm an old basket with a few withered sweet potatoes in it. Behind the woman was a young girl with bright eyes so blue that she seemed blind in the sunlight. She was beautiful in spite of her dirt-streaked face and the baggy, patched dress she wore.

"My husband is sick and ain't been able to work," Massie told Bessie. "We fresh out of food, and I'm wonderin' if you could spare us a bit?"

Bessie opened her door wide. "Y'all come on in. I'll git you somethin'."

The women followed Bessie into her kitchen. She beckoned toward the kitchen chairs and said, "Y'all set down."

After the women had sat down, Ellen, the young girl, said, "You sho' got a nice place. I ain't knowed colored folks lived like this."

Bessie smiled. "Colored folks do all right here in Smyrna. We work hard to git what we got."

"What work you do?" Massie asked Bessie.

"I'm a midwife. I help birth little babies."

Ellen began giggling. Her mother touched her arm for her to stop. "You got to overlook Ellen," Massie explained. "She don't know nothin' 'bout birthin'."

Bessie filled the woman's basket with cold biscuits, pieces of ham, sausages, and some baked chicken she had had for dinner the night before. Then she asked, "Y'all like pound cake?"

The woman's eyes lit up. "We ain't had no pound cake since last Christmas. I'd sho' like a piece."

Bessie cut a huge chunk of the cake, wrapped it in paper, and put it in the basket. Then she spread one of her towels over the food in the basket and handed it to Ellen. When Ellen stood up with the basket, Bessie gazed at her body, then asked, "How old you be?"

"Sixteen."

"You old enough to know 'bout birthin' babies," Bessie remarked.

The woman quickly changed the subject. "I'm ever so 'bliged to you, Miz . . . Miz . . . ."

"Jest call me, Bessie."

"I'm Massie Kelley and this heah is my girl, Ellen. We live over yonder in Hustellar's woods."

"Hustellar's woods?" Bessie asked. "You mean in one of them ole rottin' shacks?"

"We only stopped there for a short spell," Massie explained. "Soon as Bob—he's my husband—gits up and 'bout, we goin' move on back to Virginia where my folks is. My folks got a big ole farm with horses, cows, and chicken." She paused as tears welled up in her eyes. "I sho' miss my folks."

"How come y'all come heah?" Bessie inquired.

"Bob was in these parts when the war was goin' on. When he come back to Virginia, he ain't wantin' to live with my folks no more. He lit out for Cowpens." She looked down at her feet. "He ain't found no work 'round heah. Guess we best git."

Bessie walked with the women to the door. "You best be careful not to let ole Hustellar know you're in his woods," she warned. "That ole man ain't lettin' nobody livin' off his land if they ain't payin'."

As Bessie stood in her doorway watching the women go, Massie suddenly turned around and ran back to her, put her arms around Bessie's waist, and gave her a big hug. "God goin' bless you for this!" Then she quickly ran off the porch.

"God goin' bless you for what?" Enoch asked as he came to the porch. He had overheard Massie. Looking at the two women walking down the road, he asked, "Who is them peoples?"

"Said they live over in ole Hustellar's woods," Bessie replied.

Enoch cupped his hand on his forehead to shade the sunlight from his eyes. "They be Bob Kelley's wimminfolks. What they be doin' heah?"

Bessie frowned at Enoch. "How you know who they is?"

"I go over in them woods lookin' for rabbits to shoot," Enoch quickly replied defensively. "I done met Bob. He a good man. Down on his luck."

"If you say he's a good man, he must be a drankin' man," Bessie said accusingly. "You been over in them woods drankin' with this heah Bob?"

"Aw, Bessie, I jest told you I go over there huntin' rabbits. I run into him one day. He told me he live in one of them ole shacks."

Bessie looked skeptically at Enoch. She knew that he was in the woods drinking whiskey, not shooting rabbits. "Hustellar goin' put some shots in your butt if he catches you in his woods."

Avoiding a confrontation with Bessie, Enoch asked, "What them wimmins want?"

"Somethin' to eat, that's what!" Bessie snapped. "If this heah Bob be shootin' rabbits, they wouldn't be beggin'!"

Jesse Hustellar was a strange-looking man. His head seemed too big for his thin, gangly body, and his eyes were sunken into a face pockmarked with scars from a severe case of acne.

Hustellar wanted a wife because he had a huge sexual appetite and needed a woman to appease his carnal desires. Although Hustellar was wealthy, few single women in Cowpens wanted him for a husband. Each time he came courting, he was politely sent away.

One day when Enoch and Bob Kelley were drinking whiskey together in Hustellar's woods, Hustellar's game warden saw them and threatened the men with his gun.

"Get off Hustellar's land, you drunken bums, or I'll shoot!" the game warden yelled.

Bob jumped up from the ground, rolled up his sleeves, and screamed obscenities at the game warden. "Come on, sonofabitch! Fight me like a man! I'll beat your ass with one hand!"

Enoch grabbed hold of Bob's arms. "We do what the man say, Bob. We ain't wantin' no trouble."

The game warden raised his gun and took aim at Bob. "Ain't no need to shoot, mister," Enoch shouted. "We be goin'!"

Pulling and yanking, Enoch forced the cursing, drunken Bob down to the riverbank where Amos kept his boat. He tumbled him in it and then he rowed across the river to the other side.

On the other side of the river, the men could still see the game warden prowling along the riverbank.

As they sat hidden in some tall reeds, Bob swore he'd get back at Hustellar. "I ain't goin' let no man insult me!" he said angrily, taking another swallow of whiskey from Enoch's bottle. "I fought in the war!"

"Ain't nothin' you kin do to him," Enoch replied. "Ole Hustellar gots plenty of money. He kin shoot you on sight and nobody goin' do nothin' 'bout it."

Suddenly, Enoch began laughing and slapping his thigh. "You know somethin'? I heer'd ole ugly Hustellar is tryin' to git a wife, but none of the wimminfolks in Cowpens will have him! They ain't carin' if he gots a big bag of money. He too ugly!"

Bob was silent for a moment, then said, "You sure this is true?"

"Cross my heart and hope to die," Enoch said, and made a cross with his fingers on his chest. "My wife Bessie told me and Bessie don't lie!"

Bob then laid back and stretched out in the reeds and put his hands under his head. After awhile he said, "So . . . Hustellar wants a wife. Enoch, you and me goin' git ourselves some money!"

"How we goin' do that?" Enoch asked as he lay beside Bob.

Bob hesitated for a few minutes, then answered, "You jest wait 'til I give you the word."

"Hope it be soon," Enoch replied.

Resting in the warm sun, the two men fell asleep in the reeds on the riverbank.

The next day, Kelley, limping on a hickory stick, went up to Hustellar's mansion. He told Hustellar a sad tale about having been a soldier in the Confederacy and how he had been wounded in the war, and because of his disability he couldn't find work after the war. His wife had recently died, and he had two hungry daughters at home and he needed work.

Jesse had been a staunch supporter of the Confederacy, even though he himself had secretly evaded the fighting. He believed Bob's story and offered him work doing odd jobs around his house.

Kelley soon began regaling Hustellar with tales about his escapades as a spy against the Northern troops and how he had been shot while carrying out a spying mission.

In a few weeks, Kelley had gained Hustellar's confidence. Hustellar confided to Kelley that he was looking for a wife.

Kelley then told Hustellar that his oldest daughter was not married and invited him to call on her. "My daughter Massie is in her late thirties. She'll make you a good wife."

At first, Hustellar turned Bob Kelley down, saying he wanted a woman in his own social circles, someone he would be proud to show off to his neighbors. But as time went by and Hustellar wasn't successful in finding a woman who'd have him, he decided to take Bob's offer.

Bob convinced Hustellar to entertain his daughter in his mansion since Bob didn't have proper accommodations for a man of his standing. Hustellar agreed. When Bob brought Massie to the mansion, Ellen came along too.

Hustellar was immediately smitten by the fair-haired Ellen, forty-four years his junior. He wanted her instead of Massie for his wife.

"Sorry, Mr. Hustellar," Bob told him at the time Hustellar asked for Ellen. "You're goin' to have to take my eldest daughter, Massie. There's an old custom in my family, never let the youngest marry before the oldest."

For weeks, Hustellar insisted on marrying Ellen. "Name your terms," he told Kelley one afternoon when he was raking dead leaves in the yard. "I want that woman!"

Finally, Bob relented, saying, "You want my daughter Mr. Hustellar, it's going to cost you. As you know I was wounded in the war, and I need money to buy medicine for my war injury."

"Name your price," Jesse said eagerly as he tried to hold back his excitement.

"Five hundred dollars." Jesse said.

"You bring her to me tomorrow and I'll put the money in your hand!"

"Preacher goin' be here, Mr. Hustellar?" Bob inquired. "I won't have her livin' in sin."

"I'll take her out to the county seat next week and have Judge Binny marry us. But for now, she'll stay at my house until we do."

That afternoon Bob sought out Enoch. "I got us a bottle," he called from some bushes when he saw Enoch weeding Bessie's garden. "Come on down to the river."

It took Enoch just a few minutes to slip off from work and go to the river. He was glad Bob had a bottle because he was out of whiskey and money. He had asked Bessie that morning for some money, but she refused him.

"You jest want my money for whiskey!" Bessie scolded him. "Well, you ain't gittin' it! Now, you git out to that garden and go after them weeds!"

As the two men sat drinking together in the woods, Bob told Enoch he was going to leave Smyrna and take his wife and daughter back to Virginia. He needed Enoch to row them across the river using Amos' boat.

"I ain't knowed 'bout that," Enoch said skeptically, "Amos ain't lettin' me use his boat now. He say I'm wearin' it out."

"Amos ain't got to know," Kelley insisted.

Enoch reached over, took the whiskey bottle out of Bob's hand, and took a big swallow of whiskey, then gave a satisfied burp. "Well, you be my good drankin' man, I'll do it. When you aim on goin'?"

"Tomorrow night."

"Hey, wait a minute! what 'bout all this money you and me wuz gittin'?"

"I'm goin' to have to see you in the short rows, Enoch," Bob confided.

Enoch frowned. "You be a fast talker, Bob Kelley. Where you goin' git money?"

"Back in Virginia."

"Yeah, yeah," Enoch said. "You ain't goin' git no money in Virginny."

"If you don't believe me, come on with me!" Bob said.

"Nope," Enoch said definitely, shaking his head. "I ain't leavin' Bessie."

Then in a convincing voice, Bob said, "In no time I'll be back here with a pocketful of money!" He playfully slapped Enoch on the shoulder. "Now, will you put me and my family across the river?"

"I kin use me some secret money," Enoch muttered. "Bessie jest give me little dribbles."

Bob laughed boisterously. "Bessie knows if you lay your hands on big money, you'll drank it all up."

Enoch laid back on the ground and smiled. "Bessie ain't goin' know 'bout this money."

The next evening Bob and Ellen went to Jesse's house. Ellen was wearing a clean dress and carrying a stuffed burlap sack.

"Go on upstairs to my bedroom," Hustellar told her, "and put your things in it. I've got some business with your pa."

As soon as the girl was upstairs, Hustellar reached into his pocket and pulled out a big wad of bills, counted out five hundred dollars, and handed it to Bob, who quickly stuffed it into his pocket.

"Not a word of this to anyone," Hustellar warned. "This deal is between you and me."

Sounding remorseful, Bob with eyes cast downward, replied, "I'm not proud of this deal, Mr. Hustellar. I'll not talk."

Hustellar stood counting the rest of his money. "Don't come around here again asking for more money. You won't get it!" he said arrogantly.

"I'll only come to see my daughter, Mr. Hustellar. Not to ask you for money."

"You'll stay away from Ellen!" Hustellar ordered. "My wife will be in my circle of friends." Then, like a proud peacock, he strutted over and yanked open his door, indicating for Kelley to leave.

As soon as Kelley had gone, Jesse went to his wine cabinet, took out a bottle of his best wine, sat down in his big easy chair, and poured himself a glass of the wine and slowly drank it. Feeling proud of his deal, he pushed back deep into his leather chair and relaxed until he had consumed most of the wine.

While he was drinking the wine, Hustellar heard his hounds barking furiously. Since he was in no mood to go see why his hounds were barking, he just sat there savoring the thoughts of things to come later that night. Besides, his dogs were safely locked in their pen and couldn't go chasing off.

An hour had passed before Jesse felt he was ready to consummate his deal. It didn't matter to him that he had not married Ellen. He wanted her, and he wanted her now.

Upstairs in the hallway he set the lit lamp down on a table, stripped off all his clothes, and went naked to his bedroom door to open it. But to his surprise, the door wouldn't open. He yanked on the doorknob, but the door seemed stuck.

"Ellen, open the door from your side," he said tenderly. There was silence. He tried pushing on the door and then realized it was locked.

"Open this door, bitch!" Jesse yelled in a harsh voice and began banging and jerking the doorknob, but still the door wouldn't budge.

Naked and angry, Jesse raced downstairs to where he kept his tools, grabbed a screwdriver, and ran back upstairs. He'd take the damn door off its hinges!

Within a few minutes, he was able to shove open the door. He snatched his horsewhip off the table where he had set the lamp. He'd give Ellen a beating for locking him out! Breathing hard, he angrily stepped inside the room with whip in one hand and the lamp in the other. All he saw was the burlap bag. Ellen was gone!

When he saw the open window, he realized that the girl had climbed down the trellis to the ground, and that was why his hounds were barking.

Well, he'd go and bring the bitch back. No poor white trash was going to outsmart him.

Without putting on his trousers, Hustellar rushed down the stairs and out to his barn where he threw a saddle across his horse's back, leaped onto it, and raced through his woods toward the old house where Bob Kelley lived.

Enoch was tying Amos' boat to a tree. He had just returned from rowing Bob, Massie, and Ellen across the river when he heard some loud yelling. Believing it to be Amos, he ducked into some bushes and hid. He'd better not let Amos see him.

"Kelley! Kelley!" Jesse yelled as he rode frantically up to the old house, jumped off his horse, rushed up onto the rotted porch, and then suddenly crashed through the porch's floor up to his armpits. Stuck there, he saw the old door standing wide open. Inside, the house was empty. The Kelleys were gone.

Hearing all this commotion was Enoch. He peered through the bushes and in the moonlight saw the naked, cursing Hustellar extricating himself from the broken rotted planks and then ride off into the night.

"Bob Kelley, you in big troubles with ole Hustellar!" Enoch said to himself as he stood looking across the river. "What you done did now? I bet I ain't never goin' see the money you done promise me. You be too scared to come back heah!"

Three years after Bob Kelly and his family had left Hustellar's woods, Jesse was still too ashamed to tell his friends about the deal he had made for a wife and how he had been swindled. This episode remained his secret.

Before the Civil War, Amanda Spriggs, along with her mother and father, had joined a religious group in Virginia called "The Saints of God." This group believed that the way to defeat slavery was to educate the slaves.

When The Saints of God built a school in a small Virginia community to teach black people, the white people in the area hooked up their oxen, tied heavy ropes around the schoolhouse, and pulled it off its foundation, but the group rebuilt the school. The new schoolhouse was used only a month before it was burned to the ground and threatening notes were nailed on the members' doors that read, "LEAVE, OR WE'LL BURN DOWN YOUR HOUSE WITH YOU IN IT!"

Believing they were in danger, The Saints of God left the area. The Spriggs moved to Philadelphia, where Amanda taught in one of the movement's schools until the Civil War was over.

After the war had ended, Amanda Spriggs came south to Cowpens to teach at Wingate, The Saints of God's all-girls school. Even though Wingate was a religious school dedicated to helping the poor, the girls enrolled at the school came from the wealthy families in Cowpens.

Wingate School was in a dark, Gothic, brick mansion with medieval arches, steep gables, and stained-glass windows. There were four big chimneys pointing up from the brown slate roof. Inside was an octagonal foyer with an inlaid oak floor. The entry hall opened into a large parlor, where an ornate staircase led up to the floors above. The parlor was dimly lit by kerosene lamps scattered about the hall on heavy oak tables and on the mantelpiece above the big fireplace at the far end.

The headmistress' office was a room in back of the parlor, and beyond it was the kitchen where the girls took their meals. All the classrooms were on the second and third floors.

Amanda was forty-five when she came to Cowpens. She was six feet tall, big-boned, and plain-looking. Her complexion was swarthy, and she had large, penetrating brown eyes and a serious countenance. She always wore her heavy gray-streaked hair wrapped in a tight bun pinned up on top of her head.

Dressed in a long, black cotton dress with a white collar, black stockings, and high buttoned-up black shoes—and always carrying a large black Bible—Amanda gave an appearance of a Puritan preacher.

Five women teachers worked at Wingate along with the headmistress, Mrs. James. The teachers' manners and the way they dressed were impeccable.

Amanda, who taught reading, felt out of place at Wingate because she was so different from the other women, who thought her strange. She felt lonely until she met Lindy and Ilia, the eight-year-old twin daughters of Jacob and Minnie Flowers, who lived in a small cottage on the grounds of Wingate. Jacob was the groundskeeper at Wingate and Minnie was the school's cook. Amanda recognized immediately that the twins were gifted and asked Minnie one afternoon when she was visiting why she and Jacob were not sending the girls to the Freedman's Bureau school. This school had been opened for black people by the government.

"That school's too far away, Amanda," Minnie told her. "It's way over on the other side of Cowpens. Five miles away! I want my girls to learn readin' and writin', but I ain't goin' to chance sendin' them off by themselves."

Amanda told Minnie she'd be willing to teach the girls at Wingate, but she'd first have to get permission from Mrs. James.

Two days later, Amanda had a talk with the headmistress. She asked her if she could teach Lindy and Ilia in her class. "The twins are very bright, Mrs. James. It's shameful that they aren't going to school."

"Teaching the twins at Wingate will be against the school's rules," Mrs. James informed Amanda.

"Why is that?" Amanda asked. "The Saints of God are committed to educating poor children and black children."

Mrs. James' face turned slightly red. She didn't like the tone of Amanda's voice, always so self-righteous. "Jacob and Minnie do not have the money to pay Wingate's cost for the girls to attend here," was Mrs. James' answer.

"Then I'll pay for them," Amanda said. "I earn more than enough money for my needs."

"That's really not what is at issue here," Mrs. James said. "Lindy and Ilia are black, and at this time Wingate does not enroll black students."

"The Saints of God built schools for black children. I even taught in one in Virginia."

"Amanda," Mrs. James pleaded. "This is the South. We just can't ignore customs."

"Then give me permission to teach them in the kitchen," Amanda said.

"During school hours?" Mrs. James queried.

"When my classes are finished," Amanda answered. "It is the Christian thing for Wingate to do."

Mrs. James was annoyed by Amanda's statement. She spoke as if she were the only Christian in the school. In a well-measured voice, Mrs. James answered her. "Miss Spriggs, I am a Christian, and Wingate is a Christian institution. You know very well that I conduct vespers every morning to start our day. Now, our government has gone to great lengths setting up schools for black people. If this were not true, I'd gladly invite Lindy and Ilia into the Wingate family. They are, as you say, quick to learn. Jacob and Minnie will have to find a way to get them to their own school."

In a determined voice, Amanda said, "Then I'll teach them in their home in the evenings during my free time."

"Your free time in the evenings are to be spent helping Wingate students who may be having difficulties with their subjects," came Mrs. James' reply.

Amanda became incensed at what she had just heard. How dare this unchristian headmistress decide what she was to do with her own time. "Mrs. James," she replied, "I cannot allow you to tell me what I must do with my free time."

Mrs. James steadied herself. She mustn't lose her temper. That would not be the Wingate way. "I am the headmistress here, Miss Spriggs," she said calmly, "and if you are to teach at Wingate, you will follow my instructions."

"Then I cannot continue to teach at Wingate," Amanda retorted. "My free will won't let me do otherwise."

"Perhaps it is best that you leave," Mrs. James replied, "if you believe that Wingate will be impinging on your free will."

Upon hearing this, Amanda walked out of the office and went back to her classroom where she gathered up her large book sack and her Bible and walked out of Wingate's door without looking back.

She went to the small room that she had rented at a shabby boardinghouse not far from Wingate and pondered what to do next. She decided to seek employment at the Freedman's School for black children.

On the day she went to the school, the school principal told her all teaching positions were filled, but she was expecting more children to enroll. If they did, she would consider Amanda. For two weeks, Amanda waited, thinking perhaps the Freedman School might enroll more students and offer her a job, but it didn't happen. She decided to leave Cowpens.

On the morning that Amanda was packing her trunk with her books and three dresses to go back to Philadelphia, her landlady knocked on her door.

"Miss Spriggs," she called. "There's an odd sort of fella at the front door asking to speak with you."

At first, Amanda was puzzled. Who could it be? Then she thought it must be someone from the Freedman School and quickly went to see what the man wanted.

On the porch was an unshaven white man wearing plowshoes and bib overalls. Upon seeing Amanda, he quickly took off his dusty felt hat, revealing a thatch of matted brown hair. "You Miss Spriggs, the schoolteacher?" he asked.

"I am," Amanda replied, and before she could invite the man into the parlor, her landlady who had come to the doorway was standing determinedly in it. She meant not to allow this scruffy-looking man into her spotless parlor.

Amanda pointed toward a chair on the porch. "Would you like to sit down, Mr. . . ."

The man didn't say his name and he didn't sit down. "I'm in a hurry, ma'am. Got to git back to my plowing. I come to fetch you back to Double Oaks."

"Double Oaks?"

"Double Oaks is a big plantation over near Smyrna about five miles from here," her landlady explained. She looked suspiciously at Amanda. "I didn't know you knew Hustellar."

"I don't."

"Then how come he's sending for you?"

"Perhaps this gentleman will tell us," Amanda said. She turned to the man, who was still standing with his hat in his hand. "What does Mr. Hustellar want?"

"It be about our school, ma'am, The Old Field School. You see, we need a teacher to teach at our school."

The landlady had now sat down in the chair next to Amanda. She leaned over toward Amanda and said, "I've never heard of this Old Field School. No such place."

"We just built it," the man quickly added. "Mr. Hustellar heard about you, so he wants you to come out to Double Oaks and talk with him about the job."

"I'll get my bonnet," Amanda said and went back into the house followed by the landlady.

"You don't know nothin' about this man, Miss Amanda. You ought not go off with him. No tellin' what he'll do to you."

"It would be unchristian of me not to hear what Mr. Hustellar has to say," Amanda told her landlady.

The landlady took hold of Amanda's arm. "I'm not one to spread gossip, but I heard Hustellar's got a bad reputation. He's got money, but no reputation."

"We must trust our fellow man" was Amanda's reply. She put on her white bonnet, got her Bible, and came back to the porch. "I am ready," she told the man.

Her landlady stood frowning on the porch as she watched Amanda, who was dressed in black and wearing her white bonnet, climb up on the man's wagon in front of her boardinghouse.

Amanda sat down in one of the chairs that was in the wagon bed and the man sat in another chair. He took the reins of the two big horses and the wagon rumbled down the road and out of sight. The man was silent as he drove the wagon toward Smyrna, passing several patches of stunted corn and pea vines growing in front of some tired-looking shacks in need of repair. Finally, the man said, "We be passin' the ole Margrace Plantation soon as we get out of these woods. You can see the big house from the road."

As soon as the wagon emerged from the woods, the man pointed, "There. Margrace."

Amanda saw a large white house that set back from the road in a grove of shade trees. The fields around the house lay uncultivated.

"Nobody lives there now," the man explained. "But it used to be the largest slave plantation in the valley. The Au Bignons were real rich. Just before war broke out, they up and sold their place. Ole man Dobbs bought it, then later he sold it."

"Who owns it now?" Amanda said as she looked back at the house.

"Don't know. Last we heard is some rich woman in Cowpens bought it. I wonder why she don't move out here? That's a real fine house."

"She must have a gardener," Amanda remarked. "The lawn and flowering trees are well kept."

They rode on in silence, passing all of Margrace's empty fields. Then the man suddenly said, "Double Oaks!" He turned the horses onto a road that led through some massive oak trees planted on each side of it.

Soon they came up to a white mansion that had a wide veranda and a beautiful lawn of verdant grass. Rosebud trees near the house were in full bloom. On the veranda a man sat in a wicker chair smoking a pipe.

The driver pulled the horses to a stop, got down off the wagon, and came around to help Amanda down. She walked up the graveled path toward the porch.

The man made no move until Amanda had reached the porch, then he stood up and extended his hand. "Glad you could come, Miss Spriggs. I'm Jesse Hustellar. Come on up on my porch and sit down next to me."

After she was seated, Hustellar began. "I was out to Cowpens yesterday asking around where I might find a schoolteacher. I was given your name." He paused as he looked up and down Amanda. To him, she was a very plain-looking woman, even ugly. Her breasts were flat, and she had the appearance of a mustache over her lip.

"As you were saying, Mr. Hustellar," Amanda said, breaking the man's chain of thought.

"Oh yes. My sharecroppers came to me and said, 'Mr. Hustellar, we want our boys to learn to read, write, and cipher numbers.'" He gave a nervous chuckle. "I agreed. White boys ought to be able to read and write. So, I told them they can use one of my buildings for a school. I won't charge them much for its use. Now, they need a teacher."

"You offering me a position, Mr. Hustellar?" Amanda asked.

"Speaking for my sharecroppers, yes. I'll see to it that they pay you twelve dollars a month. Is that agreeable?"

Amanda sat quietly for a moment, looking out at the peaceful surroundings as she gave the proposition careful thought. She didn't want to go back north because here in the South there was much work to do, and twelve dollars a month was two dollars more than what she was paid at Wingate.

All the time Amanda was silent, Hustellar was studying her. Why was she carrying a Bible, and why was she wearing such a long, black dress? What was she hiding under that dress?

"Where would I stay out here?" she finally asked. "Smyrna is five miles from Cowpens, and I don't have a horse and buggy to drive out here."

"Stay with me," Hustellar said, looking at her intently. "I have plenty rooms."

Amanda gave him a disapproving look. "It's not proper for an unmarried woman to be living alone under the same roof with a man, Mr. Hustellar."

"I'm a man of principles, Miss Spriggs," Hustellar said. "I respect women."

"I stand on my Bible, Mr. Hustellar."

In spite of Amanda's homeliness, Hustellar found her exciting and he wanted to know her better. "Very well, Miss Spriggs. I'll hire Tessa to come stay nights with you."

"Who's Tessa, Mr. Hustellar?"

"She's a colored woman who lives in Smyrna. She used to cook for Mary Pettigrew until she passed on."

Amanda didn't like that suggestion. He'd be taking the woman away from her family, and that was not right. She wasn't sure she could accept this.

Sensing her uncertainty, Hustellar reached over and patted Amanda's hand. "Don't worry, Miss Spriggs. Tessa's a good colored woman. You'll like her."

Amanda didn't like his familiarity. However, she liked the idea of having her own school. "If you can get Tessa to stay here nights until I can find my own place, I'll take the position." When Hustellar reached for Amanda's hand again, she quickly withdrew it.

Old Field Schools were now being established all over the South by poor white sharecroppers who wanted their sons educated. Since they didn't have money to send their boys to private schools like the rich landlords who had refused to build public schools for poor children, the tenant farmers started their own schools.

Hustellar had offered his sharecroppers an old building on a useless piece of land. The farmers shored up this old, one-room building that sat in the middle of an eroded field that Hustellar had abandoned.

The school had two windows with no glass in them, and were shut tight with wooden shutters. A creaky door had to be kept open at all times because the room was so dark. Six long plank benches set in rows facing a well-used kitchen table that served as the teacher's desk. In the middle of the floor was a wood-burning, pot-bellied stove. Behind the stove was a large box where firewood and wood chips were kept.

On the morning Amanda moved into Hustellar's house, Tessa was waiting for her. As soon as the wagon stopped in front of the house, Tessa walked out to it.

"I'm Tessa," she said, smiling at Amanda who had climbed out of the wagon. "I'm goin' be stayin' nights with you."

Amanda took hold of Tessa's hand and shook it hard. "I'm Amanda Spriggs, the schoolteacher. I hope your staying here at night with me won't cause a hardship on your family."

"Nate, my husband, is home every night. He goin' look after Ozell," Tessa told her.

"Who's Ozell?" Amanda asked.

"He our son."

"A baby?"

"Ozell is ten." Tessa thought for a moment, "Yep, he ten 'cause he's a year older than Webster. He's nine."

"You have two boys?"

"No. Webster is my best friend Bessie's boy. She live in Smyrna too."

Amanda felt pleased that Tessa was going to be staying nights with her. She was a warm and cheerful woman and would be good company.

"I hep you git settled," Tessa said and lifted a large brown box off the wagon.

"That box's too heavy for you," Amanda said. "It's filled with my schoolbooks."

"I been usta carryin' heavy things," Tessa replied and began walking with the box toward the house.

Amanda quickly caught up to her. "I'll help."

The two women carried the box inside the house. "We'll let the driver bring in my trunk," Amanda said after they had carried the box upstairs to a room that Hustellar said she could use.

It was afternoon before Tessa left the Hustellar house. On her way home, she saw Bessie, who had been waiting on her porch all day to hear about this teacher.

"Come on and sit a spell," she called. "Ozell ain't home. Nate left him here to play with Webster. They in the back playin'."

As soon as Tessa was on the porch, Bessie said, "What's that teacher like?"

"She ain't pritty," Tessa replied. "Real tall and bony, but she be real nice. I likes her."

"Oh Tessa, I be so relieved!" Bessie cried and clapped her hands. "This make me very happy!"

Tessa was puzzled by Bessie's reactions. Why was she so happy about the teacher? She wasn't giving up her nights to stay with her.

"Now, I know you sayin' to yourself, 'Why Bessie so happy?' I'll tell you, Tessa. That teacher be the best thang that come to Smyrna!"

Bessie put her an arm around Tessa's waist. "Now, this is what you got to do. You got to ask that teacher 'bout teachin' Ozell and Webster, 'cause I done teached them all I know. Now, they need a real teacher."

Tessa was taken aback by what Bessie wanted her to do. "Bessie, I jest see'd this teacher. I can't jest start askin' her to teach Ozell and Webster! 'Sides, she is a white woman!"

"Miz Pettigrew taught us. She was white."

"Miz Pettigrew was not like other white wimmins. She give us our freedom."

"Tessa, white wimmins is teachin' black children over in Cowpens. I know this 'cause the last time I help birth a baby over there the wimmin-folks told me. They got a school now."

She lowered her voice. "I been thinkin' 'bout sendin Webster to Cowpens. But now I ain't got to. We got a teacher right here in Smyrna!"

Tessa wasn't convinced. "I don't know 'bout that, Bessie. She goin' be teachin' white boys."

"Why can't this Miz Spriggs teach our boys? We kin pay. All you got to do is ask. Don't the Bible say, 'Ask and you will git'?"

Tessa was silent, digesting what Bessie had said. "I wait 'til I gits to know her some more," she finally told Bessie.

"Don't you wait long. Our boys need to be learnin' jest like them white boys. I ain't wantin' Webster playin' all the time. He and Ozell goin' git in some kind of trouble."

On the day Amanda opened her school, five farm families all dressed in their Sunday clothes came with their children. After Amanda had enrolled six boys, she turned her attention to the girls.

"No need to write down the girls' names," one man said. "They ain't comin'."

When Amanda inquired why, the farmer told her that they didn't want their daughters attending school with boys.

"How are you going to educate them?" Amanda inquired.

Cliff Parker, the sharecropper who had driven Amanda from Cowpens to Smyrna, replied, "Girls will git husbands. They ain't needin' schoolin'. They be havin' babies and takin' care the houses."

Amanda cringed when she heard this and waited for the mothers to say something, but they all kept silent. Since she didn't want to start a controversy on the first day of school, she too remained silent. But not for long. She meant to convince the mothers to send their daughters to school along with their sons.

Three weeks after school had begun, Amanda began her campaign to convince the mothers to send their daughters to her school. She visited them at their homes, explaining how important it was for the girls to come.

None of the mothers complied with sending their daughters to school until one afternoon Amanda had a visitor. It was Cliff Parker's wife. She explained that she really wanted her two daughters to attend school, but didn't want to defy her husband. Her own life was so hard, and it was all because her father wouldn't let her go to school when she was young. She meant not to let her daughters end up with a life like hers. She was going to save some money so they could come.

Amanda told Mrs. Parker she'd teach her girls for free, but the woman wouldn't hear of it. "I pay for them or they don't come."

The two women had talked for a long time at the school, and it was dark when Amanda finally arrived at the Hustellar house.

Tessa always cooked her supper and tonight she was hungry, so she went directly to the kitchen.

"Miz Amanda," Tessa said, "I was real worried about you. So is Mr. Hustellar."

"Why is Mr. Hustellar worried about me?" Amanda said. "I'm a grown woman."

Tessa shrugged. "Don't know. He was waitin' in the parlor with Cliff Parker. But Parker left. Mr. Hustellar said for you to come to him jest as soon as you git heah. Oh, when you git through talkin' to Mr. Hustellar, I wants to ask you somethin'."

"Tessa, I'm hungry," Amanda said. "Let's eat." She sat down at the table and laid her Bible next to her. "Mr. Hustellar can wait," she announced. "Now, what is it that you want to ask me?"

Tessa first brought Amanda a plate of food that she had kept warm in the stove. Then she sat down next to her. "I told you 'bout my friend, Bessie." Amanda nodded as she ate some of the food.

Tessa sighed. "Well, Bessie ain't give me no peace. Ever day she ask me if I asked you."

"Asked me what, Tessa?"

"You see, Bessie got big plans for her boy, Webster. She been teachin' him herself, but he's real smart. Now, she need a real teacher for him. What Bessie want me to ask you is, will you teach her boy?"

Amanda's face brightened. "You want me to teach Ozell too?"

"Yes, but I ain't pushin' as hard as Bessie. I told her to wait 'til you got started with the white boys."

Amanda smiled broadly at Tessa. This was the first time Tessa had seen her smile like this. She looked so different, even happy. She was always so serious all the time, and Tessa wasn't sure what to make of it.

"We pay, jest like the white folks," Tessa quickly added.

"Of course I'll teach the boys. And if there are other children in Smyrna, I'll teach them too. Only thing is we'll have to find a place for a school. I don't think the parents at the Old Field School will want your children mixing with their boys."

Just then Hustellar burst into the kitchen. He seemed angry when he saw the two women sitting at the table chatting. "Tessa, didn't I tell you to tell Miss Spriggs I wanted her in the parlor?"

Tessa took umbrage at Hustellar's accusing voice and snapped, "I did!"

"Well?" He turned to Amanda as if to say "Why didn't you come when I summoned you?"

"Mr. Hustellar, what is it that you want?" Amanda asked wearily and put another forkful of food into her mouth.

"I'd prefer to speak to you in my parlor," he said and stormed out of the kitchen.

Amanda took her time eating. She was beginning to be annoyed with Hustellar. She didn't like the way he addressed her tonight and the language he had used the night before when he told Tessa she could go home at midnight. When Tessa asked him why, he told her to mind her "own damn business."

In the parlor, Hustellar was waiting angrily because Amanda hadn't come when he had summoned her. When she did come to the parlor, she refused to sit down. "Say what you want quickly, Mr. Hustellar. I am ready for my bed."

Hustellar replied, "Cliff Parker came to see me and told me you are interfering in the sharecroppers' family matters."

"How so?" Amanda asked.

"You're trying to change the way the farmers want to educate their boys. I want it stopped!"

"Mr. Hustellar," Amanda replied calmly, "if the parents at the Old Field School have something they wish to discuss, they are to come to the school and I will listen to them. You have no authority to tell me when and what I will do."

"I speak for them," Hustellar replied harshly.

"No, Mr. Hustellar, the parents must speak for themselves. Since there is nothing more for us to discuss, I will bid you goodnight."

Tessa followed Amanda upstairs to her bedroom. "Miz Amanda, I ain't got nothin' to do with it, but you best watch out for ole Hustellar."

Amanda told Tessa not to worry. "If God is for you, who can be against you? He holds me in the palm of his hand."

The next day Tessa told Bessie about what had transpired the night before as they sat together talking.

"Ole Hustellar tryin' to git back at Amanda 'cause he wants her in his bed at night," Bessie surmised after she had heard the story.

"I don't know 'bout that," Tessa said. "He be hard up to want Amanda. She ain't no looker."

"Tessa, Tessa, the mens ain't lookin' at a woman's face in the dark," Bessie said. "I hope ole Hustellar close that school."

"What a mean thang to say, Bessie! Amanda is a real good woman. She don't need no bad luck."

"It won't be no bad luck, Tessa. It be good luck! If she can't teach them little white boys, she kin teach for us! Did you ask her?"

In her zeal to tell Bessie about the big fight Amanda had with Hustellar, Tessa had forgotten to tell her that Amanda said she'd teach the boys. "I plum forgot to tell you. She said she'd be glad to teach our boys."

"Oh, praise the Lord!" Bessie cried and began dancing around and around. "Praise the Almighty!

"Bessie," Tessa remarked sarcastically, "did the Almighty tell you where we goin' git a school?"

Bessie sat back down quite out of breath. After she caught her breath, she explained her idea to Tessa. "I been givin' that some thought. Now, since Miz Pettigrew died, her ole house been closed up. If all the folks in Smyrna put their money together, we kin buy that house and turn it into a school."

"Aw, folks in Smyrna don't care 'bout no school. They ain't goin' give their money for that."

"Tessa, black folks in Smyrna care 'bout their children. They want them to git a better chance at life. They know they got to educate the youn' folks. You jest leave it to me. I'll git the money for a school. You jest tell Amanda that we wants her for our teacher. She ain't got to stay at ole Hustellar's. She kin stay in the Pettigrew house. It be big enough for her and the school."

"I'll tell her," Tessa said reluctantly, "but she ain't left the Old Field School."

"She will."

"How you know that?"

"'Cause ole Hustellar goin' make her skeedaddle!" Bessie replied. "She be gone inside a week."

Bessie's prediction proved true. Two days later, Ozell, Tessa's son, became ill. Nate, his father, went to the Hustellar's house to inform Amanda that Tessa couldn't come that night. Since Amanda was at school, Nate told Hustellar. When Amanda came in from school, Hustellar told her the news.

After Amanda had cooked and eaten her supper, she went up to prepare for bed. She put on her long, thick gown, tied a scarf around her hair, and said a long prayer on her knees, then got into bed. As she had done every night, she laid her Bible across her chest and blew out the lamplight. Putting her Bible on her chest at night was Amanda's way of staying in touch with her God.

Around midnight, Amanda was awakened by something she felt under her gown slowly moving up her naked leg. She opened her eyes and saw the shadow of a man down on his knees close to her bed.

Quickly, Amanda grabbed her Bible off her chest and whacked the figure with a mighty blow over the head. Her blow was so forceful that it sent the attacker reeling head-over-heels backwards onto the floor.

Like a wild tiger, Amanda leaped out of bed and hammered him blow after blow with her heavy Bible. Without making a sound, the attacker scrambled on hands and knees out of the room and into the darkened hall.

Because Amanda couldn't see in the dark, she rushed back into the room, lit her lamp, and ran back into the hall. All was quiet. No one was there.

She stood there for a few minutes looking up and down the hall, wondering if the attacker would come back. She was not worried, because with God's help she could take of herself.

The next morning when Amanda arrived at the Old Field School, Cliff Parker was waiting on his horse. He told her that the farmers had decided to close their school and they wouldn't be needing her anymore. Without another word, he rode off.

Newcomers to Smyrna

Bessie begged and prodded the people in Smyrna for money, and she soon collected enough to buy the Pettigrew house for a school. Amanda was hired to be the teacher, and the students' accounts of her were as a strict disciplinarian as well as a good instructor.

Webster was nine when the school opened. He had grown into a handsome lad. His tawny-colored skin set off his large grayish-blue eyes. A mop of jet black hair framed his round face. He was taller and stronger than the other nine-year old boys in Smyrna.

Webster had a quick mind. He was curious about life and often bombarded his mother with questions, especially about girls.

"You ain't old enough to know these things," Bessie told him. "You just stick to them books and wait 'til you get some hair on your chest."

"If I don't ask, how will I know what to do when I get hair on my chest?" Webster replied.

Bessie frowned. "What Ozell been tellin' you?"

With a sly smile, Webster answered, "Things men and women do."

"Well, you ain't no man, yet," Bessie snapped. "And whatever Ozell told you, you kin just knock it right out of your head! I'm goin' to speak to Tessa 'bout Ozell's fresh mouth!"

"Don't do that, Mama!" Webster pleaded. "Ozell will get real mad with me!"

Bessie reached down and tousled his hair and smiled. "Just you stop askin' me grown folks' talk."

Webster loved being alone in the woods and fields around Smyrna, and he often spent hours exploring, fishing, and swimming in the ponds and streams that were nearby.

Amanda even held classes in the summer, which angered Webster to no end. When he complained to his mother that school shouldn't be held in the summer, she firmly told him that learning was far more important than playing, and she didn't want to hear him whining. "So, crack the books!" she'd say.

One hot summer morning while on his way to school, Webster decided not to go. Instead, he went swimming in a creek near the Bumgarter shack. Bumgarter was a hogkiller. In early winter he went from farm to farm butchering farmers' hogs that they had raised for meat. Bumgarter lived with his wife Annie Mae and their thirteen-year-old daughter Lula at the edge of Finley's woods. These woodlands separated Smyrna from the hills to the north. The woods and the shack that Bumgarter lived in were owned by an eccentric old man named Halowell Finley.

Finley refused to allow sawmillers to cut down his trees even though he was poor and could use the money he'd get from selling his wood. "My woods are for hunting and fishing," he said. "I don't post them. Anybody who's got a mind for hunting and fishing can do so. It's the natural way of things."

The Bumgarters were a strange lot. In late fall they could be seen roaming the fields and the bottomlands walking one behind the other. Each carried a burlap sack filled with creesy greens, a wild plant, and leftover turnips they had gathered from farmers' fields and in the marshland near the creek.

One day when Bessie and Webster were at Caleb's store, the Bumgarters came in to buy some supplies. Bumgarter had a rank smell about him, and so did his wife and daughter.

Lula fixed her eyes on Webster, and with a silly grin on her face she watched his every move. When Bessie noticed her doing that, she told Webster to wait outside the store.

"Why?" Webster asked.

"I don't want that ole crazy gal looking at you," Bessie whispered. "She ain't got good sense!"

Webster was annoyed that he had to leave the store. Outside, he began skipping pebbles up and down the road as he waited for Bessie and was unaware that Lula had come out of the store too.

"What be your name, boy?" a voice asked.

Webster turned and saw the smiling Lula standing close behind him. "What be your name?" she asked again.

As Webster stood staring at the girl, Bessie came out of the store. "We be going," she snapped, and thrust a bag of supplies in his arms and stormed off. Webster followed.

"Them peoples is silly," Bessie said angrily to Webster. "When God was givin' out brains, he left a big ole hole in them Bumgarters' heads!"

Bessie stopped in the middle of the road and wagged her finger at Webster. "You stay away from that ugly ole gal! Its gals lack her that will git you strung up to a tree! I won't have you foolin' 'round with her! You heah me!"

"I don't know her, Mama!" Webster protested. "I never spoke to her!"

"You sho' you ain't see'd her on your way to school?"

"Cross my heart and hope to die!" Webster replied and made a cross with his thumb on his chest.

"Anytime you see her comin', you go the other way!" Bessie warned. "That gal in heat!"

On the morning Webster decided to play hooky from school he knew he'd be in trouble with Amanda, but he'd think of something to tell her when he returned to her class. He was sick and tired of school taking away his playtime. Since he didn't want anyone to see him, he decided not to swim in his favorite swimming hole near the settlement, but instead ran through the pines toward a new swimming hole he'd found the afternoon before when he was exploring the woods. He'd swim there.

The new swimming hole was surrounded by big sycamore trees and saplings, and beyond the trees was a blackberry thicket. As soon as Webster came to the swimming hole, he paused for a moment, looking down into the quiet water, then quickly stripped off his trousers and shirt and plunged in.

The water wasn't too deep. It just came up to his neck, and it felt so cool and refreshing that he swam over to some large tree roots and rested his head against them. Soon he closed his eyes.

Little did Webster know that Lula was watching him from the thicket where she had come to pick blackberries. Quietly, she set down her bucket, came out of the thicket, took off her clothes, and sneaked down to the stream's edge to the swimming hole. There, she stood naked looking down at Webster.

Sensing that someone was there, Webster opened his eyes. Upon seeing Lula, he was at first speechless. Then he yelled, "Get on away from here, you silly gal!"

Grinning broadly at Webster, she pointed to her breasts. "You want to feel 'em?"

Webster stared up at her big, white breasts with pink nipples and shouted, "No! Now you get away from me!"

Lula ignored Webster and climbed down into the water and waded over to him as the frightened Webster tried to climb up the bank over the tree roots.

"Go on, feel 'em," Lula demanded and came toward Webster, who was scrambling up the creek bank. Lula reached out and locked her heavy legs around Webster's wet slippery body and held him like a vice. "I told you to feel 'em, boy," she said harshly and squeezed him hard.

Kicking and thrashing about, Webster struggled to get free, but Lula held onto him tighter. He was so close to her that he smelled her body odor. It reminded him of rotting fish.

"Take one," she commanded and jerked his face up to her breast. "It ain't goin' bite you!"

By now, Webster had panicked. He knew he had to do something drastic to get away because he was in big trouble. He closed his eyes and bit down hard on one of her breasts! Lula screamed out in pain and grabbed her wounded breast, letting go of Webster.

With great strength, Webster heaved his slippery body up to the bank and, shaking with fear, he grabbed his clothes and raced headlong through the woods. As he fled he could hear Lula screaming obscenities at him.

By the time Webster reached the woods near his house, he was drenched in sweat and was winded. His naked body was scratched and bleeding because he had fallen down several times as he leaped over tree stumps and logs trying to get away from that horrible creature.

When he reached the path to his house, he could go no further. His legs were trembling and he was having difficulty breathing. He had to rest. He flung down his damp clothes, crawled under some thick bushes, and laid very still, trembling with fear that Lula was coming after him.

As he lay resting, he heard a rustling down the path. Fearing that it was Lula, Webster blindly reached around and found a large rock. If the creature wanted a fight, she'd get it. With rock in hand, Webster crawled out from under the bushes and stood up ready to strike out at his tormentor.

"What's the matter, son?" a voice said. "Did I scare you?"

At first, Webster could not see who the voice was because his view of the path was obscured by some pokeberry bushes. Then a heavy-set black man came into view. The man was wearing a white straw hat, and his shirt-sleeves were rolled up. A black suit coat was folded over one arm, and he was carrying a suitcase. Beads of sweat were on his brow, and he was breathing heavily. "Is it hot enough for you?" the man said as he neared Webster. "Looks like you've been swimming," he said, looking at the boy.

Webster remembered he didn't have on his clothes. Without saying a word to the stranger, he dropped the rock, picked up his damp trousers, and slid into them. Then he put on his shirt and left it unbuttoned.

The man walked closer and extended a hand. "I'm Hezekiah Bates. Reverend Hezekiah Bates." He waited for the glum Webster to shake his outstretched hand. When he didn't, Reverend Bates set down his suitcase. "This is Smyrna, ain't it?"

Webster nodded and sat back down in the leaves. His open shirt revealed the bleeding briar scratches on his chest.

"Looks like you been pickin' blackberries," Reverend Bates said good-naturedly. "I passed several big patches on my way heah."

The silent Webster remembered it wasn't berry picking that caused his wounds, it was that crazy ole gal!

Reverend Bates could tell that the boy was in no mood to talk, so he'd better ask his question and get on his way. He reached into his pocket and pulled out a piece of crumpled paper and glanced at it. "I'm looking for a Mrs. Bessie Epps and a Mr. Nate Pettigrew. Can you tell me where they live?"

Webster's eyes opened wide and his heart did a little flutter. This preacherman was looking for his mother. Why?

When Webster didn't answer, the man said, "Heard the people in Smyrna be lookin' for a preacher."

"Smyrna ain't got a church." Webster answered sullenly.

"I know," the man replied. "That's why I'm here. To start a church."

Feeling a bit more relaxed, Webster reached over, broke off a twig, stuck it in his mouth, and sat chewing on it.

"Do you know these folks?" Reverend Bates asked again.

All the time the man had been talking, Webster was sizing him up. If he said where Bessie lived, he'd tell her who told him. If he didn't, he'd find his house anyway and tell her about seeing a boy on the path. Maybe he could make a deal with the reverend.

Finally, Webster said, "If I show you where Bessie Epps live, will you not tell her you saw me?"

Reverend Bates' smiling face became serious. "What devilment you been into, son?"

"No devilment," Webster replied with wide-eyed innocence, hoping the man couldn't tell by looking at him about the encounter he'd had with Lula.

"Then what you be hidin'?" Reverend Bates probed.

Webster cast his eyes downward. He couldn't bring himself to tell the stranger about Lula because he was so ashamed of what happened. He replied, "I went swimming instead of going to school today, and she might get mad!"

"Why Mrs. Epps goin' be mad at you?"

"She's my mama."

Reverend Bates paused for a moment, then gave a hearty laugh. "Son, I remember when I was your age I did the same thing. There ain't a swimmin' hole 'tween heah and Charleston I ain't been in on a hot day! School or no school, I went swimmin'!" His merriment caused Webster to join in nervously.

Then the man squatted down beside Webster and asked, "What's your name, son?"

"Webster."

"I'm right proud to know you, Webster," and offered his hand again to the boy. This time Webster shook it. "Now, don't you worry," Reverend Bates assured the boy. "I'll keep your secret. It be 'tween you and me."

Webster smiled at the stranger, then stood up and pointed toward the path. "Follow this path until you come out of the woods. The first house on the main road will be ours."

The man struggled to his feet, tipped his straw hat to Webster, picked up his suitcase, and headed off toward the main road.

Webster stretched back out in the leaves and watched him go. He was still too shaken to go home. As he lay there, he swore to himself that he'd never go near that swimming hole again.

Reverend Bates settled down in Smyrna and started his church, The House of God. His fiery sermons were about hell and damnation, good and evil, and God's eternal goodness. The message to the people was for them to be "born again" and get "saved and sanctified."

At first, Reverend Bates held church services in different people's homes until they had saved enough money to build a church. The church was built with a tall steeple right in the center of Smyrna. Reverend Bates wanted the church built there to remind the people of Smyrna that God was the center of their lives.

Because Reverend Bates was so dynamic and such a powerful speaker, nearly every man and woman in Smyrna became members of his church.

Soon, the word spread outside of Smyrna and into the county about this great preacher, and people from miles around came on Sundays to hear him preach the Word of God. It wasn't long before The House of God had a large congregation. Many prosperous black people in Cowpens moved their homes and businesses to Smyrna so they could be near their church. These people built homes and shops, and opened stores. Within a few years, Smyrna had a Main Street, and it became a thriving, bustling little town.

Bessie went to church every Sunday and sang in the church choir. Although she made Webster accompany her to church each Sunday, Enoch wouldn't budge.

Because Bessie believed her family ought to worship together on Sundays, she always asked Enoch to go with her.

"I ain't believin' in no God!" Enoch told Bessie one Sunday morning when she again urged him to come with her.

"Why you say that?" Bessie inquired as she cleared away the breakfast dishes. Then she went to her bedroom to get dressed for church. Enoch followed her there and stood in the bedroom doorway.

"I say that," Enoch explained, "'cause black folks was slaves of white folks." He took a sip of black coffee from the cup he had brought with him from the kitchen and made a face at the taste of the coffee. He'd rather it had been whiskey, but Bessie always hid his bottle on Sundays.

"There'll be no drinkin' and cussin' on the Lord's Day," she told him when he once complained to her that she was taking away his pleasure. "On the Lord's day we goin' keep it holy in this house" was Bessie's reply.

Bessie had gone over to her dresser to brush her hair. "What's slavery got to do with God?" she asked and began brushing.

"There ain't no God," Enoch announced and drank some more coffee. "He be made up."

Bessie stopped brushing her hair, turned around, and frowned at Enoch. "Stop talkin' crazy, Enoch Epps! God ain't made up! God's real!"

"Is God good?" Enoch queried her.

"You know God's good!" Bessie replied and snatched up her brush and began vigorously brushing her hair again.

"If he be good," Enoch went on, "why he let white folks make slaves of black folks?" He shook a finger at Bessie. "You answer me that!"

Bessie ignored Enoch. She wrapped her hair in a ball and stuck a large stickpin in it to hold her hair tight. Then she opened a box on the bed and took out her new hat. It was a white straw hat with yellow flowers sewn around its band. Bessie had saved for months to buy it from Miss Edna, who made hats in Smyrna.

She stood admiring herself in her hand mirror, trying to ignore Enoch's questioning.

Enoch, however, refused to be ignored. He walked over closer to the dresser where Bessie was standing and said. "Slavemaster done made up God."

Bessie glared at him, but Enoch went on explaining. "You know why them ole slavemasters done made up God? To make the slaves so scared they ain't run away! 'Cause if they do, God will send his devil after them and take 'em to hell! That's what the ole masters stick in their heads!"

Bessie gasped. She couldn't believe what she had heard. Why was Enoch saying these awful things and on Sunday? Was it because she had hidden his whiskey bottle and he was trying to get back at her?

Enoch then drank the last of his coffee. By now it was cold, but that didn't deter him from further explaining his theory to Bessie. "Slavemaster jest lack a fox! Whilst slaves be on their knees prayin'," he explained, "slavemaster be makin' money off them! They keeps the poor, ole black folks callin' on a made-up God, askin' him not to let his devil git them! They be tricked!" He smiled at Bessie, feeling proud of himself.

Bessie put her new hat on her head, picked up her pocketbook, and said, "Enoch Epps, I don't understand why God do what he do, but that ain't no reason for me NOT to believe!" She left the room and went looking for Webster.

Enoch yelled after her. "All ole Bates wants is your money! He jest lack them ole slavemasters! He gots you peoples bamboogled by his hollerin' and jumpin' up and down in that ole church! The more money he gits from the peoples, the more he holler! You is a fool, Bessie, to give him money. Can't you tell when you gittin' skunked?"

Bessie rushed back to the bedroom door where she had left Enoch. "Reverend Bates be a man of God!" she shouted. "I'm goin' ask him to preach the devil out of you!"

Then in a loud voice, Bessie called to a sulking Webster, who was hiding in his bedroom. "Come on outta your hidin' place, Webster! God's waitin'!"

After Bessie had rushed out of the house, Enoch began laughing. He laughed so hard that he fell across the bed in hysterics! When he finally got control of himself, he stood up off the bed and began to search for his bottle of whiskey that Bessie had hidden.

Two years after The House of God Church had been established, Sadie Whiteside came to Smyrna.

It was early one May morning just as Amos was setting his coffeepot to boil on the stove when he heard a noise outside Johnson's store. He went to see what it was. There he saw a black buggy drawn by two sleek, black horses. A hefty black woman was sitting in the buggy seat holding the horses' reins. The buggy had stopped in front of the store.

Two young black girls dressed in white sat on each side of the woman. The girls' eyebrows were arched in a thin sliver, and they were wearing heavy makeup. A swath of pink rouge made from pokeberries was reaching up on their cheeks to their hairlines.

Their lips were painted bright red. All the women's hair was puffed up in a pompadour, and one girl had wilting wildflowers stuck into her hair. The girl with the wilting wildflowers in her hair smiled coyly at Amos, flashing her perfect white teeth.

"We jest blew in from Red Springs," the hefty woman said in a low, husky voice. "We be lookin' for a house to rent." The big woman smiled broadly and winked at Amos. "You know where we can find one, honey?"

Amos was too startled to talk. He just stood there gawking at the beautiful girl who had smiled at him. To Amos, that girl looked like an angel sitting there in the morning sun.

"You do know Red Springs, don't you?" the woman asked. Amos swallowed hard and nodded his head.

What man in the county didn't know about Red Springs? It was a grubby little place in the hills ten miles south of Cowpens and was known all over the valley as a place of ill repute because of its red-light district. Many times the sheriff from Cowpens shut down the houses, but they always opened up again.

Although the county officials professed to be God-fearing Christian men, they continued to allow prostitution to flourish in Red Springs. It was rumored that Judge Manny Hero, the tough, no-nonsense county judge, was a frequent customer of the women of the night. Whenever the sheriff closed down the madams, they just went to see Judge Hero and soon their doors were opened again for business.

"Sadie asked you a question, big boy," the smiling girl said to the tongue-tied Amos. "What's the matter? Cat got your tongue?"

The hefty woman turned and frowned at the girl. "You keep quiet, Ruby. I'll handle this business."

"Yes, ma'am," the girl replied meekly.

"Now, Mr. . . ?"

"Jest call me Amos," Amos interrupted.

"Amos, I wants to find a house for me and my girls here in Smyrna. I'm thankin' 'bout startin' a business."

"What kind of business?" Amos managed to ask.

"A saloon. I done heer'd Smyrna is bustin' out at the seams and it be a good place for hardworkin' people to settle down in."

Amos grinned broadly. "You goin' want to be on Main Street. It be down near the church. Lot of folks done opened up there. I tell you the mens in Smyrna goin' be happy to have a saloon to do their drankin' in. Cowpens quite a piece off."

Sadie leaned forward. "Did you say down near the church?" she inquired.

"Yes, ma'am."

She shook her head resolutely. "A saloon ain't got no business bein' near a church. Prayin' and drankin' don't go together! Nope, not at all. What I needs me is a place off from town where the mens kin come and go without a preacher tellin' them 'bout sin."

"Oh, I see," Amos replied thoughtfully. "You wants to be off by your-selfs."

"That's it!" Sadie replied, agreeing with Amos. "I want to be in town, but out of it. You catch my drift?"

Amos understood exactly what Sadie was talking about. She wanted the men who'd come to her saloon to do so in private, and being on Main Street would deprive them of that. The only place he could think of was the old Benny house on the other side of the creek.

Benny had been a prosperous moonshiner in Cowpens County. As he grew old and could no longer make whiskey, his friends deserted him. Bitter with anger and disappointment, he left Cowpens and came to Smyrna. He bought the old house in the woods on the other side of the creek and refused to have anything to do with people, black or white. Two years after Benny had moved to Smyrna, he fell gravely ill. When Reverend Bates heard that the people in Smyrna did not help Benny because he was a white man, he admonished them in one of his sermons.

"The Bible teaches us to care for the poor and the needy," Reverend Bates told his congregation. "God wants us to take care of the poor and needy, regardless of skin color! Benny is a child of God, and we must treat him as God wants us to do. He lives among us and it's our Christian duty to look after him until God calls his name."

Reverend Bates along with the black church members in Smyrna nursed and took care of Benny until he died. On the day Reverend Bates found the old man dead in his bed, he notified the Cowpens sheriff. The sheriff sent the undertaker for Benny's body. The undertaker refused to take it until he knew who was going to pay him for his services. Since no one knew if Benny had any kinfolk, Reverend Bates and his congregation agreed to pay for Benny's embalming. Benny's body was brought back to Smyrna to the House of God church. There, the choir sang joyfully, Reverend Bates preached Benny's funeral, and the people of Smyrna buried him in the House of God's graveyard.

Benny's old house had been empty for well over a year because no one wanted to move into it.

"You might want to go on over the creek and look at old man Benny's house," Amos advised Sadie. "It's in the woods. It ain't a pretty sight, but kin be fixed."

Before Sadie could ask where Benny was, Amos quickly added, "Benny's been dead well over a year."

Sadie was pleased at what she'd heard. "Me and the girls will go on over there and see what we find." She lifted the horses' reins, then paused. "I ain't told you my name. I'm Sadie Whiteside." She pointed to the smiling girl, "This is Ruby." Then she pointed to the other girl. "This heah is Mabel."

Amos took off his cap and bowed deeply. Sadie then snapped the horses' reins and drove off.

Within a year, Sadie's Saloon was a thriving business.

New Lessons Learned

As Webster grew older, he spent a lot of time exploring the woods. Bessie grew worried about him. "I don't like you bein' out there in them woods by yourself," she scolded. "Somethin' kin happen to you."

"Nothing going to happen to me," Webster answered. But he still remembered vividly his near rape by Lula and he kept an eye out for her. The thought of her gave him shivers.

Enoch took no interest in Webster. Even when he was a baby, Enoch had little affection for the boy, and as Webster grew older, Enoch's dislike for him grew. He'd threaten Webster with a whipping for the smallest infraction.

Bessie often had to keep Enoch from abusing the boy. When she did, he'd storm out of the house and go to Sadie's Saloon. There, he'd drown his anger in whiskey for hours and was often late coming home at night. When this happened, Bessie would send Webster to Caleb's store to tell Amos to go bring Enoch home, because she refused to set foot in Sadie's house of ill repute.

More than once, Amos found Enoch in the saloon drinking himself senseless.

"Enoch, you gots to stop drinkin' and carousin' at Sadie's and spend more time with Webster," Amos scolded. "Your boy is becomin' a man and he goin' be tryin' manly thangs. He be needin' advice."

Enoch's answer was always the same. "If he gits hisself in trouble, he goin' have to git hisself out! Ain't no need callin' on me!"

Amos bristled at Enoch's answer. Amos loved Webster and believed that Enoch was a poor example of a father. Yes, Webster was stubborn and a little hard to manage at times, but with the right kind of guidance from Enoch, he'd change. The way things were, the boy didn't get any attention from Enoch and too much from Bessie.

One day Amos witnessed a verbal fight between Webster and Enoch. He had spoken to Bessie earlier, and she told him she was going to Cowpens to help a woman in childbirth. Amos decided to visit with Enoch, but just as he walked around to the back porch, he heard loud, angry voices.

"You ain't foolin' me none," Enoch yelled at Webster. "Your ma done told you to hide my bottle!"

"That's a lie!" Webster yelled back.

Enoch balled up his fist and jumped down off the back porch into the yard where Webster was standing and said, "You callin' me a liar? I'm goin' knock your head off!"

"Liar! Liar!" the angry, red-faced Webster screamed at Enoch and ran off into the woods.

Enoch ran after him but stopped when he saw Amos and came back to the porch steps, flopped down, and began pounding one fist into the other.

Amos watched him with disdain. Finally, he said, "You gots to stop blamin' Webster for the least little thang. The trouble with you, Enoch, you is jealous of the boy. You jealous that Bessie loves him more than you."

Enoch jumped up from the steps and yelled as he looked off in the direction where Webster had gone. "That ain't it! He be smart-ass! He tells me I be dumb!"

Amos tugged at Enoch's shirtsleeve. "Come on. Set back down."

Breathing hard and sweating profusely, Enoch slowly sat down. "I tell you, Amos, Webster be the root of all our fussin' and fightin'!"

"Whose fussin' and fightin'?" Amos asked.

"Me and Bessie! Sometimes I wish we ain't had him. I wish we left him where he was!"

Shaking his head as he disputed Enoch, Amos replied, "Now, I knows you don't mean that, do you?" He reached into his back overall pocket and handed Enoch his half-empty bottle of whiskey. "Take a drank."

With relish, Enoch took a big drink from the bottle, smacked his lips, and burped. "I guess you be right, Amos." He looked off in the distance for a few moments, then said, "If it ain't been for Webster, where, oh where would I be now?"

Amos grinned at him. "You'd be settin' heah drankin' up my whiskey."

Enoch ignored Amos' statement and began shaking his head ruefully. "Don't thank it ain't weigh on my mind from time to time." He frowned. "Bessie sho' won't let me forget it!"

Then Amos realized that something serious was on Enoch's mind. "Where would you be?" Amos probed.

"I be so po' that I be leanin' up aginst a tree."

"What Webster gots to do with you not bein' po?" Amos probed further.

"It be a lon' story and I ain't goin' talk 'bout it!" Enoch quickly replied. He looked down at his hand and said quietly, "It be a deep secret."

Amos had never heard Enoch talk this way before. Something was troubling him, so he tried to cheer him up. "So, you been stealin' from Sadie!" Amos said and slapped Enoch on his back and laughed.

Enoch didn't laugh. He just sighed deeply. "I tells you, Amos, that's why I dranks so much."

In a serious voice, Amos said, "If somethin' be on your mind, Enoch, spit it out."

Holding onto Amos' whiskey bottle between his legs, Enoch shook his head determinedly. "No, Amos, I gots to let it be."

Amos reached over and took the bottle from between Enoch's legs, twisted the cap back on it, and stuck it into his back pocket. "We best put this ole bottle away. Bessie be comin' home soon. If she sees us drankin', she be on us lack a bee on honey!"

"Aw, Bessie try to run my life!" Enoch protested when he saw Amos put the whiskey bottle in his back pocket. "She want ever'body to do what she sez!"

"She be a Christin woman, Enoch. Christins ain't believin' in drankin' and whorin' 'round," Amos explained.

"Christin folks need to keep their snoots outta other folks business! They always rootin' 'round lack a hog tryin' to git somethin' on you so they kin tell you what to do. Is they God?"

"God or not," Amos said, "I ain't wantin' to mess with Bessie. Time for me to go."

Little by little, Webster turned to Amos for friendship. Soon Amos became more like a father to him than Enoch. They did everything together. Amos taught Webster how to seine for fish in the streams, make rabbit boxes to catch rabbits, and shake opossums out of trees at night. When Webster told Amos he wanted to go deer hunting, Amos decided to take the boy up into the hills to Indian Woods.

Bessie grew concerned when Webster told her about the trip he and Amos were planning, so she went with Webster to Caleb's store to see Amos. "I ain't wantin' my child huntin'," she told Amos. "The next thing I know he'll git shot!"

"The only thang that's goin' git shot is them ole deer we be shootin' at," Amos told Bessie. "Webster be a big boy. He kin handle a gun."

"Quit worrying, Mama," Webster assured his mother as he set about getting supplies for Amos and himself to take on their trip. "Amos taught me how to shoot a gun."

"It ain't your shootin' I worried 'bout," Bessie said to Webster. "It be them Indians up there. They ain't lackin' folks killin' off their animals. They be done strung y'all up to a tree!"

"Indians won't do that!" Webster replied with confidence. "Indians don't do stuff like that."

Bessie walked over to Webster, who had now piled up a lot of supplies on the counter and said, "Well, I see'd how that Indian looked at me the other day when I was right here in this store." Bessie gestured with her hand. "I jest spoke to him, friendly lack. He ain't said nothin'. Jest gives me a mean look!"

"Them Indians ain't thankin' 'bout you." Amos explained as he checked the supplies Webster had put on the counter. "I done see'd Indians come in heah lots of times and they ain't bothin' nobody. They jest gits what they wants and leave."

"Indians won't BE in the store," Bessie retorted. "They're goin' to BE up in their woods. And they be actin' different!"

"Bessie, Bessie," Amos pleaded, "I done hunted and fished up in them hills more times than I gots finger and toes and the Indians never come near me."

Bessie wagged a finger at Amos, who had now begun putting supplies into a burlap sack. "Don't be so sure, Amos. One of these days you're goin' see the rough side of them Indians!"

Amos quickly defended the Indians again. "All I'm sayin' is Indians be real good to black folks, Bessie. I heer'd they hid black folks when they run away from slavery."

Still not convinced but not wanting to say more about who was good and who was bad, Bessie asked, "Where you goin' stay if a big rain comes? I ain't goin' have my boy catchin' his death of cold! Them woods kin git real cold after a rain."

"Last time I was up in the woods huntin' I found this ole shack," Amos said. It musta been built a long time ago, 'cause it was all covered over with vines and briars. Me and Webster goin' fix it up."

"You gonna fix up a shack on them Indians' land?" Bessie cried. "Amos, you is crazy!"

"Say what you want, Bessie," Amos replied calmly, "I done already started clearin' away some vines. All me and Webster gots to do now is finish it off. Since we goin' be huntin' a lot, we goin' be stayin' a spell in the shack."

"Yeah," Webster agreed as he helped Amos pack their sacks. "We might stay a week at a time if we want to."

"You best talk this over with Enoch," Bessie warned. "He might be needin' Webster to spell him in the garden."

Amos reached over and patted Bessie on the shoulders. "I done had speaks with Enoch, and he want me to teach Webster how to hunt."

After much wrangling, Bessie finally gave in and went home. Amos and Webster then set off for the hills.

The deserted cabin had been built deep in a hollow near a stream of clear water. It was invisible until you were very close to it because the cabin was surrounded by a profusion of thick bushes and saplings. The cabin's back was pushed up against a steep hill covered with an underbrush of vines and briars that extended far up toward the tall trees near the crest of the hill.

Amos had found the cabin quite by accident. He had gone fishing in a pond up in Indian Woods and after he had caught several trout, he went looking for frogs. Amos loved fried frogs' legs. He followed a stream that emptied its water into that pond for a mile or two but found no frogs. As he sat resting on the stream's bank, he glimpsed something shiny through some briars that grew near the water. Not knowing what it was, Amos decided to find out. It took him some time to break through the briars to reach the shiny object. To his surprise, it was an old tin pot lying near the door of the vine-covered cabin that was made of logs and had a large stone chimney.

It took Webster and Amos an hour to walk to the cabin. They rested for awhile then set about cutting away the vines that were growing over the heavy door. Then they forced open the door that had been stuck from debris blown up against it. Inside the cabin was a large stone fireplace, a handmade table, a chair, and a bench. On each side of the fireplace were two crude hand-made beds nailed to the wall. Several rusting pots lay about the room.

Bessie had given them two old quilts, some cooking pots, a frying pan, and an old coffeepot. She also gave them two tin plates, two well-stained cups, three bent forks, two knives with parts of their blades broken off, and two old spoons. Amos had brought a lantern from the store, a can of kerosene, a box of matches, an ax, and a broken-handle shovel.

"We gots our work cut out for us," Amos told Webster, "so let's git to it."

Amos took his hunting knife, went out, and climbed up on the roof to cut away the vines that were growing down the chimney. He left the vines that covered the roof. While Amos was on the roof, Webster swept out the cabin.

When Amos came back, he said they had to clean out the fireplace. "We ain't wantin' to set ourselfs afire," Amos said as they dug out huge mounds of leaves, twigs and animal waste from the fireplace and up into the chimney.

"I wonder why there ain't no windows?" Webster asked.

Amos explained. "Well, the folks who built this house be way out heah all by themselves, and when the folks go to bed at night they ain't wantin' nothin gittin' in the window whilst they be sleepin'. So, they ain't built windows."

When the fireplace was cleaned, Amos and Webster walked to the creek bank, dug out a bucket of clay with the shovel, and mixed it with some water to make mud. With the mud they chinked up the big cracks in the cabin to keep out the rain and cold.

Before they could settle in for the night, Amos informed Webster that they had another chore to perform. "We best git in some firewood," he said. "We goin' need some for cookin'."

As the two were gathering the wood, Amos decided to camouflage the cabin's sides and door with several dead tree branches. He didn't want other hunters and fishermen using it when he and Webster were not there. It took well over an hour for the two to chop some firewood and to gather enough dead branches to hide the hut. When they had finished piling the tree branches around the hut, only a small hole was left open for the door.

It was early fall. The hills were ablaze in color, and there was a chill in the air. Webster made a fire in the fireplace and Amos opened one of the knapsacks that had been packed with food.

"Let's git some of Bessie's good eats," Amos said and began putting some cold fried chicken and baked sweet potatoes onto the tin plates. "My ole stomick is growlin' lack a hound dawg."

The cold food tasted good, and after eating the two sat by the fire talking. Amos sat on the chair and Webster lay on his quilt that he had spread in front of the fireplace. During their talk, Webster told Amos he wished Amos was his father instead of Enoch.

"Why you say that?" Amos asked.

"Because I hate Enoch!"

Amos threw some of the sticks they had gathered earlier onto the fire. Then he leaned down and patted Webster on the head. In a comforting voice, he said, "Enoch ain't bad. He come up the hard way. I know. I was right there with him. Ever day it was do this, do that! Ole Au Bignon acted lack you ain't had a brain in your head. And ole Brute never lets you forgits he had the whip! Yep, bein' a slave wuz ter'ble!" Amos paused for a few minutes. "It wuz the time we lived in, me and Enoch."

"How's that?" Webster asked, not understanding that statement.

"You take Smyrna," Amos began to explain. "Smyrna was a free place long 'fore the war come. True, there wuz slave plantations all 'round Smyrna, but black folks wuz livin' there free. But me and Enoch wuz livin' jest down the road apiece. We wuz slaves. White folks owned us and black folks owned us. It be a queer world we wuz livin' in."

Webster raised up from his quilt to look at Amos. "What you mean by saying black folks owning black folks?" He asked.

Amos shrugged his shoulders. "Jest what I say. There be black folks 'round heah who own other black folks!"

Shaking his head in disbelief, Webster said emphatically, "I don't believe that!"

"Now, it wuz told to me by Phil," Amos replied. "You 'member I told you 'bout Phil?"

"The one who died and you went to his funeral over in Cowpens last year?"

"That be Phil," Amos agreed.

"So what did Phil tell you?"

"Well, Phil wuz owned by Au Bignon lack me and Enoch. Phil wuz sold off to the Gidney plantation jest over on the other side of Nebo River. One night Phil swims back over the river to see me. Me and Phil wuz real good friends and he be missin' me a lot. When he be leavin', I slip down to the river with him and we jest set there talkin' when he stops and looks at me real hard. Phil look so scared! Lack he see'd a ghost! I sez, 'What be the matter with you?'"

By now, Webster was sitting up on the quilt. "Well, what was wrong?" he urged.

"Jest hold on," Amos cautioned Webster. "I be tellin' you the story." He cleared his throat. "Now, I wuz thankin' he done heer'd the paddyrollers and we best git! But that ain't it. Phil sez, 'Amos, I done see'd somethin' I ain't b'lieve!' I sez, 'Phil, go on spit it out! . . .'"

Amos pushed his chair back from the fire and picked up a piece of wood and threw it on the fire. Then he sat back down and stared into the blaze.

Webster was anxious to hear the rest of the story. "Well . . . ," he urged Amos.

"This be hard for me to tell," Amos said.

"Just try," was Webster's advice.

Amos sighed deeply and began to tell the story. "Phil sez, 'I see'd a black man who wuz a slave of 'nother black man!' I sez, 'Phil, black folks tryin' to git us out from under the yoke of slavery. They ain't puttin' the yoke 'round our necks too!' Phil jest shakes his head and sez, 'I sho' hope that man made it up north!'"

Amos grew silent again and Webster became anxious. "How'd Phil meet this man?"

"Phil say one night when he wuz in the barn pitchin' hay to the cows, he stuck his pitchfork into a big ole pile of hay. The sound that come from that hay wuz so loud it hurt his ears! Then he saw him! A black man in tatters, all skin and bones, come crawlin' outta that hay. Phil done stuck his fork in him!"

Amos' eyes teared as he continued the story. "That man told Phil all his troubles. How he wuz worked and treated by 'nother black man! He wuz runnin' away and he meant to git up north to Canada! Phil wuz scared, but he hid that man in the hay and fed him for days 'til he wuz well enough to git outta there!"

Webster stared at Amos. "Why would black folks own slaves?"

"Guess they love money too," Amos replied sadly.

"Why didn't Phil go with that man?"

"I can't rightly say. Maybe he ain't had the guts, jest lack a lot of us didn't."

"You believe Phil's story?" Webster questioned.

"Phil sez it be true. I b'lieve Phil."

Webster laid back down on the quilt and stared blankly into the fire. Both were silent for a few minutes, then Amos finally said, "Now, you kin see how a man kin git mixed up. Enoch got a lot on his plate."

After a few minutes had passed, Webster said, "Enoch's always getting drunk and telling me he's going to beat my butt."

"You ain't gots to pay no never mind to Enoch. He all talk," Amos said.

Webster turned over on his back and lay looking up at the ceiling. Then he said, "I know something Enoch thinks I don't know."

Puzzled, Amos asked, "What's that?

With a pleased look on his face, Webster replied, "I know he's been slipping off to Sadie's Saloon to see a woman! If he mess with me again, I'm going to tell Mama! She'll kick his butt all over Smyrna!"

"Now, look heah, Webster," Amos warned. "Don't you go tattlin' to yo' ma 'bout Enoch." He kicked Webster playfully with his foot. "Us mens gots to stick together. We gots to keep some secrets from the wimminfolks!"

"But he's cheating on Mama!"

"Well, jest a little bit," Amos replied, chuckling slightly. "You see, boy, there be certain thangs a man need from wimmin. It be the way he made. Now, if he ain't gittin it from one woman, he go to 'nother. For some time your ma ain't wantin' to give Enoch what he need, so he slip off to Sadie's."

"What does Enoch need?"

Amos gave a belly laugh and slapped on his knee. "You sho' lack to ask questions, boy. One of these days I be tellin' you." He leaned over and looked Webster in his eyes. "You ain't wantin' to upset your ma and git her mad, do you?"

Webster shook his head. The last thing he ever wanted to do was get his mother angry, so he just lay there feeling angry at Enoch.

After awhile, Amos asked, "How you know 'bout Enoch?"

"I followed him."

This didn't please Amos because he thought Webster had seen Enoch with a woman. "Enoch ain't seein' wimmin. All he be doin' at Sadie's is drankin'. He ain't doin' nothin' else."

Webster then said sarcastically, "One of these days I'm going into Sadie's, sit down on one of her big settees, cross my legs, get me a drink, and put my arms around one of them women there."

Amos nearly fell off the chair. "You'll do no sech thang, boy! Them wimmins be done ruint you for life!" He stared at Webster. "How you know 'bout this?"

With a smug smile on his face, Webster replied, "I heard Enoch telling you about what he did at Sadie's. Why should he be having fun when Mama ain't? He ought to be home with her where he belongs!"

"You ain't gots no right eavesdroppin' on your pa and me. Your pa got a right to his secrets."

"I wasn't eavesdropping," Webster replied. "I just happened to hear him. He's got such a big mouth! I heard him talking about the women at Sadie's and the way they walk." Webster jumped up off the quilt and demonstrated a walk by swaying his hips from side to side. Then he fell back on the quilt and laughed and laughed.

Amos was becoming anxious. He wasn't prepared to talk to Webster about sex because he felt Webster was too young to know certain things. "You jest git your mind off them wimmins at Sadie's," he warned. "I ain't come all the way up here to be talkin' 'bout them!"

Amos was silent for a few minutes and leaned back on the rickety chair and closed his eyes. "Slavery sho' wuz a bad thing, Webster. You take me and Enoch. We is free now and we ain't free."

"How do you mean?" Webster asked and got up to his knees. "How can you be free and not free at the same time?"

"I mean we is free in our bodies but not in our minds. You see that wuz the real bad thang 'bout slavery. It ruint the mind. Got you b'lievin' you ain't worth nothin', and when you ain't worth nothin', folks do all kinds of thangs to a nothin'!"

"But you know better than that," Webster said. "You know you're a man, just like all other men."

"I know it now, but there's still folks who ain't freed up their minds lack me."

Amos looked down at the serious-looking boy and playfully slapped him on the back. "You thank you big enough to beat me, don't you?"

"Yeah," Webster answered confidently and got up on his knees into a crouch and motioned at Amos.

Then without warning, Amos grabbed hold of Webster's shoulders and yanked him onto the floor. The two began wrestling in front of the fire. Over and over they rolled, first Webster on top, then Amos. Soon, Amos realized that Webster had learned his wrestling lessons well from him.

"We best stop," Amos said, breathing hard. "I ain't wantin' to hurt you."

"I was just getting started," Webster cried. "Let's go at it again!" And he pranced around and around Amos feigning wrestling movements.

"We go at it agin in the mornin'."

The disappointed Webster sat back down on the floor. After a few minutes he asked, "Did you know my mama and pa?"

Amos was surprised at Webster's question and had to fumble for words. "You . . . you know I know Bessie and Enoch, boy! You tryin' to play a trick on me?"

"They ain't my real folks," Webster replied.

"Who told you that?" Amos inquired.

Webster brushed his hair back from his face and gave Amos a knowing look. "I ain't a fool. I look in the mirror every day."

"They your folks," Amos insisted, "'cause they love you."

"Mama loves me and I love her, but she's not my real mama." Webster paused. "You know Ozell?"

"Tessa's boy?"

"Yep. Ozell told me that my mama told his mama I was part Indian. Is that true?"

Amos spit into the fire and frowned. "That ole rascal don't know nothin' 'bout who you is! Ozell be spreadin' bad news!"

Webster patted Amos on the knee. "Don't get so mad. I'm glad to be Indian! Maybe while we're up here in the hills, I might see some Indians. They might even be my kinfolks!"

"I ain't goin' spend no time lookin' for Indians, Webster. That ain't what we come up heah for." Amos stood up and yawned. "It be gittin' bedtime."

Early the next morning Amos awoke, opened the door, and went down to the stream. He washed his hands and face. Then he brought back a pot of water for coffee.

When he came back to the cabin, Webster was still sleeping. "Sun's comin' up, Webster," Amos said. "I'll git a fire goin' whilst you git the sleep outta your eyes. Go on down to the water and git your face washed."

While Webster was washing his face down at the stream, Amos built a fire in the fireplace and set his coffeepot near some hot embers. When Webster had finished washing his face, he returned to the cabin, put some fatback meat into the old iron pan, and fried it over the fire.

"Fry me some eggs," Amos said.

Webster scrambled the eggs in the fatback grease and put some fried meat and eggs on the plates. He heated some of Bessie's cold biscuits over the fire and put them on the plates. Then he poured two cups of the black coffee.

"Let's eat," Amos said, and the two sat down at the table.

As soon as they had eaten, Webster took the dishes to the stream and washed them while Amos got the shotguns ready.

Deer had become scarce in the woodlands of the Bushy Mountains, and Amos and Webster had been looking for them for well over two hours. Just when they decided to give up and look for rabbits, they heard a slight rustling in some bushes. Amos motioned to Webster to stand still. As the two stood perfectly still and quiet, the antlers of a buck were glimpsed through the underbrush.

Amos silently raised his shotgun and blasted. The racket from the gun was thunderous, so loud that Webster fell backwards on the ground. In a fleeting moment, the deer's antlers went moving quickly through the trees.

"I think I hit him!" Amos shouted. Then he and Webster raced down the hollow, jumping over dead tree branches and rotting logs, and dodging saplings as they chased after the deer.

Suddenly came loud shouts and yells from high atop a steep hillside. The sounds were hideous to Webster, and he looked up in the direction from where the sounds had come. He saw four men running down the side of the hill toward them.

"Indians!" Webster cried to Amos. "I wonder what they want?"

Amos gazed up the hillside at the oncoming shouting men with raised guns. "We best git outta heah!"

"Why?" Webster asked. "Indians won't hurt me. I'm just like them!"

"I ain't so sho' 'bout this bunch! They ain't runnin' lack they be friendly!"

When Webster hesitated, Amos shouted, "Git movin', boy!"

Back up the hollow they ran until they came to the edge of a gully. Amos slid down into the gully, causing a mountain of dust. Webster fell into the cloud of dust and tumbled head over heels down the gully after Amos, crashing against bushes and dried bunches of grass.

Amos reached out and jerked the falling Webster behind a pile of dead branches. Webster's heart was pounding so hard he thought he could hear it beating.

"Lay still," Amos whispered.

The two were as quiet as the dead. They could not hear nor see the four young Indian boys who were bent over with laughter standing at the gully's edge. After peering down into the gully for a few minutes, they left.

After lying behind the dead branches for awhile, Amos cautiously crawled out and looked up toward the gully's edge. He didn't see anyone. "We best git," he told Webster.

Webster crawled out from the hiding place and wiped the dust from his face and eyes. "Why did they come after us? Couldn't they see we were black?"

"Guess skin color don't matter when you be goin' after folks' eats. Indians jest lack ever'body else. They looks after themselfs!"

Webster shook the dust from his pants. "They sure gave me a scare! I thought they'd get us for sure! Guess they couldn't run as fast as me and you."

Amos wiped off his face and neck with his hands. "If them Indians want us, they kin git us! I done see'd Indians run lack the wind! No, they ain't wantin' us this time. They be wantin' to scare off our pants!"

Webster pulled up his baggy pants that had now fallen to his knees. "I think they did."

The two walked slowly back to the cabin. When they reached it, Amos began stuffing their things into the burlap sacks. "We best go on home," he said. "We ain't wantin' them Indians gittin real mad at us. If they find us agin tryin' to kill off their animals, we might not be so lucky."

"Where we going to hunt?" Webster asked.

"There lots of woods 'round Smyrna that ain't posted," Amos told him. "We kin go over to ole man Finley's woods. He don't mind folks huntin' there."

Webster grew pensive. He remembered his encounter with Lula and started to tell Amos about the incident but changed his mind. He was too ashamed. But if he and Amos ever hunted in there, he'd keep an eye out for Lula. To him, she was real scary.

"Aw shucks!" Webster said and reluctantly threw some of their stuff into a sack. "I thought we'd be hunting, not going home."

"We best not tell yo' ma 'bout this," Amos warned. "She ain't wantin' us comin' up heah in the first place. I tell her I gots to finish off a pair of boots. If we tell her the truf, you ain't never goin' go huntin' up heah agin."

When the sacks were filled and the fire was put out with water, Amos closed the cabin door. Then he and Webster piled the tree branches around the cabin until it was well hidden and they left for home.

Bessie was surprised to see Amos and Webster come home so soon. "Guess them Indians done run y'all off!" she teased.

"Amos had to get back to finish off a pair of boots," Webster quickly said.

Bessie looked quizzically at Amos. "Ain't you knowed that 'fore you set off? Caused me to do all that cookin' for nothin'!" she snapped.

Ruby

Late in the afternoon a few days after Webster and Amos had returned from their hunting trip, Bessie sent the boy to Caleb Johnson's store to buy a box of baking soda. "Your pa want some soda biscuits for supper," she said. "Make haste."

At the store, Webster asked Caleb where Amos was. "In the basement," was Caleb's reply. Webster went down to the basement for a short visit. As he made his way down the dark, steep basement stairs, he heard laughter. Peering through some horse saddles and ropes hanging near the entrance to Amos' quarters, he saw Enoch sitting on a barrel next to Amos. Sitting on a chair he had brought out from his bedroom, Amos was working on a pair of shoes. Amos often retreated to the basement to work when he wanted privacy.

The two men were laughing and talking as Amos hammered sporadically on a shoe sole. They hadn't heard Webster come down the steps, and he was wondering what was causing the men to laugh so boisterously.

"She be hea'en on earth!" Enoch blurted out through gales of laughter.

"You best not let Bessie heah you say that, or it be hell on earth!" Amos teased. "Enoch you is bad! Real bad!"

Enoch leaned toward Amos and replied gleefully, "Once you done had this gal, you be knowin' what life be lack!" He again burst out laughing. "I tells you Amos, you be missin' a lot!" Enoch then reeled with laughter.

Grinning slyly at Enoch, Amos replied, "I be plum wore out! Ain't nothin' I kin do for the wimmins 'ceptin' talk, and wimmins be needin' more than talk!"

"Talk ain't goin' make it, Amos!" This time Enoch laughed so hard he nearly fell off his barrel.

The eavesdropping Webster became enraged at Enoch for talking about women when his mother was at home cooking his dinner. Why was Amos listening to Enoch's dirty talk? Didn't Amos have any respect for Webster's mother? If only he were older, Webster'd put a stop to Enoch's escapades!

Webster grew so angry that he ran out of the store forgetting to buy the box of soda. Blind with anger, he ran down the path behind the store until he came to the big chestnut tree that stood a few feet off the path. Webster flung himself angrily on the grass in the chestnut tree's shade.

"Damn you, Enoch!" he shouted angrily, shaking his fist at an imaginary Enoch. "Just you wait 'til I'm bigger! I'll show you!"

After calling Enoch as many curse words as he knew, Webster laid on his back and looked up at the sky.

Silently watching some puffy white clouds drift by, Webster's rage subsided. He soon felt at peace as he lay in the undergrowth, where the wildflowers were wilted from the dust and the heat. The shade felt good to Webster and he reached out, broke off a dead flower stem, and stuck it into his mouth, then closed his eyes.

As he lay there in the quiet woods dappled with sunlight, he heard someone coming on the path. Webster quickly got to his knees and looked down the path in the direction of the sound. There were three women walking up the path toward him.

He squinted his eyes from a glint of sunlight to get a better look. The women must be from Sadie's Saloon, he thought. But why where they coming this way? Didn't they know they were not welcome in this part of Smyrna?

As the women came closer, Webster got a better look. He recognized the chunky woman in front whose hair looked as if it were on fire: the infamous Sadie, madam of the saloon. She was wearing a red satin dress that was stretched over a crinoline petticoat which gave her the look of several women's weight. Red rouge was smeared on Sadie's face all the way back to her ears, covering a zigzagged scar that ran along the side of her face. She looked mean and fearsome.

Following Sadie was another woman wearing black. Webster couldn't get a good look at her face because she walked with her head down as she passed by. One thing for sure, Webster surmised, the woman wasn't getting enough to eat! Walking behind the woman in black came another young woman dressed in white.

The first two women rushed by Webster as if he were not there. But the woman in white paused, then sauntered over to the wide-eyed boy sitting up on his knees.

"Well, well," she said in a husky voice. "What's a pretty boy like you doin' settin' under a big ole tree by yourself? Need some company, honey?"

Webster was so dazzled by the woman that he couldn't speak. Not that she was pretty, but she was all dressed in white, her cheeks were painted red, and she smelled like honeysuckles!

Staring up at the woman, Webster remembered he'd seen her before, one day when he and his friend Ozell were playing down near the creek. They'd seen her coming in the distance and had slipped into a clump of bushes and watched as she walked up the hill toward Sadie's Saloon, swaying her hips from side to side. When she was out of sight, he and Ozell mimicked her walk down by the creek bank.

"That's Ruby," Ozell had told him.

"How you know her name," Webster had asked.

"Kin I tell you a secret?" Ozell asked.

"Cross my heart and hope to die!" Webster responded, making a cross on his chest with his fingers.

Upon seeing that, Ozell told him the secret. "My ma found out that Pa was sneakin' over to Sadie's at night visitin' a woman. Uncle Jeff told Ma that the woman Pa was seein' was Ruby! So Ma went over to Sadie's and called Ruby out to the porch. Ma gave her a piece of her mind!"

"How did you know what Ruby looked like?" Webster asked.

Ozell smiled deceptively. "I followed Ma and hid in the bushes. I got a real good look at her." He smiled again. "When I git me some money, I'm goin' go lookin' for Ruby. She's a real honey!"

All the happenings of that day came back to Webster. And now, here was Ruby standing in front of him, smiling and showing her buck teeth.

"What's the matter, pretty boy?" she purred. "Cat got your tongue?"

"Ruby!" the chunky woman in red yelled in a harsh voice. "You ain't got time to fool with a baby! You git on up heah! We got to git home."

Ruby lifted up her dress so Webster could glimpse her lace pantaloons. She winked at him, then ran and caught up with the other women. Before the women disappeared into the thick woods that led down to the creek, Ruby turned and waved to Webster and, swaying her hips wildly from side to side, she went out of sight.

Webster just sat there mesmerized. He had a mind to follow. Then he remembered the baking soda. He wasn't going back to the store for it. Let Enoch eat flatbread, Webster thought, because he didn't deserve soda biscuits!

"What kept you?" Bessie inquired as Webster came through the door. "I've been waitin' quite a spell."

"Mama," Webster said, "you ain't going to believe who I just saw."

Looking at Webster's empty hands, Bessie asked, "Where's the soda?"

When Webster didn't answer, Bessie asked, "Caleb's out of it?"

Believing that the store didn't have baking soda, Bessie said, "I can't make biscuits without soda. Go on over to Tessa's and git me some soda from her."

Bessie, who was preoccupied with getting the supper ready, ignored Webster. She opened the cabinet over the kitchen stove, got a can of lard, and set it on the table. Then she went to get some flour and her large mixing bowl that she kept in the pantry.

When she came back with a bag of flour and her mixing bowl, Webster was still standing in the kitchen doorway. "Mama, I saw some women in the woods just now," he said. "One was so pretty! She was dressed in white from head to toe. Boy! She looked like a ripe peach, and I wanted to take a bite out of her!"

Bessie gave Webster a disdainful look as she shook some flour from the bag into her mixing bowl. "Peach may look good on the outside, but you might be biting into a worm," she snapped. "Jest 'cause a woman look good don't make her good."

Webster came closer to his mother. "How you know?" he quizzed.

Bessie pointed her stubby, flour-covered finger toward her head. "This ole head ain't filled with gray hair for nothin'. For ever' gray hair on my head mean I done learnt somethin'! And I sho' got a lot of gray hair."

"So . . . ?" Webster asked.

"So, that means I know plenty! Now you best git on to Tessa's."

"I'm going," Webster assured her, "but I first want to tell you what I learned. I found out her name."

Bessie now had put a handful of lard into the mixing bowl. She stopped short of mixing it with the flour. "Who you talkin' 'bout?"

"The woman I saw in the woods." He walked over to the table and stood behind Bessie and said in a syrupy voice. "Her name is Ruby!"

Bessie nearly knocked over her bowl of flour as she twirled around and grabbed Webster by his shoulders and shook him hard. "You be gittin' too big for your britches! You stay away from that trash! You hear me?"

"Why?" the startled Webster asked and pulled away from Bessie's grip.

"Because I say so!" Bessie yelled in his face. "Next thang you know, you be gittin' the 'bad disease'!"

Webster primped up his face in disbelief. "She looks so pretty, Mama."

"You be taken in by a pretty face, 'cause you jest a child! Wimmin lack her got all kinds of bugs crawlin' inside them. Them bugs will put you in your grave! You git that ole bad disease, and it will rot off your swimps!"

Webster knew Bessie was talking about his penis. She always called a penis "swimps." "You mean. . . ."

Bessie interrupted him. "That's 'xactly what I mean, you little fool!"

"Aw, Mama. Ruby ain't got syphilis," Webster protested. "People who got the bad disease stink! Ruby smells like honeysuckles!"

Bessie began shaking Webster violently and screamed, "Where you been smellin' her? Over at that whorehouse?"

"No, no!" Webster cried. "I just told you I saw her on the path in the woods."

By now Bessie was fuming with anger. Webster had never seen her so angry, not even when she and Enoch were having a fight.

"You know what I'm goin' to do?" she yelled. "I'm going to git Reverend Bates and the churchfolks and we goin' go over there and run them wimmins out of Smyrna! The likes of her ain't got no right walkin' the streets of Smyrna where decent God-fearin' folks live! Let 'em get on back to Red Springs with their mangy bodies!"

She angrily jabbed her hand into the flour and squeezed the lard into little lumps. Still angry she said, "Jest think that ole Sadie lettin' a little boy in that whorehouse!"

"Mama," Webster pleaded and touched her on her back. "I ain't been to Sadie's."

Bessie whirled around. "You better not!" This time Bessie yelled so loud that Webster was momentarily deaf for a few seconds. "'Cause I'll beat your pants off!" She grabbed him by the hand and shoved him out the kitchen door. "Now you git over to Tessa's and git me some baking soda before I whack your butt!"

Webster ran down the road toward Tessa's house talking to himself. "Mama is just saying that Ruby's got syphilis because she's mad at Enoch for sneaking off over to Sadie's."

A few weeks had passed since Webster had met Ruby on the path. He was still thinking about her and at night he dreamed about her. It wasn't so much her face he thought about, but it was the way she smelled. He'd go back to the big chestnut tree and lie under it, close his eyes and imagine that he was at Sadie's, sitting on a sofa with Ruby who smelled of sweet honeysuckles. They'd be sipping cool mint water from the same glass.

Soon Webster's imagination became obsessive. All he could think about was Ruby. Then he began slipping off down to the creek and lying in the bushes hoping to catch a glimpse of her. When he no longer could bear his secret, he decided to tell his best friend Ozell.

Since Webster wanted to talk about his secret out of the range of Bessie's ear, he asked Ozell to come fishing with him one morning. They took their fishing poles and a can of freshly dug worms and headed for a fishing hole in the deep part of the creek.

As soon as they reached the fishing hole, Ozell quickly put a worm on his hook and threw in his line. But instead of fishing, Webster laid down on his back in the grass, put his hands under his head, and closed his eyes.

"Them fish ain't gonna jump out of the water into your bucket," Ozell teased. "Come on, throw in your line. I promised Ma we'd have fish for supper."

Webster just lay there with his eyes closed. Finally, he said, "Ozell, I'm in love!"

"Love?" Ozell asked.

"Yep, love," Webster confessed.

Ozell tied his fishing pole to a bush to keep his hook in the water and went and sat down in the grass next to Webster. He was not at all surprised at what Webster said because they were always talking about girls and the ones they wanted to court.

"I bet I know," Ozell replied, grinning at Webster. "It be Mary Lou. I saw you givin' her goo-goo eyes in church Sunday."

"Nope. She ain't the one."

"Then it's her sister, Emma Jane, 'cause she was settin' next to Mary Lou." Ozell paused. "But she fifteen. You only ten."

"Ten going on eleven," Webster corrected him. "But she's not the one either."

Ozell quickly jumped up and ran over to inspect his fishing line. He thought he had caught a fish. When he discovered he hadn't, he came back to Webster. "It best not be my gal, Bertha. She was settin' next to Emma Jane."

"No, it isn't!" Webster replied emphatically.

"Good!" Ozell said. "Bertha be fifteen, but I'm a man even if I just turned twelve," he bragged. "I kin take care her."

"I ain't in love with a gal, Ozell. I'm in love with a woman!"

"A woman? What woman?" Ozell asked.

In a dreamy voice, Webster said, "Ruby." He opened his eyes and gazed at the bewildered Ozell. Then he closed his eyes again.

After a few minutes, Ozell shook his arm. "You be talkin' 'bout Ruby over at Sadie's?"

Webster nodded his head. "She's the one."

Ozell began laughing. It took him some time before he could control himself. Finally, he said through spurts of laughter, "That woman old enough to be your ma!"

Webster just lay there as if he were helpless. "I can't help myself."

"You be ten . . . going on eleven," Ozell said. "Ain't no such thang as a ten- . . . I mean going on eleven-year-old boy being in love with a woman in her fifties!"

Webster sprang up to his knees. "Twenties!" He put in.

"Forties," Ozell replied.

"You didn't think she was forty when you said you wanted to go see her! And she ain't in her forties, Ozell! Stop lying!"

"All right, but I was just teasin' 'bout going to see her." He paused, "But she be in her twenties and that be twice your age. Well, almost twice."

When Webster didn't respond, Ozell asked. "How'd you meet her? You go over to Sadie's?"

Webster sighed deeply and laid back on the grass. "Mama would kill me if I went over to Sadie's." Then a dreamy look came into his eyes. "I saw her in the woods walking, she smelled of honeysuckles, and I fell in love!"

Ozell was perplexed at his friend. He had a mind to tease him about falling in love with a smell, but the look in Webster's eyes told him not to.

"Ozell," Webster went on. "I want to go over to Sadie's and see her."

Not knowing what to say, Ozell said, "Well?"

Webster sat up again and began pounding his fists together. "I can't get up the nerve! I once went down as far as the creek, but I couldn't cross over it! I just couldn't go any further!" He looked at Ozell for a moment. "Maybe if I had someone to go with me, I could do it."

"Don't be lookin' at me," Ozell quickly said. "I ain't got the nerve neither!"

"But you're my best friend, Ozell," Webster pleaded. "You got to help me!"

The two then sat there in silence for a few minutes. Then Ozell said, "Maybe if we got some likker in us we could do it."

"Likker makes me sick," Webster said and made a face. "I once took a swallow of Enoch's and I threw up for days!"

"My pa says when a man gits likker in him, he ain't scared of nothin'! Not even the devil!" Ozell elbowed Webster in the side. "You wants to go see Ruby, you got to drank likker!"

Webster sat there for a few minutes and began tossing stones into the creek. He was thinking over what Ozell had proposed. Soon, he concluded that, if the only way he could get the nerve to go see Ruby was to drink some whiskey, he'd just have to make the sacrifice.

Finally Webster said, "Tell you what, Ozell. I'll steal a jarful of Enoch's likker. Tomorrow we'll meet down at the creek, drink it, then we'll go to Sadie's."

Sounding a bit frightened, Ozell asked, "What if Enoch catches you? There'll be hell to pay!"

"Aw, Enoch ain't going to catch me," Webster assured Ozell. "He sleeps 'til twelve. We'll go early."

The boys shook hands, and both of them went back to fishing.

Webster was up early the next morning. He took a bath, put on a clean shirt and trousers, and slicked down his hair with Vaseline. He went out to the backyard where Bessie was busy washing clothes in a tub. "How do I look?" he asked.

Bessie stopped scrubbing a shirt she had on her washboard. "What you so dressed up for?" she asked.

"Ozell and me are going fishing."

Eyeing Webster with a frown on her face, Bessie said, "Since when did you have to git dressed up for fish?"

Webster strutted in front of her. "I don't want the fish to be afraid to bite."

"And you thank if you slick down your hair and git all dressed up, the fish goin' come jumpin' outta the water to you." She stared at Webster momentarily. "You and Ozell ain't goin' fishin'."

Webster's heart began to beat fast as fear gripped him. Had Bessie guessed where he was going? What if she asked if he were going to Sadie's Saloon?

Webster's fears were over when Bessie said, "Y'all goin' over to ole man Hughes' place tryin' to git a glimpse of Mary Lou and Emma Jane." She smiled at Webster. "You boys ain't foolin' me none. I done see'd the looks passed back and forth in church on Sundays."

Webster liked his mother's explanation of where he was going. Better she believed he was going over to the Hughes place than where he was really going.

"You boys ain't tryin' to get fish," Bessie continued. "Y'all is tryin' to git a girlfriend!"

Smiling, Webster said unconvincingly. "Mama, we aim to catch a mess of fish."

Bessie waved her hand at Webster. "Go on before I make you take off your nice clothes."

She watched him go, thinking that her boy was growing up. However, she didn't mind Webster keeping company with the Hughes girls. They were nice folks. Mary Lou was in Webster's class at school. She was real pretty and smart too. She'd make something of herself one day.

Webster only pretended he was going to Ozell's house, and when he'd gone down the road a short distance, he slipped into the woods and came back to the cowshed behind his house. The night before, he had hidden a small jelly jar with a cap there.

Inside the shed, Webster knew where Enoch hid his whiskey bottle. He felt under a damp sack of cow feed and found the bottle. Carefully, he poured the jelly jar full of whiskey, screwed the cap on, and put the bottle back in its hiding place. Then he sneaked out of the shed and ran down the path through the woods.

Down on the creek bank, Ozell was waiting. He stood up when he saw Webster. "You git it?" he called.

Webster held the jar up high and hurried down to where Ozell waited.

"We best go 'cross the creek and set in the bushes to do our drinkin'," Ozell advised. "We ain't wantin' Enoch sneakin' up on us."

"Yeah," Webster agreed, but he wasn't afraid of Enoch coming that way until it was dark. If, however, Ozell wanted to go across the creek it was all right with him.

The two boys crossed the creek by jumping from stone to stone that lay in the shallow water. On the other side they crawled into a clump of bushes and sat down. Webster unscrewed the jar cap and handed the jar toward Ozell. "You go first."

Ozell pushed the jar back toward Webster. "No. You go first."

Webster took a deep breath, held his nose with one hand, and with the other trembling hand he brought the jar up to his mouth and took a big swallow. When the strong whiskey rushed down his throat, he gagged, then blurted, "Aaaww!" He fell sideways onto Ozell.

Ozell shoved him away and cried, "What's the matter with it?"

"This stuff taste nasty!" Webster cried as some whiskey dribbled down onto his chin.

"It's suppose to taste nasty!" Ozell explained. "That's how it gives you nerve."

Webster wiped his mouth on his shirtsleeve and handed the jar to Ozell, who took a little swallow and handed the jar back to Webster.

"Drink some more," Webster urged and put the jar up to Ozell's lips. "You just took a little bit!"

Ozell frantically shook his head and pushed the jar away from his mouth. "Webster," he retorted. "I ain't the one who wantin' to see Ruby! You be the one, so you need to git up your nerve to talk to her. I jest only need to git up nerve to go with you to the house!"

When Ozell saw the angry look in Webster's eyes, he yanked the jar from Webster's hand, spilling some of the whiskey down the front of his shirt. He took another swallow and shoved the jar back in Webster's hand. "Finish it off!"

Webster pinched his nose with his fingers and took a huge gulp, and all the whiskey was gone. Gagging violently, he rolled over on his stomach trying to keep the whiskey down.

After a few minutes he cried, "My stomach's on fire! I'm going to puke! Git outta the way, I'm going to really puke!"

Ozell jumped astride Webster's back and slapped his hand over the boy's mouth! "Don't puke it up!" he cried to the gagging, struggling boy and held him down. "You gotta let the whiskey git to workin'!"

Try as hard as he could to get up, Webster couldn't. Ozell held him firmly until the burning subsided. When Webster did try to stand up he felt dizzy and giddy, and he fell back down onto Ozell.

"Git off me," Ozell cried and pushed Webster over into the bushes. Then the two began tumbling over each other, giggling and laughing as they rolled in the dry bushes.

Suddenly, Webster gave a big hiccup and yelled, "Let's go see Ruby!"

"Yeah!" Ozell replied, "Ruby, here we come!"

The boys brushed off the dust and leaves from their clothing, and arm-in-arm, they started up the dusty, eroding hillside toward Sadie's Saloon.

"Ruby! Ruby! Ruby!" They sang in lusty voices as they stumbled forward. "Ruby! Ruby!"

Sadie, who had been sleeping, was awakened by the racket. Since it was before noon, this disturbance caused her great displeasure. She climbed out of her big feather bed, stuck her feet into a pair of slippers she kept under the bed, grabbed up her wooden stick from the corner of her bedroom, and angrily went out to see what it was that had disturbed her rest.

Out on the porch, she peered down the path toward the edge of the straggly woods that were in front of her house and, to her amazement, she saw two boys, their clothing rumpled and dirty, arm-in-arm, staggering, stumbling, laughing, and chanting Ruby's name, coming toward her house.

Sadie stormed down off her porch and went to confront the boys. "Where the hell do you thank you be going?" she bellowed and shook her big stick at them. "If you don't git, you be feelin' my stick on yo' butts!"

Sadie looked so mean and fearsome that she frightened Ozell, who stopped short and stood frozen in place and whispered, "We best git, Webster! I ain't wantin' no stick upside my head!"

Webster, who was now too drunk to be frightened, stood facing Sadie. Weaving back and forth, he stuttered, "I . . . come . . . to . . . see . . . Ruby and. . . ."

"I'll give you Ruby!" Sadie shouted and came at them shaking her stick. Ozell jerked away from Webster, who then went crashing to the ground!

Ozell raced back down toward the scraggly woods and in a few minutes was out of sight. Webster tried to get up, but each time went crumpling back down. The last time he fell, he began shaking violently.

Sadie was now standing over Webster and had raised her stick to give him some whacks when she saw him double up in pain. His lips had turned blue, and he was holding his stomach with his hands as big tears rolled down his cheeks.

"Hey! You gals in there!" Sadie shouted. "Git out heah, quick!"

By the time several women had rushed out to the yard, Sadie had lifted Webster up in her strong arms and had carried him over to a bench under a tree and sat down with him on her lap. "This child be sick," she announced to the women who had gathered around her.

Ruby, who was among the women, asked in a worried voice, "What's wrong with him?"

"He musta drunk some bad whiskey," Sadie replied. "He smell like a still. We got to git some raw eggs in him. That'll brang it up!"

Then she began barking orders to the women, "Go beat some eggs! Git some water boilin'! Brang me a blanket! Hurry!"

The women quickly followed Sadie's orders. While they were gone, Sadie stripped off Webster's clothes and began walking the naked boy back and forth in the yard as she supported him with her arms.

As she kept him on his feet, she spoke gently to him. "Come on, son, you got to brang that stuff up! Come on now!" All the time she spoke, she kept slapping the gagging Webster on his back.

By now, Webster couldn't hold up his head. His eyes were blurred, his legs had become putty, and his stomach felt like a tightly blown-up balloon ready to burst. He just knew he was dying.

Webster could barely hear Sadie asking him, "Where you git the likker, son? Who give it to you?"

Even though Webster wanted to tell her, he couldn't talk. But Sadie was so insistent on walking him, slapping his back, and asking him about the whiskey that he finally was able to blurt out, "Enoch . . ."

When the women returned, Sadie said, "That bastard Enoch will drank poison! The boy done got hold of his bad likker. Let's git the raw eggs into him first."

One woman held Webster up, and Sadie forced open his mouth with her strong fingers. Then another woman poured the raw eggs down his throat. Within a few seconds, Webster began vomiting so violently that he thought his intestines were coming up. When he tried to stop vomiting, Sadie belted him on the back and he vomited still more. Webster was now so weak that his eyelids were closing off and on.

"Drink this, son," Sadie commanded, and she gave him a glass filled with green liquid. Since he was too weak to protest, he just drank the funny-tasting concoction. Then he slid out of Sadie's grasp and crumpled to the ground.

"Is he . . . ," the frightened Ruby asked.

"He all right now," Sadie told the women. "The mint juice makes him sleepy. We got the poison outta him." She looked at the naked boy covered with dirt and vomit. "I'll wash him up and put him in my bed. He can sleep there."

After Sadie had given Webster a bath on the bench in her yard, she carried him into the house, put one of her big gowns on him, laid him in her big featherbed, and covered him. Webster was now deep in sleep.

Sadie then questioned Ruby. "You know who this child is?"

"No," Ruby responded, blinking her eyelids rapidly and trying to look innocent.

"Then why was them boys callin' out yo' name?" Sadie retorted accusingly. "Now, you best tell me the truf! I won't have my gals messin' 'round with children!"

In a nervous voice, Ruby said, "He looks like the boy I saw in the woods the day when we were comin' back from Cowpens."

Sadie thought for a moment, then remembered who Webster said had given him the whiskey. "He be Enoch's boy. Your nightman!" She frowned at Ruby. "Did you give Enoch's boy cause to come over heah wantin' to see you? If you did, git yo' thangs packed!"

The frightened Ruby denied that she had given Webster any reason for him to come and see her. "I guess he be feelin' his oats like little boys do, Sadie."

"Well, you git on back to your work," Sadie snapped. "You keep away from this child!"

Ruby quickly left the room and Sadie got a knitting basket from her bedside table, pulled up her plush chair near a window, and began knitting. She loved to knit.

It was late in the afternoon when Webster woke up. He was in a strange room and in a strange bed. "Where am I," he thought as he looked around. In a chair by the window he saw a woman knitting. It was Sadie.

She smiled at him when she saw him looking at her. "I been lookin' after you all day," the woman said. "How you feelin', son?"

"Better," Webster replied weakly. As he lay there watching her knit, he wasn't afraid of her anymore. She had gotten rid of his terrible stomach pain.

After a few minutes, Sadie asked, "When did you take to drankin' whiskey?"

"I hate whiskey," was Webster's reply.

Sadie went on with her knitting, then stopped momentarily and said, "Guess you done learnt your lesson then."

"Yes, ma'am," Webster replied submissively.

Just then Ruby came into the room. "Sadie, we got supper ready." She then walked over to the bed where Webster lay and he got a good look at her face. This time she didn't look pretty, and she didn't smell like honeysuckles. "You be wantin' some supper, child?" Ruby asked him.

"No, ma'am," Webster said. "I best be going home now."

"Get him his clothes," Sadie said, and she stuffed her knitting needles back into her basket.

"Where did you put them?" Ruby asked.

"I washed them," Sadie snapped. "So they be on the clothesline!" She set the knitting basket back on the side table. "Ruby's goin' brang your pants and shirt," she told Webster and left the room.

When Ruby came back with his shirt and trousers, she laid them at the foot of Sadie's bed, grinned, and winked at him. "Here your clothes, big boy," she said in a low, husky voice.

Webster quickly turned his head away from her in disdain, because he suddenly knew that he did not like Ruby!

Webster kept his back turned to her and refused to talk. Ruby soon left the room. Then Webster quickly dressed himself and quietly slipped out into the hall and out the front door.

On the porch he saw Sadie rocking in her porch swing. She had now changed into a red satin dress and was heavily made up with pink rouge on her cheeks and her lips painted red.

With his eyes cast downward, Webster quietly walked down the steps. He felt so ashamed because he'd made a fool of himself. But when he reached the edge of the yard, he turned around and went back up to the porch. He could not bring himself to leave without saying something to the woman who had shown him so much kindness.

"Miss Sadie," he said and extended his hand to her. "Thank you for curing me!"

Sadie smiled and shook his hand vigorously. "Jest you keep away from that ole bottle, son."

After saying good-bye, Webster quickly ran off down the path toward the creek. Upon reaching the bushes where he had been drinking, Ozell jumped from the underbrush. He had been waiting all day for Webster to come back.

"You all right?" he inquired anxiously. "I been so worried!"

"Why were you so worried?" Webster asked nonchalantly.

"Last time I see'd you, you was rollin' on the ground holdin' your stomach! You was real sick!"

Webster stood facing Ozell. "You didn't stay to help me!" he said. "You just ran off!"

Ozell shrugged and stepped backwards. "Ain't nothin' I could do. You ain't see'd the look in that big, ugly woman's eyes! I ain't wantin' to git knocked upside my head!"

"You are a coward!" Webster yelled and started walking away.

Ozell caught up to Webster and kept pace with him. "You ain't see'd how mad that woman was 'cause you was rollin' on the ground!" He grabbed Webster by the arm and stopped him. "Did she beat you?"

"No!" Webster said and jerked away from Ozell.

Ozell grabbed hold of Webster again. "Well, what did she do?"

Again Webster jerked away from Ozell. "If you want to know what she did, you just go on back up the hill and ask her! I'm going home!"

Webster then ran down to the creek and began jumping from rock to rock, crossing over it to the other side.

Ozell stood looking back up the hillside toward Sadie's Saloon for a few minutes, then he turned and ran after Webster.

Secrets

By the time Webster was twelve, he had grown tall and lanky. His tawny-colored skin complemented his large grayish-blue eyes. A mop of jet black hair framing his round face hung down to his shoulders. He was fairly even-tempered, not a bully like his friend Ozell. However, Ozell knew better than to threaten Webster, because he'd get the worst of it.

Webster had a quick mind with a generous helping of curiosity, especially about girls. Even though he remembered the episode with Ruby, that still didn't stop him from talking and thinking about girls. He and Ozell spent many hours together sitting on the creek bank, laughing and discussing the girls in Smyrna and the ones they liked best and wanted to court.

Jacob Warren moved his wife and daughter Emmaline from Cowpens to Smyrna in the spring of 1874. There, he bought a dairy farm from Mary Gaines, a widow, whose husband had recently died. Since some of the Gaines' land bordered the Epps' land, Enoch and Bessie soon came to know their new neighbors, the Warrens.

One summer after school had let out, Jacob was busy with his haying and asked Bessie if she'd let Webster help him out with milking his cows. Bessie said yes, but only if she didn't have work for Webster to do at home.

Webster liked helping Jacob Warren milk his cows and pitch the newly mowed hay into the hayloft.

Emmaline Warren, Jacob's daughter, was fifteen, plump, and awkward. Whenever Webster was alone in the barn milking the cows, she'd come to the barn and talk with him.

One day Emmaline asked Webster if he'd like to make love to her. Webster quickly declined because he really didn't like Emmaline. She reminded him of Lula, the big girl who had tried to rape him the time when he had gone swimming alone in the woods. But Emmaline wouldn't let go of the subject. Every chance she got she'd talk about sex, and how much she enjoyed it; furthermore, she had had sex many times before when she lived in Cowpens.

Because Emmaline gave Webster no peace, he decided to talk to his best friend, Ozell, about what Emmaline kept proposing.

"Go on, try it! I did!" Ozell told Webster.

Webster didn't believe Ozell because he was always bragging that he had done things when he really hadn't. "Why didn't you tell me about it?" Webster asked.

"A man don't go 'round talkin' 'bout private matters," Ozell replied. "Havin' sex is a secret."

Webster was still undecided. "I ain't old enough," he said.

"Sez who?" Ozell asked.

"Sez Mama. She told me I was too young to be talking about being with a girl. That was what men and women did."

Ozell looked astonished. "You talked 'bout sex with your ma?"

"Yeah. Why not?" Webster answered.

"Ain't I jest told you that havin' sex is a secret?" Ozell admonished Webster. "You can't tell nobody when you git sex, 'specially not your ma!"

"I don't keep secrets from my mama," Webster said. "I tell her everything."

"Oh," Ozell replied accusingly. "Did you tell her 'bout Ruby?"

"That was different," Webster replied. "Mama got so mad when I mentioned Ruby's name that I thought it best to keep that a secret. I think Enoch laid with Ruby!"

"Look," Ozell said, "if you want to be a man, you got to lay with a girl. Emmaline is willing so take her up on it." He shook a finger at Webster, "But you got to keep it a secret!"

Webster had this dreaded feeling that Ozell's advice would get him into trouble, like the time they stole Bessie's locust beer.

Every fall, Bessie gathered the dried locust pods from the locust tree in back of her house to use for making beer. First, she'd put a layer of the long, black, ripe fruit and a layer of straw and salt into a big pottery jar, then she'd pour in some water and cover the jar so that the straw, salt and locust would ferment. Next, Bessie would dig a hole and bury the jar underground. Within a few weeks the locust and straw fermented and she'd have a strong, potent beer. One fall before the mixture fermented, Webster and Ozell, who had helped bury the pottery jar, dug up the jar, uncovered it, and dipped out a cup of the brew and drank it. They then put the jar back into the ground and pledged to each other that they'd keep this a secret. But Ozell kept on stealing the drink without Webster's knowledge, and when Bessie finally uncovered her jar, there was no beer. She was furious. Webster too was furious that Ozell had stolen the beer. He wanted to tell his mother what he and Ozell had done, but out of loyalty to Ozell he kept silent. However, after the beer fiasco, Webster decided that he'd never again keep a secret from his mother.

And now, here was his best friend advising him to do it again, to keep a secret from his mother. He wasn't sure he ought to listen to Ozell.

Days after Ozell had given his advice to Webster, he still had not given in to Emmaline's wishes. But she gave him no peace. Twice, he had tried to talk to Bessie about it but somehow just couldn't bring himself to do it. He felt too embarrassed to bring up the subject.

Late one afternoon as Webster was pitching hay into the loft, Emmaline came to the barn. She grabbed Webster's hand and the two climbed up the ladder into the darkened loft filled with fresh cut grass. This time, Webster did not resist her. He had decided he must find out what it was like to be with a girl.

After reaching the loft, Emmaline laid down into the hay. "Quick," she whispered, "take off your pants and lay on top of me! I'll tell you what to do!" She pulled up her dress and her bloomers down.

Webster did as he was told. But just as he was about to kneel down to Emmaline, he heard someone climbing up the ladder. Within minutes, Jacob's head popped up at the end of the ladder.

Emmaline sprang up with lightning speed that sent Webster flying headlong into another nearby pile of hay. She jerked her dress down and yanked up her bloomers and screamed, "Daddy!" and pointed her finger at Webster. "He's trying to make me do something I don't want to!"

The poor frightened Webster struggled up out of the pile of hay and tried to get on his pants before Jacob reached the hayloft. He had one leg into his pants when an angry Jacob confronted Webster. Jacob tried to grab hold of the pitchfork that was stuck into the hay pile where Webster was putting on his trousers, but the boy kicked it out of the way and nimbly leaped out of the man's reach.

"So, you tryin' to lay my daughter, you low-down rascal!" Jacob yelled.

"He forced me up into the hayloft!" Emmaline added. "I kept on tellin' him, Pa, to leave me alone!"

"You're a liar!" Webster yelled. "You wanted me to come up here!"

Jacob sprang at the boy and grabbed hold of his shirt. "I've a mind to cow-hide you!"

"Let me go, you damn bastard," Webster cried as he struggled to free himself from the two-hundred-pound man.

"You cussin' me, boy?" Jacob yelled and tossed Webster from the hayloft into a big pile of hay below. "You got bad blood!" He yelled to Webster and began climbing down the ladder. "I'm gonna tear you into scraps and feed you to my hounds!"

Webster didn't wait for Jacob to get down the ladder. He ran out of the barn and into the woods and was soon out of sight.

As he ran toward his home, he grew angrier and angrier. Emmaline had told her father that big lie when she knew she had been the instigator. Hadn't she badgered him for weeks to come up to the hayloft? Why was she pretending to be an innocent victim? Because of her treachery, he was now in big trouble. Jacob was surely going to tell Bessie.

Webster stopped before he reached home, trying to think what to do. He knew he should never have listened to Ozell and Emmaline. They had given him bad advice. Finally, he decided to keep his own counsel. Although he felt ashamed of what he had gotten himself into, he'd tell his mother the truth. No more secrets.

Bessie was hanging out her wash when Webster arrived home. She was puzzled when he walked past her without speaking and on into the house. She waited for him to come back to the yard, but when he didn't, she went inside to look for him. She found him sitting on his bed in his bedroom with the shades pulled down.

Bessie knew immediately that Webster had something on his mind, because whenever he was troubled he'd go to his room and sit with the shades drawn. She quietly entered his bedroom and sat down on the bed beside Webster and waited for him to talk.

When he didn't, Bessie said softly, "You want to tell me 'bout it."

Webster was now trembling with anger and with fear, but he was determined to make a clean breast of his predicament. "It wasn't all my fault!" he finally said. "She just kept on after me until I listened to her! Then she tried to blame it all on me! She's a damn liar!"

Bessie frowned. "You jest watch your tongue, son. You know I ain't standin' for no cussin' in my house, and surely not from my boy! Now, what ain't all your fault?"

Webster cast his eyes downward. "Emmaline and me went up to the hayloft and Jacob found us together," he said in a voice that was almost a whisper.

Bessie sighed. "You and Emmaline layin' together?"

"No, Mama," Webster quickly said. "We didn't have time! Jacob came!" And then he said angrily, "Emmaline told Jacob I made her go up to the hayloft when I didn't! And he believed her!" In a pleading voice, Webster said, "I didn't!" And he then buried his face in his mother's bosom and began crying.

Bessie put her arms around him and patted him on the back. "I believe you. You know why? Ain't no way in the world you goin' get big Emmaline up a ladder if she ain't wantin' to go. She make two of you!" She then dried Webster's eyes with her apron.

"Mama, I'm real ashamed of what I did," Webster confessed.

"Webster, you got to stop lettin' that ole devil tempt you. You got to be strong and resist his temptin'! Ain't I been teachin' you this?" Bessie turned Webster toward her and looked into his face. "Now, I know you git-tin' big and you wantin' to test things, but that gal, Emmaline, ain't the one to do the testin' with. She's the kind of gal who will point her finger at someone else if she git caught! She be dangerous!"

"I don't even like her," Webster put in. "When she kept on asking me to go up into the hayloft and I kept putting her off, Ozell told me to try it."

"So, it be Ozell agin!" Bessie retorted. "That boy always got his mind on menfolk stuff! You stop doin' what Ozell tell you! The quickest way to git into trouble is takin' someone else's advice! Use your own mind!" She waited for a moment. "Now, I want you to be rememberin' this the next time you tempted by the devil! You heah me?"

"Yes, Mama," Webster said meekly, happy to be getting off so lightly. "Mama, I'm hungry. Will you make me an apple pie?"

Bessie hugged him tightly and then said, "Come on in the kitchen and peel me some apples."

A few days later, Webster met Ozell down on the riverbank in their favorite secret spot and told him what happened. "I'm never going to do what someone else tells me to do just to please them. I'm not going to keep any more secrets!"

"Not even from me?" Ozell asked.

"Not even from you, but you've got to tell me all your secrets."

"All right," Ozell said, and the two shook hands.

Then Webster inquired, "You keeping anything from me?"

Ozell then confessed to Webster that he had kept a secret from him, as to what had happened after their episode with Ruby. He had become so engrossed with the women at Sadie's that he stole some money from his father and sneaked out of his house one night after telling him that he was going to bed.

Ozell had climbed out the window in his bedroom and took a circuitous route to Sadie's Saloon so he wouldn't be seen by the numerous men who went back and forth there during the night.

When he finally reached the saloon, he hid in a clump of bushes underneath one of the windows, and when he thought it was safe, he stood up to look inside the house.

"The room was painted red," Ozell said dramatically, "and there was a big bed that had lacy, white covers and big, fluffy pillows on it."

"I didn't see that," Webster interrupted. "The room I was in wasn't painted at all."

"Webster," Ozell said. "You ain't been in them rooms where the mens go at night! You was in Sadie's bedroom."

"Well, what else did you see?" Webster asked anxiously.

"There was a fireplace and over the mantelpiece was a picture of a big, black woman smiling. She was dressed in red and had a black umbrella opened over her head. It was Sadie."

"How'd you know it was Sadie? It could have been her grandma," Webster said sarcastically.

"Cause it was the same woman who come at us with that big, ole stick when we went there. Remember?" Ozell then chortled.

When Webster frowned, Ozell said with a snicker. "You was too drunk to know who you was! You ain't see'd nothin'!"

Webster frowned again. He hated it when Ozell reminded him of that awful day and remarked snidely, "How could you see all that stuff in the dark?"

"'Cause there was a table between two chairs and it had a lit kerosene lamp on it. I could even see a round hooked rug on the floor." Ozell explained. "You know the kind of rug my ma and your mama make in the winter. It was red and white."

"Seems like you wasted a lot of time just to see a red room in the dim kerosene light," Webster added sarcastically.

"I'm gittin' to the good part," Ozell said and slapped Webster playfully on his thigh. "A pritty woman came in and started taking off her clothes."

This statement got Webster's attention. "Was it Ruby?"

"I don't think so. I was too busy watchin' her pull off all them things she was wearin' right down to her petticoat."

"Did she take off her bloomers?" Webster asked excitedly.

"I don't know," Ozell replied, "'cause somebody knocked on the door and I had to duck down. I waited for awhile, and when I looked again she blew out the light."

Webster was clearly disappointed at Ozell's story. To him, the story wasn't worth telling. "Aw shucks!" he said, and yanked off a twig from a nearby bush and stuck it into his mouth.

Sensing Webster's disappointment, Ozell said with a big grin, "But I went back two nights later."

"Well, what did you see this time?" the bored Webster asked.

"There was no light in the room," came Ozell's reply.

"Hell, Ozell," Webster snapped, and jumped up off the ground where he had been lying. "Why you keep telling me nothing!" He started to leave.

"Now, wait a minute," Ozell said. "Set on back down. I got more to tell."

Reluctantly, Webster flopped down beside Ozell. "This better be good," he warned Ozell.

"Just as I was 'bout to leave," Ozell began, "the woman lit the lamp again! I knocked on the window. When she saw me, she came over and said, 'What you doin' peepin' at me, boy? Your pa and ma know you out this late . . . ?'"

Webster smiled. The story was getting better. "What did you say?"

"I say, 'I'm a man!' She say, 'What you be wantin', sonny?' I say, 'I be wantin' you!'"

Upon saying that, the two boys began laughing and punching each other and rolling in the grass. Then Webster reminded Ozell he hadn't finished telling the story.

Ozell continued with his story. "That woman giggled lack a little gal. She say, 'Jest 'cause you want don't mean you goin' git.' I jest reached in my pocket and held up my five dollars."

Webster yanked on his sleeve. "Where did you get five dollars?"

Without hesitation, Ozell said, "I stole it from Pa." Then he continued talking. "I say, 'I got money!'"

"What did she do?" Webster urged Ozell to tell him more quickly.

"That woman leaned out the window and planted a kiss on my forehead! And she grabbed my five dollars! Then she say, 'I don't do business with little boys. Little boys can't handle me!'"

Webster began laughing, but Ozell didn't join in.

"That woman say, 'Come back in a few years. I'll jest keep this money 'til you git back!'"

"Did you put up a fight?" Webster inquired.

"I sho' did. I say, 'You got my five dollars, so I ain't waitin' for later. I'm comin' in, now!'"

"Did you climb in the window? Did you?" Webster asked excitedly, waiting for Ozell to tell him what he had done after he had gotten into the room.

Ozell shook his head vigorously. "Just as I got up on the windowsill that woman reached over in the corner and grabbed a bullwhip! She snapped that whip over my head three time! She say, 'If you don't heed my words, you goin' feel the sting of my whip on your butt! . . .'"

Webster frowned deeply at Ozell because he knew how the story was going to end, and he didn't like it one bit. Ozell wasn't going to get into that woman's room.

"I fell back into the bushes and I got outta there, fast!" Ozell said.

Upon seeing the disappointment on Webster's face, Ozell quickly added, "But I heard her callin' as I run away, 'Come back in a few years.'"

Webster closed his eyes and lay there for a few minutes. This was the worst secret Ozell had ever told him. Imagine being stupid enough to let that woman trick him out of his money.

The boys lay there in the grass for a moment. Then Webster opened his eyes and looked right into Ozell's face. "You didn't hear that woman say that, Ozell. You just made that up!"

The Decision

Webster had developed a desire to know the names of his birth parents. Once when he asked Bessie, she didn't reply. When Webster saw that she didn't want to talk about it, he let it go but decided to ask Amos. Amos told him he didn't know. Since there was no one else to ask, Webster was left wondering who his real parents were.

In the spring of 1877, Webster turned sixteen. He was nearly six feet tall and had grown into a handsome young man. It was whispered that all the girls in Smyrna were in love with him. Webster had long forgotten about Ruby and his infatuation with her, but he often remembered Sadie and how kind she had been to a foolish ten-year-old boy who became desperately ill from drinking bad whiskey. In Webster's mind, Sadie had saved his life and he'd never forget her.

Now, whenever his mother said unflattering things about Sadie and about the degrading things that went on at her saloon, Webster defended her.

"He who is without sin cast the first stone," he said, reminding Bessie that Reverend Bates had preached a sermon about tolerance to his congregation using those words, when rumors surfaced that the church women had planned to storm Sadie's Saloon and run her off.

"Why you stickin' up for them lowdown wimmins?" Bessie asked Webster, when he reminded her of this sermon.

"I believe in live and let live," he answered. "As long as people aren't doing you harm, you ought not to do them harm."

Webster's philosophy did not please Bessie because she didn't like his rebellious attitude of defying her. She, however, never guessed the real reason that Webster always defended Sadie.

That summer when school let out, Webster, along with six other students, had completed all the grades at Amanda Spriggs' school. All the people who lived in Smyrna came together and participated in a big celebration for their first graduates.

The graduation ceremony was held at The House of God church because the school was too small to hold the audience. Reverend Bates' fiery speech to the graduates about how a common religion is the glue of a community, and how this glue serves as the common thread for all of Smyrna to rally around, set the people talking.

The day after the graduation, Tessa and Bessie sat talking in the swing on Bessie's porch drinking mint water. Bessie had brought out a pitcher of cool water with several sprigs of freshly picked mint leaves in it. Drinking mint water on a hot day always helped the women to cool off. Soon their conversation turned to Reverend Bates' speech that he had made to the graduates.

"Reverend Bates is right when he tells us to have one kind of religion," Bessie said as the two women rocked slightly in the swing. "It's how the white folks git ahead."

"How so?" Tessa asked. "How havin' one way to serve God gits you ahead?"

"'Cause the people won't be in splinters," Bessie explained. "If folks in Smyrna all b'lieve the same way, they can help each other by poolin' their money. A big sack of money can do a lot more than a little pocketful of it."

"Hadn't thought of it that way," Tessa said. "That Reverend Bates is real smart!"

Bessie replied, "I been knowin' that for a long time. Smart folks know how to git on in life. That's why my Webster goin' be a big man in Smyrna one day."

"Guess that's why he got one of them scholarships from Amanda," Tessa remarked.

Bessie stopped the swing from rocking with her feet. "What scholarship?"

"Ain't Webster got a scholarship?"

Sounding annoyed, Bessie snapped, "Tessa, if Webster got a scholarship, wouldn't I know it?"

Tessa then told Bessie that Amanda had given a scholarship to Mary Lou Hughes to continue her education at The Saints of God's Preparatory School in Philadelphia, a school her parents had established.

"How you know about this?" Bessie inquired.

"Yesterday, after the graduation, Amanda told me to stop by her house for some T-cakes and coffee," Tessa said. She paused and took a sip of her mint water. "We been real good friends since the day she moved into ole Hustellar's house. We got to talkin' and she told me that if Ozell hadn't dropped out of school she would have give him a scholarship like the one she give to Mary Lou Hughes. So, I jest thought she give Webster one too."

Tessa tried to start the swing again, but Bessie stopped it with her feet. "Why Amanda give Mary Lou a scholarship?" Bessie inquired. "She ain't been the smartest in the class! It's been Webster all along!"

Tessa agreed. "Ever'body in Smyrna know that Webster was the smartest in the class."

"Then why she ain't give him that scholarship?" Bessie retorted.

"I can't rightly say," Tessa quickly replied. "Maybe she plan on giving him a scholarship too."

"Is that so?" Bessie said and jumped up from the swing and stood in front of Tessa. "Ain't I been the one who got that school started? Didn't I beg the folks in Smyrna night and day for money? You know why?" She wagged a finger in Tessa's face. "Havin' no learnin' is the worse thing for black folks! It makes them thank everthing is fine, when it ain't, 'cause they ain't knowed no better! The only way for youn' black folks goin' git a better life is to fill their heads with learnin'!"

Tessa nodded in agreement. She now wished she had kept silent about the scholarship.

Bessie kept on talking to her silent friend. "Now, I ain't wantin' Webster to have somethin' he ain't got no right to. But if Amanda's givin' away learnin', she give it to the one who been the smartest! Not to a pritty little gal! Maybe that woman got eyes for gals!"

"Oh, no," Tessa quickly refuted Bessie's statement. "Amanda only got eyes for God. She be real holy!"

"Well, I mean to find out why she slighted my boy!" Bessie replied angrily and put on her straw hat that she had left on a chair near the table. Tessa knew it was time for her to go home. When Bessie was defending Webster, she had no equal. She quickly set her glass on the little table, put on her straw hat, and said good-bye to the fuming Bessie.

Leaving her glass next to the pitcher of mint water on the little table, Bessie strode off the porch and up the dusty road to the old Pettigrew house that was now the school.

She found Amanda in the classroom working behind her desk. Sweating profusely as she came into the room, Bessie said, "I come to talk." She then squeezed herself into a seat in front of Amanda's desk.

No sooner was she seated than Bessie began to ask Amanda questions.

"Why," Bessie asked, "you ain't give Webster a scholarship? Ever'body in Smyrna knows how smart he is! I want him to go to that school you sendin' Mary Lou Hughes!"

The solemn Amanda was at first taken aback by Bessie's abrasiveness and was unprepared for her aggressiveness. But having taught Webster for seven years, this didn't surprise her. She knew that she'd better tell Bessie immediately.

She stood up from her desk and in a calm voice spoke to Bessie. "Webster was my brightest student, and he was the one I first offered the scholarship to All Saints Preparatory School. He refused it."

"What!" Bessie cried in disbelief.

"You see, Bessie, Webster and I have been having long talks about his future and what he wants to do with his life. He told me he first wants to find out some things about himself before he continues his education. There's no doubt in my mind that Webster would be a fine scholar at All Saints Preparatory School, and I wanted him to accept, but I respected his right to take care of the things that are weighing heavily on his mind first. Since the scholarship needed to be honored this fall, I offered it to Mary Lou Hughes, who was second in the graduating class."

"You talkin' in riddles," Bessie retorted. "Webster ain't got nothin' on his mind!"

The usually calm Amanda grew agitated and she chastised Bessie. "Webster needs to know his identity. Knowing who your parents are is very important, Bessie, because it helps to shape your thinking."

"Webster been talkin' to you about wantin' to know his real folks?" Bessie asked.

"He has," Amanda replied. "And I think that Webster is old enough to know the identity of his real mother and father."

"You keep your nose outta my family matters, Amanda," Bessie said, as she struggled out of the tight seat. "If I want you in it, I'll let you know!" She left the classroom and went back down the dusty road to her house. She meant to find Webster and have it out with him. Imagine him talking about private family matters to Amanda, a woman who never had a husband. What did she know about bringing up a child?

Webster had had every intention of telling Bessie that he had turned down a scholarship, but he wasn't sure how Bessie would take it, so he had hesitated. What was on his mind now was to find work, earn some money, and go on his quest. He meant to go up to the mountains and look for the Indian tribe that his mother belonged to. If he found her, he'd ask her who his father was.

Bessie had seen Webster hoeing vegetables in her garden behind the cowshed. While working, he had seen his mother going up the road toward the center of town and wondered why she was hurrying on such a hot day. Maybe some woman was giving birth. But just as he had finished his work and was putting his hoe into the shed, he heard Bessie yelling from the back porch.

"Webster!" Bessie called. "You git in heah! I want to heah 'bout this scholarship!"

From the tone of her voice, Webster knew she was angry. She must have gone to the school and Amanda had told her that he had turned down the scholarship for that fall. Since he wasn't prepared to talk with his mother about refusing the scholarship, not just yet, Webster ignored her because he wanted first to talk with Amos about giving him work.

So, instead of going into the house, Webster slipped through the weeds in back of the cowshed, and onto the path that led through the woods to Caleb's store.

It didn't take him long to get to the store. Inside the store, when he didn't see Amos' workbench, he knew Amos was downstairs working in the basement. Amos often moved his workbench down to the basement on hot days.

Webster carefully made his way down the steep basement stairs. The stairway was dim and smelled musty from the dampness. A host of spider webs engulfed Webster's face when he reached the bottom of the stairs. Quietly, he made his way through the dim light until he was near Amos' workbench.

"You're going to go blind working in this dim basement," Webster said to Amos, who hadn't heard him coming.

"Hey," the startled Amos cried and stopped hammering. "What you doin' heah?"

"I said, you're going to go blind working in this dim place," Webster said again.

"I kin see a teeny spider ten feets away," Amos retorted. "I kin move upstairs anytime I wants to," he boasted. "But I lacks workin' down heah. It be quiet and I gits more done. Set down." He pointed toward an upturned barrel.

"It stinks down here," Webster said. "All this old junk piled up in here," and he walked over to a pile of things. "Look at it! Old, wore-out horse bridles, ropes, bent buggy wheels, and all these boxes of stuff. I ought to throw out all this stuff and make this place nice for you."

"That be good stuff, boy," Amos replied happily, "so you jest leave it be."

Webster came back over to Amos and peeped into his bedroom. The bedroom had no windows and there was an unused door that led to Caleb's root cellar directly in front of that door. Amos had pushed his iron bed up against it. Near his bed was a wooden table with an old empty tin can on it. Webster had once asked Amos why he had his bed there? His reply was that air blew through the root cellar and helped him sleep better. When Webster pointed out that if he moved his bed to the other side of the room and left his door open he'd get more air, Amos told Webster to leave his bed be.

Although Amos kept his body clean, his room had a funny odor, between damp and musty because the basement didn't have a fireplace to dry it out from time to time nor to keep it warm in winter. On cold nights Caleb had offered Amos to come and share his bedroom upstairs because he had an extra bed in it. But Amos refused. When he grew cold in his room he'd take his quilts, go upstairs to the store, and make a fire in the big, iron stove that kept the store warm during the day. There he'd sleep on the floor.

After surveying the little room as he had done so many times before, Webster said, "Well, if you won't clean this place, come live with us. We've got an empty room."

Amos guffawed at what Webster had proposed. "You ain't never goin' git me to live under Enoch's roof! He my friend but I ain't goin' live with him!" He paused and said in an inaudible voice, "'Sides, I ain't wantin' to heah Bessie's tongue a-fussin' all the time."

Webster finally sat down on the barrel next to where Amos was working. "I came to talk to you about a serious matter," he said. "You know I finished school."

"Yeah," Amos replied with a proud look on his face. "I wuz settin' right there in the front row of the church happy as a bunch of bees!"

"Amanda offered to give me a scholarship to go study at All Saints Preparatory School in Philadelphia," Webster then told him.

Amos seemed not to understand the word "scholarship," so Webster defined it. "I wouldn't have to pay for my schooling at this school."

Amos dropped his hammer, leaned over, and happily embraced the boy. "Ain't that somethin! You be goin' up north! Ain't that somethin!"

"I turned it down," Webster said.

Amos loosen his grip from around Webster's waist. "You turnt down goin' up north to study? Your ma know 'bout this?"

"That's what I came to talk to you about," Webster said. "I didn't tell her, but I think she knows." He hesitated when he saw the puzzled look on Amos' face. "You see, Amos, I do plan to go to school, but not just now. What I want to do now is to get a job so I can have some money."

"If you git more schoolin', you kin make more money." Amos advised. Then a far-off look came into his eyes as if he wished it were him getting more education. "You be givin' peoples orders, not takin' them."

"I'm going to go on to school, but later," Webster assured Amos again. "Maybe I'll be another Blanche K. Bruce."

"Ain't never heard of him," Amos confessed. "Who he be?"

Happy to show Amos how smart he was, Webster recited, "Mr. Blanche K. Bruce . . . from Mississippi . . . was elected to the . . . United States Senate!"

"He a black man?" Amos inquired.

"He sure is!" Webster replied proudly.

"Well, what he do?"

"Amos," Webster said forcefully. "Mr. Bruce is helping make the laws that govern our country! He's in Washington, D.C., where the President lives! When I finish my schooling, I might join him! Then I can really give people orders!"

Amos didn't seem impressed about Senator Bruce, nor Webster's talk about joining him one day. He began hammering on the shoe he had been working on.

Finally, he replied, "I ain't lackin' them folks makin' laws. They talk outta both sides of they moufs at the same time."

Webster just shrugged. It didn't matter to him that Amos was unimpressed with Bruce, because that wasn't what he had come to talk about.

Amos felt deep disappointment that Webster was not going on to school. Here was an opportunity for him to really make something of himself and he was just squandering it on wanting a job. What kind of a job did he think he was going to get? It was hard enough for grown men in Smyrna and Cowpens to find work. Whatever job he'd get would be menial. Even though Amos had learned long ago that people didn't listen to advice, that didn't stop him from offering it to Webster.

"God done give you smart brains, Webster. You gots to use them in the right way. Why, smart as you is, you kin make a pile of money 'fore you git my age."

"You're right, Amos!" Webster cried enthusiastically. "That's why I want you to teach me how to make shoes! Then you and I can move to Cowpens and open a shoe store. We can make a pile of money there!"

"Hey," Amos interrupted, "that ain't what I means. I means you gots to git more learnin'. 'Sides, I ain't never goin' live in Cowpens agin, no siree! You 'member that story I told you 'bout Cowpens when you wuz a little fella?"

"Not sure," Webster replied, hoping Amos wouldn't tell him another story about slaverytime. He knew it was important for him to know about slavery, but right now he was seeking a way to find out the identity of his mother and father and where they had gone. He needed money to find them.

Amos paid no attention to Webster's seeming lack of interest in his tale. He just began telling his story.

"I done see'd this wif my own eyes," Amos pointed to his eyes. "It wuz right after I got my freedom from Margrace and wuz workin' in Cowpens makin' shoes in the back lot of the seed store. I sees this wagon pullin' in the back lot. I looks up from my bench and see this big, black fella, wearin' a stovepipe hat, all decked out in a big, ole swallowtail coat, and a stiff white shirt. He wuz actin' lack he own the world! He stop his wagon so close to my workin' bench that I had to jump outta the way 'cause his wagon wheels be done run over my feets! On the back of that wagon set a skinny, ole black man settin' up on some big ole sacks with a passel of hound dawgs."

Webster closed his eyes hoping Amos would see how bored he was, but Amos was so engrossed in his story that he had forgotten Webster was even there.

"I sez 'Mornin'," Amos went on. "That ole, stuck-up man jest looks outta the corner of he eye and act lack he ain't knowed the King's En'lish. 'Git this wagon unloaded,' that uppity man barks!"

Amos breathed deeply several times and then continued talking. "That ole, half-bent man who wuz wearin' rags and no shoes jump off the wagon and start pullin' them big sacks off. He stagger over to the store door and drop them down." Amos made a rocking motion with his hands. "Then he come runnin' back as fast as git-out, to git 'nother one. All the time that ole dressed-up black man jest set on his tail lettin' that ole man carry them heavy sacks! Then I look hard at the uppity man and found him to be Jonah Blue!"

"Jonah Blue?" Webster asked.

"Yeah, he wuz a slave at Margrace and he gits his freedom the same time I gits mine! He wuz making cabinets over on the other side of Cowpens and done hired this ole man to work for him cause that ole man ain't got no place to go! I start shakin' lack a leaf on a tree 'cause I got so mad I wants to go for ole Jonah Blue's throat!"

After sitting for a moment looking off into space, Amos said, "I ain't never goin' forgit that! I made up my mind to leave Cowpens right then and there! I ain't wantin' to live in no place where black folks treat other black folks lack slaves! That place be hell!"

Amos then hit his fist down hard on his workbench because the thought of Jonah Blue caused him to become angry and upset. It was some time before he was calm again.

After Amos had calmed down, Webster asked, "You going to teach me how to make shoes?"

"I might," Amos replied. "But I gots to have speaks with your ma first."

"No need to tell her until I learn shoemaking," Webster said.

Amos wagged a finger at Webster. "Your ma and me is good friends. I ain't goin' spoil it by goin' 'round her back."

"I'll tell Mama," Webster then said confidently. "It'll be better that way."

Webster left the store and went back home. There he braced himself for what he knew was to come, but he meant to hold his ground. His mind was made up.

The minute he came through the front door, Bessie began her fussing. "You git in heah and set down!" Webster sat down in the chair nearest the door.

Bessie came and stood in front of him and demanded to know why he had turned down Amanda's scholarship. "I wants to know why you ain't wantin' to git more learnin' lack Mary Lou Hughes is," she accused. "Your answer best be a good one!"

"Mama," Webster began quietly, "I plan on going to school, but not right now. I'm going to work first."

"Work?" Bessie shouted. "Where you goin' find work? Ain't no peoples in Smyrna goin' hire you! Peoples got their own young'uns workin'!"

"I plan to work with Amos."

"With Amos!" Bessie cried in disbelief. "He ain't nothin' but a shoemaker. It don't take no brains to cut leather and hammer in nails!"

Webster knew there was no point in trying to convince Bessie about him getting a job. He also knew that if he stayed and listened to her, she'd anger him and he might say something to her he'd later regret, so he got up from the chair. "Let's not talk about it anymore."

"You set right back in that chair," Bessie commanded and blocked his way from going out the front door. "You ain't Amos' boy!" she yelled. "If he wants a boy, he best git one! He ain't goin' tell my child what to do. Amos . . ."

Webster couldn't listen to Bessie berating Amos, who was like a father to him, who he loved very much, almost as much as he did Bessie. He bolted through the kitchen and out the back door. He could hear his mother yelling for him to come back, but he didn't.

Webster ran off deep into the woods to a place where he'd gone many times when he felt lonely and disturbed. There, he climbed upon a big gray rock that jutted out from an outcropping of a bigger rock and sat there to think. This was a quiet place where he could sort things out. He knew he was different from the other boys and girls in Smyrna because he was not black like them. When he'd asked Bessie why his skin color was different from the other children, she said, "Ask God."

She knew the answer but refused to tell him. Why? Why was she keeping his identity a secret? They'd never kept secrets from each other. Since she wouldn't tell him, he'd find out for himself.

After sitting on the rock for awhile, Webster climbed down and wandered through the woods to the Margrace mansion and onto its grounds. For some reason he was drawn to the place because Margrace was indelibly intertwined with the people of Smyrna. Many people in Smyrna had their beginnings and endings with the Au Bignon family who had once owned the plantation. For sure, Enoch and Amos were directly connected to the place. Standing looking at the mansion, Webster wondered what it would be like to live in such a house? Why did the Au Bignons sell this beautiful house and its grounds? Where were they now? Dead?

The next morning, Bessie rose before sunrise, and without making her coffee that she had to have every morning before getting started for the day, she put on her straw hat, went out back to her washtubs, got her washing stick, and set off for Caleb's store. She meant to have it out with Amos.

As she came in sight of the store, the sun was rising and she knew Caleb would be opening his store. He and Amos always started work at sunrise.

Upon reaching the store, Bessie saw that Caleb was unlocking the door. He called out cheerfully. "Good morning, Bessie. You're up and about early."

Without speaking, Bessie stormed pass Caleb, nearly knocking the bushy-bearded man over. On she went, passing the counters piled up with dry goods, wheels of different kinds of cheeses, barrels of pickles, dried beans, and kegs of nails until she came to the stairway that led to the basement.

"I come to beat your tail, Amos!" Bessie yelled and started down the stairs. "Git ready for me!"

Amos had just started hammering on a pair of boots, but he stopped when he heard her call because he knew why she had come. He rushed over and met Bessie at the bottom of the stairs.

In the gray light of the cellar he saw Bessie's wash stick, and she knew how to use it. The frightened Amos raised his hands to defend himself from her oncoming stick. "I ain't had nothin' to do with Webster not goin' on to school. That be the Gawd's truf!" Bessie jabbed Amos' chest hard with her finger and walked him backwards. "So, you goin' teach my boy how to make shoes, eh? I'll teach you the lesson of your life if you mess with my child! You heah me, Amos?" She bellowed and raised her wash stick to strike.

Amos leaped deftly out of the stick's reach. "I ain't gon' do no sech thang, Bessie. I don't aim to teach Webster shoemakin'! You ain't got to worry none!"

Bessie strutted over closer and eyed Amos angrily. "You best be tellin' me the truth! If you ain't, I'll be back and you won't git off so easy!" She abruptly turned away and stomped back upstairs.

Caleb had heard the angry yelling in the basement and had come to the stairs. "What's the matter, Bessie?" he inquired as she came up the stairs.

"Git outta my way, Caleb," Bessie shouted and shoved him over a saddle that was lying on the floor. "When I wants you in my business, I be askin' you!"

When Bessie shoved Caleb, her straw hat fell off her head. She reached down, retrieved it, jammed it on her head, and yelled back down to Amos. "You jest 'member what I been tellin' you, Amos!"

After this encounter with Bessie, Amos absolutely refused to teach Webster shoemaking, and no amount of pleading from Webster changed his mind.

Rataree's Raiders

Matt Rataree had been a well-respected banker in Cowpens before the Civil War. His mother, Ellen Davis Rataree, was a second cousin of Jefferson Davis, who later was named president of the Confederacy, when the South formed its own nation.

Rataree, who had never married, lived with his mother on a large plantation that he owned outside of Cowpens. He was not a slaveholder because he held a deep contempt for black people and refused to have them living on his premises. He rented out his land to poor, landless white farmers who lived in the area. However, his relatives in Mississippi were slaveholders, and he believed they had that right.

When rumors spread in 1860 that the South was going to war with the Union over the slavery question, Cowpens, like many other small mountain towns, was undecided whether it would support a war. Since few people in Cowpens owned slaves, the town officials called a meeting to discuss the issue.

It was a warm April evening when the meeting was held. Most of the town's leading citizens came to Town Hall to listen to speeches and to decide what Cowpens would do if war broke out. The tiny room was packed, and many people had to stand. Sitting in front of the audience were the elected officials: Thaddeus Green, the mayor; Walt Bingham, town secretary; and Matthew Rataree, town treasurer.

Thaddeus Green was the first speaker. He made a fiery speech against going to war. He said the people of Cowpens should not be put at risk for a few rich slaveholders. "If they want a war, let them fight it!" he said as he ended his speech.

Then Rataree rose to speak. He spoke in support of the war and backed the slaveholders implicitly: "We are all Southerners, cut from the same cloth!" he told the audience. "We must stick together!" Then he challenged Green's pronouncements by wagging his finger in Green's face. "You're nothing more than a Yankee stooge!" he said angrily. "If you won't stand with the South, go north!"

After hearing their two most prominent citizens, Rataree the banker, and Thaddeus Green the mayor, the townspeople, not wanting to alienate either of the men, voted to take a wait-and-see posture.

The following year, the Civil War actually began. Still, the citizens of Cowpens were undecided as to what the town should do. Rataree, however, financed the Confederate cause heavily, all the time trying to persuade the town to do likewise. By the second year of the war, he had spent all of his personal fortune. Since he believed so passionately in the South's cause, he began embezzling some of the bank's funds for the Confederacy. Then, when the South printed its own currency, Rataree secretly converted large amounts of the depositors' money into Confederate money.

It wasn't until after the South had surrendered in 1865 that the people of Cowpens learned the truth about their bank president. Rataree National Bank was bankrupt, because most of its assets had been converted to Confederate currency, which was now worthless.

When Thaddeus Green learned what Rataree had done without the depositors' consent, he had him arrested by the northern military government that had now been installed in Cowpens.

Rataree was brought before a military court at Fort Belton and tried as a traitor for stealing and converting U.S. currency into Confederate dollars to benefit the South. He was convicted and sentenced to serve ten years in a military prison.

After Rataree had served his ten years, he was released and was now an angry, embittered man. He was somewhat demented from brooding over the South's loss of the war and his conviction and imprisonment.

On the day he left Fort Belton, two prison guards rowed him in a military boat across the Nebo River. When they reached the other side of the river, the men offered their hands to Rataree to wish him well. He refused to shake hands. "I have served an unjust sentence," he declared. "I will not shake the hands of my tormentors!"

Rataree then scrambled up the riverbank to the road that led to Cowpens. With his head held high, shoulders erect, he walked proudly in a shabby suit over to an old wagon hitched to a tired horse that was waiting. In the wagon was his cousin, William Elliott, who owned a rundown farm and a ramshackle house that was on a hillside near the Nebo River.

Elliott had once been a prosperous farmer before the Civil War and had supported the South, but now he lived in near poverty because he'd lost all his possessions. He was nearing seventy, his first wife had died, and he had now married a young girl who had run away from her father, who had had an incestuous relationship with her.

At his cousin's house, Rataree learned that his mother had moved back to Mississippi and that all his property in Cowpens had been confiscated by the town, auctioned off, and the proceeds had gone to pay the bank depositors who had lost their money.

"So that's why her letters came from Mississippi," Rataree told Elliott. "But why didn't she tell me what had happened?"

"She didn't want you to know," Elliott replied. "She said you were suffering enough."

"True, true," Rataree nodded his head in agreement. "Dear mother always worried about my well-being."

It wasn't until Elliott told Rataree how the community of Smyrna was flourishing that he became enraged. "Them black people caused the ruination of you and me!" he yelled as he banged his fists together hard. "Because of them we've lost our way of life, money, possessions, and our families! We have suffered at their hands!"

Since Rataree had a deep hatred for black people, he reasoned they were responsible for the Civil War and ultimately the South's defeat, and because of the South's defeat a terrible fate had befallen him.

However, he was in total shock when Elliott told him that his once proud bank, Rataree National, was now owned by his chief accuser, Thaddeus Green! The bank at Cowpens was now called Thaddeus Green National Bank!

After hearing about his property being sold, his mother moving back to Mississippi, and the loss of his bank, Rataree spent weeks brooding about his predicament. The more he thought about it, the angrier he became. He wanted revenge, for in his mind Smyrna, Cowpens, and Fort Belton all had done him an injustice.

He told his cousin he wanted to stay for awhile before going on to Mississippi to join his beloved mother. There were things in the Nebo Valley he meant to set right.

Although Elliott had shared with his cousin what little he had, Rataree was totally unhappy living there under these dire conditions. Another reason he was unhappy living with Elliott was because of his young wife, Mary Lou. What a mistake his cousin had made by marrying her. The girl was crude and uncouth and flouted her body shamelessly in his presence, hoping to entice him into a sexual union with her. The girl needed a good flogging, Rataree thought.

One day at supper, Elliott told Rataree about four men who were living up in the Bushy Mountains. He had found out about them during a blizzard when the men had come down from the mountains to his house looking for something to eat. He shared his food with them and learned they were "outcasts" from their communities because they had been perceived of some wrongdoings.

When Rataree learned of these misfits, he believed they were just the men he was seeking, so he borrowed Elliott's old horse and rode up into the mountains looking for them.

The first of the men that Rataree met was Eli Bean, who was staying deep in the woods in a shabby, hideout camp that had once been a hideout for men who had deserted the armies, both North and South.

Bean was a strange sort of fellow—tall and skinny, with protruding front teeth. He spoke with a lisp and in a high tinny voice. Being gregarious, Bean welcomed Rataree to his quarters by offering him a cup of tea made from the bark of a Sassafras tree.

While sitting on a fallen dead tree and sipping his tea, Bean told Rataree his sad story. When the Civil War ended, he had gone back to Cowpens to live. One night he went to a roadhouse a few miles out of town. There, he met two well-known men who lived in Cowpens, the owner of the feedlot in town and a local jackleg preacher.

At the roadhouse, the men plied him with whiskey and then asked him to perform certain sex acts upon them. When he asked for money, they became infuriated and set upon beating and kicking him, and in loud voices for all to hear, accused him of lewd and lascivious behavior.

Upon hearing this, other men who were drinking at the roadhouse joined in the fray and Bean barely escaped with his life. Since he was too frightened to go back to his home, he fled to the deserter's camp, where he had once hid to avoid the fighting.

Too afraid to return to Cowpens for fear the men would come after him again, the frail Eli stayed at the camp and made a living by wildcrafting—gathering wild herbs and plants that were used for medicines. He sold these plants to farming people in the valley who often had no access to a doctor.

Rataree, who was homosexual, slept with Eli that night. This was his first sexual encounter since he had left Cowpens ten years before. The next morning he told Eli that he'd come back to him later, but now needed to find Jinxie Red, the man Elliott had spoken about who also lived up in the mountains.

Jinxie Red was living in a lean-to made of burlap sacks and broken cedar boughs in a hollow not too far from Bean. Eli had offered to share his lodgings with Jinxie, but he refused. His idea of a good time was sleeping with a woman, not with another man.

At first, Jinxie was suspicious of the dark, gaunt, brooding man with the bushy eyebrows, but when Rataree told him about being imprisoned wrongly, Jinxie opened up to him.

Jinxie recounted his story of how he had come back to the mountains. After the war had ended, he couldn't find work and soon became desperate for food, so he broke into the general store at Cowpens one night to get something to eat. Just as he crawled out a window in the rear of the building with a sack of food, the sheriff grabbed him. Being stronger than the sheriff, Jinxie overpowered him and escaped.

Jinxie Red's real name was Jinxie Parker, but he was called "Red" because of his red hair and his red-hot temper. Before the war, he was known to the Cowpens sheriff as a petty thief who stole what he wanted. To the sheriff, Jinxie was a one-man crime wave, and Jinxie kept the lawman busy chasing him for crimes he had committed.

At the time the Civil War broke out, Jinxie was being hunted for having robbed a farmer who lived in the Nebo Valley. Afraid of getting caught and being sent to prison, Jinxie joined the Confederate Army, believing it was better to be in the army than in a harsh North Carolina prison.

Jinxie, believing he'd gotten a better bargain was proved wrong, because in the army he was placed under the command of Colonel "Make or Break" Bumgarter, who was a hard taskmaster and drove his raw recruits relentlessly during their training.

Jinxie soon grew to hate being in the army because Colonel Bumgarter was the devil incarnate. Jinxie became determined to get out of the army, so he began trying all kinds of schemes to bring about his discharge.

Once Jinxie told Colonel Bumgarter he had contracted a "dirty affliction." He'd gotten it from a loose woman who had sold herself to him back in Cowpens. The colonel had him examined by the army doctor, who pronounced him free of any venereal disease.

A week later, after his first scheme boomeranged, Jinxie came up with yet another. He knew how much Bumgarter glorified being a man and all manly things, so Jinxie just knew this time his scheme would work. However, he would have to be careful how to get the information to the colonel, and he decided that the soldier who shared his tent would do the telling.

One morning he called out in pain to his tent-mate saying he was hav-ing severe cramps in his stomach.

"Must be that rotten food we ate last night," the soldier replied as he laced up his boots. "You'd think they could at least feed us good meat! After all, we're laying our lives on the line!"

"Nope," Jinxie said, reeling back and forth clutching his stomach. "It's not the meat. I'm bleeding!"

The soldier jumped up off his bunk and came to him. "You shoot yourself with your rifle?"

Jinxie saw the frightened concern in the soldier's eyes and he quickly said, "No need to worry, it's my female period."

"A female period?" the startled soldier questioned and stared dumb-foundedly at Jinxie.

"Yep, I get one every month," Jinxie replied calmly.

"You must be going crazy," the soldier said sounding concerned. "A man ain't got no place for the blood to come out, my friend." And he leaned over and patted Jinxie on top of his head.

"The blood comes outta my penis!" Jinxie replied coyly, as he smiled and fluttered his eyelashes seductively at the soldier.

The soldier stepped back away from Jinxie. "You're a damned liar!" he retorted through clenched teeth and stormed out of the tent. In a few min-utes, he stuck his head back inside the tent and shouted, "From now own, keep you stinking butt on your side of the tent!"

After the soldier left, Jinxie doubled up in gales of laughter. He was now sure his tent mate would rush off and tell the colonel about him, and of course, the colonel wouldn't allow a woman to be in his he-man troop, even if she did look and act like a man. To be in the colonel's troop, you had to be a man cut to the bone.

Jinxie thought, all he had to do now was wait for the colonel to come storming into his tent and kick him out of the army. He waited and wait-ed, but the colonel didn't come. The soldier saw through Jinxie's lie and didn't bother to tell anyone.

Once again, Jinxie was disappointed and at his wits' end trying to think of another scheme.

Months went by and Jinxie began to realize that he was stuck in the army for the duration of the war. Not until February 1865 did Jinxie finally solve his problem of escaping from the army. Only this time, he didn't wait to get kicked out; he took the initiative. Colonel Bumgarter had received orders that the South was planning an all-out attack on Fort Belton. Northern troops held the big, cement-walled fort that overlooked the Nebo River, and from their position they could see and destroy any Confederate boats that came up the river with supplies for Robert E. Lee's troops in southern Virginia. The eager Colonel Bumgarter, who was spoiling for a fight, quickly marched his tired, ill-fed troops down out of the foothills, where they had bivouacked for weeks, and joined other Confederate companies of soldiers on their way to the fort. A cold February wind had come up, the temperature soon fell below zero, and heavy snow began falling. Under the cover of darkness, the Southern forces slipped into the deep woods that were behind the fort, planning a surprise attack at dawn. The soldiers were not allowed to build fires for fear of giving away their position, so groups of weary men huddled and shivered in the bitter cold behind trees, bushes, and dead logs, trying to keep out of the piercing wind. Jinxie found a half-rotted tree trunk and crouched down against it.

At first light, there came shouts from soldiers in the woods, yelling that some men had frozen to death. Jinxie was stiff from the cold, so when a soldier came to him and asked if he was all right, he didn't respond. He pretended to be dead too.

Without waiting to bury his dead, Bumgarter ordered the attack. The soldiers rushed out of the woods toward the fort. Jinxie waited until he knew all the live soldiers had gone, then he crawled away deeper into the snowy woods.

He soon came upon a group of deserters from the Northern army and the Southern Army, all living together in a filthy makeshift camp deep in the mountains. Desperate and frightened, these young men had taken to the woods. They robbed and stole what they needed to survive.

When the war ended in 1865 and the news slowly filtered into this camp, these men dispersed. Jinxie, however, stayed on in the mountains because he had grown to love the life of an outlaw.

The third man Rataree found in the mountains was Bernard O'Brien, secretly called Brute by the slaves on Margrace Plantation near Smyrna. Brute had been hired as an overseer by Karl Au Bignon, whose wife owned Margrace.

When the Au Bignons sold Margrace, Brute found himself out of a job. He looked for another overseer job on other slave plantations, but with the impending war, slaveholders would not hire him. He finally found work as a paddyroller, one who hunted down runaway slaves, but this job sent him into hostile communities that harbored the runaway slaves. When he tried to exercise his authority, he was often threatened with bodily harm. In one community he was set upon and beaten severely, and he lost the sight in his left eye.

Three years after the war had begun, Brute tried to join the army, but when he went to enlist he was turned down because of his physical disability. Brute then headed further south, where he was sure he'd find work on one of the larger slave plantations, but to his dismay, ruins were everywhere; plantations destroyed, great mansions burned, and the slaves were gone!

Fearing he might be captured by freed slaves or by the Yankees, Brute secretly made his way back to the Nebo Valley where he knew he'd find a place to hide.

The best hiding place was with the deserters who camped deep in the Bushy Mountains. Brute had little fear of being captured there because the military police were afraid to come into this den of desperadoes. His fear, however, was how to stay alive in this deadly place.

Since Brute had no place to go after the war had ended, he stayed on at the deserter's camp. He was now eking out a living as a bounty hunter by capturing wanted men and turning them over to the sheriff for a price. His life now was far different from his glory days when he lived at Margrace. Now he barely knew where he'd get his next meal.

Tom Biggers was a black Indian. He was the last man that Rataree met in the mountains. Tom Biggers' mother was a Peedee Indian. She had fallen in love with his father, a runaway slave. When his mother became pregnant and wanted to take his father as her husband, her father refused to allow it, saying Indians must marry Indians.

One night, his father and mother left the Peedee Indian village for the mountains of West Virginia. During childbirth, his mother died, and his father, not wanting to take care of a newborn, brought him back to his Indian grandparents and left him.

His grandfather, who was chief of the Peedees, refused to let the baby grow up in their settlement because he wasn't pure Indian. Instead, he took the baby to an encampment on the fringe of Indian Woods where other black Indians were allowed to live.

The baby was given to Rebecca, who turned the baby over to her daughter, Tallaquah, a young black Indian girl, whose father was a Peedee Indian and her mother, Rebecca, a runaway slave. Tallaquah was living in the encampment with other black Indians. Although she didn't want to look after the baby, her mother, who was now infirm, told her she must because the chief would otherwise make all the black Indians leave the encampment. Tallaquah named the baby Tom Biggers.

After several years, Tallaquah fell in love with a young Indian named Moonstar. She soon gave birth to a boy and called him Skelly Moonstar, and six years later she gave birth to a baby girl and named her Tai.

Tom Biggers grew up in two different worlds, half Indian and half black. He now was an angry man because he believed he had been denied his rightful Indian heritage.

After meeting and talking to the four men, Rataree invited them to come a week later to Elliott's house for a good meal. He believed a home-cooked meal was a way to get the men down from the mountains and he could lay out his plans to them.

When Rataree returned to his cousin's house and told Elliott what he had done, Elliott agreed with him and said he'd get his wife, Mary Lou, to cook the meal, but Mary Lou said she wasn't going to cook a meal for a bunch of strangers. Elliott told her that if she didn't obey him, he'd take her out to the barn and horsewhip her.

On the evening the men came, Mary Lou had spent the entire day in the kitchen preparing a big pot of pinto beans, cornbread, and fried chicken.

In the meanwhile, Elliott and Rataree waited in the parlor as the men straggled in, looking grubby and suspicious. Eli Bean was the first to arrive, then Jinxie and Brute, and the last to arrive was Tom Biggers. When the last man came, Elliott called to Mary Lou, who was in the kitchen, to put the supper on the table and then go to her room.

Angrily, Mary Lou banged down onto the kitchen table the pot of cooked pinto beans, a platter of tough fried chicken, and a plate of cornbread she had broken into pieces with her hands. Without saying the food was on the table, she stormed off to her bedroom, flopped down on her sagging mattress, and pouted.

During the meal, the grubby men ate ravenously and in silence. Elliott watched in amazement and thought it must have been a long time since these men had eaten to devour Mary Lou's cooking like that!

Rataree did not join in the meal. He could not stomach Mary Lou's bad cooking. She had an unclean way of not washing her hands and wiping her nose on her apron. Instead, he sat in a rocking chair in the parlor, sipping a cup of coffee that he had brewed, staring out the window into the dark night.

When the men had finished eating all the food that was on the table, Elliott invited them into the parlor where Rataree was waiting. Elliott pointed toward an old sofa whose cushions were ripped and worn thin. The four men squeezed onto it and waited. Each man was wondering what the strange man wanted of them.

Slowly, Rataree stood up and walked over to the window, pulled back the ancient lace curtain, and looked out for a few minutes. Then he turned to the men who were watching him intently. "I suppose you are wondering why you were invited to this house to partake of a fine meal." He sighed deeply. "When I met you up in the mountains and we talked, I realized that you are the men I'm looking for, because you too have been wronged as I have! You have been mistreated and cheated, and it is our duty to put things right again!"

All four men held grudges and hatred toward someone or something, and they listened eagerly to the demented Matt Rataree, who began to expound on the injustices that needed to be set right.

"Look at all them uppity black folks in Smyrna," Matt told the men. "They're living like white folks! They've no right to that kind of living! I want to strike at them when they least expect it. Take all the valuables from each house, store, and business, then burn Smyrna down!"

The idea of stealing from former slaves had great appeal for Brute. It would be an extreme pleasure for him to set fire to Smyrna. He remembered the beating he'd gotten there one night by several unknown men disguised as paddyrollers when he went there looking for runaway slaves.

Tom Biggers didn't care one way or another about uppity blacks living in Smyrna. What did interest him was money and things he could turn into money. He needed to hear more from Rataree.

"Next," Rataree continued, "on to the heart of Cowpens!" He began pacing back and forth as if he were a caged animal. "The bank! They've changed Rataree Bank's name! That's my bank! They had no right to change the name of my bank to my enemy's name, Thaddeus Green! I'll take every red cent from that bank because that money belongs to me!"

Jinxie was now thoroughly enthralled when he heard about robbing a bank. This was just the thing to whet his appetite, all that money within his grasp. He could hardly wait! He tried to ask when were they going to get started, but Rataree droned on as if he were possessed by some demon spirit and couldn't control himself.

Suddenly, he cried out in pain as if someone was thrashing him and he was ducking the blows. "Fort Belton! Fort Belton!" he yelled. "That miserable old dank wall of crumbling, stinking cement! I'll blow you to kingdom come! And everyone in it! I'll blow up all your foot soldiers and your arrogant officers!"

Rataree shook a fist at an imaginary person. "You mistreated me! Fed me rotten meat, bread with worms in it! You degraded me by forcing me,

Matthew Rataree, bank president, to clean out your stinking outhouses! You'll rue the day that you ever heard of me, Matthew Rataree, kinfolk to the great Jefferson Davis, the president of the Confederacy. Then he screamed in a guttural voice, "Long live Jefferson Davis!"

Eli Bean, who had remembered the night he had slept with Rataree and was prepared to follow him at any cost, jumped up off the sofa and repeated, "Long live Jefferson Davis!"

Rataree smiled weakly at Eli. "Are you willing to join me to set things right?"

"I am!" Eli responded lustily.

"And you other men?" Rataree queried.

"Ready and able," the three other men replied emphatically.

Rataree's brows knitted together and he spoke in a cadence. "We will strike at the heart of our enemies—silently and swiftly—until we wipe them out!"

On that April night Rataree's Raiders were formed from a group of ragtag, angry men.

Two weeks later the four men met again at Elliott's farm, and Rataree laid out his plan. Eli Bean was to go to the Nebo Valley near Smyrna, gather information about the bank in Cowpens and the shops in Smyrna, and get that information back to Rataree. In the meanwhile, Rataree and the other three men were to plan the destruction of Fort Belton.

Brute quickly challenged Rataree about blowing up the fort. He struggled up off the sofa and stood near the window. "The wall around that fort is three feet thick, made of cement," he said, "and a guard is settin' up there with a big gun in a little ole house lookin' out all the time. If he see us sneakin' 'round that wall, we'll be shot dead!"

Brute paused for a moment, then said, "Remember how them ole Yankees whipped our tails when we tried to take that fort during the war? We best keep our eye on gittin' that bank money and robbin' them niggers!"

Upon hearing a slight toward his beloved Confederate Army, Rataree nearly fell into a fit. And it was then that the men saw his immense anger and dark rage. He leaped up off his chair where he had been sitting and plunged at Brute. The big, burly man fell backwards, and his huge head banged hard against the window, which sent glass flying all over the parlor!

Before Brute could get his balance, Rataree screamed into his ear. "Don't you dare impugn the valor and bravery of my army! Don't question my plan, you fool! You just be ready to act when I give the orders!"

Elliott rushed over to his cousin and pulled him off the stunned Brute. "He didn't mean any harm, Matthew," Elliott said quietly. "A man has a right to question if he's to do a dangerous job."

The other three men were too shocked to move. Never had they seen a man who had reacted that way. Then Tom Biggers went and helped Brute up off the floor and brushed off some of the broken glass. "You cut yourself?" he asked.

Brute shook his head, cracked his knuckles, and glared at Rataree, whom he wanted to flatten. But he held himself back. If he weren't in dire need of money, he'd make scrapmeat out of this madman. Just as soon as he laid his hands on some money, Rataree would feel the blows of his fists on his head, thought Brute.

Still angry, Rataree then pounded down hard on a table in the parlor. "Are you going to take orders from me?" he yelled at Brute, Tom Biggers, Jinxie, and Eli. "'Cause if you aren't, get out now!" He ran over and jerked open the door. But the four men stayed put.

Elliott calmed his cousin again. "Come on, Matthew, sit down and tell us your plan."

Slowly, Rataree sat back down in the rocker and began rocking back and forth, back and forth with his eyes closed. The four men stood silently near the broken window. Glass was everywhere in the room, so Elliott called out, "Mary Lou, bring the broom in here and sweep up this glass."

Mary Lou had been listening behind the parlor door, wanting to know what all the commotion was about. She also was trying to find out why her husband had made her cook a meal for these men and why she wasn't allow to eat with them. Why had they come back to the house? What was her husband, Rataree, and these men up to? They were planning something, and she meant to find out.

Ever since Rataree had come to live with them, Elliott had been behaving strangely toward Mary Lou. The two often went to the barn to talk, and once when she came upon them talking, they quickly stopped. Rataree never allowed her to be near him and refused to hold a conversation with her. What a strange man!

Mary Lou sauntered into the parlor with a broom and slowly began sweeping up the broken glass, her hips swaying from side to side as she swept. Jinxie watched her intensely, and when he caught her attention he winked at her.

When Rataree saw Jinxie flirting with Mary Lou, he yelled, "Leave the sweeping, woman, and get out!" Mary Lou looked over at Elliott, expecting him to say, "Don't yell at my wife," but her husband turned and looked the other way. She then primpt up her lips, frowned at Rataree, and as she left the room, purposely stepped on his foot.

Rataree waited until he thought Mary Lou was out of hearing range, then he began talking. "I was riding along the Nebo a week ago and saw stacks of material on its bank. I asked some men what were they planning to do. One replied that the county was going to build a bridge across the river over to Scroggs Island."

"Why they need to build a bridge?" Jinxie asked. "Ain't there a trestle over to the island?"

"They're tearing down that trestle," Rataree snapped.

"How they going to do that?" Brute inquired.

"Dynamite! They'll blow it up!" Rataree paused and then said, "We'll go get some of that dynamite, a little at a time until we have enough to do our job."

"The dynamite is stored along the river?" Jinxie asked.

"No," Rataree replied. "They'd never do a foolish thing like that. That dynamite is stored over in the rail yard in Cowpens."

"How are we to get it?" Eli asked.

"We'll ride over to Cowpens rail yard at night, steal it, then carry it across the trestle to Scroggs Island. We'll hide it in that old asylum," Rataree said.

"I ain't ridin' on a horse with a box of dynamite at night across that ole trestle," Tom Biggers declared. "I've seen what it can do! Next thang I know I'll be seein' my Maker!"

"Yeah," Jinxie concurred. "I'm willin' to rob a bank, but carryin' dynamite at night across that old trestle, that's somethin' else."

The two men then started toward the door to leave, but Rataree stopped them.

"Come on back," he commanded. "We'll hide the dynamite on this side of the Nebo River until we're ready to use it."

Rataree's statement appeased Tom Biggers and Jinxie, and they came back into the room. He then turned to Eli Bean, reached out, and took his hand. "You need to get on your way to Smyrna. Keep watch. I'm depending on you. You other men can go on back to the mountain and wait until I come for you."

Without another word, Rataree rose and left the room. The men then departed.

Draying

Eli Bean, with instructions from Rataree, went down to the Nebo Valley to Manny White's farm. Manny was a former Confederate soldier and a friend of Elliott. He had lost an arm in the war and was struggling to make a living on his twenty acres of farmland. Since Manny had no family to help him farm, he eagerly took Eli in because he needed help on the farm and he also believed in Rataree's cause.

Manny's farm was near Smyrna and about five miles from Cowpens, an ideal spot for what Eli was sent to do. By working for Manny, Eli could easily go into Smyrna and Cowpens for supplies and listen for information that Rataree needed to know. Since most people in the valley considered Manny touched in the head—that is, a little crazy—they paid little or no attention as to who was living with him.

Eli had a problem getting information to Rataree until he went one day with Manny to Smyrna. Manny always traded at Caleb's store when he didn't have money because Caleb extended him credit, as he did for all the farmers in the valley. However, when Manny had money, he'd shop in Cowpens. He told Eli he hated having to shop in a nigger town.

That day, while Manny was getting his supplies at Caleb's, Eli wandered into the back of the store. There he saw Amos working on a pair of boots. He watched for a few minutes and suddenly it came to him. His problem was solved. He knew how he'd send information back to Rataree.

～

Since the close of school, Bessie and Enoch argued often about Webster not working. It wasn't that Webster didn't want to work, but every time he got a job Bessie found fault with it and interfered so much that he'd have to quit.

By July, Webster had had enough of the bickering between Bessie and Enoch and went to Amos to ask for help in getting him another job.

It was late in the afternoon when Webster arrived at the store. Amos was busy cutting out leather for a pair of boots. A huge pile of leather scraps and broken and bent nails surrounded his workbench. Upon seeing the pile, Webster remarked, "How come this place is in such a mess?"

"Ain't had no time to sweep up," Amos replied. "I've been mindin' the store for Caleb and tryin' to do my own work." He stopped working and held up his hands. "I only got two hands."

Webster walked over and got a broom from the corner and began sweeping up the scraps of leather and bent nails that were strewn about the floor. "Caleb sick?" he asked.

"Nope," Amos replied and took aim at a tack in the boot sole and banged it in. "He ain't got back from takin' stuff out to the valley. And whilst he be gone, I'm left mindin' the store."

"Why can't the farmers come in and get their own stuff?" Webster asked.

"They say they be too busy with their plowin', so Caleb got to takin' their stuff to them. He tried to git me to do it, but I told him if the peoples want stuff they need to come and git it! 'Sides, I'm too old to be settin' up on a wagon rattlin' these old bones."

Webster stopped sweeping. "You mean Caleb has started a draying service?"

Amos nodded his head. "Is that what it be called?"

"Yeah," Webster said, bending down and picking up a handful of leather scraps he'd swept into a pile. He walked over to a big rusty oil drum Amos used for a trash barrel and threw the scraps in it.

Amos stopped hammering and said, "I told him he done started somethin' them folks goin' want him to keep doin', and it's causin' trouble."

"Why so?" Webster inquired.

"Cause when he's out, ain't nobody heah to watch his store and take care of folks when they come in to buy. I've been tryin' to take care of the folks." He frowned. "I'm fallin' way back with my own work. I promised Ben Butler this pair of boots, and he complainin' 'cause I jest can't seem to git 'em done."

"Sounds like Caleb needs a hired hand."

Amos looked up from his work at the tall, sun-tanned youth and retorted, "Where Caleb goin' git a man to drive his wagon? The mens in Smyrna is busy with their own work." Shaking his head determinedly, "Nope, what Caleb needs to do is stop takin' stuff to them folks. If they wants stuff, they need to come and get it!" He hammered another nail into the boot sole with one blow.

"I'll do the draying for Caleb," Webster said.

Amos looked surprised. "You dray?" He smiled faintly. "You don't know nothin' 'bout drayin'. You can't even handle a hoss."

"Yes, I can," Webster countered. "I take care of Enoch's mule all the times."

Amos snickered, "That ole mule almost dead. He can't cause no trouble."

"I can handle horses, Amos," Webster insisted. "I learned to drive a team of horses last summer, when I worked on Cissom's farm."

Amos thought for a moment, then replied. "Webster, you might run into them robbin' people we been heerin' 'bout up in them hills. They be done robbed you of stuff people paid good money for."

Sounding skeptical, Webster said, "I take that robbing story with a grain of salt."

"Why you say that?" Amos asked.

"I don't believe nothing that comes from Manny White's mouth. He's crazy and he's a proven liar."

"Well, I ain't so sho'," Amos said. "He could be right."

Webster flexed his muscles, then grabbed Amos around the neck in a playful chokehold. "I'll do this to them robbers!"

Amos waved him off good-naturedly. Webster then sat down on the bench next to Amos, who gave Webster an approving look because he was so strong.

As he prepared to work on the other boot, Amos said, "Why don't you go on out to Cowpens and git you one of them store job? I heer'd some black folks who run them stores be lookin' for help. Now, that job be more to your ma's lackin'. She ain't wantin' her good-lookin' boy drivin' a team of mules. She wants her boy doin' smart folks' work."

Webster looked up at the ceiling in exasperation. "Quit worrying about Ma," he replied firmly. "I've already talked to her, and we made a bargain."

'What kind of a barg'in?'

"I told her that when I've saved enough money, I'm going to go to The Saints of God's Preparatory School and not before." In an earnest voice he asked Amos, "How can I keep my bargain if I can't get a job?"

Sounding skeptical, Amos questioned him. "Your ma agree to that?"

Webster threw up his arms in a defeated gesture. "Amos, I just told you!"

Amos went back to work for a moment, then said, "I ain't wantin' Bessie comin' at me with her broomstick!"

"She's not going to do that," Webster assured him. "Will you ask Caleb if he'll give me the job?"

Amos sighed. "Looks lack I ain't goin' git no peace if I don't. I speaks to Caleb, but I don't know what he goin' say."

It had been three days since Webster had spoken with Amos about the job, and still Amos hadn't asked Caleb. Amos had put it off because he just didn't want to deal with Bessie.

That morning Caleb went out early to make his deliveries and left Amos in charge of the store. As it was getting on toward the evening, Amos grew anxious when Caleb had not returned. Had something happened to him? Several times Amos went outside the store and looked up the road for Caleb's wagon.

It soon grew dark, and Amos had now become very worried. Had Caleb carried a lantern? What could be keeping him? Could there be some truth to what Manny White had whispered?

Reluctantly, Amos locked the store, lit a lamp, and started downstairs to his room. Just as he reached the bottom step, he heard the rattling of a wagon coming from around the back of the store.

Quickly, Amos rushed back upstairs with his lamp, unlocked the store's door, and called out into the darkness toward the back. "Caleb! Is that you?"

"It's me," came a faint reply. "Come help me unhitch the horses."

Amos hurried around to the store's back where Caleb had driven the wagon. "Where you been?" he asked. "You been gone all day!"

"I stopped on the road to rest," Caleb replied, "and I fell asleep." He wearily climbed down off the wagon and slowly made his way into the store.

Amos unhitched the horses from the wagon and took them to the small barn. Then he went back into the store. There, he saw Caleb flopped in a chair with his eyes closed.

Amos went to the potbellied stove where a coffeepot sat and poured some black coffee into a tin mug. The coffee had been simmering on the stove since morning and had become very strong. He went over to Caleb and shook him on the shoulder to wake him up. When Caleb opened his eyes, Amos handed him the mug. "You too old to be drivin' a wagon all day. You goin' git busted up if you keeps doin' it," he warned.

With trembling hands, Caleb held the mug and took a swallow of the black brew. "I think you're right, Amos. I'm real tired." He yawned and handed the mug back to Amos. "I need to go up to bed." Slowly, he lifted himself up off the chair and walked stiffly toward the stairs.

"You be needin' a hand to help you out," Amos called out after him.

Caleb stopped and grabbed hold of the stair rail to steady himself. "What?"

"You be needin' a hand to do the drayin'. Then you kin git back to takin' care of the store." Amos poured himself a cup of the thick, black coffee. "I can't keep my eye on the store and do my own work. I jest found the man you be needin'."

When Caleb didn't answer, Amos went on. "Enoch's boy. Webster. He lookin' for work. He be willin' to dray for you."

Caleb looked pensive for a moment, then asked. "How old is Webster?"

"Goin' be eighteen soon, but he goin' on thirty." Amos gave a little laugh.

Caleb sighed deeply and replied, "Let me think on it. Right now, all I want to do is get in my bed."

The next day was Saturday, always a busy day at the store. This was the day that the farmers came to Smyrna to buy their supplies for the week. By the afternoon, Caleb had sold out most of his staples.

Jacob Coffin, the youngest son of Israel Coffin, was now in charge of his late father's large peach orchard north of Smyrna. Late that afternoon, he came to the store for his supplies. Caleb told him he'd have to come back on Tuesday to get the goods he wanted because he needed to drive to Cowpens on Monday and buy more supplies.

"That means I'll have to take a day off from work to come back in here!" Coffin replied indignantly. "I've got hands picking my peaches, Caleb. I can't take time off to come back to Smyrna!"

Jeb Franklin, another farmer who had come in the store, heard Caleb tell Coffin he was out of supplies and said, "I can't take a day off neither, and I can't live with my missus if she ain't got her morning coffee. She's got just enough for a couple of days."

When the men said they couldn't give up a day's work to come back to the store, Caleb went back to where Amos was busy working. "You think Webster can take these supplies out to the farms?"

"Webster kin do that," Amos replied confidently. "You give Webster the job, and he'll git it done."

Caleb walked back to the men and said, "I'll get your supplies to you on Tuesday."

By that time, two other men had come into the store: Preacher Mathers, as he was called, and another man, who was a stranger in Smyrna. After Mathers had given his order and Caleb had told him he'd get his supplies on Tuesday, he left.

The stranger had wandered around to the back of the store where Amos was hammering on a pair of boots. He came to Caleb and asked, "Did I hear you say you make deliveries?"

"Sure enough," Caleb replied. "What do you want and where do I take it?"

"Not sure," the stranger answered. "I'll come back on Monday."

"We won't be making deliveries until Tuesday," Caleb reminded him.

After the stranger had gone, Caleb told Amos he'd pay Webster a dollar a day. "That's all I'll give him. If he wants the job, he's to come on Tuesday and get started." Caleb then went upstairs to his room to take a nap.

Amos was still working when Webster came to the store and heard the good news. "Caleb wants to hire you to do the drayin' for him."

Webster looked pleased. "He'll pay you a dollar a day," Amos continued. When he saw Webster's pleased look dissolve in disappointment, Amos quickly added, "He might raise you later on. I'll tell your ma."

"Amos, I don't need you to tell Ma what I'm going to do," Webster replied sharply. "I decide for myself!"

"Now you listen to me, boy," Amos replied, shaking his finger at Webster. "Your ma been heerin' whispers 'bout robbers up in them hills. Now, if you goin' take Caleb's job, I needs to set her mind at ease. So, you 'gree to me tellin' her, or I'll tell Caleb not to give the job to you."

When Webster saw the determined look on Amos' face. he said reluctantly, "Tell Enoch about the job, not Ma."

It was Enoch's habit to visit Amos every Saturday after the store had closed. There, he could drink his whiskey in peace and not have to deal with Bessie, who always started an argument with him whenever she saw him drinking.

So, that Saturday evening as usual, Enoch came to the store and knocked on the door. Amos let him in and realized he had been drinking heavily and was in a foul mood.

Enoch stumbled down the stairs to where Amos stayed and stood weaving back and forth in front of his door. "I needs me a drank," he yelled.

"Look lack you done had enough," Amos cautioned. "Go on in and lay down on my bed. I git you some black coffee."

"I ain't wantin' coffee," Enoch said as he stumbled over and flopped down on the bed. "I needs me whiskey!"

"Well, that's what you goin' git," Amos retorted, and went upstairs to the store where Caleb kept a pot of coffee simmering. He poured a big tin mug of the strong black coffee and went back downstairs.

"Raise up, Enoch, and drank this," Amos ordered, and waited until the drunken Enoch struggled up from the bed and sat on its side. He took a swallow from the mug that Amos held up to his lips. He spit the coffee out.

"I needs me a drank," Enoch yelled.

"I ain't got no bottle, Enoch. You done finished off the one I had the last time you wuz heah!"

Enoch fell back prone onto the bed and closed his eyes. "It be Bessie's fussin' all the times that be gittin' to me! She fuss so much I can't heah my ears if they be talkin'!"

He rolled over onto his side and looked up at Amos with his blood-shot eyes. "I tells you, Amos, Webster be a curse to us! It be him not wan-tin' to go on to that fancy school up yonder!" He waved an arm weakly to indicate somewhere off in the distance. "Bessie now be mad at me!"

Enoch motioned for Amos to sit down on the bed beside him. After Amos had sat down, Enoch raised up onto his elbows and leaned close to him. "Webster be jest lack he mammy. That woman wuz the meanest cuss in this world and the next!"

"What wuz her name?" Amos asked.

"Mar . . . grac . . . ," Enoch blurted out.

"Margrace? Was that her name?"

Because Enoch was in a drunken stupor, he spoke incoherently, "He . . . ma . . . from . . . Mar . . . " Then he flopped over onto the bed.

Amos thought for a moment. Margrace was the name of the planta-tion where he and Enoch had been slaves. Then he asked, "You talkin' 'bout Au Bignon?"

"Ole sonofabitch!" Enoch replied with his eyes closed. "He sell Noah!"

"Yeah," Amos eagerly replied. "What 'bout him?"

"Noah . . . go! Sonofa . . . ich!" Enoch struggled to say.

Amos pulled Enoch up to a sitting position because he wasn't making sense. Enoch teetered from side to side as Amos tried to question him. He wasn't interested in Noah. What he wanted to know was the name of Webster's mother. "You ain't said the name of Webster's ma," Amos said.

Enoch's head drooped down toward his chest and nodded off for a moment. "Noah . . . comin' outta hayloft . . ."

Amos pulled up his chair and sat on it instead of the bed because the intoxicated Enoch was leaning so close to him and might vomit at any minute.

"I . . . Noah . . . jest laffs . . . ," Enoch said, his voice trailing off.

Enoch gave several big hiccups and then his eyes drooped closed.

Amos couldn't figure out Enoch's story, so he grabbed up the mug of black coffee and put it to Enoch's mouth. "Drink some more of this." He tried to force open Enoch's mouth. Enoch fought him off, but Amos was too strong for him and was able to get a little of the coffee into Enoch's mouth.

Enoch gagged after he swallowed the strong coffee. "That stuff be awful! Git me a drank!" His head fell back again against the pillow and some of the coffee trickled out one corner of his mouth.

Since Amos was anxious to hear the rest of Enoch's story, he quickly took the lamplight over to a big straw basket in the corner of his room and reached down under a pile of his clothes and found his bottle of whiskey. Carefully, he kept his back to Enoch because he didn't want Enoch to learn Amos' hiding place and sneak in his room when he wasn't there and drink all of his whiskey. Amos poured a small amount of whiskey into a jelly jar he kept in his room for water, went to the bed, and gave the jar to Enoch, who quickly took it with trembling hand and drank all of the whiskey in one big gulp.

Enoch burped. "Ain't you got no more?" he asked, looking at Amos with his red eyes. "That jest wet my throat."

"It be all you goin' git," Amos said and sat back down on the chair near the bed. "Now, you wuz tellin' me 'bout who Webster is."

Enoch didn't answer, because he was snoring hard on the bed. Amos tried to awaken him, but to no avail.

Amos sat there looking at the snoring Enoch and tried to piece together what he had heard. Someone named Ma'grac was Webster's mother. She must be kin to the Au Bignons because her name is Margrace, the name of the Au Bignons' plantation. But why was Enoch talking to him about Noah, a slave, who had once lived on the Margrace plantation?

Amos meant to tell Enoch about Webster's job that Saturday night, but didn't. Enoch was too drunk. So, Monday morning he went to Enoch's house to tell him. He knocked on the front door, and when no one answered, he went around to the back and saw Bessie washing clothes.

"I be lookin' for the men of the house," Amos called cheerfully.

Without looking up from her scrubbing, Bessie answered, "Webster over at the Cissom farm helpin' pick strawberries."

"Enoch too?"

"No!" Bessie retorted, and went over to a boiling, black pot of water and took a bunch of hot clothes out of it with her broomstick. She brought the clothes back to her washtub and dropped them into it. Then she turned and faced Amos, "Enoch layin' on his tail in the bed! He say he be sick but I know better!" She began angrily scrubbing a shirt on her washboard.

Amos could see that Bessie was in a bad mood. If he were to tell her about Webster's job, he'd have to be careful how he approached the subject. So he rolled up his shirtsleeves and started helping to scrub the hot clothes with his hands.

Bessie stopped scrubbing for a moment, wondering why Amos was helping her wash. He wants something, she thought, but what? Oh well, she'd wait for him to say.

As Amos kept on scrubbing the clothes, Bessie grabbed up an armful of the clothes she had washed, took them over to the boiling pot of water, and threw them in.

Finally, Amos said, "I come to have a little talk with Enoch but seein' he be sick, I'll jest tell you." He glanced over to where Bessie stood punching down the clothes into the pot with her broomstick.

Bessie stepped back from the hot fire, wiped her face with her apron, walked over, and stood in front of Amos with her hands onto her hips. "'Bout what?"

"It be 'bout a job."

"For Enoch?" she asked sarcastically.

Amos almost laughed but knew from Bessie's tone of voice she'd not entertain frivolity. So, he replied cautiously, "No. For Webster."

Without moving, Bessie answered, "I see."

Amos waited for her to say more but when she didn't, he asked, "Ain't you wantin' to know what kind of job and who be offerin' it to Webster?"

"I'm waitin' to hear," Bessie replied.

"It be a job workin' for Caleb."

"What kind of work can Caleb give Webster?"

"Caleb need a drayman, and he goin' give the job to Webster."

Bessie stepped back from Amos and exclaimed in a loud voice. "A drayman? Did I heah you say 'drayman'? You talkin' 'bout Webster drivin' a team of mules?"

All the time Amos had been talking to Bessie, he had kept his head down as he washed her clothes. But her voice sounded angry and he wasn't sure what she'd do to him, bent over scrubbing her clothes, so he quickly stopped washing and stood up.

Shaking her finger in Amos' face. Bessie replied, "You tell me how my boy goin' be turnt into a man? If Caleb need a drayman, let him find a man!"

"Webster be close to eighteen," Amos reminded her. "You eighteen, you be a man! Let the boy work, Bessie. It be what he want."

"You know what I think, Amos? Caleb can't git a man to go up in them hills 'cause the word is there be robbers up there!"

"Aw, that jest be talk," Amos assured her. "Who goin' b'lieve ole Manny White? Ain't no soldiers up in them hills takin' what they wants."

"One of these days, folks in Smyrna goin' find out if ole Manny be speakin' truth," Bessie replied.

Amos went over and draped his arm around Bessie's shoulder. "You best let him do it, Bessie. If you don't, Webster will jest up and leave. Now you ain't wantin' that to happen, do you? Webster be real smart. He kin take care himself."

Slowly, Amos guided Bessie over to the chestnut tree in her backyard where some weathered wicker chairs were. He helped her down into one and then sat in the other chair.

The two sat there silently for a few minutes, then Bessie said, "I guess you think I'm too hard on my child, but I love him and I be wantin' all the best things for him." She paused and looked out at her vegetable garden nearby. "You know, Amos, I dream of seein' my Webster all dressed up in a swallowtail coat with a starched white shirt standin' in Smyrna's church pulpit preachin' the Word of God on Sunday mornin'." She smiled. "Oh, he'd be somethin' to see!"

Amos chuckled. "Webster ain't never goin' be a preacher, Bessie. He might be lack Blanche K. Bruce."

Bessie seemed puzzled. "Who is that?"

"He be a lawman up in Washin'ton helpin' make the laws."

"Is he black?"

"He sho' is," Amos replied proudly. "Webster kin do that."

"True, true," Bessie agreed, "but I wants him to be a preacher, that be my dream."

"Ever'body need a dream," Amos said, agreeing with Bessie.

"I ain't never goin' be nothin' important," Bessie confessed. "Ain't had no chance, but I want Webster to be all the things I ever wanted to be."

Amos was a little surprised to see tears in Bessie's eyes. He'd never seen that before. She was always so strong, never letting her emotions get in the way when she was making a decision.

Amos reached over and patted her on the shoulder. "You could be a good preacherwoman, Bessie. Ole sinners ain't stand a chance if you wuz in the pulpit."

The two laughed heartily at what he had said. Then Bessie became serious again.

"If Webster go on to The Saints of God Prepatory School, he can climb that ladder right on up to the top!" She clapped her hands loudly to make her point.

"Webster goin' be goin' on to school jest as soon as he save up some money. He told me so." Amos explained softly. "So, quit fussin', Bessie."

Bessie seemed relieved at what Amos had told her. She wiped her teary eyes with her apron and replied, "I'm glad to heah he plans on goin' to school!" She leaned her head back against the chair and closed her eyes to hide the fact that she was crying.

Amos waited until Bessie regained her composure, then said, "We best hang them clothes on the line, woman."

That night at dinner, Bessie told Webster what Amos had told her about the job Caleb was offering him. In a cheerful voice she said, "You got to hit the floor 'fore sunrise tomorrow mornin'."

At first, Webster was puzzled by Bessie's cheerful disposition. Why wasn't she putting up an argument with him? Then he reasoned that perhaps she had begun to see things his way, so he went around the table to where she sat and took both her hands in his. "You know how much you like ice cream, Ma?"

Bessie smiled, "Yeah, I do."

"When I first get paid, I'm going to buy you that big ice cream churn you've been looking at every time you go to Caleb's store." Webster said. "And whenever you want ice cream, you can make yourself a churnful!"

Bessie smiled broadly. "I like ice cream!"

"Well, you won't have to borrow Tessa's old broken-down churn," Webster explained. "You'll have a new one!"

They both laughed, remembering how they always had to repair the handle of Tessa's ice cream churn that fell off every time Bessie used it.

The next morning Webster rose early. He could hear Bessie's and Enoch's snoring coming from their bedroom. He went quietly to the kitchen where he buttered three cold biscuits that had been left over from last night's dinner, put them into a brown paper bag, and slipped out the kitchen door.

The path to Caleb's store led through damp woods because the sun's rays had not penetrated them. As he walked through the quiet woods, he felt so happy that he began whistling. Soon, he emerged from the woods and saw the store. As he came closer, he saw a wagon in front of it. The wagon seemed bigger than the one he'd seen Caleb driving, and he became a little anxious.

"Ready to go to work?" Caleb asked as he greeted him from the store's porch.

"Yes, sir," Webster replied confidently. "Hope I didn't get here too early."

"The earlier, the better," Caleb replied. "I want a day's work for a day's pay."

When Caleb saw Webster glancing over at the wagon he explained, "I had to change the wagon. Broke an axle on the other one." He motioned for Webster to follow him and went over to the bench in front of his store and sat down.

Caleb said to Webster. "There's some things I need to go over with you. Try and avoid strangers. Just conceal yourself until they're gone." Seeing the concerned look on Webster's face, he said, "I don't believe there's anything to the talk about robbers that's going around here in Smyrna, but it won't hurt to be cautious. Don't push the horses too fast. When they are tired, let them rest. Remember, I want you to make the deliveries, not to get my horses sick. If it gets too late, just spend the night and come back to Smyrna in the morning."

"Where do I sleep, if I can't get back?" Webster inquired.

Caleb shrugged. "Oh, someone will let you sleep in his barn." He stood up. "We'd better get the wagon loaded."

Webster didn't like the idea of sleeping in some stranger's barn. He wanted to question Caleb more about it, but decided to let it go for now.

Caleb handed Webster a piece of paper with the names of Coffin, Mathers, Franklin, and Elliott written on it. Webster recognized all the names but Elliott. Amos had pointed out Coffin to him one day when he came to the store. Coffin stood well over six feet tall, had piercing blue eyes, and a Roman nose.

"He Pa thought he wuz a prophet," Amos told Webster.

"Where is he now?" Webster asked.

"He be dead. I heer'd they lock him up on Scroggs Island," Amos replied. "But it be funny. Some people say Coffin's wife be actin' strange, jest lack that ole prophet."

Before Webster could go over in his mind information about the other men, Amos came around from the back of the store leading two brown horses and hitched them up to the wagon.

After the horses were hitched to the wagon, Amos and Webster began loading it. Back and forth they went into the store getting supplies and putting them into the wagon bed. They brought out four sacks of flour, four bags of coffee, six small sacks of sugar, a new horse's bridle, and a roll of new rope.

"We got it all loaded," Amos called to Caleb.

"Wait a minute," Caleb called back and came outside with a scruffy pair of boots.

Amos stared at the boots, then asked, "Where you git them ole beat-up shoes?"

"That man who was in the store on Saturday brought them in yesterday and asked me if I'd deliver them to William Elliott. I told him not 'til this morning." He handed the boots to Amos.

Amos seemed puzzled for a moment, then said, "I 'member that fella. He come back where I wuz workin' Satday, and watched me work. I asked him if he wants me to make him some boots. He jest smiled and walks away."

"Who is William Elliott?" Webster asked.

"Oh, I knew him a long time ago," Caleb replied and paused for a few moments. "I thought Elliott was dead."

"How you know he ain't?" Amos asked.

"Don't know for sure," was Caleb's answer. "This fella wouldn't be sending him boots if he were, now, would he?"

"Them ole boots be tore up," Amos remarked. "He need to throw them away and let me make him new ones."

"It's not for us to decide," Caleb said. "I told him I'd deliver the boots."

"I'm not sure I know how to get to Elliott's farm," Webster said.

"His farm is north of Smyrna. Just go in the direction of Fort Belton," Caleb instructed him. "It's the old farmhouse that sets up on the hill across the river from where that old asylum used to be."

When Caleb hesitated, Webster said, "Sounds like a far piece."

"Oh, not more than ten miles," Caleb replied and went back inside the store.

"Guess this be all," Amos said. "Now you sho' you know where you is goin' and who gits what?"

Webster looked again at the written paper Caleb had given him, then he recited the information off to Amos.

"First, I go to Coffin's place and leave the bridle, two bags of sugar, a bag of coffee, and two sacks of flour. Then on I go to Mathers' house. He gets two bags of sugar, a sack of flour, a bag of coffee, and the rope. Next, I go to the Franklin farm and leave two sacks of flour, two bags of coffee, two bags of sugar." Webster looked over at Amos who was holding the scruffy boots. "Then I'll try to find the Elliott house and give him them boots."

Amos grinned proudly. "You sho' got it down pat. Oh, I'm forgittin your viddles! A man can't work on a empty stomick. I jest run in and git them."

Before Webster could say he had some food, Amos had rushed into the store. Soon he came out with a big straw basket covered with a checkered cloth.

"I put in a hunk of cheese, six biscuits, and six sausage balls," Amos announced. "Oh yes, I give you a slug of my pound cake." He handed the basket to Webster.

Webster felt a little embarrassed. Amos was still treating him like a child. "You didn't have to cook me some food. I brought along some buttered biscuits. I don't need much."

Amos frowned. "Biscuits ain't goin' hold you up when that ole sun gits hots and them hosses be pullin' on their bits. Now, you git on up on the wagon and git goin'."

Webster climbed up to the wagon seat with the basket, took hold of the reins, and held them steady.

"Wait, wait," Amos said and picked up the boots from the ground where he had left them when he had gone into the store to get the basket of food. He handed the boots up to Webster, who promptly dropped them down in the wagon bed.

"Git up," Webster commanded the horses, and slowly the animals pulled the wagon away from the store. Webster turned and waved to Amos, who was standing in the road watching him leave.

Webster was off on his first big job. He felt satisfied and happy as the wagon rolled away from Smyrna and out toward the countryside.

The rutted, dirt road wound its way through the farmlands where men, women, and children wearing wide straw hats were bent over at their waists, harvesting ripe vegetables and fruits in the hot sun. Webster was glad that he no longer was picking strawberries. He hated working all day for Cissom doing backbreaking work in the hot sun for a few pennies. Now, he had a man's job and was going to earn a man's pay.

The red, dirt road cut straight through the wheat fields, waist-high with heavy-headed wheat turning golden in the hot sun. In a few weeks the farm workers, using scythes, would cut down the ripe wheat and the dusty threshing would begin.

The moving wagon had stirred up the wheatbugs. Although the bugs were so tiny one could hardly see them, they had voracious appetites. Webster began feeling their effects as he slapped at his face and neck.

Soon, he was out of the wheat fields and a large orchard, ripe with peaches, came into view. Webster knew he was nearing the Coffin farm because Jacob Coffin had the largest peach and apple orchard in the Nebo Valley. Off in the distance he heard voices talking and laughing, and he knew the fruit pickers were at work.

Webster was happy he wasn't picking the ripe peaches because he knew it was an itchy job. Once he and Bessie picked peaches for Coffin, and he got a terrible red rash on his hands, neck, and face from the peach fuzz. For him, the only good thing about picking peaches was you got to eat a lot of the sweet, juicy fruit.

After passing the peach orchard, Webster soon saw the Coffins' white frame house setting back from the main road. Even though Jacob Coffin was a rich man and could have lived in a mansion, he chose to live simply.

At the house, Webster pulled the horses to a stop and climbed down off the wagon and went to the front door and knocked. There was no answer. He knocked again, only this time much louder. After waiting for a few minutes, he saw the curtains at the front window move and he saw the face of a woman.

"Mr. Coffin," he yelled. "I brought your goods from Caleb's store."

Slowly, the front door opened, and a gray-haired, pinched-face woman, clad in a cotton flowered dress and wearing a white apron, stood inside the screen door.

"I'm looking for Mr. Coffin," Webster said to her.

The woman pointed toward the orchard.

"I just came that way and didn't see him," Webster said. "If you like, I can unload your goods for you."

Watching Webster intensely and not saying a word, the woman pointed her finger toward a long wooden table on the porch.

Webster went to the wagon and got a sack of flour and a bag of coffee and brought them back to the table. Then he went and got two bags of sugar and the bridle from the wagon and put them on the table.

Looking at the piece of paper that Caleb had given him, he said, "I think that's all. Much obliged to you, ma'am." He walked down off the porch to the wagon, climbed up on it, and took the reins. "Git up," he commanded the horses in a firm voice and skillfully turned the animals around toward the main road and drove off.

When Webster glanced back at the house, he saw that the woman had come onto the porch and was watching him go. "Amos was right about you, Mrs. Coffin," Webster said aloud.

As Webster drove on, he gave the horses a gentle tap with the whip. At the rate he was going, it would be time to eat before he could reach Jim Mathers' house. Every now and then, he glanced at the basket of food Amos had given him. He could almost taste that piece of cake in the basket.

Webster wasn't looking forward to seeing Jim Mathers. Jim was called a religious zealot by some people in the valley, but others weren't so sure what to make of him.

Mathers ambled about the countryside carrying his Bible trying to save souls. He'd preach a sermon to anyone who was willing to listen, and his sermon was always about the story of Sodom and Gomorrah. He'd preach vigorously and emotionally about the vile and lascivious appetites these people of the Bible had engaged in.

Amos once told Webster that Mathers' preaching was merely a disguise to keep people from learning the truth about him. He had heard that Mathers had once run a whorehouse in Renlo, a hamlet twenty miles south of Cowpens. The good Christian folks in Renlo tarred and feathered him one night and chased him out of their town. With the money he'd earned from operating a whorehouse, Mathers came to the Nebo Valley and bought a piece of hard-scrabbled land that he didn't farm.

Whether or not this was true, Webster felt a bit unsettled going to Mathers' house. He remembered the time when he and his friend Ozell had been hunting in the woods for muscadines to make some wine, and they came out of the woods near Mathers' house. It had been a hot day, and the two decided to go to the house and ask for water. As they neared the house, they saw Mathers sitting naked on his porch smoking his pipe. When he saw the boys staring at him, he began jumping up and down on his porch, holding his genitals and shouting, "Jesus is coming! Jesus is coming!"

His hideous yelling and the way he looked frightened the two boys, and they ran back into the woods.

Soon, Webster came in sight of Mathers' ramshackle house near a grove of scrub pines. When he reached the house, Webster pulled the horses to a stop, climbed down off the wagon, and went up onto the porch. Just inside the open door on the floor was an old quilt where Mathers lay sleeping. His naked body heaved up and down from his heavy snoring. Just an arm's distance away from his quilt sat a jug, and Webster quickly surmised the man had been drinking whiskey.

Webster meant not to awaken him, so he tiptoed off the porch and went back to his wagon for Mathers' supplies.

First, he carried the bag of flour and eased it off his shoulder down onto the porch. Then he brought over the two bags of sugar and coffee. All this time, Mathers continued to snore loudly.

When his work was done, Webster hurried back to his wagon and quietly gave the command for the horses to get going. In his haste to get away undetected, he had forgotten to leave the rope.

"I'm sure as hell not going back there," Webster said aloud when he saw the rope still in the wagon bed.

Down the road from Mathers' house was the Franklin farm. Webster decided he'd make that delivery and then drive over to the meadow near Bear Creek and let the horses get some water and rest. There, he'd eat his dinner.

It was getting on toward twelve by the time he reached the Franklins' big, rambling house. The grass in the yard was turning brown and sunflower heads had begun to droop along the fence where they were planted. It was hot.

Webster thought the Franklins would be home for dinner, but when he knocked on the door no one answered. Caleb had told him to leave the supplies on the back porch if no one was home. So he drove the wagon around to the back and went to the screened porch, opened it, and put the two bags of flour, coffee, and sugar inside.

He had now made all the deliveries except the boots, and he didn't have any idea how far the Elliott farm was. Well, he'd think about that later. Right now, all he could think of was eating that good food Amos had given him, especially the cake. Webster headed to Bear Creek.

At Bear Creek, Webster stopped the horses in the meadow, unhitched them, and led them down to an opening where they drank deeply of the cool water. When the horses had finished drinking, Webster tied each one loosely to a nearby tree so they could graze on the meadow grass. Then he took the basket from the wagon and went over to a shady spot under a small tree and flopped down on the soft grass.

234

From where Webster lay, he had a panoramic view of the farms, hills, and railroad tracks that snaked alongside the river in the Nebo Valley. To the south was Smyrna, and to the north were some high pockmarked limestone bluffs overlooking the river.

The bluffs were slowly eroding away because water had leached down into the limestone, making small caves inside them. Webster knew about the caves because he and Ozell had once gone exploring there.

Out in the middle of the river he could see the outline of Scroggs Island where the asylum had been built and was now abandoned. Webster stood up, shaded his eyes, and tried to see the old trestle that connected the island to the mainland, but the glare was too great. All he could see in that direction was a profusion of green where saplings, bushes, unruly vines, and large briar patches hugged the sides of the bluffs.

After Webster had eaten all the food Amos had given him and his own buttered biscuits, he felt sleepy, but he knew he'd better get going. Caleb had said that the Elliott farm was beyond the bluffs, and if he was to get there and back to Smyrna before sundown, he needed to get a move on.

The Strange Boots

Webster quickly gathered up his food basket and took it to the wagon, rounded up the horses, hitched them to the wagon, and headed toward the bluffs. It was slow going because the road had not been maintained. Big dirt boulders that had tumbled down from the bluffs lay in the road where sturdy, huckleberry bushes and creeping vines grew so thickly that at times the road ruts disappeared. When Webster saw signs of gophers he slowed the horses, because if they were to step in one of their holes, that move could cause a disaster.

Because he had to travel so slowly, Webster worried that he might not get the boots delivered and back to Smyrna before nightfall. It wasn't until after he had driven though a patch of woods, then up a steep hill bordered by what seemed to be an endless dense thicket with briars, bunch grasses and vines growing right up to the bluffs that he finally saw a farmhouse in the distance. That had to be Elliott's house because it was the only one nearby. If not, he'd just turn the horses around and go back to Smyrna. He'd not be wandering in these lonely hills at night.

Webster soon reached the ramshackle house in need of repairs and painting. He could see that the farm had once been prosperous, but not now. Signs of neglect were everywhere. Several planks were missing from a hulking barn that stood in back of the house, and horses' stalls on the inside could be seen from the outside. Some rusty barbwire dangled from posts that now enclosed an empty pasture tall with weeds and grasses. The henhouse had rotted away, and so had several sheds. All that remained of them were their blackened, rotting roofs surrounded by jimsonweed.

Webster stopped the wagon at the edge of the front yard, got off, and walked up onto the porch. Before he could knock, the door was jerked open by a chubby, ruddy-faced young girl with stringy brown hair that hung to her shoulders.

"You be lost?" she asked, revealing a gap in her front teeth.

"I'm not sure, ma'am," Webster replied. "I'm looking for Mr. William Elliott's farm."

"You be at the right place," the girl said and smiled broadly at Webster.

"Who is it, Mary Lou?" a voice called from inside.

"It's a man," the girl yelled. "I don't know who he is!"

"Well, you just come on back in here," the voice commanded. "I'll talk to him."

In a few minutes, an old man with white hair, a handlebar mustache, and a blotchy complexion appeared in the doorway. He motioned for the girl, who had now sat down in the porch's swing, to go back inside. She gave him an angry look, jumped up from the swing, and as she pushed pass him in the doorway, she gave him a slight shove.

The old man teetered backwards for a moment.

"You Mr. Elliott?" Webster asked.

"I am," Elliott replied as he got his balance.

"I'm draying for Caleb Johnson and I have a delivery for you."

"Caleb Johnson?" Elliott seemed puzzled.

"He owns the general store in Smyrna," Webster explained.

"Caleb Johnson?" Then the old man remembered. "Why I haven't seen or heard from Caleb since before the war. What in the world is he sending me?"

"A pair of boots," Webster replied.

"Boots? Now, why is Caleb sending me boots?"

"Oh, the boots aren't from Caleb," Webster explained. "A man named Bean sent them to you.

This confused Elliott. "Bean?" he asked, staring at Webster. "I don't know a Bean."

As the old man stood scratching his head trying to remember who Bean was, a tall man wearing a white shirt with his sleeves rolled up came to the doorway. Towering over Elliott, he sized Webster up with brooding dark eyes that seemed to penetrated through him.

In a solemn voice, the man said to Elliott, "The boots are from Eli." When he didn't see the boots, he asked, "Where are they?"

"They're in the wagon," Webster said. "Wasn't sure I was at the right place. I'll get them."

Webster went to the wagon, retrieved the boots, and handed them to Elliott, who passed them back to the tall man who took the boots inside.

Webster was surprised that the man didn't remark about the condition the boots were in, but that wasn't his concern. He'd made the delivery and now wanted to get on his way back to Smyrna.

"I'd like to get some water for my horses," Webster said.

"You hungry?" Elliott asked. "Mary Lou can put some leftovers in a bag."

"I'm much obliged to you," Webster replied, "but I'm not hungry. All I need is water for the horses."

"The watering trough is around back. You'll have to draw the water up," Elliott told him.

Webster drove the wagon around to the back of the house where a stone well stood near the barn. The well had a large wooden bucket tied to a well-worn rope that was wrapped onto a chunk of an oak log nailed between two posts that were on either side of its opening.

Slowly, Webster unwound the rope as the bucket descended into the well. Then he heard a splash and knew the bucket had reached the water below.

An oaken bucket filled with water is quite heavy, and Webster's muscles strained as he pulled the bucket up out of the well. When it reached the top, Webster poured the water into a long wooden trough and sent the bucket back into the well.

From the amount of water the horses needed, Webster knew he'd be there a long time. His arms ached just from pulling up the first bucket of water.

As he stood resting from the hard work, a voice called from the barn. "That ole bucket be real heavy." Webster looked in the direction of the sound and saw the young girl sitting in the shade of the barn.

Not wanting to appear weak, Webster wiped his brow on his shirt-sleeve and replied, "This sun is hot!"

She giggled and Webster could see that her blouse was unbuttoned, showing the outlines of her ample breasts. "Come on over and rest in the shade."

Now, Webster was always attracted to women, but not this one. She reminded him of Lula, the hogkiller's daughter, and the ugly experience he'd had with her. So he quickly replied, "I'm not tired," and continued drawing up the water with the heavy bucket.

As soon as the watering trough had been filled, Webster unhitched the horses and let them drink. When they had finished drinking, he hitched them back to the wagon.

All this time, Mary Lou hadn't moved from her position. She just sat there, watching his every move. Webster felt relieved when he drove away from the barn and onto the road.

"Elliott needs to take his daughter out to the woodshed," he said aloud and gently tapped the horses on their rumps with his whip.

Soon, the farmhouse faded into the distance and the wagon rolled on past the huge briar patch and on toward a steep hill and some woodlands that were a few miles away. Webster was confident he'd get to Smyrna before sundown.

Just before the horses reached the bottom of the steep hill, Webster saw two horsemen riding hard, bearing down on him, and he didn't have time to hide the wagon as Caleb had warned him to do when he saw strangers.

The horsemen rode straight at Webster, who was forced to give ground so much that the wagon went careening off into the bushes. It took all his strength and skills to hold onto the horses to keep the wagon from over-turning.

By the time Webster had reined in the horses, the two men had stopped and were busy laughing and pointing at him. One man was big and burly with mean eyes, and the other man was muscular, had a swarthy complexion with an ugly scar that ran down the side of his face to his lip, and heavy black hair that hung to his shoulders.

Then the burly man leaped off his horse and lumbered toward the wagon. Webster became frightened because he thought these men were the robbers that Amos had spoken about.

The burly man yanked Webster off the wagon and flung him headfirst into the thicket. "I'm gonna kick your ass, bastard," he snarled as he snatched Webster up to his feet, and drew back his balled-up fist. Suddenly, there came an ear-splitting whistle and the burly man's fist was frozen into place.

A short distance away at the top of the hill, a man on a horse was beck-oning. When the swarthy-looking man saw the man on the horse, he quickly rode off toward the hill.

The burly man angrily tossed Webster back into some briars and yelled as he left. "Next time, your ass be mine, bastard!" Then he struggled up onto his horse and raced off after the other two.

Webster extricated himself from the briars and hurried to the wagon, grabbed the reins, and yelled, "Git up!" When the horses didn't respond, he used the whip.

It was twilight when Webster finally reached Smyrna. Amos was wait-ing for him on a bench in front of the store. "How'd it go?" he called.

"Went fine," Webster replied and drove the wagon around to the back. Amos followed. After the horses had been unhitched, watered, and were taken to the barn, the two went inside to Amos' quarters.

Even though it was late, Webster knew that Amos wanted to hear everything, so he began telling him about each delivery. Finally, he told him about Elliott and the horsemen, but he didn't tell all. He didn't tell that he had been tossed into some briars and threatened. He wanted to keep his job.

"Who you thank they be?" Amos questioned.

"Don't know," Webster replied nonchalantly. "Probably some drunken mountain men."

It had been two months since Webster had been draying, and he had had no more unpleasant encounters. He had saved forty dollars.

One morning as the sun was just rising, he set out from the store with a wagon load of goods to be delivered. He had taken the north road from Smyrna, the same way he had come on his very first trip.

After traveling a few miles out of Smyrna, he saw a man standing in the middle of the road waving for him to stop. As Webster came closer, he saw that the man was waving a pair of boots, which frightened his horses. They reared up on their hind legs, and Webster had to strain to control them.

"What the hell do you think you're doing?" Webster shouted after he managed to calm the horses and bring the animals to a halt.

"You be the drayman, ain't you?" the man asked.

"Hell, yes!" Webster shouted. "You caused my horses to buck! What the hell's the matter with you, sonofabitch?"

The man held up a pair of new boots. "I want you to take these boots out to Elliott."

Webster glared down at the scrawny, shifty-eyed man who had a tight smile on his lips. "You mean the Elliott up in the hills?" The man nodded his head. "Too far," Webster snapped. "It would be nightfall before I could even get there."

"Mr. Elliott need his boots," the man insisted.

"Well, take them yourself." Webster said.

"I can't," the man replied and coughed. "I just got out of a sick bed."

"I just took a pair of boots to Elliott a couple of months ago," Webster said. "Now why is he needing another pair?"

"Them boots be too small," the man answered. "I bought him this new pair in Cowpens and got sick 'fore I could git 'em to him." Then he began coughing again. When he finally stopped, he said, "If you take the boots to him, I'll give you two dollars." He reached into his pocket and held up two one-dollar bills.

Webster believed the coughing spasm was faked, but if the fool was willing to give him money he'd take it. "Make it five," he said.

"Five!" the man replied.

"It's five, or I don't go!" was Webster's reply.

"All right." The man reached into his pocket and held out a five-dollar bill.

For a moment, Webster hesitated. His good judgment told him not to accept the offer, but then again five dollars was a lot of money, a week's pay for him. He reached out and took the money. The man handed up the boots.

"Who's sending these boots?" Webster asked.

"Bean. Eli Bean," the man replied and ran off into the woods.

Webster wasn't sure he'd deliver the boots, but he knew for certain he was going to keep the money.

After Webster had gone that morning, Caleb went back upstairs to his bed because it was too early to open his store for business. Amos went to work because he needed to finish making a pair of shoes.

Suddenly, there came a loud banging on the store's door.

"Now who in the world is it?" Amos said aloud as he went to the door. "Don't folks know the store hours?"

When Amos saw Manny White, he opened the door and said, "Store ain't open." Ignoring what Amos had said, White shoved him out of his way and came inside. "I told you the store ain't open," Amos yelled to him.

"Where's your master?" he said in a demeaning tone.

"Master? I ain't got no master!" Amos retorted indignantly. "Now, you go on and git! You gots to wait 'til store hours!"

Ignoring Amos again, Manny shouted in a loud voice, "Caleb! Caleb!"

In a few minutes, Caleb called from the top of the stairs, "What's going on down there?"

"It be ole crazy Manny," Amos called back. "He won't git outta the store. I done told him the store ain't open!"

Manny threw back his head and yelled as if he were out in the woods, "Caleb! I need coffee and sugar!"

By now, Caleb had come down the stairs, wearing his nightshirt. He tried to reprimand the man. "Manny, have you lost your wits? Don't you know the good people of Smyrna are still sleeping?"

"I come for a bag of coffee and sugar." Manny turned to Amos with puckered-up lips and angrily shouted. "Git it!"

"I'll git it," Amos snapped. "We ain't goin' git no peace 'til you gits what you come for."

Amos went behind the counter and reached up onto a shelf. He took down a bag of coffee and a small bag of sugar and put them on the counter.

Manny gathered up the bags and started for the door. "Put this on my bill."

"Nope," Caleb said and took the bags away from Manny. "I'll take cash. No more credit until you settle up with me."

"But I ain't got no money, Caleb," Manny whined.

"You owe me from two years back," Caleb said. "I know you've been spending money in Cowpens. Saw you there myself. So, if you spend your money at them stores in Cowpens, you'll have to get credit from them."

When Caleb saw how disappointed Manny was, he remarked, "I won't deprive you of coffee for your breakfast, so I'll give you a little."

Caleb went to where he kept his coffee and put some in a bag, then he shook some sugar into another bag and came back to Manny. "Just remember who your friends are when you're spending money in Cowpens."

Manny snatched the bags from Caleb's hand. At the door he turned and angrily shouted, "I won't be askin' you for credit agin! The raiders goin' swoop down in Smyrna lack locusts and burn this hellhole to the ground! You and all these niggers goin' go up in smoke!" He slammed the store's door and was gone.

"They're going to be taking Manny to the asylum real soon if he keeps on talking about raiders," Caleb remarked and went back upstairs.

Amos wasn't so sure about Manny being crazy. He remembered that Webster had told him about two men he had encountered. Could there really be raiders up in the hills? Did Manny know what he was talking about?

All day long Manny's words about burning Smyrna tugged at Amos. He needed to talk to someone, so he went to see his preacher, Reverend Bates.

The two men sat talking quietly in one of the church's pews.

"I ain't wantin' to git peoples scared," Amos confided to Reverend Bates, "but I been thankin', what if there really be raiders? Them robbers kin ketch us by surprise and no tellin' what kin happen!" In a hushed tone, Amos continued, "I b'lieve there still be white folks who hate us black folks. Jest cause we be black!"

"You're right about that," Reverend Bates concurred. "Some old Confederate soldiers are still fighting the war in their hearts. They'll still be doing it ten, fifteen, twenty years from now. Them old soldiers will never give up!"

"I bet them raiders be ole soldiers who be hell-bent on real fightin'!" Amos remarked. "What we goin' do, Reverend Bates? Jest set heah and let 'em come?"

Reverend Bates patted the agitated Amos on his back. "Amos, we're not sure there are raiders. But to ease your mind, I'll form a watchdog group to keep an eye on things at night."

"Maybe we ought to git the sheriff over in Cowpens to handle that," Amos suggested.

In a determined voice, Reverend Bates replied, "No, Amos. Black men must protect Smyrna! We can't run to the white man to solve our problem!"

Amos had never heard Reverend Bates speak so forcefully; he quickly agreed. "It ain't goin' matter who do the watchin', jest as long as there be watchin'."

"I'll get our community leaders together," Reverend Bates told Amos. "We'll form a united black front to keep watch at night. You're not to breathe a word of this to anyone, because this must be done in secrecy."

The two men shook hands, and Amos left the church and went back to work.

It was late in the day when Webster made his last delivery. He was hot, tired, and very hungry. In his haste to leave early that morning, he had forgotten to put some food in a bag. He stopped near a cornfield, thinking he'd take a couple of corn ears and roast them over a fire. But the corn was too hard, not suitable for eating unless he wanted to break a tooth. He had long passed the orchards and the vegetable farms, but he remembered there was a blackberry briar patch up near the bluffs. He'd go there.

When Webster reached the briar patch, he saw nothing but berrycaps on brown thorns because the birds had stripped the vines clean. Not a berry was to be found! As the famished Webster stood surveying the huge blackberry briar patch, his stomach gave a monstrous growl. He needed food.

Even though Webster had decided early on that he'd not deliver the boots, he changed his mind. Why not deliver the boots and ask Elliott for some food? He'd been offered food when he first went to his house, and this time he'd brought him another pair of boots. Surely he would offer him hospitality.

As the empty wagon rumbled toward Elliott's farm, Webster reached down and set the boots up on the wagon seat near him. The more he looked at the boots, the more curious he became. Why was Bean sending another pair of boots to Elliott? Why had he sent the dilapidated pair before? Why? Something was going on with these boots, thought Webster.

Webster stopped the wagon and examined the tough leather boots thoroughly for broken seams or tears on the outside and found nothing unusual. Then he put his hand inside and felt around for lumps. Nothing was out of the ordinary there. These were just plain, heavy, hobnailed boots with big thick soles that farmers wore while working in their fields.

By the time Webster reached Elliott's house, the sun was low in the sky. The old man had seen him coming and had walked out to the road to meet the wagon.

"I came to make another delivery," Webster said as he pulled the horses to a stop.

He climbed stiffly off the wagon and reached up and got the boots. "Eli Bean sent you another pair of boots," he said, and handed them down to Elliott. "He said the other pair was too small."

"Oh, yeah, they were," Elliott agreed and started toward his house.

"Mr. Elliott," Webster called to him, "because I had to come way out here to make your delivery, I missed getting something to eat. I'm wondering if you could spare me a bite? I'd be terribly obliged."

Elliott hesitated for a few minutes, then said, "Come around to the kitchen. I think we've got some leftovers from dinner."

Webster drove the wagon off to the roadside, unhitched his horses, and brought them around to the watering trough. After they had drunk some water, he tethered each one to a pasture post to graze. Then he went to the kitchen door.

Elliott gave him a plate with several pieces of fried rabbit and some cold biscuits. "You can eat it out at the barn," he said.

Webster took the food, thanked Elliott, and walked out to the barn. An old, empty, rusting barrel lay in a sea of weeds on the side of the barn. Webster turned the barrel upside down and sat on it. Even though the burnt rabbit meat was tough with no seasoning and the cold biscuits were hard, Webster wolfed the food down.

By the time Webster had finished eating, it was dark and he didn't want to set out for Smyrna because the road was too dangerous. He'd go off over the bluffs. Webster decided to ask Elliott if he could spend the night in his barn.

This time when he knocked on the door, Mary Lou opened it. He could see Elliott sitting at the kitchen table eating. "I wanted to ask Mr. Elliott if he'll let me sleep in his barn tonight," he told the girl.

"Now, why you want to do that?" she inquired.

"It's too late for me to head back to Smyrna," Webster replied.

Mary Lou went to the table and talked to Elliott. After a few minutes, she came back. "Elliott said he want you gone at sunrise."

"I'm much obliged to him for the food and letting me stay," Webster said.

At the barn, he untied his horses from the posts and put them in a rickety stall. In a corner of the barn, Webster stretched out on a thin pile of hay.

The hay felt good to his aching body, and he tried to go to sleep but couldn't. Something was bothering him. It was the boots. Why would Elliott need hobnailed boots when he wasn't farming?

Webster sprang up from the hay. "I've been a fool," he said aloud. "I should have torn open the boot soles! I bet Bean is secretly sending Elliott money and hiding it in those big thick soles!"

Webster didn't wonder why Bean had to hide money in the boots. He didn't wonder how he got the money. All he knew was Bean had money. Hadn't he given him five dollars that morning? He wanted that money, but how to get it?

Webster laid on the hay trying to think of ways to get back the boots when he saw a dim light coming toward the barn. He got up and walked over to the opening to see what it was. It was the girl carrying a dimly lit lantern and an old quilt.

"Thought you might need this," she said and walked over to the corner where Webster had been lying and spread the ragged quilt over the pile of straw and patted it out. Looking up at Webster she said, "This quilt's real soft. It be big enough for two." And to Webster's astonishment, she stretched out on the quilt.

Feeling nervous, Webster quickly said, "You better get on back to the house. Your pa will be needing you in the kitchen."

"You can't tell me what to do!" the girl retorted, pulling her dress up to her waist and showing a puffy pair of torn bloomers. "He ain't my pa. He's my husband."

"Your husband?" the stunned Webster replied. "He's old enough to be your grandpa."

Mary Lou giggled and said, "I married him 'cause he's got money. When he's dead, all this will be mine!" Smiling up at Webster, she paused for a few minutes. "You ever laid a woman?"

Ignoring the girl's brazen question, Webster asked, "Why does your husband need hobnailed boots?"

With a pouting look on her face, she snapped, "I ain't talkin' 'bout some ole boots. I want to get laid! Elliott's so ole he can't do nothin'!" And she pulled down her bloomers, revealing her heavy, milk-white thighs.

The sight of her lying with her thighs agape disgusted Webster. He nearly vomited because flashes of Lula, the hogkiller's daughter, pressing his face onto her big breasts came to him. He wanted to run away from the girl as he had done with Lula. But this time, he knew he couldn't. He was now a man, not a nine-year-old boy.

Webster knew Mary Lou would yell rape if he didn't do what she wanted him to do, so he quickly said, "Look, we don't have enough time now. Elliott hasn't gone to sleep. Come back before daybreak."

When Mary Lou hesitated, Webster said firmly, "Go on back to the house before he misses you!"

Reluctantly, the girl got up off the quilt. She wagged her stubby finger in Webster's face. "You best keep your word, 'cause if you don't, I'm gonna holler!"

"I aim to keep my word," Webster assured her.

Webster knew he had to leave right away. He'd rather take a chance on the dangerous road than stay there and get shot, and he was certainly not going to have sex with Mary Lou. The thought of her turned his stomach.

Webster didn't want to wait too long before making his move. The girl might come back. So when he thought it was safe, he quietly led the horses from their stalls and hitched them to his wagon that he had left on the roadside. He knew wagons make racket, so he needed to make sure Elliott and Mary Lou were sound asleep. The only way to know for sure was to look in on them.

Quietly, Webster pushed open the kitchen door and went in. He heard loud snoring coming from down a hall. Was the girl asleep? He'd better find out; he tiptoed down a narrow hallway to a room where he heard loud snoring and peeped in.

Inside the room, a dim ray of moonlight filtered through some dirty window curtains. Webster could barely make out the old man lying on a four-postered bed, with his arms wrapped around the girl. Both were snoring.

Without tarrying, Webster left the room and hurried down the hall. In his haste to get out of the house, he tripped on something. Not wanting to awaken Elliott, he stood very still for a few minutes. While standing there, he thought he saw a pair of boots next to his feet. Bending down, he felt boots. Without making a sound, he carefully lifted them up, then slipped out of the hall, through the kitchen, and out the back door.

With the boots in hand, Webster made a dash to the wagon where the horses were hitched and drove away in the dark.

The faint moonlight lit his way as he drove past the dangerous bluffs and on beyond. Soon he came to the briar patch that stretched from the woodlands up onto the bluffs where their vines covered the entrances to the caves. The road from there became rougher and rougher, and Webster knew it wasn't safe to go on. He was now far away from Elliott's farm and decided to sleep in the woods until dawn, then go on to Smyrna.

At first light, Webster awakened. When he saw the boots he had thrown into the wagon, he decided to open the soles. With his jackknife he ripped open one boot sole. His heart was pounding because he expected to find money, but there was nothing. He quickly pried open the other boot. Again, no money. As he felt around in the inside of the sole, he discovered a lump stuck at the toe of the boot. He pulled the lump out and saw that it was a tight, rolled-up ball of brown paper.

At first, Webster started to throw the ball of paper away, but then he unrolled it. On a scrap of paper torn from a brown paper bag were a bunch of poorly scrawled numbers: 17- 21- 9- 20. What in hell did this mean? Webster thought. Could it be a code? If so, what did it mean?

Webster sat puzzling over the numbers, trying to decipher what they meant. After a time, he gave up and started for home. He stuck the paper in his pant pocket and decided to give the boots to Amos, who could repair and sell them.

The sun was now high in the sky and Webster was preparing to leave, but he heard the sound of horses' hooves coming in his direction. Afraid it might be Elliott coming after him, he quickly drove his wagon deep into the thicket of trees where it couldn't be seen.

After the riders had passed through the woods, Webster jumped off the wagon and ran through the thicket and out of the woods, trying to see the direction the riders had gone. If they were going toward Smyrna, he'd have to find another way to get there.

He sneaked up the grassy hill, keeping close to the thicket and hoping to get a better view. At the top of the hill, he looked toward the bluffs and saw a cloud of dust; he believed the riders were gone. What he didn't see was a horseman relieving himself on the hillside.

When the man spotted Webster, he jerked up his pants, and holding onto them with one hand, the man came running toward him. Webster couldn't get back to his wagon, so he leaped off into the briar patch hoping to hide.

"I'm gonna fix your ass this time!" a voice yelled as Webster crouched in the briars. He recognized that voice. It was the same burly man who had tossed him into some briars on his first trip to Elliott's farm.

When several bullets whizzed over his head, Webster fell to his knees and began crawling through the tangled vines, grasses, and blackberry briars.

On hands and knees Webster crawled deeper and deeper into the briar patch as the sounds of gunshots continued to ring out. He could hear loud shouting and cursing. If that man wanted him, he'd have to crawl in and get him.

After awhile, the shouting and cursing stopped, and Webster thought the man had given up and left. But then he smelled smoke. Webster rose up to his knees and looked back toward the road. A trail of black smoke twirled skyward. The man had set the briar patch afire. He meant to burn Webster out.

Webster knew he couldn't get back to the road, and he had to get out of that briar patch. The vines and grasses were bone dry, and soon the briar patch would become an inferno. If he could get to one of those caves, he might save himself.

Furiously, Webster crawled through the briars, even as they ripped open his skin and cut his face and hands. Bleeding and coughing, with his shirt and pants in tatters and several long cuts across his back, he came to a small opening in the hillside. With all his might, Webster yanked up a bush that was blocking most of the opening and squeezed his body through.

He lay there for a few minutes in the damp, dank cave, breathing heavily and coughing sporadically. He was completely exhausted. But then Webster smelled a whiff of the smoke inside the cave and knew it was only a matter of time before the smoke would reach him.

The dank cave was dark, and Webster could only see a few feet in front of him. When he tried to stand, he discovered he was taller than the cave. Because his knees were so bruised and painful, he'd never get out of the cave by crawling. He'd have to walk stooped over.

But how was he to find his way in the dark? Webster remembered that one summer when he and Ozell were exploring inside a cave up in Indian Woods, they became lost, but found their way out of the dark cave by running their hands along the cave's wall as they walked until they found an opening to the outside. He'd try that.

With his hands rubbing against the slimy cave's wall, and shoulders stooped to keep his head from banging into the cave's roof, Webster sloughed through some rainwater that had collected in the dark cave. He trudged on, losing track of the time. The only thing he knew for certain was he had escaped the smoke.

When he felt he no longer could walk and believed he'd surely die in that cave, Webster saw a glimmer of light in the distance. Half-falling and stumbling, he went toward the light.

After what seemed like an eternity to Webster, he finally broke out of the darkness into the bright sunshine. Bruised and battered with torn flesh, he flung himself down on the ground in the woods, and in a few minutes he was fast asleep.

When at last Webster woke up, he just laid there looking up at the puffy white clouds, so glad to be alive. Although Webster was not religious, he believed it was a miracle that he had gotten out of that cave.

Finally, Webster went looking for the horses and had not gone far when he saw the wagon leaning precariously on the bank of a small creek. The horses had pulled it there and had gotten tangled up in the reins that had wrapped around the oak. Luckily, this had kept the wagon from over-turning and the horses from injury. Another miracle, Webster thought.

With great haste, Webster untangled the horses and led them up the hillside and out of the thicket to the road. All the time he was doing this, Webster reminded himself that he'd taken a terrible beating for five dollars.

Raine

September was a busy time for the farmers in the Nebo Valley. It was harvest time, and few farmers came to Smyrna to buy goods because they were busy bringing in their crops. Whenever they needed supplies, Caleb had Webster deliver them. Webster was now working long hours, and by the time he came home at night, Bessie and Enoch were asleep.

September was also the month that school opened in Smyrna. This time, the town was abuzz with talk about one of the new teachers Amanda Spriggs had hired to teach the fourth grade. She was Miss Raine Parker, from Rutherfordton, a small town north of Smyrna near the Virginia state line.

"She's a real looker," Bessie told Webster the night she had waited up for him.

"I've seen pretty women before," Webster said, pretending to be uninterested in the teacher. What he didn't tell Bessie was that Amos had already told him about Raine Parker two days before.

"Oh, she speak so proper," Bessie went on excitedly as she sat at the kitchen table in her nightgown.

"How you know how she speaks?" Webster asked, and went over to the stove with a bowl and spoon, taking the lid off a pot that set on the back of the stove. He filled the bowl with black-eyed peas, came to the table, and sat down across from his mother and began eating.

Bessie explained, "Tessa and me knowed the school needed hands to help with the openin', so we went up yesterday to help out. And Amanda let us meet her."

Webster chortled. "You and Tessa didn't go to the school to volunteer your time. You went trying to meet that teacher."

Bessie smacked him playfully on his hand. "You shet up!"

"And you just happened to tell her you had a son," Webster said accusingly.

Bessie smiled. "Yeah, I did."

Webster quickly finished the bowl of peas and went to get some more. Bessie waited for him to ask her some questions about the teacher, but he didn't. When he came back to the table, she asked, "Ain't you eat your dinner?"

"Sure," Webster replied.

"Then how come you eatin' two bowls of peas for supper?"

"Ma," Webster said, "I work long hours. A man has to keep up his strength."

"Ole Caleb be workin' you lack a mule," Bessie snapped. "I'll be glad when you quit that ole job!"

Webster then jokingly said, "I guess I'll have to buy me a piece of land, put some sharecroppers on it, and make a pile of money! Then I won't have to work for Caleb."

"Don't talk silly," Bessie replied. "I ain't stayed up this late to hear silly talk."

"So, talking about Miss Raine Parker isn't silly?" Webster replied.

"No, it ain't," Bessie answered and leaned across the table. "What you need to do is to git to know her. Go up to the school and meet her. She be sech a fine woman."

"So, you think I ought to try and court her," Webster said.

Anxiously, Bessie replied, "You should git to her 'fore other mens in Smyrna do." She paused. "The mens goin' be standin' in line."

"She might not want me," Webster teased. "I ain't got much schooling."

Bessie stood up from the table and shook a finger at him. "Webster Epps, you is the best-lookin' man in Smyrna. And you is real smart! Any woman turn you down is a fool!" Upon saying that, she stormed out of the kitchen, went to her bedroom, and slammed the door.

Webster chuckled to himself. This Raine Parker had made quite an impression on his mother to have her get this upset. But he wasn't looking for a woman to court. He was having too much fun not being committed.

Two days after Webster and Bessie had talked about Raine Parker, he met her, quite by accident. Webster had the day off and was on his way to visit Ozell. When he was passing the church, Raine came out the side door carrying an armful of hymnals. When she tried to close the door, all the books fell to the ground. Webster saw what had happened and went to help.

As he gathered up the books for the petite, brown-skinned woman with curly, black hair, he remarked, "These books are too heavy for you, Miss. I'll carry them for you."

"I do not take offers from strangers," she replied. "So, if you will give them to me, I'll be on my way."

Holding onto the books, Webster said, "I'm Webster. Webster Epps."

Unimpressed, she said, "I see."

"You must be Raine Parker, the new teacher."

"And how would you know my name and what I do?" she questioned Webster in an affected voice.

"I know everybody in Smyrna," Webster said, and to drive home his point, he added, "I grew up here."

"I am Miss Parker," the woman replied. "Now, I'll have my books."

Webster placed them into her waiting arms, and she then sauntered off up the hill toward the Teachery, the house where the teachers boarded.

Webster watched her go. He didn't like the way she acted, all stuck up and putting on airs. Did she think he wasn't good enough to carry her books? Well, the hell with her!

Webster went off to find Ozell. His mother had told him that Tessa and Nate were worried about their son. He had taken to drinking and was sneaking off to Mush Creek, a place of outcasts, derelicts, thieves, and red-light houses. There, Ozell could get bootlegged whiskey with no questions asked.

Sadie's Saloon had moved to Mush Creek after the women in Smyrna closed her down. She had now opened another house of ill repute.

Webster was nearing Ozell's house when he saw Tessa in her garden digging some white potatoes. He went to help. Webster liked Tessa and her husband Nate. They were really good friends to his mother and him.

"Webster," Tessa said as they dug the small white potatoes from under the potato plants, "I want you to talk to Ozell. He's gettin' just like your pa, Enoch."

"So, he drinking too much and whoring around," Webster remarked.

"You got that right," Tessa agreed with Webster. "Evertime he gits his hands on a piece of money, he be off to Mush Creek." She wagged a finger at Webster. "And you know the kind of lowdown folks who live in Mush Creek. He be hangin' 'round the drankin' places and them whores!"

"I thought Ozell was working over in Cowpens," Webster said.

"He lost that job!" Tessa replied. "He thank I don't know." She paused. "He lost that job 'cause he can't make time in the mornin'. He be too tired. Folks ain't goin' pay you good wages if you ain't able to do the work! Now, I wants you to talk to him."

"Ozell knows how to take care of himself," Webster said. "He doesn't need me to tell him what to do."

Tessa pleaded with Webster. "I be beggin' you to talk to him! I can't sleep at nights 'cause I be so scared they goin' be brangin' him home one of these nights dead!"

When Webster saw the fear in Tessa's eyes, he remarked, "Why don't Nate talk to him? Ozell and his pa always got along, not like me and Enoch."

"Webster, Nate done talked to Ozell 'til he be blue in the face!" was Tessa's response. "So, he jest give up on him!"

After Tessa had filled her basket, she and Webster walked to the house. "Go on in the bedroom and give him a talkin'," Tessa said, and opened the door to Ozell's bedroom.

Webster really didn't want to counsel his friend. He knew how unresponsive Ozell was to advice and remembered vividly how he had begged Ozell not to quit school, but was told to stay out of his business.

So, with some trepidation, Webster went into the room and over to the bed. "When you going to get your butt up out of this bed?" Webster said jokingly as he shook the sleepy Ozell's shoulders. "The sun's been up for hours."

Slowly, a red-eyed Ozell yawned, stretched, then sat up in bed. "Oh, it's you, Webster."

"Yeah, it's me. You expecting someone else?" Webster replied.

"I thought you were Ma," he yawned again. "She's been on me for days." Ozell stretched again.

"For drinking?" Webster asked.

"Yep, and I lost my job." He yawned widely this time. "I guess I've got to get me another job just to keep Ma from fussin' at me."

The room needed an airing, so Webster went over, opened a window, pulled up a chair, and sat down. "Your ma's only fussing at you because she's real worried about your drinking."

Ozell frowned. "I kin handle my likker. I drank 'cause it makes me feel good, and I ain't wantin' no advice!" He glared at Webster. "I'm a man!" He paused for his words to sink in because he sensed his mother had sent Webster to try and interfere in his life. Ozell liked Webster because they had been boyhood friends, but now that they were older, they had drifted apart.

Ozell got up from the bed and stood stretching his arms. "I guess Caleb keep your nose to the grindstone that you ain't had time to find out what's goin' on in Smyrna."

"Yeah, he keeps me busy. But I don't aim to work for Caleb much longer. I've got bigger fish to fry."

Both Webster and Ozell laughed. Then Ozell asked, "Have you met Miss Raine Parker?"

"Yeah. I ran into her this morning," Webster answered.

Ozell grinned slyly, "And what did you think of Miss Raine Parker?"

"I think she's stuck on herself," Webster replied disdainfully. "She's got her nose in the air like she's smelling something. You know what I think, Ozell. I think that little gal thinks she's better than the folks in Smyrna."

Ozell pulled his trousers off the foot of his bed and slipped into them. Then he yanked his shirt off the bedpost and put it on. "Miss Raine Parker IS better than the folks in Smyrna," he announced.

"The hell she is!" Webster shot back. "I know women twenty times better looking than her."

"But she's educated, Webster. That puts her in a different stead than the twenty good-lookin' women you know." He winked at Webster. "She's got a cute way of walkin'." Ozell took a few steps, swaying his hips from side to side to mimic the way Raine walked. "You know somethin'; she can have any man she wants. Any man in Smyrna worth his salt will be willin' to set her up! You too, Webster Epps!"

"Like hell I will," Webster replied, vigorously denying Ozell's statement. "Say, ain't you going to get in the tub?"

"Tub?" Ozell asked as he laced up his shoes. "What tub you talkin' 'bout?"

"The one with the water and soap in it," Webster said. "You stink."

"Ain't got time," Ozell said. "I've got to get out of here and go look for a job."

The two left the house without telling Tessa, who was busy in her kitchen. They slipped out the front door, down the steps, and headed for the center of town. Ozell told Webster that he was going to Mush Creek.

"To get drunk?" Webster quizzed. "Look, Ozell, Mush Creek ain't no place to be hanging around. That place is nothing but trouble."

"I ain't goin' to Mush Creek to get drunk," Ozell snapped. "I'm going to look for that guy who's tryin' to sell his land. I might buy it after I save some money."

"You going to buy land in Mush Creek? Ozell, you're talking foolish!"

"No," Ozell retorted. "You see, I met this black Indian last week when I was in a drinkin' joint, and he told me he had some land for sale. He didn't say where the land was. Hey, I gotta go."

Ozell ran off in the direction of Mush Creek and Webster went home. His mother was mending socks on the porch in the swing. Webster came and sat down beside her.

"I met the famous Miss Raine Parker," he told his mother.

Bessie's eyes lit up. "Now, ain't she the prittist and nicest little thing you ever did meet?"

"Nope. She looks fair and she's stuck up," Webster replied.

Bessie gave Webster a kick on his leg and he winced. "Oh, she ain't stuck up! She be proper like educated folks act!" was Bessie's reply to Webster.

Rubbing his leg, Webster said, "Amanda doesn't act that way. She's educated."

"Amanda be white," Bessie replied. "White educated folks and black educated folks don't act the same way."

Before Webster could challenge her, she went on. "Miss Raine's grandpa started a college for black wimmin up in Wilkesboro. Her pa is now in charge of that college, and her ma is a teacher there."

"So, that makes it right for her to look down her nose at us fools in Smyrna?"

"Webster, quit judgin' Miss Raine. You know what the Bible say, 'Judge not, less you be judged,'" Bessie warned.

Bessie was silent for a few minutes as she and her son rocked together in the swing. Sitting with Webster was always a pleasure. She stopped the rocking with her feet. "Now, Webster," she said. " I want you to come to church with me on Sundays so you kin git to know Miss Raine." She smiled broadly as she looked at Webster. "You know, she always wear white gloves to church, and she only takes them off when she be playin' the piano for the sangin'."

Puzzled, Webster asked, "Why is she playing the piano for the singing? Don't the gospel choir raise the hymns?"

"Yeah, they still do that. But Miss Raine done got a junior sangin' group goin' and them youn' folks sang with piano music! Oh, Miss Raine plays that piano and it be lack bein' in heav'n! Ever'body in Smyrna is talkin' 'bout it!" Bessie closed her eyes and looked up toward the sky.

"They don't have pianos in heaven," Webster teased.

"Stop bein' so sassy," Bessie said. "Now, I wants you to come with me to church this Sunday."

"Why?" Webster inquired.

"To serve the Lord," was Bessie's reply.

"Is that all?" Webster probed.

Bessie continued her mending for a few minutes, then confessed. "Miss Raine told me this morning that she wants you to join her sangin' group lack the other youn' folks in the church."

"That's it!" Webster said, and jumped up from the swing. "You just tell your Miss Raine that Webster Epps ain't going to sing for her!"

"Set down," Bessie commanded and waited for him to sit. "I ain't finish talkin' to you. Where did you go?"

"Go?" Webster replied, confused at what his mother was asking.

"Yeah, go! I see'd Miss Raine when I wuz comin' from Caleb's and she told me she done talk to you early this mornin', so when I gits home you ain't here."

"I went to see Ozell."

"I bet Tessa be whinin' 'bout his drankin' to you."

Webster nodded. He really didn't want to talk about his friend to his mother. So, he tried to talk about something else. "Where's Enoch?"

But Bessie wasn't having it. She meant to counsel Webster about keeping company with the wrong people.

"Now, you listen to me, son," Bessie began. "I ain't wantin' you hangin' round with low-lifes. I loves Tessa lack a sister and Nate lack a brother, and I know what they be going through with Ozell. But I won't have my son goin' to the dogs! And that be where Ozell is headin'. You lay down with dogs, you git up with fleas. You fool 'round with Ozell, he pull you down. Leave him be!"

Webster thought for a moment and said, "So, you want me to give up my best friend?"

"Honey," Bessie pleaded, "there ain't nothin' wrong with bein' with the best folks, 'cause you be good folks." She leaned over and kissed Webster on his cheek.

All that next day, Webster thought about his mother's warning and whether or not he was going to do what she wanted. He decided that a friend was a friend and you didn't turn tail and run when they were in trouble. He wouldn't desert Ozell. He'd stand firm on his friendship.

A few weeks later when Webster came home from work one Saturday evening, he found his mother in the kitchen preparing Sunday's dinner. Bessie often cooked the dinner on Saturdays when she had planned to spend all day Sunday at church. As she went about preparing her food, she told Webster that Ozell had joined Miss Raine's singing group. "If you had any sense in your big head, you'd be sangin' too!" She then set her big iron skillet on the iron stove and dropped in a chunk of lard.

"I see we going to have fried chicken again for Sunday dinner," Webster said.

"Never you mind 'bout Sunday dinner," Bessie retorted. "You eatin', ain't you?"

"Don't make no difference to me," Webster said. "I love chicken."

Bessie floured her cut-up chicken and put the parts into the hot grease and covered the pan with a tin lid. "You ain't been listenin' to me, Webster. I just told you Ozell done join Miss Raine's sangin' group. Now what you think he be up to?"

Webster sat down at the table and stretched out his long legs under it. "I can't say what the ole boy is up too. Ozell is hard to figure out these days."

"Well, I kin figger him out! He be after Miss Raine! And you jest set-tin' 'round lettin' him go after her!" Bessie retorted.

"I don't own Raine Parker. I don't even like her," was Webster's response and he stood up. "You want me to turn over the chicken? It's frying fast."

Bessie became thoroughly annoyed at Webster. Here she was trying to tell him important information and he was worrying about chicken! "I do the cookin' in this house! Now, you set back down at that table and hear me!"

Webster did as she commanded. He knew she was getting upset at his indifference, and the last thing he wanted after a hard day's work was to make his mother angry.

After Bessie had turned over her frying chicken, she came and sat down at the table where Webster waited. "Now, I ain't wantin' to heah no foolishness from you. In the mornin', you be comin' to church with me. I done starched and ironed your white shirt, and Enoch done polished your shoes. All you got to do is git your washin' and jump in your suit."

Webster nearly fell off his chair when he heard that Enoch had polished his shoes, Why, Enoch didn't polish his own shoes. And in a disbelieving voice, the astonished Webster asked, "Enoch? Polished my shoes?"

Bessie gave him a sly look. "Well, it took some doin' but he did."

"What kind of doing?"

"I give him some of my pokeberry wine," Bessie replied. "Before I let him drank it, I slapped the shoe polish in his hand and put the shoes next to him. I say, 'Polish!'"

"And he did?"

"He did. 'Course he ain't knowed what he be doin', but he wanted that pokeberry wine!" Bessie chuckled. "The shoes ain't lookin' they best, but they do for one wearin'," Bessie remarked.

Webster couldn't contain his laughter, and soon he and Bessie were laughing heartily. Webster thought that if his mother had gone to these lengths, he'd have to accommodate her and accompany her to church on Sunday.

At the church that Sunday, Webster was surprised to see so many young men singing in Raine Parker's choir. Seeing his half-sober friend Ozell sitting in the choir trying hard not to fall asleep was truly funny, and it was hard for Webster not to laugh.

Just before the church services ended, Reverend Bates rose and said Miss Raine Parker would sing the closing hymn, "Precious Lord, Take My Hand."

Everyone in the church congregation believed Raine would play the piano and sing. Raine, who was dressed in a delicate pink silk dress and wearing a wide pink straw hat, slowly rose from the piano bench and walked deliberately to the center of the pulpit and stood there silent for a few moments with her eyes cast downward. Then she looked up, breathed deeply, and began singing her solo a cappella.

Webster knew she had pitched her song too low and was singing off-key. But this didn't seem to bother the congregation, because when the services were over, many people went up to her, gave her hugs, and told her how well she had sung.

Webster waited for Bessie outside in the churchyard as she talked and greeted other church members, but after a time he decided to find Ozell. On his way he saw a knot of men following Raine out the church's side door, and there was Ozell among them congratulating Raine on her singing. Webster couldn't believe what he was seeing and hearing! Why were these men, young and old, gawking and fawning and throwing themselves at her? There were lots of pretty girls in Smyrna, much prettier than Raine.

Webster decided not to seek out his friend but instead started to leave, when he heard someone calling, "Mr. Epps, I want a word with you."

He stopped and saw Raine Parker rushing to catch up to him. When she did, she remarked disdainfully, "I just had to get away from all those people."

"Seems like they were admiring your singing," Webster replied as they walked away from her admirers.

"Yes, they were. I'm pleased that they are beginning to appreciate good music." Then she paused, "Why haven't you joined my choir?"

"Don't have time," Webster said nonchalantly.

"Oh, yes, you do draying," she said in a less than admirable tone.

Webster stopped short and looked down at the proud woman with her pouty mouth and upturned nose. "I dray because I want to, and I like what I do."

"Oh, Mr. Epps," Raine replied condescendingly. "There's nothing wrong with working with your hands. It's a quality that is admired the world over."

"And do you admire people who work with their hands?" Webster retorted and waited for her superior answer. If she wanted to match intelligence with him, he was ready for her. But instead of challenging Webster, Raine turned the conversation to something else.

"I've heard that you scored the highest in your graduating class this year and that you were offered a scholarship to The Saints of God Preparatory School in Philadelphia, but you turned it down."

"Who told you that?" Webster asked.

"Miss Spriggs. She said you were so very intelligent. Too bad you didn't take it, because The Saints of God Preparatory School is one of the very best. Why didn't you go?"

"Amanda Spriggs shouldn't be telling my business," Webster replied. "But since you're sticking your nose into my affairs, I'll tell you why I didn't take the scholarship."

Raine stopped walking and smiled up at the tall, handsome Webster. "You don't have to tell me."

"I know that, but I want to," Webster replied. "I'm working and saving my money and when I've saved enough, I'll go to a school of my own choice. I won't be beholden to Amanda Spriggs, nor my father and mother. I'm my own man, and that's the way it's going to be."

Raine smiled and took hold of his hand. "Mr. Epps, would you have supper with me this evening at the Teachery?" With flirting eyes, she added, "There'll just be the two of us."

Webster was taken aback by her forwardness. Wasn't she supposed to be the dainty, high-brow young woman? In his books, young women didn't invite men to their homes when no one was there.

"Not tonight," Webster replied. "My ma and pa are waiting dinner." He hurried off, leaving Raine standing in the middle of the road.

The next time Webster saw Raine was at the church's September picnic. The weather was still hot, so when the food table was set up, Webster got a plate of food, found a shady spot under a nearby tree, and sat down on the grass. Just as he bit into a fried chicken leg, Raine came with her food.

"Mind if I join you?" she asked, standing in front of him.

Because Webster's mouth was full of food, all he could do was nod his head.

Raine took a white handkerchief from her pocketbook and spread it out on the grass, then sat down. "You enjoying the picnic, Webster?"

Between chews, Webster replied, "I always enjoy the picnic."

"So, you only attend church for the picnic?" she said accusingly.

Right off, Raine annoyed Webster. He glared at her and said, "You ask stupid questions." He fully expected her to go away, but she didn't. Instead, she shrugged her shoulders.

Then Webster asked, "Why don't you go and join the women and leave me be?"

"Because I want to know who your parents are," Raine said calmly. "It's obvious that Bessie and Enoch aren't your mother and father."

That did it. She was the most irritating woman Webster had ever met. He put down his plate and snarled, "What the hell is it to you who I am?"

Raine was unfazed by Webster's crude language and continued talking. "Now I know you aren't all black, because of your skin color, eyes, and straight hair. Bessie must have told you where she got you."

Webster grabbed his plate, scrambled up, and stood looking down at Raine, who had begun to eat. "Go to hell, Raine Parker!"

Webster then took his plate of food and went home where he didn't have to be bothered with Raine Parker.

Bessie was in a furious mood when she came home, and the first thing she did was to question Webster on why he'd embarrassed Miss Raine by leaving her alone to eat. Hadn't she taught him better manners than that?

Webster wanted to use his favorite curse words to describe Raine, but he held back. He knew his mother wouldn't tolerate cursing in her presence, so he told her that he felt sick and needed to come home.

Two days later, he saw Raine and she invited him again to visit her at the Teachery. He declined. But Webster's refusals didn't stop Raine from constantly asking him to visit her. Her insistence became so intense that Webster began avoiding her. It was as if he was the only man in Smyrna. Why wouldn't Raine leave him alone? She could get any man in Smyrna.

Webster began to believe that Raine had developed an obsessive attraction for him. He also believed she didn't even like him and that her attraction could be dangerous.

Webster began slipping in and out of Smyrna like a thief just to stay out of her way. He had once thought of talking with Amanda Spriggs about Raine Parker's strange behavior, but changed his mind. He knew Bessie would never forgive him if he did.

It was now late October, and Webster hadn't seen Raine for well over a month. He was feeling free and invigorated because this was his favorite time of the year. October is a time of great beauty in the North Carolina mountains. The air is clear and crisp, and huge white clouds stack up in the blue sky as they lazily float over the forest dotted with colors of green, yellow, orange, and red. Immense flocks of birds of every description gather for their annual fall migration. It is the time of the hunter. This October was the time Webster made his decision.

One Saturday, when Webster returned to the store, he told Caleb that he was quitting his draying job. When Caleb inquired as to why, Webster told him that he needed to move on because he wanted to do something different.

"How you goin' git your schoolin' money?" Amos asked him when he heard the news.

"Oh, I've saved quite a bit," Webster said. "I think I'm going to try to parlay it into more money, and when I do, I'm off to Philadelphia."

"Webster," Amos admonished him. "Stop usin' big words. I ain't knowed what this 'parlay' is."

"It means, Amos, that I take what money I've got and use it to make some more."

"And how you goin' do that?"

"Haven't thought about how, but I will."

"Boy, your head is full of suds," Amos replied. "There ain't but one way you goin' git more money. It be by the sweat of your brow."

Webster laughed. "Amos, there are more ways than one to skin a cat! Now, I better get on home."

That evening Bessie had cooked a big dinner and was waiting at the table for Webster. On the table set a platter that held a big roasted chicken with onion stuffing, a large bowl of green beans, and butter beans. Sweet potatoes were in another bowl, and cornbread cut into small squares was in a large plate. A big chocolate cake was on the sideboard.

Enoch was annoyed because Bessie wouldn't let him eat until Webster had come. The minute he opened the front door, Enoch yelled, "Come on and git to the table, boy!"

"You'll do no such thing," Bessie called back. "Git cleaned up first! We got company!"

"Company?" Webster said and came through to the kitchen. He didn't know what to make of what he saw. There was Enoch, sitting at the table dressed in his worn gray Sunday suit, and Bessie was wearing the yellow dress that Tessa had made her for Easter. And what really stunned Webster was Raine! She was also sitting at the table, dressed in a soft white dress and wearing bright beads around her neck. She smiled sweetly at him.

What is going on here? Webster thought as he stood looking at all the food on the table. Was Raine leaving Smyrna? Why were they sitting there waiting for him? Bessie had never done that before. When she cooked, she ate. One thing for sure, he wasn't going to get dressed up. He wasn't even going to wash his hands. He just plonked down in a chair at the table with a frown on his face.

"Ain't you goin' wash up?" Bessie reminded sweetly.

"Nope. Enoch's hungry and so am I."

"Yeah," Enoch snapped. "My stomick is sinkin' in."

Webster knew his mother wasn't pleased with him, but she didn't start an argument.

She'd let it pass for now, because she wanted to make a good impression on Raine. She had hoped that Raine and Webster would fall in love, and since Webster wasn't making the right moves, it was left up to her.

Bessie often asked Webster why he didn't visit Miss Raine. Webster knew he couldn't tell her he believed Raine to have a dark side. All his mother could see was Raine, the schoolteacher, and she wanted her son to better himself by associating with high-class folks.

267

Raine dominated the dinner conversation. It was as if she couldn't get enough of talking about herself and how important her family was in the town where she was born. She said that her grandfather owned lots of land in Wilkesboro and that he had given a piece of his land and some money for the black women's college that she had attended.

When Bessie tried to enter into the conversation, Raine ignored her and continued talking about her family. This didn't bother Enoch, because he was busy stuffing himself with all that good food. But all Raine's talk about her family wore thin on Webster's nerves.

After the meal, Bessie suggested that Webster walk Raine back to the Teachery. Webster didn't want to go, but his mother kept insisting, saying it was too dark for Raine to walk by herself, so he gave in.

As Webster and Raine were walking toward the Teachery, she abruptly stopped and, to Webster's astonishment, tried to unzip his trousers.

"What the hell are you doing?" Webster cried and jerked her hand away. "You trying to get me to lay you?"

Then without warning, Raine flew into a wild rage, screaming and yelling at him. "How dare you talk nasty to me! You're nothing but trash! No breeding! Uneducated dray boy! I'd never let you put your filthy hands on my body!" Then screaming as loud as she could, Raine ran off into the darkness.

The astonished Webster just stood there in the dark trying to comprehend Raine's strange behavior. Why did she try to unzip his pants? Did she want sex? And if so, why did she become so angry? Why was she constantly putting herself in his way? She's sick in her head, Webster concluded.

The next day Webster went to see Amos and told him about dinner with Raine. "I tell you, Amos, I wanted to haul off and smack her in the mouth. All this blabbing about her educated family."

Amos laughed. "She be gittin' next to you, eh? You lack her?"

"No."

"Why not? She real cute," Amos said.

"Amos, there's something wrong with Raine. I can't put my finger on it, but it's like she's got another person in her skin."

"Sounds lack she ain't wantin' to do what you had in mind," Amos quipped. "Some wimmins be lack that."

"Amos, I didn't have anything in my mind about her. Ma made me walk her home and then she just started unzipping my pants! I asked her what she wanted and she changed into another person! She went wild as if I meant to rape her!"

Webster sat silently for a few minutes, then said, "You know what I've a mind to do, Amos?"

"I hope you ain't thankin' 'bout tellin' folks what Miss Raine did. She be actin' that way 'cause some man musta got to her when she be little," Amos remarked.

"I'm not thinking that," Webster said. "As far as I'm concerned, I hope I never see her again. That gal means to get me into trouble!"

"Now why you thank that?"

"Amos, she's been pestering me ever since I met her. I think she's a little crazy!"

"Well, maybe you look lack the man who hurt her. Maybe she want to git even," Amos said.

"I don't believe that one bit!" Webster replied angrily. "The woman is a man-hater. I've read about her kind in a book I found at Amanda's house when I washed her windows. A woman like that sets her sights on you, and she won't stop until she's gotten you trouble!"

Amos stared at Webster in disbelief. "I ain't never heer'd that 'bout wimmins. Wimmins be nice and warm, all cuddly lack little kittens." He winked at Webster.

"Not this one. She's a wildcat with sharp claws."

"You said you got somethin' in mind. What is it?

"I need to get away from Smyrna and this woman's craziness. I'm going to take off after I look up that man in Mush Creek."

"What man?" Amos asked.

"I told you that I plan to parlay my money," Webster explained. "I'm going to buy this man's land and then sell it for more money."

"Who in Mush Creek sellin' land?" Amos inquired.

"I don't know who he is," Webster said. "Ozell told me about him."

"You can't b'lieve Ozell," Amos told him. "That ole likker done scrambled he brains. 'Sides, Mush Creek ain't no place for you to be goin', Webster. Folks real bad there. They see you with money, your life ain't goin' be worth a plugged nickel."

"Ozell goes there," Webster said.

"Ozell is a fool. God look after fools and babies," Amos paused. "Hey, you 'member that Bean fella?"

"The one who was sending boots back and forth to Elliott?"

"Yeah, that be him. I heer'd he done run off with crazy Manny White!" Amos chuckled. "They jest up and left. Guess ole Elliott ain't needin' no more boots."

Suddenly, Webster remembered the numbers he had seen on the scruffy piece of paper found in the boots, 17-21-9-20. "Amos," he said, "you good at numbers?"

"Enough so that folks can't cheat me. Why you ask?"

"What you make of 17-21-9-20?" Webster asked.

Amos mulled the numbers around in his thoughts for a few minutes, then said, "I can't make nothin' of them. Now, if they wuz the ABCs, I might figger out what they be tellin'."

"That's it!" Webster shouted and startled Amos. "It's a code! Each number stands for a letter in the alphabet."

Webster quickly scribbled down the alphabet and assigned numbers to it and wrote 17=q 21=u 9=i 20=t: Q-U-I-T.

Puzzled, Amos remarked, "Why Bean be sendin' that word to Elliott? Why didn't he just spell out the word? You know somethin'? Bean wuz up to somethin' and it ain't good."

"What did he mean by writing 'quit,' and by using a code?" Webster puzzled. "It doesn't sound important."

"It be important to Bean," Amos put in. "Why else wuz he sendin' it?"

"Didn't you just tell me that Bean and Manny had run off together?" Webster asked.

Amos nodded his head.

"Well, that explains it," Webster said. "Bean must have been part of something secret going on up in the hills, and he sent information back by putting it in the soles of boots. So that's why Elliott was getting all those boots. Guess Bean didn't want to belong any more and quit."

Amos snapped his fingers. "Elliott is runnin' a gang of robbers! I knowed it! I knowed it! Them robbers be who ole Manny wuz talkin' 'bout. He done learnt it from Bean!"

When Amos saw how perplexed Webster looked, he explained. "I done went to Reverend Bates and told him what Manny told Caleb, the morning when Caleb wouldn't give him credit at the store. Manny said raiders wuz coming and wuz goin' to burn down Smyrna!"

Then with a satisfied look, Amos said, "Reverend Bates done got the mens in Smyrna ready if them ole robbers come messin' with us!"

Skelly Moonstar

Webster found Ozell at home, alone in bed, sleeping off yet another drunken binge. He was in a haze of booze and needed black coffee, so Webster went to the kitchen to make a pot of coffee for him.

Webster knew where Tessa kept her coffee because he'd seen her make it many times. First, he made a fire in the stove. When the stove was hot, he threw some coffee into a coffeepot and filled it with water. It didn't take long for the coffee to boil.

With a steaming cup of strong coffee, he returned to the bedroom. "Ozell," he commanded, "sit up and drink this."

Slowly Ozell opened his bloodshot eyes and looked up at Webster. "I thought you was Ma."

He reached for the cup, but his hands were shaking so badly that Webster had to hold onto the cup to keep the coffee from spilling.

It took Ozell some time to drink the coffee, and during this time Webster observed his condition. "You've got to stop hitting the bottle so much," he told Ozell. "You're getting the shakes!"

Ozell grunted as he massaged the temples of his aching head. "Yeah, I guess you be right. I'm goin' quit drankin'."

"When?"

"Soon as I git a chance." Ozell replied, yawning and stretching his arms. "Don't you go gittin' on me too," he told Webster. "I hear enough fussin' from Ma and Pa. Git me another cup of that coffee."

When Webster brought him the second cup of coffee, Ozell gulped it down, burped, and yawned again. "Come on, let's set in the parlor," he said to Webster. "I got to git outta this room or I might go back to sleep."

The two went into Tessa's shabby parlor. Bessie always said her friend was a rotten housekeeper, and she couldn't understand how Tessa could keep Mrs. Pettigrew's house so nice and clean and her own house was such a mess.

In the dark, musty parlor, Webster threw a few dirty shirts off a chair near a window, and kicked a clump of old shoes out of his way and sat down. Ozell flopped down in another chair where the stuffing inside the chair cushion was oozing out.

"Tell me about the man in Mush Creek who's selling land," Webster said.

"Well, he say he got land, but I ain't see'd it," Ozell replied. "All I know is he been askin' folks in Roy's Saloon down in Mush Creek if they want to buy his land."

"What kind of looking fella is he?" Webster asked.

"Ugly!" Ozell chortled. "Say, you ain't aimin' on takin' him up on his offer?"

"I might."

"You got money?" an anxious Ozell inquired.

Webster knew he'd have to be careful about telling him how much money he'd saved, because Ozell always needed money, so he replied, "A little, and I aim to make it work for me."

"How you going to do that?" Ozell inquired.

Webster then laid out his plan. "If I buy land cheaply and clear it, I'll sell it for more than I paid for it. Then I can buy a lot more land and sell that for more than what I paid for it too. It's called doubling your money."

"Well, ain't that somethin'," Ozell remarked. "You always was smart, old friend. With all that money you plan on making, you'll be a big man on a pole!"

Denying that he wanted to be big man on a pole, Webster revealed what he wanted to do. "All I want is to get enough money so I can go to All Saints Preparatory School in Philadelphia."

"I heer'd you turned down help," Ozell remarked.

"I did. Didn't want to be beholden to folks."

Ozell grinned slyly, "Yep, you did the right thing. Just think, if you'd gone away you wouldn't have met Miss Raine Parker!" He wagged a finger at Webster. "Now don't tell me that you don't like her."

"I don't," Webster said.

Ozell was suspicious of Webster's answer. All the men in Smyrna liked Raine and wanted her for their very own. Why wouldn't Webster?

"I don't like her," Webster said emphatically again. "So, let's just leave it at that." He chose not to tell him why he didn't like Raine. Anyway, Ozell wouldn't believe him because he was so smitten with her.

"If I buy this man's land and it needs clearing, will you help me?" Webster asked Ozell.

"You goin' pay me?"

"Sure."

"Let's git to Mush Creek," Ozell replied. "My pockets be empty."

"Not now, I first got to see if I can buy the land," Webster said. "And you must promise that, if I do buy it, you've got to keep your mouth shut. I don't want you telling your ma, and then she'll tell my ma. This deal is between you and me."

"I hear you," Ozell agreed, and reached over and clasped Webster's hand, and shook it hard.

At first light the next morning, Webster began the three-mile walk to Mush Creek. He left Ozell at home because he wanted to make his deal alone.

As Webster walked in the early morning, he remembered the time when he and Ozell were boys and had sneaked into Mush Creek to explore, when they were accosted by two burly men, and how it took all their wits and skills of evasion to elude them. After that experience, Webster never went there again. The place held no appeal for him.

Webster walked along a well-defined path from Smyrna to Mush Creek. The path first led through the bushes along the riverbank and then into a grove of scrub oaks and pines, and then the path terminated at the edge of the settlement.

Where the path ended, Webster could see a cluster of ugly, drab buildings that had long been abandoned by some early settlers who had left them there to decay. These settlers were the same people who had settled the town of Cowpens. Now, these old buildings were occupied by outcasts: thieves, alcoholics, prostitutes, derelicts, men hiding from the law, people hiding from their families, and all kinds of lowlifes.

Webster walked toward the buildings and soon came upon a grizzled old man sleeping on a pile of rags up against an old building where some faded letters spelled out Feed and Grain Store. Webster cleared his throat to awaken the man. The old man's eyes flew open and glared up at Webster, who asked him which way to the saloon.

"Saloon?" the man repeated. And closed his eyes again.

It was useless to ask the man again, so Webster walked through some tall weeds until he came to a ramshackle building that had Roy's Saloon painted in big, black, bold letters on a dirty windowpane.

This must be the place, Webster thought, and entered the dim, dank saloon that smelled musty. The rickety floor made a crunching sound as Webster walked over to the counter and sat down on a shaky barstool that felt as if it were going to give way. On another nearby barstool was an inebriated man leaning over his shot of whiskey as two yellowed, sticky flypapers covered with trapped flies hung from the blackened ceiling. The flypapers turned slowly round and around, making scratching sounds as they went. These sounds didn't awaken the man on the barstool, who was lost in a haze of booze.

In a few minutes, a narrow-faced man with dirty blonde hair and a skimpy blonde mustache came from a backroom to the counter. He was wearing a stained white apron over tight woolen trousers. His shirtsleeves were rolled up to his elbows, and the white cotton shirt was unbuttoned at his neck, revealing a sparse bit of chest hair.

The man came and stood behind the counter in front of Webster.

"Are you Roy?" Webster asked him.

The man puckered his thin lips and replied, "I am."

Not wanting to be too forward by inquiring first about land for sale, Webster told the man that he came in to get something to eat.

Roy raised a hand and counted off on his fingers, "I can give you hot grits, some fried sausage balls, and a couple of scrambled eggs."

When Webster told him he'd like that, the man quickly left the counter and went through a small door in the back of the saloon.

Soon, Webster smelled frying sausage, and after a few minutes Roy came back with some grits on a plate with two sausage balls and two scrambled eggs.

"That's going to cost you twenty-five cents," Roy remarked sweetly as he set the plate in front of Webster.

Webster tossed a quarter on the counter and Roy quickly picked it up and put it in his cash register.

Webster took one look at the lumpy grits, runny eggs, and burnt sausages and instead of eating started a conversation with Roy. "Any land around here for sale?"

"You plan on settling down here?" Roy asked inquisitively.

Unperturbed by the man's prying, Webster answered, "Maybe."

Roy leaned across the counter and lowered his voice. "It's not the best-looking place around here, but what I like about Mush Creek is people don't stick their noses into your business like they do in other places." He smiled at Webster. "It's live and let live!"

"Sounds like a good place to live," Webster said, trying to sound sincere. "But first, I've got to get me a piece of land."

"Money's burning a hole in your pocket," Roy joked, and a sly smile curled up at the corners of his mouth.

"The sooner I get me some land, the sooner I can settle in," was Webster's reply.

Roy rubbed his pointed chin as if he were trying to remember something. "Now let me see. Oh yes, I did overhear Skelly Moonstar saying in here just the other day that he wanted to get rid of some land."

"Skelly Moonstar?

Roy smiled. "Sounds queer for a name?"

"It tells him who he is," Webster replied.

Roy shrugged.

Just then, the man on the barstool struggled up, put on an old dusty, black felt hat, and staggered out of the saloon.

After the man had gone, Webster asked Roy where could he find this Skelly Moonstar.

Roy replied uncertainly, "Don't rightly know where he's now." Then he quickly added, "but he comes in here every morning, downs a couple of locust beers and several shots of whiskey. Then he leaves."

"So, he's a drinking man," Webster remarked.

"No more than most men in Mush Creek." Roy leaned over the counter closer to Webster. "Why don't you come back here tomorrow morning? I'm sure Skelly will be here."

When Webster hesitated, Roy made him an offer. "You can spend the night here with me. I often take in strangers, and my place is just over the saloon."

Webster turned him down. He knew what Roy meant, and sleeping with a man had no appeal for him whatsoever.

Although Webster could have easily walked back to Smyrna, he decided not to. He didn't want to go home until he'd concluded his business. He'd just wait around until tomorrow, but not in Mush Creek. So, he went down to the riverbank and crawled under some dense bushes that concealed him. In the quiet coolness of the bushes, Webster fell asleep.

When he awoke it was morning, so he stripped off his clothes and dove naked into the river. The water was brisk and he didn't tarry too long in it. With a handkerchief he carried in his pants pocket, he wiped off as much water as he could, then put on his trousers and shirt and headed to the saloon.

Roy was working behind the counter and saw Webster come into the saloon. He nodded his head in the direction of the back. There, sitting at a battered old table, drinking a glass of locust beer, was a grimy-looking, dark skinned man. His ragged shirt was held together with one button and the rest of the shirt fell open to his waist, revealing clumps of straggly hair on his thin chest.

When Webster approached him, the milky-eyed man raised his glass to Webster. "My breakfast," he said, smiling a snaggle-toothed grin.

"You Skelly Moonstar?" Webster asked.

"Yep. That's me." He motioned for Webster to sit down.

Webster pulled out a chair from under the table and sat down. "I hear you have land for sale."

"Got twenty acres."

"Where?"

"'Bout a couple of miles from here. Up near Indian Woods," Skelly told him and took a big swallow of the beer. "Why? You lookin' to buy?"

"If the price is right," Webster said. "But first, I've got to see it."

Skelly finished his beer, wiped his mouth on his shirtsleeve, and stood up.

Webster saw that Skelly was in need of a good meal. His baggy pants were held up by a piece of greasy rope tied around his thin body. No wonder he wanted to sell his land.

"I got my mule out back," Skelly said. "We can ride out to see the land."

Webster followed him out the back door of the saloon into a dirty alley strewn with all kinds of garbage; rusty cans, old busted buggy tires, and a sea of ragweed. A tired old horse hitched to a spindly tree waited patiently.

"We ride double," Skelly informed Webster.

"I'm not sure that mule can carry both of us," Webster replied.

"Old Turtle is real strong," Skelly remarked and climbed up onto the mule's back. "Climb up."

Up on the mule's back, Webster felt its backbone pressing into his buttocks as the two set off. Webster felt compassion for the mule carrying him and Skelly, but was happy Old Turtle was carrying him away from that stinking alley.

Between the swarms of green flies and the awful stench of rotting vegetables and food, Webster had begun to feel sick. No wonder the people in Smyrna called this place Mush Creek, he thought.

The old mule lived up to his name, plodding along on a rutted, bumpy dirt road until they came to a panoramic view of the valley that extended up to Indian Woods and the Bushy Mountains beyond.

"Whoa," Skelly said and the mule stopped. The men climbed off the poor beast and Skelly walked over to the road's edge.

"You see that strip of land over yonder?" He said to Webster, pointing toward some woods on a hillside.

Webster said he saw some land that was dotted with small bushes and vines.

"That's it," Skelly remarked.

From where Webster was standing, he could see the red bluffs where he'd gone to deliver Elliott's boots and the old rusting trestle that spanned the Nebo out to the old asylum. He could also see the train tracks that curved around the bluffs and most of Fort Belton that was setting high on a hilltop.

"Pretty land," Webster remarked.

"Yep," Skelly replied nonchalantly.

"How much is yours?"

"'Bout twenty acres," Skelly said, then he explained. "Startin' where you see the river and runnin' up the hill to the woods."

"How'd you come by it?" Webster asked.

"Indians," Skelly said.

"Why did the Indians sell you their land?"

Skelly didn't answer Webster. He just said, "I'm Indian."

Looking at the dark-skinned man, Webster remarked skeptically. "You? An Indian?"

"Black Indian," Skelly replied. As if to make his point, he pointed toward Indian Woods. "I live up there."

Webster wasn't sure whether to believe him or to disbelieve him. True, Skelly had a headful of silky black hair, and Webster had heard of black Indians. Why should he doubt him? He, too, was part Indian.

Standing there, looking out at the view, Webster repeated, "So . . . the Peedees gave you this land."

Skelly shrugged. "Indians got plenty."

"Why you want to sell it?" Webster questioned.

"Don't want to work it."

Webster saw that the land was covered with bushes, vines, and brambles. And looking at Skelly, Webster knew, the man didn't have the strength to clear that land so it could be worked. "How much you asking for it?"

"Two dollars an acre."

"Too much," Webster remarked. "I can buy cleared land for that price."

"It'll be real good for corn growin' . . . ," Skelly answered.

"If it's cleared," Webster remarked.

Skelly wandered over to a nearby sapling, broke off a twig, stuck it in his mouth, and thought for a moment. "Well, seein' you is young and needin' a foothole, I'll knock down my price to a dollar an acre. But that's as low as I'm goin' to go."

Webster pretended he was thinking it over. He wandered over to the same sapling, broke off a twig, and stuck it in his mouth. He knew that the land was worth far more, and he'd make a good profit because he was going to get Ozell to help him clear the land. Then he'd sell it for three dollars an acre, triple the price he'd paid for it.

"Let's go back to Mush Creek and talk business," Webster finally told Skelly.

It took well over an hour for Turtle to get the men back to the saloon. Since Webster wanted to do his business and get away from that stinking place, the two quickly went to the same table where they had sat that morning and Webster counted out twenty dollars.

Before Webster put the money in Skelly's hand, he wrote on a scrap of paper the amount of money he'd paid Skelly, and the date that Skelly had sold him the twenty acres of land north of Mush Creek between the river and up to Indian Woods.

"Sign this," Webster told Skelly and handed the scrap of paper to him.

Without reading the paper and in big bold letters, Skelly printed his name, SKELLY MOONSTAR and gave the paper back to Webster, who then gave him the twenty dollars.

"Guess you be a landowner," Skelly said, stuffing the dollar bills into his pocket and flashing his snaggle-toothed grin at Webster. "This deal calls for a drink! Hey Roy," he yelled, "brang us two locust beers!"

Roy quickly came with two glasses of beer and set them on the table. Skelly grabbed up one glass and took a huge swallow. "I just sold my land!" And he winked at Roy.

"The drinks are on me," Roy told Webster. "It's not every day a man comes in here and becomes a landowner."

"I don't drink," Webster replied as he folded the piece of paper and put it in his pocket.

Skelly reached over and took the other glass of beer that was meant for Webster. "Can't let this go to waste."

Webster didn't engage in any conversation but quickly left the saloon and walked the three miles back to Smyrna. Before going to his home, he stopped at Ozell's house and told him to be ready to go with him the next morning to help clear his land.

The next morning, Ozell and Webster left at dawn with two axes, two shovels, and a box of matches. By the time they had walked the three miles to the land, the sun was rising from behind the mountains.

The morning sky at sunrise at the foot of Indian Woods was overwhelming for Webster, especially so because he now owned a piece of land. Not that twenty acres was worth a lot, but he had worked hard for the money he'd paid for it.

At the land Webster and Ozell decided to burn off the underbrush, then dig up the tree stumps after they had been burned. They puzzled over where to start the fire and soon concluded that the best place was on the hillside in the dried grasses and let the fire burn down to the river where it would burn itself out.

Ozell made a fire, and with some coaxing, it began burning the damp grass and soon was sending up heavy, black smoke.

As the two watched the fire burn, they noticed three men coming out of the woods some distance from them. As the men came closer, Webster recognized them to be Indians because he had seen one of the men in Caleb's store. Indian men often came to Caleb's store where they traded and bought supplies. Once, when he was younger, he wanted to talk to them, but Bessie stopped him. When he asked her why, she just repeated he was never to talk to Indians.

The light-skinned men seemed friendly, even though each carried a gun. Perhaps they were going hunting, Webster surmised as he watched them come.

The men walked up close to Webster and Ozell and stood in a semi-circle. Then the oldest man said, "Who set this fire?"

"I did," Webster answered. "I'm clearing my land."

The man frowned at Webster and said, "This is Peedee land."

Upon hearing this, Webster quickly explained. "I bought this land just yesterday." And he pulled out the scrap of paper that Skelly had signed and offered it to the man.

The man refused to look at the paper and repeated, "This is Peedee land."

Looking bewildered from one man to another, Webster remarked, "How can it be Peedee land now? I just told you I bought this land yesterday. All twenty acres from here down to the river. I have a signed piece of paper as proof." He offered the paper again to the man.

Still the older man refused to look at the paper. "Did you buy this land from a Peedee?" The man questioned.

"He didn't say he was a Peedee," Webster said. "All I know is his name is Skelly Moonstar and he's a black Indian who sold this land to me."

"Black Indians don't own land," the man snapped.

Ozell saw that Webster was agitated and was becoming angry, so he tugged at his shirtsleeve and said, "You done bought a pig in a poke! Let's not git into it with these Indians. They got guns! Let's just go."

The man turned to leave but stopped and said, "Stomp out that fire before you leave." And the three men walked away back toward the woods.

Webster knew he'd better obey the Indians' command, because they really hadn't left. They were watching from the woods.

Fuming with anger and cursing loudly, Webster lashed out at Skelly. "Damn you, Skelly Moonstar! You're a bastard and sonofabitch!" He had been swindled. He meant to find Skelly Moonstar and get his money back, then he'd give Skelly something to remember him by.

Because the fire had gotten a good start, Webster and Ozell had quite a time beating the fire out with their shovels. All the time as they worked, they sensed the Indians were keeping an eye on them from a distance.

When at last the fire was out, Webster and Ozell hurried off to Mush Creek to look for Skelly. Ozell was just as eager to find Skelly as was Webster because he knew now he wasn't going to get any money, and Ozell meant to take it out of Skelly's hide.

In Mush Creek, the two went immediately to the saloon.

"Where the hell is Skelly?" Webster yelled to Roy as he came through the door.

With a look of innocence, Roy gave a snippy answer. "How should I know?"

With his fist clenched, jaw set, and seething with anger, Webster shouted again as he menaced Roy. "I asked you where the hell is Skelly?"

Seeing how angry Webster was, and also seeing the angry Ozell standing behind him, Roy meekly asked, "What you want Skelly for?"

Ozell jumped in front of Webster and shouted, "He sold my friend some damn Indians' land, and we aim to get his money back and kick Skelly's ass! So you best tell us where the bastard is!"

The scared Roy quickly responded. "Skelly pulled out of here! Left yesterday!"

Webster then reached across the counter and grabbed hold of Roy's shirt. "Where did he go, bastard?"

Struggling to free himself, Roy answered. "Skelly went back home. Up in Indian Woods. Please, turn me loose!"

Webster loosened his grip on Roy's shirt and punched him. He fell backwards against the wall. Rubbing his hip, Roy whined, "I didn't have anything to do with Skelly's deal! Why you picking on me?" He reached down under the counter, got a bottle of beer, yanked off the cap with his teeth and took a swallow.

Webster was so furious now that he banged his fist down on the counter so hard that the glasses stacked behind the counter rattled.

"You knew what that thieving bastard was doing!" Webster said, glaring at the frightened Roy. "That's why I'm picking on you! I'm going up to Indian Woods and kick his butt! And if I find out you were in cahoots with him, I'm coming back and kick your butt!"

Webster then stormed out of the saloon, leaving Ozell there.

Because Webster was so angry, he didn't go home; instead he went to see Amos at Caleb's store. He found Amos cutting out some leather for a pair of shoes at his workbench.

Webster strode in and without speaking went downstairs to Amos' quarters. He fell across Amos' bed. He was unable to speak because he was so angry at himself for being taken in by Skelly Moonstar. Now, a portion of his hard-earned savings was blown in the wind. How could he have fallen into such a trap? He should have known better, Webster thought.

Amos hurried to his room to see what was the matter with Webster. When he saw him lying on his bed, he knew something was terribly wrong. "What's the matter?" he asked.

At first, Webster was too embarrassed to tell Amos because he had been warned not to go to Mush Creek. Greed had gotten the best of him. But with a lot of prodding from Amos, Webster told him what had happened.

"You ain't the first man to be made a fool and you sho' ain't goin' be the last," Amos told him. "Jest you let this be a lesson to you. You can't trust all folks."

In a determined voice, Webster said, "I'm going after this Skelly! I'll get back my money!"

"Jest let it be," Amos counseled. "Don't you go runnin' up to them mountains, 'cause this Skelly ain't there. I bet he's off somewheres jest drankin' up your money."

"I can't let it be," Webster replied. "What really bothers me is that he's part Indian like me! How could a person do that to his kinfolks?"

Amos grew silent for a few minutes, then said, "Webster, I got to tell you somethin' that been on my mind for a long spell. I been wrestlin' with it and I ain't goin' git no peace lessin' I tell you." He sighed deeply and closed his eyes for a moment. Then he reached for his Bible that he kept on a little table near his bedside. "You got to swear on my Bible that you will never tell your ma and your pa!"

Webster had never seen Amos sound so solemn and look so serious. What was he going to tell him?

"What is it?" he asked.

Amos laid his Bible on his lap. Even though Amos could barely read the Bible, he believed deeply in its word. He once told Webster that all he had to do was touch his Bible and it gave him courage to face any adversity.

"Put your hand on the Bible," he commanded Webster.

When Webster hesitated, not knowing what he was going to swear to, Amos insisted. "If you ain't goin' swear, I ain't goin' tell you."

Because Webster was so anxious to find out what Amos was going to tell him, he put his hand on the Bible.

"Swear 'fore God what you goin' hear, you ain't goin' tell your folks."

Webster complied, "I swore, now what is it? Did you kill somebody?"

"Naw, boy. I ain't that bad," Amos replied and sat down on the bed next to Webster. He cleared his throat several times and began talking. "Your ma ever tell you who your folks is?"

"Ma's never told me," Webster replied, "but I sort of know. I found it out from Ozell because Ma told Tessa and she told Ozell."

"Yeah, you done told me that," Amos replied impatiently.

"I know my mother was an Indian and father was a white man," Webster said.

Amos lowered his voice as if to tell Webster a secret. "You got it all wrong. I b'lieve your pa ain't white."

Webster's body stiffened, and he drew back from Amos. "Run that by me again."

"I b'lieve your pa be black," Amos repeated.

Webster had known a long time that Amos hated the idea that he wasn't black and was always prying information from Enoch to validate his belief. Amos felt this way because he loved Webster as if he were his son. So, he was black and wanted his son to be black also.

Amos continued in a monotone voice. "You be black 'cause your Pa wuz a slave on Au Bignon's plantation."

"A slave?" Webster managed to ask.

"Yeah, a slave, lack I wuz," Amos reaffirmed.

Webster and Amos had talked many times before about who his parents might be, and he'd always made him swear not to tell Bessie. He'd go along with it because he didn't want to hurt Amos' feelings, but he really wished Amos would stop trying to find out who he was. He knew who he was.

"I got it out of Enoch," Amos confessed. "He come in heah one night and wuz a little drunk and he talks 'bout Noah. Now, Noah wuz at Margrace Plantation when me and Enoch wuz there. I didn't git to talk much to him lack Enoch did. He wuz a field hand and I work in the house. Then Noah wuz gone. Guess Au Bignon sold him."

All the time Amos was talking, Webster was only hearing snatches of what he said. His mind was on Skelly Moonstar and what he was going to do when he found him.

Amos hadn't noticed that Webster wasn't listening to him and kept on talking. "Enoch be so drunk he ain't knowed what he tell. He keep on sayin' 'Noah, Ma'grace Ma'grace, Noah.' So, I done figgered out what he be tellin' me. He be tellin' me Noah who lived on Margrace Plantation wuz your pa."

Webster's patience had worn thin. He had come to Amos for solace and understanding, and here he was talking about what Enoch had told him. This was all he could take of Enoch's gossip.

Webster jumped up from the bed and shouted, "Enoch is a damned liar! Why do you listen to him, Amos?"

Amos was taken by surprise at Webster's response to him. So he tried to explain. "Webster, you lack my own son and I wouldn't be telling you this if I thought it be a lie."

"Amos, whoever this Noah is, I hope he's alive and well. I'm not angry with you. It's Enoch! He'd lie about me at the drop of a hat! I know who my folks are."

"Your ma tell you?"

"Not in so many words, but when I told her that Ozell told me I was part Indian, she didn't deny it, just said Ozell had a big mouth!" Webster paused and informed Amos again. "I'm Indian and white. Not black! "

Amos bristled at Webster. "You got somethin' 'ginst black? Ain't Bessie black? Ain't I black? You ain't wantin' to be lack us?"

"Amos, if I had a choice to be like someone, it would be you and Ma. So let's not keep talking about it."

But Amos did talk about it. He told Webster what was on his mind. "You say you be angry' cause that Skelly person be lack you. That jest makes my blood boil! He ain't lack you at all! Now, I ain't got nothin' 'ginst Injuns. They be good folks and bad folks jest lack black folks and white folks. Good and bad come in all colors!"

"I know that, Amos." Webster replied.

"Jest you remember that," Amos snapped.

Tai

Amos' bushy eyebrows had knitted together as he angrily glared at Webster on the morning he came to the store and told him he was going after Skelly. "You got a hard head, boy!" Amos said. "What's it goin' take for me to git through it? Them Indians done told you to stay off-a their land. They'll take your hide off if they ketch you there agin!"

"I'm not going to bother the Indians," Webster retorted. "I'm looking for that Skelly fellow."

"You ain't got no business messin' 'round in them hills! Jest let it be!"

"Amos, I'm not going to let it be," Webster replied emphatically. "So quit telling me to."

"Where you goin' stay up there in them mountains?" Amos asked.

"In the shack."

"It ain't no place for you to be stayin'," Amos fumed.

With his jaw set firmly, Webster retorted, "I'll stay there until I find the bastard!"

Amos had seen Webster's jaw set like this before and knew it was useless for him to try and change his mind. "You told your folks 'bout this?"

"Nope," Webster said. "Ma worries too much. If she comes asking you, don't tell her."

"I'll do no sech thang! I ain't mixin' up in this!" Amos replied. He was now thoroughly annoyed at Webster and frowned deeply at him. "That ole cabin done fell down. You know how long it's been since you and me went there?"

"It's there," Webster replied with confidence and dropped down a gunny sack he was carrying that had some food, an ax, a knife, and a gun inside.

"What you got in the sack?" Amos inquired.

"Stuff I'll need." Webster said. "I'll shoot a couple of rabbits and fish a little."

Looking into the sack, Amos saw the gun and asked, "Ain't that Enoch's gun?"

"Yep."

"You done stole it?"

"No! I'm just borrowing it," Webster responded defensively. "And I want to borrow your mule."

Shaking his head, Amos said, "I ain't so sho' I kin do that. 'Cause I ain't knowed how long you goin' be gone."

When Amos saw the disappointed look on Webster's face, he changed his mind and reluctantly agreed to lend him his mule. "I guess I kin trust you, but I want my mule back heah in two weeks time."

Amos took another look in the gunny sack, then looked up at Webster with fatherly eyes and said, "If you goin' be up in them woods wanderin' 'round you goin' need some viddles." He walked behind the counter and began taking down some staples from the shelves.

On the counter, he laid a slab of salt pork, a small sack of flour, sugar, salt, coffee, and a box of baking soda. From underneath the counter he pulled out a big butcher knife, opened a large, wooden, round box that held sharp cheese and hacked off a hunk, and put the cheese next to the other supplies. Next, he took a box of saltine crackers from the shelf. From a clear jar that sat at the end of the counter, Amos took several handfuls of peppermint candies that were Webster's favorite and dropped the candy into a brown paper bag.

After Amos had collected the supplies, Webster told him he couldn't take the supplies because he couldn't pay for them.

"How you plan on eatin'?" Amos asked.

Sounding pompous, Webster's answer was he'd live off the land.

"Don't talk foolish!" Amos admonished him. "You start stealin' them moun'in folks' stuff, you'll git a butt full of lead! Caleb will put this stuff on my bill."

While Webster stuffed the staples in his sack, Amos went downstairs to his room and came back with an old quilt and a sheet. "It gits cold up in them woods at night," he said, stuffing the quilt and sheet into the sack with the food.

"Benny's out in the shed," Amos informed Webster. "Go on and git him."

Webster gathered up the sack and went out back to the shed where Amos and Caleb kept their horses. He saddled Benny and rode off.

Amos watched him go from the store's porch. In a strange sort of way, he was proud of Webster. The boy's becoming a man, he thought.

First Webster rode north until he came to a patch of woods not far from Smyrna.

There he followed a stream of clear water that flowed down from the hills. Webster believed this was the same stream of water that flowed by the old shack. If he followed the stream, it would lead him to the shack.

Soon, the landscape changed. It became rough and plunged downward to a steep hollow where the vegetation became dense with bushes, vines, and saplings that crawled up the sides of the ravine. The stream of water had become a trickle, and it was too dangerous for the mule to navigate this terrain.

Webster then rode the mule out of the woods and came into a meadow. The meadow stretched away to a purplish outline on the horizon. Those low, rolling hills in the distance was where the cabin was located. Webster and Amos had come this way when they had gone hunting. It only took them an hour to get to the cabin, but with Benny plodding along so slowly it would take Webster twice that long.

When the sun was positioned straight overhead, Webster knew it was noon and he needed to give the mule a rest. He came to a small brook that flowed through a grassy meadow dotted with a few trees. Webster pulled Benny to a stop. This was a good place for the mule to get a drink and eat some grass.

Webster climbed down stiffly off Benny's swayed back. His buttocks were sore from bouncing in the saddle all morning. He untied the gunny sack and slid it and the saddle off the mule's back onto the ground.

"Come on, Benny," he said, and led the mule to the brook. After the mule had finished drinking, he let go of the bridle and Benny quickly began munching on the deep, succulent grass.

Webster walked over to a lone tree that had recently been struck by lightning. Part of the tree's crown was burnt brown. There he flopped down, leaned against the tree's trunk, and closed his eyes to rest.

As he rested, Webster wondered if his real reason for coming to the hills was all about Skelly. After all, it was only twenty dollars. Was it about Raine? Was he trying to escape from her because he was afraid of her? He had had many encounters with women before, but nothing was ever like this. What made Raine's behavior so strange to Webster was that he had told her he didn't like her, and yet she persisted. Lately, he had begun dreaming of falling into an abyss, a deep black pit, and he couldn't get out. Coming up to the hills was like a breath of fresh air for Webster. He felt free and didn't care if he couldn't find Skelly.

After awhile, Webster opened his eyes and sat looking out at a carpet of green grass that ran up to the purplish hills. He thought about the first time he and Amos had come that way. He was just a small, excited boy, eager for adventure in the woods. It seemed like a long time ago.

Webster also remembered that at the start of this trip, he truly believed all Indians were good and kind. This later proved false when a bunch of Indian men, yelling frightfully, chased him and Amos out of the hills. This picture was still vivid in his mind. He'd have to watch his step while looking for Skelly in Indian Woods.

Webster's thoughts were interrupted because he needed to find that old cabin if he didn't want to sleep under the stars, and the very thought of sleeping outdoors had no appeal to him. He hated ants and bugs crawling on him and the feel of the hard, cold ground.

Webster stood up, stretched, went over to the brook, laid down on his belly, and drank. Then he whistled for Benny, who by now had eaten a wide swath of grass in the meadow. When the mule refused to come, Webster went and retrieved the reluctant beast, saddled him, and started out again.

The old mule was being pushed to his limits to reach the hills before nightfall. Slowly, he made his way up, up, into the low hills. When the mule came to where the land gave way to a hollow, Webster stopped him and sat there trying to remember a landmark. That cabin had to be down there, he thought. But everything looked so different. After all, it had been nearly ten years since he'd come there with Amos.

Bushes, brambles, saplings, and tangled vines grew in profusion, and there was no sign of a visible path. What Webster did remember was the cabin was near a creek and an oak tree grew in back of it. Part of the cabin was pushed up against the hillside and it had a big stone chimney.

By now, Webster reasoned, the oak would be towering above all other trees in that vicinity. As he sat in the saddle looking for a big tree, he spotted wisps of spidery smoke making its way skyward in the purple hills to the north. He rose up in his saddle to get a better view and saw a cluster of shacks stuck on a hillside with smoke coming from several of the chimneys. He also saw patches of cultivated land near the shacks. People were living up there, Webster realized. It couldn't be the Peedee because they lived in Indian Woods. Who were these people?

As Webster sat there pondering who the people on the hillside were, he spotted the crown of a giant oak tree down in the hollow. "It's down there," Webster said aloud. He didn't dare try to ride down the steep hill, so he got off the mule and led him down toward the tree.

The bushes and vines slapped at his face relentlessly as Webster picked his way, making sure Benny didn't stumble. As he came closer to the tree, he saw a sea of creeping vines wrapped around a bulky, rectangular shape, with a few visible stones poked out at the top.

"That's the cabin's chimney!" Webster said, and frantically stomped his way through the rough grasses and brambles. It didn't take him long before he'd made a path to the vine-covered cabin, and a few of its logs were discernible.

"The door has to be around here," Webster said aloud and felt along the vines until he found the door's outline. The door was cracked open a tiny bit, and Webster tried to push it open enough so he could get in. It wouldn't budge further, so he ran back a few steps in the weeds, then raced forward, and with a mighty kick he smashed the door open and got inside.

The cabin wasn't in bad shape because it had been built strong and had withstood the elements. The two hand-made beds nailed to the wall on each side of the big fireplace were still intact, as was the wooden table, bench, and chair. They were still where he and Amos had left them on that autumn day when they rushed away.

There was an old burlap sack in the corner near the fireplace. Webster opened it and saw a cooking pot, an iron frying pan, a coffeepot, and an old quilt. He smiled at the sack's contents. This was the same sack he was supposed to carry the day he and Amos ran away from the cabin. In his frightened state, he'd left his sack. Leaving that sack was good fortune for him now. In his haste this morning, he had forgotten to bring cooking utensils.

After Webster had taken Benny to the creek for water, he tied his rope to the bridle and then to a tree. The rope was long enough for Benny to walk around, eat grass, and to lie down. He'd make a pen for him later.

Back at the cabin, Webster set about cleaning it out. When this was done, he went outside and hacked a path through the brambles to the creek so that he could come and go easily.

Although he had cleaned out the fireplace, he didn't use it. He was too tired to cook, and made do with the cold biscuits and a piece of Amos' cheese. To top off his dinner, he ate a handful of the peppermint candy. After he'd eaten, Webster wrapped himself in the quilt Amos had given him and fell asleep on one of the wooden beds.

Early the next morning, Webster began looking for Skelly. He wondered where he might be living. In Indian Woods? Or could he be living with these unknown people on the hillside?

At first, Webster thought of taking Enoch's gun but changed his mind. He didn't need a gun to get his money back from Skelly. His fists could do the job.

Webster followed the creek through a small grove of trees until it flowed out into a small mountain meadow, and to his surprise, several cows were grazing there. On a slight rise above the meadow were eight or ten weathered log cabins clustered together. These were the houses Webster had seen yesterday. Could this be an Indian settlement? If so, he'd have to be careful not to antagonize them.

The only way for Webster to answer his question was to find out who lived in those houses. He slipped through the tall grass until he came to some cowsheds. Beside the cowsheds were a bunch of chicken coops surrounded by a wire fence. Inside the chickens scratched and pecked at some grains of corn spread onto the ground.

Webster knew immediately that this was no Indian settlement. Indians always kept dogs, and no dog had barked to give him away. He decided not to venture any further because it might prove dangerous. What if Skelly was really part of a robber gang that Amos believed operated in the hills, and the robbers lived there?

Webster slipped back through the grass and found a spot near the creek where he was out of sight. If Skelly did live there, he'd show up sooner or later, and he'd have to grab him before he got to that settlement.

Webster stretched out on the ground and waited. From where he lay, he could easily watch the settlement. Webster watched the houses for an hour or two, but because it was so quiet and peaceful in the meadow, he fell asleep in the warm sun. He was later awakened by the sound of a crunching noise, and when he opened his eyes he saw a black and white cow eating her way toward him.

Quickly, Webster sat up to his knees and saw a person leading a brown cow by a rope coming in his direction. He rose up a bit higher trying to get a better look.

Then he saw her. The girl had chocolate-colored skin and jet-black hair that hung to her shoulders. She was wearing a brightly colored dress that clung to her well-proportioned body as she moved with a lyrical gait, leading her cow. Webster was so enthralled at what he saw that he stood up, and the slim girl stopped short. He rubbed his eyes several times, wondering if the girl was real or was he having a good dream? She was by far the most beautiful girl he'd even seen. He gazed at her for a moment, then finally managed to say, "I hope I didn't scare you."

"I wasn't expecting someone hiding in the grass," the girl replied. "You gave me quite a jolt."

Webster didn't reply. He just kept staring at the brown-eyed girl, thinking. Was she Indian? Black? What was she?

Since Webster seemed to have been struck dumb, the girl yanked on her rope and continued on through the meadow.

"You live around here?" Webster called after her.

She pointed toward the houses. "Over there."

Webster ran and caught up to her. "I never knew black people lived up here in the hills," he said.

The girl didn't answer, just kept on walking.

Webster kept pace with her. "All the black people I know around here live in Smyrna and Cowpens."

The girl stopped walking. "You from Cowpens?" she asked.

"No. Smyrna."

"So, what are you doing up here?"

At first, Webster was ready to tell her he was looking for Skelly but held that thought because he wasn't sure if he wanted to tell a stranger about his plan. So he asked, "You wouldn't be Indian, would you?"

"What's it to you?"

"Well . . . ," Webster stammered, "you see . . . I'm part Indian, not full Indian. Only half."

The girl was amused at the way Webster was trying to explain himself. So, she put him at ease. "I'm a black Indian."

Sounding impressed, Webster answered, "Is that so? I've heard that black Indians were in the vicinity, but never knew exactly where they lived."

"We live over there," the girl said and began walking away again with her cow.

"Webster ran after her, "Say, I didn't get your name."

"I didn't tell you."

"My name is Webster, Webster Epps," he blurted out.

"What? No Indian name?" the girl responded.

Webster wasn't sure what the girl meant by saying he had no Indian name. Was she being sarcastic? But the girl explained. "I thought you'd have an Indian name since you've got Indian blood in your veins." She tossed back her hair and observed him for a moment. "I thought, here stands a big strapping, part-Indian man. I bet he's got an Indian name!"

This time, Webster knew she was being sarcastic and he matched her sarcasm, "I bet this black Indian girl with a cow has got an Indian name."

Webster could tell she wasn't pleased, but she did say her name. "It's Tai," and she walked away from him.

This time, Webster didn't try to catch up to her. He just watched her go.

So there really was a settlement of black Indians living up in the hills, and that's where he'd find Skelly, because Skelly said he was a black Indian. But how was he to find Skelly? He just couldn't walk into that settlement and ask for him. He had to find an unobtrusive way to go there.

All morning long, Webster lay in the grass watching the houses, hoping to spot Skelly, but soon his thinking wandered away from Skelly to the beautiful Tai. He'd like to know her better, but what if she was another Raine? Living up in these godforsaken hills could easily warp one's personality. Amos had once told him that the black Indians sucked up to the Peedees because they believed themselves better than the black folks in Smyrna and Cowpens. Perhaps that's why Tai acted so hostile. She thought he was black. His inner voice told him to forget about that girl.

By the late afternoon, Webster hadn't had a glimpse of Skelly, and he had grown hungry and tired. He decided to go back to his cabin and try again the next day.

The next morning, Webster took the cane fishing pole that had been left in the cabin and set out again for the meadow. He didn't want it to appear that he was watching the settlement by lying in the grass, but if he were fishing this might not be obvious.

Carefully, Webster made his way from the shack down to the creek, being cautious not to leave an obvious trail to his cabin because he didn't want Skelly finding out where he was staying. So, the best way for him to go to the meadow was to wade through the creek. By wading in the creek, he wouldn't have to stomp his way through the reeds and leave a trail mark.

Wading in the ice-cold water and slipping from time to time on the slick rocks that lay on the creek's bed was tough going for Webster, and when the water became too deep for him to wade in, he climbed out and walked along its bank.

Webster was glad when the creek flowed out of the dark hollow and into the bright clearing of the meadow. He followed the creek bank to the same place where he had been the day before. There was an opening to the water, so he dropped his fishing line into the reed-choked water and waited. Here, he had a clear view of the houses.

After an hour of watching, Webster glimpsed the girl coming through the meadow leading her cow. Even though he tried to pretend he hadn't seen her, she stopped and came closer to him before letting go of the cow's rope.

"Trying to catch a catfish for my breakfast," Webster said to her.

"You'll probably go hungry," was the girl's reply.

"No catfish in here?" Webster asked.

"No."

"Why so?"

"We've fished them out." Tai responded. Then she saw Webster's fishing line had no hook on it. "But you didn't come here to fish, did you?"

"Now, why would you say that?" Webster answered.

"You need a hook to catch fish, stupid." She then asked, "What is the real reason you're up here in the hills? You're not a black Indian." She stared at him for a moment. "I don't think you're even part Indian, as you said."

"If you say so," Webster replied, not wanting to anger the girl. "I live in Smyrna." He pointed toward the Nebo River valley. "It's down there near Cowpens. You've heard of Cowpens, haven't you?"

"Of course I have," Tai retorted. "You think I'm ignorant because I'm living in the mountains?"

"Not at all," was Webster's quick reply. "I didn't mean to insult you. It's just I'm surprised to see a black woman living in the mountains."

Webster knew from the way Tai upbraided him that she was no backwards mountain girl. She was educated. "Where did you go to school?" he inquired.

"School?" Tai said.

"Yep. Where?" Webster asked.

"In Cowpens."

"Why you living here in the mountains?"

"I told you that yesterday."

Webster motioned for her to sit down on the bank. He wasn't sure she would, but when she did, he sat down too, but not too close to her. "Why did the black Indians settle up here in these hills?"

"What's it to you?" was Tai's response.

"Just curious."

Tai sighed as she looked toward the forlorn huts stuck on a hillside. "This place has been here long before the Civil War. When slaves ran away from the plantations down in the valley, they came to the mountains. The slaves knew the Indians wouldn't allow slavecatchers on their land."

"The Indians were good folks," Webster commented.

Tai gave him a hard, cold look. "The Indians let the slaves stay, but not in their encampment!"

"Is that so?" Webster asked.

"That is so!" Tai shot back. "So the slaves built Euraw. My grandmother was one of those slaves who lived in Euraw."

"Euraw?" Webster questioned.

"That's the name of the place you see on the hillside."

Trying to cheer up the somber Tai, Webster said, "Pretty name for a town."

"A slave name for an ugly place," Tai corrected him.

Webster waited for a moment, then changed the subject. "So, you're part black and part Indian. How'd that come about?"

"You ask a lot of questions," Tai said.

"If you don't ask questions, you won't learn things," Webster replied.

"I came about the same way you came about." She stared at Webster's face for a moment, then said, "I think you're part white and part black."

Webster drew back. She'd gotten it wrong and he quickly corrected her. "I'm part white and part Indian."

"Have it your way," Tai said, "but in my school in Cowpens there were several students who were part white and part black. They were not allowed to go to the white school, so they had to come to my school. You remind me of Sally, my best friend. She was part black and part white."

Webster felt uncomfortable with her thinking but decided to let it be. So he said, "Explain to me black Indians."

"Not much to explain," Tai responded. "Some of the slaves mixed with the Peedees. When the babies were born, their heritage was part black and part Indian. And again these babies were treated like my friend Sally was."

"How's that?"

"The Indians had babies with the black people, but those babies weren't allowed to live with the so-called pure Indians!"

Tai yanked her hair back out of her face. "My mama told me that we were a whole new race of people. She called us 'bridge people'! Mama said we connected two races of people and made a whole new group! Some pitiful group!"

Tai scrambled to her feet and dusted off the back of her dress with her hand. "I must get going."

"Stay a bit longer," Webster said.

"I can't. My mama's sick, and I have to get her dinner cooked." She strode off toward the shacks, her shoulders erect and her head held high.

This was quite a woman, Webster thought. There was nothing fragile about her. She was the kind of woman he always wanted to know, strong and to the point, like his mother Bessie.

When Tai was out of sight, Webster's thoughts turned to Skelly Moonstar, the bastard who sold him land that wasn't his. "Skelly," Webster said aloud, "I bet you are hiding up there in Euraw."

Every day for a week, Webster returned to the meadow, and each time he saw Tai. He had courted many girls both in Smyrna and in Cowpens, but he had never met a girl like Tai.

Webster had developed strong feelings for Tai, but he was afraid to tell her that. He knew she was a no-nonsense girl and might tell him the time wasn't ripe for his affection toward her. He just contented himself with talking to her as he kept watch on Euraw for Skelly.

During one of their meetings, Tai told Webster about her mother, Tallaquah, who was the daughter of Rebecca, a fifteen-year-old runaway slave girl, who along with her mother and father escaped to the mountains. Upon seeing Rebecca, the Indian chief took her for his mistress. And in return, he allowed her family to stay on Indian land.

Rebecca, however, stayed in the village with the chief and became an Indian prayer woman who assisted the Spirit Priest when he administered spiritual ceremonies to the Indians.

A year after Rebecca came to the mountain, her daughter Tallaquah was born. When Tallaquah was ten years old, the chief, her father, died and his wife, Seneca, forced Rebecca and her daughter out of the village. The two then went to live in Euraw, the black Indian settlement.

Rebecca was not liked by the people in Euraw, who believed Rebecca thought herself better than they. So, although Rebecca was allowed to live in Euraw, she and her daughter lived an isolated life on a plot of land at the edge of the settlement. When Tallaquah was sixteen, Rebecca died.

After Rebecca's death, Tallaquah met Moonstar, an Indian man with a withered arm. Moonstar had refused to live with the other Indians because he felt unwelcome and he moved in with Tallaquah. They had two children, a boy and a girl.

When he died, Tallaquah took her children and went down the mountains to Cowpens where she did domestic work, and her children attended the black school that was run by the Freedman's Bureau.

"Why did your mother come back to Euraw?" Webster asked. "Cowpens is a nice town."

Without hesitation, Tai simply said, "We didn't fit in. Oh, we went to a black school and joined Prince Hall, a black Methodist church, but we were different from the other people around us, even though we tried to fit in."

"Did the people say you were different?" Webster inquired.

"No. We just felt it. Mama felt it more strongly than my brother and me. True, we didn't have playmates, but we played with each other. There was no one for Mama. She joined all the social clubs in the church and worked hard and help put on programs, but still she felt she didn't belong. So, one day she just up and brought us back to Euraw. She said it was where we belonged, even if she didn't."

"Didn't you protest leaving school?" Webster asked.

"I did, but my brother was glad. He hated being cooped up all day in a room. He never liked learning." She paused. "But I did get more schooling."

"How so?"

Tai smiled. "My, you ask a lot of questions."

Webster reached over and took her hand into his. "I like you," he said, stroking her hand with his thumb. "I want to know all about you."

"A white missionary family had built a school just over the mountains in Virginia for children of mixed heritage," Tai explained. "They came to Euraw and offered me a scholarship, so Mama let me go. I stayed there for five years and was planning to go on to school in Philadelphia, but Mama became ill, so I came back here to take care of her." She sighed. "I just hope she gets well."

"Say, I'd like to meet your mama," Webster said, trying to cheer her up.

Tai thought for a moment. "You'd be welcomed in our home."

"But I don't have an Indian name," Webster teased her.

The two laughed, remembering the first day they had met and how Tai had remarked sarcastically that he didn't have an Indian name.

Then Webster noticed two hawks flying high overhead, engaged in a mating ritual. He pointed them out to Tai as the hawks swooped and made daredevil dives by zooming high in the sky and with breakneck speed plunged downward, calling noisily as they tumbled effortlessly toward the ground.

"Hawks!" Tai said. "That's it!" She reached out and took Webster's hands and said solemnly, "I name you, Webster Epps, Webster Two-Hawks!"

"Why Two-Hawks?" Webster questioned.

"To me, you're like a hawk!" Tai explained. "Hawks are strong, intelligent, and they are survivors. No matter how hard you try to run them off, they'll pop up in the oddest places. If not in the corn patch, it'll be in the pumpkin patch or among the fruit trees. You can't get rid of them, no matter what you do. They are determined! I'm drawn to them."

"I'm drawn to you," Webster said and took her into his arms and kissed her tenderly on the lips and whispered, "Tai, I've never met a girl like you. You're really special. Come back to Smyrna with me."

Tai pushed away from him. "I can't, Webster. My mama needs me!" She scrambled to her feet. "My brother will be coming home soon. He's not well, and I need to cook some food for him and Mama."

Webster got to his feet. "What's wrong with your brother?"

Tai waved her hands in desperation. "He just drinks and drinks and drinks! He can't help himself." She smiled weakly at Webster, and he could see her eyes were teared. "I love my brother, no matter what he does. He's kind and loving, not like Tom Biggers."

Webster was confused because he wasn't quite following what Tai was telling him. "Who's Tom Biggers?"

"He's a black Indian man that Grandmama Rebecca raised after his mother died and his father gave him away. Tom Biggers is mean and cruel. I hate him! But Skelly is just the other way 'round."

For a moment, Webster was dumbfounded. Did he hear the name Skelly? She couldn't be talking about the Skelly he met. No, that Skelly couldn't be Tai's brother, Webster thought.

Although Tai had mentioned the name Moonstar, Webster had been so enraptured by her beauty that he hadn't made the connection! A beautiful, well-spoken young woman couldn't be a sister to the likes of Skelly Moonstar!

"Did I hear correctly?" Webster asked. "Did you say your brother's name is Skelly? Skelly Moonstar?"

"Yes," Tai replied eagerly. "Do you know him? Skelly often goes down to the valley."

Still not believing that Skelly was Tai's brother, Webster asked. "Did he say where he went in the valley?"

Tai thought for a moment, "Now let me see. I know he goes to Cowpens, and . . . oh what is the name of that place? It's an awful sounding place!"

"Mush Creek?" Webster asked, hoping desperately he was wrong.

Tai snapped her fingers. "Yeah! That's the awful sounding place where he goes. You saw him there?"

"I, I may have seen him," Webster managed to say.

"I'm sure you'd remember him. He's real bony and likes to talk a lot."

He's a fast talker, Webster thought as he nodded his head. "Yeah, I may have seen him."

Tai waited for Webster to say more about meeting her brother, but when he didn't she announced, "Gotta go!" and ran off toward the houses.

"Bastard! Bastard! Bastard!" Webster said angrily as he pounded his fists together. He wasn't so angry that Skelly had tricked him as he was that he was Tai's brother. What a damnable position for him to be in. Here was a girl he could easily love, and she was this lowlife's sister! Tai won't have anything more to do with him when she learns he is after her brother. Her love for Skelly runs deep. She had told him so.

For the rest of the day, Webster lay in the meadow feeling sorry for himself. His life was a mess when it came to women. First, there was Lula, then Ruby, Emmaline, then Raine, and just when he had found Tai, a girl that he really liked, he was going to lose her. His mother had been right all along. He should have taken the scholarship and gone on to school in Philadelphia, and now because of his poor judgment, he was being punished.

It wasn't until the sun was slowly going down that Webster headed back to his cabin. Just as he came to the edge of the hollow, he glimpsed a shadowy figure on the other side of the creek coming through the trees. Webster squatted behind a clump of bushes and peered out. To his surprise, it was Skelly. He'd know the bastard anywhere.

Webster crept out from behind the bushes and silently sneaked back toward the meadow. There, he slipped across the shallow water to the other side and hid in the tall reeds waiting for Skelly to come that way.

Soon, he heard the crunching of Skelly's feet as he walked through the grass. When he thought he was near, Webster leaped out and grabbed Skelly by the throat. "Gotcha, bastard!" he yelled, flinging the thin Skelly headfirst into the reeds.

Standing over Skelly with one foot on his neck and his fists balled, Webster said, "You sold me Indian land! Now, if you don't give my money back, I'll take my twenty dollars out of your hide!"

The look on Skelly's face was that of disbelief. At first, he wouldn't talk, just laid there passively in the reeds looking up at Webster with large, sunken eyes. Finally, he said, "I needed money."

"For likker?" Webster shouted.

"Nope. My mama's sick. I had to git money for her medicine."

Looking down at the frail, unkempt Skelly, Webster suddenly felt a tinge of pity for him. He knew Skelly hadn't wanted money to buy medicine for his mama. He needed whiskey. What satisfaction would he get from beating up this poor, lost soul? The whiskey had already beat him long ago. He reached out his hand, grabbed hold of Skelly's hand, and yanked him up from the ground.

Believing that Webster was going to beat him up, Skelly was resigned to it. "All right, go ahead and kick my ass," he said. "Your money be long gone."

Webster glared at him for a moment, then flung him back into the reeds and walked off back toward the hollow.

Noah

In the spring of 1864, Karl Au Bignon, owner of Margrace Plantation, sold twenty-year-old Noah to Jeb Herndon. It was a year before Robert E. Lee surrendered to General Ulysses Grant at Appomattox.

Herndon's wife, Missy, had inherited a small farm fifteen miles south of Margrace Plantation, and when her father died he left her the farm, a slave called Jesse, and a little money. Because Jesse was old and sick, the Herndons used the inherited money to buy another slave, Noah.

Noah was tall and big-muscled, with leathery black skin and a vicious temper. Noah was determined to get his freedom and had run away many times from Margrace Plantation. Each time he was captured, tied up, and horsewhipped by Brute, Au Bignon's overseer.

These beatings, however, did not deter Noah from trying to escape again and again. Au Bignon, fearing Noah might escape permanently, decided to sell him and get rid of the problem.

Au Bignon had told Jeb Herndon to watch Noah closely. So each day, as Noah worked in the fields alongside Herndon and Jesse, Missy stood guard with a loaded pistol and a gun belt with bullets strapped around her massive waist. If Noah or Jesse attempted to run off, she'd shoot. She did not intend to lose her inheritance.

When the men were brought home at night, Herndon, with Missy holding the gun, chained the men to a heavy log-chain that had been soldered into the cabin's wall. After the men were securely locked to the log-chain, Missy would drop the key into a pouch she hung around her fat neck.

The Herndons were religious zealots who often sang and gave praise to God as they mercilessly worked their slaves from sunup to sundown. And before the men were given food at night, Missy forced them to get onto their knees while her husband read from his Bible and prayed.

When Herndon had finished praying, he'd remind Noah and Jesse who he was. "I'm the master," Jeb would say. "God commands me, the master, to obey Him. You're my slaves, and I command you to obey me. If we don't keep God's commandments, we'll all burn in hell!"

With her pistol aimed at the men's heads, Missy would chant. "Amen. Praises to God!"

After having prayed a long and boring prayer, the wizardly old man would carefully set a tin plate with cold pinto beans and a chunk of cornbread on the floor in front of each man to eat by a dim candlelight.

Outside the cabin, Herndon would lock the cabin door and prop up a heavy log against it. After that was done, he and Missy would go up to their house and eat a sumptuous dinner by a kerosene lamplight at their dining room table.

Noah hated Jeb Herndon to the core, but he hated Missy more. She was an evil woman who gave them little food, worked them relentlessly, and treated them in a subhuman way. Every day, he wished her dead.

Missy had named her farm Archadale, because all the big slave plantations had names, and she believed that giving her tiny farm a name gave her status in the community.

Every waking moment Noah spent at Archadale, his thoughts were about escaping. If Missy hadn't had that gun pointed at his head, he'd have been long gone. For now, he'd wait. His time would come.

Each night after the Herndons had left, the men would talk, and Noah always talked about escaping from Archadale.

"We wait," was Jesse's advice. "The war goin' free us."

"I don't aim to hang 'round heah that long," Noah told Jesse. "I be leavin'!"

"How?" Jesse asked. "We can't break these log-chains."

"We need that key," was Noah's reply. "I got to thank how to git it."

"You ain't never goin' git that key," Jesse replied, "lessen Missy fall over dead. That ole woman would jest as soon shoot us as she'd shoot a rattlesnake!"

It was early autumn and Noah had been with the Herndons for six months. The corn had ripened and the three men were pulling the ripe ears from their stalks and dropping them into the furrows. Later, they'd come back, gather up the corn, and haul it to the barn for winter storage.

Although it was autumn, the sun was still hot. The tall, brown cornstalks were planted so close together that it was hard to see beyond a few feet. Dried tassel dust sifted down into the workers' faces and eyes, and the heavy, stifling humidity mixed with the sun's heat created an ovenlike atmosphere in the corn patch.

As Herndon, Jesse, and Noah pulled corn, Missy, who was sweating profusely, walked behind the men holding the gun. She was a mountain of a woman and the hot September noonday sun was taking its toll. Even though she wore a wide-brimmed straw hat, her face had turned bright red and big globs of sweat poured down her back and ran down the sides of her face. Suddenly, she gave a sharp cry and crumbled face down to the ground in the hot field.

Jeb Herndon turned and glimpsed his wife falling to the ground. He ran back to her shouting, "Missy, what's wrong?" But she didn't answer. She just laid there in a heap.

Herndon dropped to his knees and whispered softly, "Missy, it's me, Jeb; I'll get you to your feet!" Carefully, he took hold of her arms and strained to turn her over onto her back. He couldn't budge her. Because Missy was so heavy, Jeb knew he might injure her. He needed help.

Standing over the fallen Missy, Jeb beckoned Noah and Jesse to come quickly.

Noah was always cognizant of the fact that Missy carried a gun, and from where he was working he believed Jeb now had it. He reluctantly walked back to where Jeb was waiting.

The limp Missy lay there barely breathing as Jeb shouted orders to Noah and Jesse. "Git over on the other side," he told Noah. "Run your hands under her so we can get her onto her back so her face won't be in the dirt!"

Noah took his time bending down. A feeling of rage shot through him. Here he was, forced to help the woman who held him against his will.

"Get your hands under Miz Herndon," Jeb snapped. "When I say go, we'll turn her over. Then we'll get her to her feet!"

Noah slowly slid his hand under Missy. It touched something. He pushed his hand under further and, to his amazement, it was the gun. Missy's fingers had it clutched to her stomach. Carefully, Noah's hand pried the gun loose from Missy, and when his hand was firmly onto it, he quietly slid it toward him, all the time watching Jeb, who was barking orders to him and Jesse.

Slowly, Noah stood up to his full height and said, "Come on, Jesse, we be leavin'."

Jeb looked up and saw Noah with the gun. "Give me that gun!" he yelled. When Noah didn't hand him the gun, he shouted, "I command you in God's name!"

As Jeb scrambled to his knees, Noah warned, "You git up and I'll shoot you right 'tween the eyes!" Herndon knew from the look on Noah's face and the tone of his voice that he'd better obey.

"Lay flat!" Noah commanded Herndon and motioned for him to stretch out next to Missy. Then he turned to the speechless Jesse and said, "We hit it!"

"But . . . what 'bout her?" Jesse pointed to Missy.

"Let her die!" Noah shouted.

When the stunned Jesse stood rooted to the ground, Noah yanked him by his hand and they bolted through the tall, brown corn toward the woods.

As they ran, they heard Jeb yelling and shouting for help. His cries, however, went unanswered because the Herndons' farm was isolated. Their closest neighbors were ten miles away.

All day long, Noah kept up a steady pace because he wanted to get into the hills where he and Jesse could hide and be safe.

Jesse struggled to keep up because the day before he had cut his leg when he was using a scythe to cut down a clump of ragweed that was giving Missy hay fever. The cut was deep and needed the attention of a doctor, but instead of getting a doctor for Jesse, Jeb prayed that he be healed and left it up to God.

All night long Jesse had been in pain, and even though he had been injured the Herndons still chained him. The following morning they made him go to the field to work.

Now, as Jesse ran through the woods dodging dead tree boughs and jumping over stumps trying to keep up with Noah, the pain in his leg was like a toothache gnawing at him. He didn't tell Noah because freedom was on his mind and nothing else mattered.

Late in the evening, the two came to a hillside that was covered with rock boulders. Noah chose a rock ledge to sleep on top of for the night. From the ledge they could see any one coming. Trying to sleep that night on a hard rock only made matters worse for Jesse. By morning he was in excruciating pain. As he lay doubled up with pain, he began babbling in several different voices.

Noah sprang up when he heard the voices. Then he realized it was Jesse talking and gave him a shake on the shoulders. "Jesse, wake up, you be dreamin'," Noah said.

When Jesse kept on babbling, Noah shook him harder. "Wake up, Jesse." Then Jesse began crying, which alarmed Noah. "What be the matter, Jesse?"

"I be hurtin', Noah," Jesse said through his tears. "I be hurtin' bad. I can't go no further. You go on."

"It be your leg?" Noah asked. Jesse nodded.

Quickly, Noah rolled up Jesse's trouser leg and saw that his leg had swollen tight and had turned bluish-purple. "I'll git some pokeberry leaves on it," Noah announced. "I see some right down there." He pointed down toward the hillside.

"It ain't no use," the dejected Jesse replied. "Jest let me stay heah. You kin be up in them hills by dinnertime."

"No," Noah replied determinedly. "We go together. You jest wait heah 'til I git them leaves."

Noah ran off down the hillside to a clump of pokeberry bushes, yanked off several of the foul-smelling leaves and came back. He spit on the leaves to moisten them and placed them on Jesse's wound. Then he tore off a piece of his shirttail and tied the leaves firmly to the leg.

"Jest thank," Noah said, trying to cheer Jesse, "you ain't got nobody tellin' you to git up and work today. You kin jest lay back!"

"Noah," Jesse recounted, "I done see'd thangs with these ole eyes last night. God comin' for me."

"You wuz jest dreamin'," Noah reassured him. "God ain't goin' be rushin' you now. You jest got your freedom! Tell God to wait."

After Jesse had rested some more, they started up the hillside. It was slow going as Jesse leaned heavily onto Noah's shoulder. It took them an hour to reach the crest. At the hill's top, Jesse was breathing laboriously as Noah carefully guided him to the shade of a large gray rock where he could rest.

"We stop heah," Noah said. As he stood looking down at a wide expanse of land dotted with Queen Anne's Lace, Black-eyed Susans, and orange and golden poppies, he remarked, "This be a real pritty place, Jesse."

Jesse didn't respond. He just sat leaning his head against the rock with his eyes closed.

"You rest heah," Noah told Jesse. "I'm goin' find us some viddles," and walked off toward a small patch of woods that bordered the field.

Noah walked through the woods and on the other side of them found a few wild crabapple trees near a tiny brook. Most of the trees were dead or dying, but one had a few tough, wormy apples.

Quickly, Noah gathered a handful of the little apples that had fallen onto the ground and began eating one. He made sure where he bit into the apple because he didn't want to eat any worms. After he'd eaten his fill, he stuffed his pockets with some apples to carry back to Jesse. Now, he needed a big drink of water.

Over at the tiny brook clogged with dying grass and water lilies, Noah laid down on his stomach, pushed aside some grasses, and drank deeply of the water. As he was lying on his stomach drinking, he spotted an old rusty tin can stuck in some debris. From the looks of it, the can had been in the water for some time.

After he had finished drinking, Noah took the can, cleaned it out, and filled it with water to carry back to Jesse.

When Noah returned to Jesse and offered him the water, he refused to drink it.

"You got to drank this water," Noah pleaded. "You die if you don't!" But each time he offered the water, Jesse refused it. Then Noah tried to force the water into Jesse's mouth, but Jesse clenched his teeth together and held his jaws tight.

"If you ain't wantin' water, then eat the apples I brung you." Noah reached out to him with a handful of the half-rotting apples. Jesse just stared at them for a moment, then closed his eyes. Noah put the apples in a heap on the ground near him.

Noah was perplexed at Jesse's behavior. Perhaps it was his injured leg that was causing him to behave strangely, but both of them had been injured many times before, and pokeberry leaves always healed their injuries. Could something bad be happening to Jesse's leg? He'd better have a look at it.

Noah crept over quietly, hoping not to disturb the sleeping Jesse, but the moment he touched the leg, Jesse began kicking wildly and thrashing about so violently that his leg slammed into Noah's groin.

Screaming out in pain, Noah rubbed his groin. Exasperated, he shouted at the angry-looking Jesse, "You goin' addled!"

From a distance, Noah sat watching Jesse and thought that there was more to Jesse's strange behavior than his injured leg. Something deep and mysterious had overcome Jesse, and there was nothing he could do about it.

Jesse refused to go any further. Noah tried and tried to coax him, saying they were just a day's walk from the Indian's land. There they'd be safe, but Jesse refused to move. It was as if he were glued to the ground. So, Noah decided to spend the night there and start out in the morning. Perhaps he'd been pushing Jesse too hard.

The next morning when Noah awoke, Jesse was gone! Befuddled and frightened, Noah ran out into the field shouting Jesse's name over and over. But he didn't answer.

All morning long and on through the night, Noah searched the field, the small patch of woods, and the hillside where they had spent the night. He even searched on the other side of the hill, but no Jesse. He had to find him. He couldn't leave Jesse alone and sick.

By noontime the next day, Noah knew he had to move on. Paddyrollers were probably now on their trail, and he'd better get to the Indian land.

Sadly, Noah walked through the field toward the woods. And then he saw him! Jesse was lying among the orange poppies in the same field that Noah had searched several times the day before. He had run over every inch of that ground. How could he have missed him? Jesse must have hid from him.

Noah squatted down to the old man. He looked so peaceful lying there among the wildflowers. "Guess God didn't wait," Noah said softly.

It took Noah several hours using a sharp rock and his hands to dig a grave for Jesse in the field of white Queen Anne's Lace, orange poppies, and Black-eyed Susans.

Finally, Noah buried Jesse. From some twigs of a nearby birch tree he fashioned a cross and placed it at the head of Jesse's grave. He did this because Jesse believed deeply in God.

"This be a nice restin' place for you, Jesse," Noah said. "It be quiet." He pointed toward the patch of trees. "Runnin' water over in them woods and lots of birds to keep you comp'ny." Looking up at the sky, he remarked, "Pritty blue sky and big, ole puffy white clouds up there floatin' 'round." He paused. "I guess you knowed Jesse, you couldn't go on and you ain't wantin' to git caught! I ain't lackin' it that you be dead, but you better off now than back at Archadale."

Noah stood silently for a few minutes over the crude grave, then he walked off into the woods.

By the time the sun was setting, Noah was far up into the foothills. He was tired and hungry, and it was a good thing he'd brought along those half-rotting apples he had put on the ground near Jesse. He quickly wolfed them down and crawled under a rock ledge that jutted out from the hillside and fell asleep.

The next morning, rain was dripping off the rock ledge and, as Noah sat up, a flock of wild geese flew up from some marshes just below him, and he saw a brilliant rainbow that radiated against a black sky. A surge of joy shot through him, the joy of freedom. Even though Noah was wet, hungry, and exhausted, it was a glorious morning indeed.

Noah stood up and stretched. He needed food. He set out hoping to find some wild berries to eat, but to no avail. Berry vines didn't grow that high up; he'd have to go downward toward the valley.

Just when Noah thought he'd die from hunger, he spotted an old shack near the bottom of a hill with a barn looking as if it were going to collapse surrounded by some scraggly apple and peach trees. An ancient corn crib, set among a patch of orange, ripening pumpkins. In a garden were some dying pole bean vines and some tomato plants. Nearby was a patch of sweet corn turning brown.

Noah sneaked closer and saw that the old barn had double doors that were heaved inward, and around the back was a dangling piece of frayed rope hanging from a rusty pulley that extended up to an opening to a hayloft.

Off to the left of the barn was a small patch of turnips whose tops had been killed by an early frost. Noah yanked up a plump purple and white turnip and gobbled it down in several big bites. He quickly devoured another and another.

The barn hayloft looked inviting, just the place where he could hide and rest. But, if people still lived in the old farmhouse, he'd be taking quite a chance. He'd wait and slip into the hayloft that night.

Noah stayed hidden at the edge of the woods until late afternoon. As he lay in the woods, he thought he heard a rooster crowing, but was too far away from the barn to know for sure. Perhaps, he wanted it to be a rooster. Where there was a rooster, there'd be hens. And where there were hens, there'd be eggs. Raw eggs would give him the energy he needed. The thought of eating raw eggs overcame Noah's fear, and he took a chance of sneaking into the barn.

At first, he'd try to heave himself up to the hayloft by holding onto the old rope and using the pulley. Noah leaped up and grabbed hold of the rope but it snapped and sent him flying onto the ground. The only way he was going to get into that barn was through its broken doors.

Noah then crept around to the front of the barn, keeping low so as not to be seen and gave the doors a little push. They made an awful squeaking sound. Noah quickly hid in the patch of ragweed and waited to see if anyone had heard the noise. After assuring himself that no one was coming, he gave the old doors another push. This pushing and hiding went on for over an hour until Noah finally cracked the door just enough to squeeze inside the barn.

It was just as he had thought. A few old hens were scratching at the barn's dirt floor for worms as a tired, old rooster sat sleepily upon the tattered top of an old buggy covered with chicken waste.

Noah didn't want to alarm the chickens, so he crept silently around, hoping to find some eggs. Inside an old barrel were two brown eggs. He quickly cracked each egg and swallowed its content, tossing the shells on the barn floor. In vain he searched for more eggs, but after a time, he swung up onto a rafter and pulled himself up into the loft.

There were a few clumps of hay scattered about in the loft. Noah kicked the clumps over into the deep recess of the loft and laid down on it. Soon he was asleep.

Noah was awakened by a sharp kick in his ribs and sprung up to face the barrel of a shotgun. Holding the gun in one hand and a lit lantern in the other was a gray-bearded man wearing a grayish uniform.

A Confederate soldier, Noah thought. He was caught. Quickly, he said, "I ain't done nothin'."

"You stole my eggs," the man snapped. "I found the eggshells."

So, it was the eggshells that had given him away. What a fool he'd been to leave them there.

"Mister, I wuz real hungry," Noah pleaded. "I ain't et for three days!"

"Git up," the man commanded.

"Where you be takin' me?" Noah asked.

"Jest shet up and do as I say."

The man forced Noah to climb down an old ladder from the hayloft, and out through the barn's side door that Noah had not seen when he had tried to get in.

The man marched Noah up to the house and through the kitchen door. Inside the kitchen on a table was another lit lamp, and around the table sat two big, mean-looking men wearing dirty gray uniforms that had several buttons missing from their coats.

With hardly a glance up from their plates, one man said, "Where'd you find him?"

"Up in the loft," the man with the gun replied. He pointed his gun toward a chair near the stove. "Git over there," he told Noah.

In the kitchen's light, Noah realized that these men didn't look like the Confederate soldiers he had seen one day passing Archadale Farm. The color of the uniforms were different. The soldiers he had seen wore bright gray, with a row of gold buttons down the front of their uniforms. Noah remembered this because, even though he hated these soldiers, they did look smart and snappy in their crisp, well-fitted uniforms.

The men around the table and the one holding the gun were wearing dark, dirty, gray uniforms with one row of white buttons down the front of their jackets. These men were not soldiers, Noah thought, they were slavecatchers, and he had fallen into their hands.

Noah waited for the man to tie him up, but instead, he went over to the stove and filled a tin plate with potatoes and two pieces of fried rabbit and handed it to him.

At first, Noah wasn't sure what to do with the food. Paddyrollers had never fed him before. Each time he'd run away and was caught, the paddyroller refused to give him food.

"Eat," the man with the gun told Noah.

Noah didn't need to be told again. He began eating the food.

Then the man stood his gun up in a corner, filled another plate of food, and sat down at the table with the other men. As the men ate, they spoke in low voices.

When the men had finished eating, the man with the gun took his gun from the corner and pulled up a chair near Noah. "Where you heading?" he asked.

Watching the gun, Noah asked, "You a paddyroller?"

"I could be."

"Then I ain't headin' nowhere," Noah said, "'cause you goin' take me back."

"What if I said I don't aim to take you back to your owner?" the man said. "What if I give you a chance to be free?"

"Why you goin' do that?"

"To work for me."

Noah first thought the man was playing a cruel joke on him. He hadn't seen much of a farm around there. But then he thought again, any man who had fed a runaway slave couldn't be all bad.

"I won't take you back," the man continued. "But from now on you'll stay with me." He waited to hear if Noah was going to protest. When Noah didn't, the man introduced himself. "I'm Big Max. What do they call you?"

"Noah."

"You can sleep in the hayloft," Big Max informed Noah. "Don't try to run off because I'll be watching. If you try, I'll shoot you."

The men that Noah met that night were Confederate soldier war deserters. They made their living by robbing and plundering the mountain people. Because the Confederate generals were so occupied with trying to win the war, they didn't go after the thugs.

Big Max gave Noah two choices: Be returned into slavery or join up with him and his men. Noah chose the latter.

The first job Noah went on was to a small settlement called Renlo, about twenty miles from where the deserters hid. Wearing fake Yankee uniforms and with their faces covered with handkerchiefs, the robbers attacked the largest house in the town one night. This house belonged to the town's doctor.

The men carried a flaming torch in their hands and rode horses up the steps of the doctor's house and onto his piazza. They broke the glass doors and rode through into the parlor, chasing the doctor and his wife into their dining room.

"Git the silver," Max shouted to Noah, who was carrying a big gunnysack.

When Noah raked a silver tea service into the sack, the doctor protested. Max then hit the doctor on his head with the butt of his rife. Then he snatched off the diamond wedding ring the doctor's wife was wearing.

The other robbers raced upstairs looking for more jewelry. After they had ransacked the bedrooms, taking whatever valuables they found, the men rode off into the night.

Some time later after that robbery, Big Max heard a rumor that the wealthy mountain people in the surrounding communities, who owned silver and jewelry, were burying their valuables so that the dreaded Yankee soldiers couldn't find them.

Max then sent Noah to inspect the mountain churches' cemeteries to see if fresh graves were there. If they were, then, at night, the robbers would open the graves. But they never found any hidden silver, only dead bodies.

The next rumor Big Max heard was that valuables had been hidden in outhouses. Noah was glad that Big Max didn't believe that. It had been spooky enough digging open a grave at night, but inspecting all the outhouses in the villages would have been a bit much for Noah.

Within a year after Noah became a robber, the South surrendered and the slaves were freed.

"We better get away from here," Jim, one of the robbers, told Big Max. "Them Yankees are gone and the people will soon find us out."

"Where will we go?" Big Max asked.

"Ohio!" Jim answered. "It's a big territory out there. I aim to buy me a little farm, get married, and settle down."

The two other men decided to join Jim, but Max said he was going to stay. He had grown up in the mountains and wouldn't be happy any other place. Noah decided to stay too, because he and Big Max had become close friends.

The men said their good-byes early one May morning in 1865, and that was the last Noah saw of them.

Eighteen years after the South had surrendered, Big Max died. Noah found him dead in his bed. He'd gone to look for him when he hadn't come for breakfast.

Noah buried Max in the old orchard behind the old barn. He didn't say a prayer over his grave or affix a cross there, because neither he nor Big Max believed in God. Noah did show his respect for Max by observing a few silent minutes at his grave. Then he said, "I be missin' you, Max."

Noah was now alone. He wasn't sure what he'd do, but he was sure as hell not going to keep on farming Big Max's hardscrabble land. Even with the two of them working from sunup to sundown, they barely eked out a living. Perhaps he'd return to robbing, but not in the mountains. All the folks there now were as poor as dirt.

So Noah headed down from the mountains to Cowpens.

A Chance Meeting

Long shadows from the setting sun fell eerily downward into the hollow as Webster made his way back to the cabin through clumps of bushy trees, wild grasses, flowers, and sedges that grew along the creek bank. He stopped for a few minutes and gazed upward toward the steep, wooded hill on the other side of the creek. Far toward the north above the tree line, he could see the misty peaks of the mountains beyond.

As Webster stood looking toward the mountains, a feeling of excitement swept over him as he thought about the beautiful, intelligent Tai, and he wanted to make love to her. But his excitement quickly turned to cold reality, because Webster believed that Tai would reject him once she learned of his dealings with her brother. He didn't want to lose Tai, but didn't know how to deal with his dilemma.

Three days before, Webster had shot a rabbit, but when he tried to cook the rabbit, it became a disaster. At first, he brought some dried sticks into the cabin and laid them down on the hearth. Then he walked down to the creek and filled the pot with water, came back to the cabin, and built a fire in the fireplace. While the fire was getting hot, he skinned and gutted the rabbit, washed it off and sprinkled some salt on it. Next, he punched a sharp stick through the rabbit, making a spit, and placed a pot upside down onto the fire, and laid it on top of the pot.

Suddenly, a huge puff of black smoke billowed out from the fireplace, and quickly the cabin filled with the stifling smoke.

"Aw hell!" Webster shouted as he began coughing. "The damn chimney is blocked!"

Making his way through the smoke with the pot of water he had washed the rabbit in, he dowsed it onto the fire. But the fire kept on burning, and the smoke kept puffing out into the cabin. Fearing that the fire may have taken hold in the chimney, Webster ran to the creek and scooped up another pot of water. Back in the cabin, he again fought through the smoke and dashed the water onto the fire. This time he put it out.

The rabbit lay burnt, blackened with soot and soaked with water. Webster yanked the rabbit out of the mess and threw it on the table. He knew that he had to climb up onto the roof and clean out the chimney.

So, armed with a dead tree branch, he shimmied up the giant oak, crawled out on a bough that hung over the cabin, and jumped down on the roof. Webster was relieved that the roof hadn't given way under his weight. It was still sound.

Carefully, he crawled over to the warm chimney and peered into it. He could see a bunch of oak leaves that were blocking the opening. With the stick, he rammed the leaves back down into the fireplace.

Webster climbed down off the roof, propped open the door, and waited outside until all the smoke had cleared out of the cabin. Then he went inside. By now, he was famished.

Although the rabbit was not fully cooked and was covered in thick soot, he bit off a mouthful of the meat. It tasted terrible. Angrily, he snatched up the rabbit and went to the door to toss it out, but changed his mind. It might come in handy later on. So, he stuck the rabbit into a pot and covered it.

This had not been a good day for Webster. He'd finally found the man he had come looking for, but to his dismay he'd learned that Skelly Moonstar was Tai's brother.

Perhaps it was time for him to go back to Smyrna. The thought of leaving Tai pained Webster, but he thought it best to go. He was running low on food, and Amos' old mule missed his daily oats. Each time Webster tossed an armful of the tough reeds to Ben, the mule would stand looking at the pile of grasses for a long time before munching on them.

Webster approached his cabin door, and because he was thinking of other things, he hadn't noticed that the door wasn't tightly closed as he always left it. Webster had kept the door closed because he didn't want varmints in his cabin who would make quick work of his supplies.

As he yanked open the door, he was met by a volley of blows to the head that sent him reeling backwards onto the ground. Before Webster got his footing, he was set upon, slammed to the ground, and straddled by a big black man with a huge head covered with a shock of gray-streaked hair. The man glared angrily into Webster's face with both fists raised. In a booming voice he demanded, "Who you be?"

Struggling to get up, Webster managed to say, "Who the hell are you?"

"Don't make me crack you one," the man threatened. "I wants to know who you is. And what you be doin' heah."

"My name's Webster and this IS my house."

The man stared down into Webster's face and loosened his grip a bit. "Thought you be a man, but kin see you jest a stripplin'."

"Let me up," Webster said.

Slowly and deliberately, the man unstraddled him, reached out with one of his thick gnarled hands, and yanked Webster up off the ground.

Watching the man closely, Webster dusted the dried bits of leaves and dust out of his hair and off his face. Then he asked, "Why were you hiding in my house?"

"Shet up," the hulking man snapped and motioned with his head for Webster to go inside. Webster did and the man followed closely behind him.

It was getting dark inside the cabin, and an uneasy feeling came over Webster. Who was this man and what might he do to him? Webster had hidden his gun inside the fireplace chimney after the incident with the rabbit because he hadn't built another fire there. Amos had told him a fire-place chimney was a good place to hide a gun because people never expect it to be there.

When Webster first came to the hills he took his gun with him wher-ever he went, but after he met Tai he left the gun behind. Now he need-ed to get to the gun. He walked over to the wooden table and announced to the man he was going to light the lamp.

Webster kept the kerosene lamp and the box of matches on the wood-en table. He took a match from the box, struck it, and lit the lamp.

In the light's glow he got a better look at the man. He was tall and heavy-set with leathery black skin, thick lips, and broad shoulders. His kinky black hair, unkempt and unruly, was streaked with gray. A zigzag scar ran down the left side of his face, and he looked mean and formidable.

The man was wearing big, baggy, well-worn overalls and a big denim coat, called a bum-jacket. Webster quickly recognized these clothes. They were the ones that prisoners on the chain gang wore. When the man moved toward the table, Webster heard a clinking sound. He looked down and saw links of chains dangling from each of the man's ankles. To Webster, this meant the man was an escaped prisoner!

Not knowing what kind of crimes this man had committed, Webster tried to appear unafraid, although he was quivering on the inside. "You're a free man?" he asked nonchalantly.

"I is now," the man snapped.

"Where you heading?"

The man ignored that question and walked over to the table and flopped down in one of the chairs that Amos had made. He pushed the chair against the wall and sat facing Webster. "Ever'body's goin' some-wheres," he finally said. "You got some eats?"

"A little," Webster answered.

"Git me some."

By now, Webster could kick himself for hiding his gun up in the chim-ney. Here he was alone and facing an escaped prisoner. He needed that gun. The man who was sitting at his table, cracking his knuckles from time to time, was giving him orders.

Webster knew the man was far too strong for him to tackle because he'd felt his strength when he tried to get up from under him. He'd better think of another way to get rid of him.

"I ought to make us a fire," Webster suggested. "It gets a bit chilly in here at night."

"Git me the eats, boy," the man snapped.

From the sound of his voice, Webster knew the man was becoming irritated, so he didn't hesitate. He went to the pot where he had put the rabbit and lifted the cover. The smell nearly knocked him over. The rabbit had become rancid.

Webster turned to tell the man the rabbit had spoiled, when he saw him abruptly get up from his chair and amble over to the fireplace. Webster's heart thumped loudly as he watched the man reach up into the chimney and pull down the soot-covered gun.

Turning to Webster with a smirk on his face, he said, "Learnt this trick when I wuz a young'un. I knowed it wuz there when you tried to make a fire. You got to git up early in the mornin' to fool me, boy."

With the gun in his hand, he went back to the chair where he had been sitting. "Git me that food, boy."

Webster picked up the pot with the rabbit and set on the table in front of the man.

The man wrinkled up his nose at the pot. "This thang stinks."

"It's food," Webster replied and moved over near the door. He expected the man to spring upon him when he removed the pot's lid. Since he couldn't beat the man, he could at least run fast. And in the dark he meant to get away.

The man snatched off the lid. The putrid smell caused him to gag as he shoved the pot away. "What the hell's in this pot, boy?"

"It's a rabbit I cooked," Webster answered.

"I ain't never smelt a rabbit lack this."

"It's been in the pot for a few days," Webster said. "I ate some of it."

The man stared at the rabbit-pot for a moment, then reached into the pot and got the rabbit. He brought it up to his mouth, took a bite, and swallowed it. He gagged violently after he had swallowed the meat, then belched and took another bite of the rabbit.

Webster watched in disgust as the man ate, but surmised that he had to be terribly hungry to eat that rabbit. Every time the man brought the rabbit up to his mouth, he'd hold his nose and take a bite.

Webster was expecting the man to vomit any minute, but he didn't; he just finished off the rabbit. He belched loudly several times. Then he took the gun, went over to the cot where Webster had been sleeping, stretched out onto it, and laid the gun across his chest.

Webster knew that there was no way he was going to get that gun. Perhaps the man meant him no harm. He had the gun and if he wanted to use it on Webster, he could. Maybe he just wanted something to eat and a place to rest.

"You got a price on your head?" Webster ventured to ask.

"Ole bounty hunters be after me but they ain't knowed who they be messin' with," the man explained.

Even though Webster didn't know what this man had done, he didn't feel he was in harm's way. He tried to find out more about this stranger. "Were you on the chain gang?"

"Work gang," the man corrected him. "Layin' railroad tracks." He closed his eyes. When Webster asked him why, he opened his eyes and snapped, "You talks a lot, boy. Jest 'cause you give me that stinkin' rabbit don't mean I got to spill my guts to you."

He burped loudly and closed his eyes again, and said, "Close that door, boy." After Webster had done so, the man went to sleep and was soon snoring as he held fast to Webster's gun.

Perhaps this was an opportunity for him to sneak out of cabin, Webster thought. But could he risk trying to get the door opened? It would make a noise. Maybe he should try to snatch the gun? No, he concluded, the man was too wily. Hadn't he known where to find his hidden gun? The man was probably lying there fooling him that he was asleep, just waiting for him to do something that would give him cause to shoot him.

So, in spite of all the dire warnings that Bessie and Amos had given him when he was a little boy about not trusting strangers, Webster decided he'd not be forced out of his house, so he went to sleep.

Early the next morning, Webster awoke and was stiff from having slept in a chair at the table all night. Yawning and stretching, he looked over at his bed to see if the man was still there. He was.

Quietly, Webster took his coffee pot off the table and a handful of matches. He also took the paper bag that held the last of his coffee and two tin cups.

Ever so quietly, he crept over to the door, hoping not to startle the sleeping man for fear he'd get shot. In a crouched position, he pushed with his shoulders against the door. It took several pushes before the old door gave way and Webster sneaked out of the cabin.

Outside, away from the cabin, near a fallen dead tree, Webster set down his coffeepot, the bag of coffee, and the cups. From nearby, he gathered some sticks and dried leaves and started a small campfire. After the fire had begun burning, he took the coffeepot, went to the creek, and filled it with water. Back at the campfire he tossed a handful of coffee into the pot and set it on the fire. Soon, the coffee was perking.

Inside the cabin, the sleeping man suddenly sprang up. He smelled coffee. When he didn't see Webster, he grabbed up the gun and cautiously kicked open the door and looked out. To his surprise, he saw Webster sitting quietly on the fallen tree bough drinking coffee.

The man didn't know what to make of this. He felt sure Webster had taken off. He could have. Why was he still there?

When Webster saw the man, he called, "Want some coffee?"

Eyeing Webster, the man cautiously walked toward him. As he drew near, he said, "Thought you'd be gone."

"Want some coffee?" Webster asked a second time.

"I kin use some," the man said and sat down on the bough not far from where Webster was sitting. He put the gun on the ground between himself and Webster.

Webster took the coffeepot off the fire and poured some coffee in the other cup. When he handed the cup to the man, he had to step over the gun. He pretended not to see it.

Seeing that Webster had ignored the gun, the man relaxed some. He gulped down the coffee with relish, smacking his lips when he had finished it. "You got some more?" he asked.

"Just a little," Webster replied and took the coffeepot over to the man and drained the balance of the coffee into his cup.

Between swallows, the man asked, "What you doin' up heah in these hills?"

"I came looking for a man who cheated me," Webster replied.

"Find him?"

"Yeah."

"What did you do to him?"

"Nothing."

The man's eyes opened wide and he shook his head in disbelief.

"You jest let him go?"

"I just let him go," Webster answered.

"What they call you?" the man asked.

Webster thought he'd not tell the man his real name, so he said, "Webster, Webster Two-Hawks."

The man took another swallow of coffee, all the time scrutinizing Webster's face. Then he said, "You ain't no Injun. I been 'round more Injuns than I got fingers and toes. I know Injuns when I see 'em. You ain't."

"I didn't say I was Indian," Webster replied.

"Then how come you got a Injun name?"

"It was given to me by a beautiful girl I met up here in these hills."

"A Injun gal?"

"She's black Indian."

The man gave Webster a blank look. "Black Injuns live 'round heah?"

Webster pointed his finger in the direction of Euraw. "Just outside this hollow."

The man frowned deeply and spit on the ground. "I ain' lackin' black Injuns. They be low-down."

"Why you say that?" Webster asked.

"Them peoples bad. I done tangled with a couple of black Injuns. Them peoples lie and they steal. They steal out your eyeballs!" was the man's reply.

"Tai's not a liar," Webster replied defensively.

"Is that the gal's name?" the man asked.

Webster nodded his head.

"She be the hen's liddle chickie, boy," he said and chuckled.

Webster was not amused at that statement. True, Skelly was a liar, a drunk, and a thief, but he was just one black Indian. He didn't want to hear more criticism of the black Indians and he didn't wish to antagonize the man, so he changed the subject and asked, "What do they call you?"

"Noah."

"Noah?" Webster repeated.

"Yeah, Noah," the man replied emphatically.

The name Noah sounded familiar to Webster. He'd heard that name before. Oh yes, it was the man's name that Amos said Enoch had spoken of. At that time, he hadn't believed there was such a person. Now, here was a man named Noah.

As Webster sat remembering what Amos had said, the man asked, "Somethin' wrong wif my name?"

"No," Webster quickly replied, "Noah's a good name."

"Thought you ain't lackin' it 'cause it ain't Injun."

"That's not it at all," Webster assured the man. "It's just I was going to ask why you were up here."

Noah leaned back against the dead tree trunk. "'Cause them ole bounty hunters ain't comin' up heah. They git lost in these hills. So, I'm jest bidin' my time." He set the empty cup down and stood up. "I'm goin' shoot me a fresh rabbit."

He picked up the gun and started to walk off. After he'd gone a few paces, he stopped and beckoned for Webster to come.

At first, Webster felt hesitant, but Noah had the gun and was waiting, so he quickly caught up to him.

They hadn't been hunting long before Noah spotted a rabbit, raised the gun, aimed, and in a flash of light the rabbit lay dead.

"Go git him, boy," he commanded Webster.

Back at the cabin Webster skinned and gutted the rabbit while Noah built up the campfire that Webster had made earlier. When Webster came with the rabbit, Noah poked a sharp stick through it, placed it over the fire, and the rabbit began roasting.

Webster was amazed at the deftness that Noah showed as he constantly flipped the rabbit over and over, causing it to roast evenly on both sides. By the time the rabbit was thoroughly cooked, Webster's mouth was watering. The two men sat down to a rabbit feast.

While they were eating the rabbit, Noah asked, "When you goin' see your gal?"

"Not sure if I'll see her again," Webster said.

Noah laughed and remarked, "You funny, boy. If that be my woman, I'd be settin' at her door."

"You got a woman?" Webster inquired between bites.

"No. But I always lacked wimmins," Noah confessed.

"Why didn't you get one?"

Noah stopped chewing. "Well, I had to put if off 'cause I wuz livin' with Max. He gone now." He smiled broadly, then announced. "I'm gittin me a woman now!" He paused for a moment. "I aim to hop a freight train and go north and jest as soon as I set feets there, I'm goin' find me a big woman!" He stretched his hands wide to indicate the size of woman he wanted.

"When you going to hop the freight train?" Webster asked.

"Jest as soon as them ole bounty hunters quit spyin' on them tracks. I'm goin' sneak down to them tracks where they go up that steep grade and when that ole train be huffin' and puffin' up that hill, I'll hop on and be home free!" He gave a belly laugh but soon grew somber. "I got to git these chains off-a my legs. Ain't no woman goin' sleep wif a man wif chains on his legs."

Wanting to know more about Noah, Webster inquired, "Why were you put on the work-gang?"

"I wuz hungry," Noah explained seriously. "When I needs to eat, I do crazy thangs! Now, I wuz willin' to work off my time. I wuz wrong stealin' them folks' chickens. I knowed that." Noah banged a fist into his hand and said angrily, "But I ain't standin' for no man to put chains on me agin! I ain't no slave! Slaverytime long be over!"

"Why did they do that?" Webster asked.

"When that ole sheriff back in Cowpens took us mens out of the jail to work off our time for the railroad, he chained all the black mens but not the white mens. I asks why? He haul off and hits me 'side my head with his club! And then holds his pistol to my head.

"'Nigger,' he sez, 'you keeps your big mouth shet! . . .'"

Webster sensed that bounty hunters wouldn't be hunting Noah just for stealing chickens. He'd done something more serious than that, so he asked, "What happened to the sheriff?"

"He be in hell, now!" Noah replied angrily. "Whilst I wuz helpin' lay them tracks that ole sheriff jest followed me' round. Pokin' me with his gun barrel. Tellin' me to git movin' fast. I jest bided my time. I knowed I wuz goin' to git him. And I did!"

"What did you do?" Webster asked.

Noah paused for a moment, then began to explain what happened. "It wuz foggy one mornin' and I wuz sent to work on the tracks way up near the steep grade. Heah comes that ole sheriff after me. He stood wif his legs spread wide, holdin' his gun and lookin' mean at me."

Noah stood up and demonstrated to Webster how the sheriff stood. "He jest be wantin' me to do somethin' so he kin shoot me. His back wuz to that steep hollow. Lookin' at him standin' there straddling a railway tie, I knowed this be my chance. I stoops down and picks up that tie and shoves it into his gut! That ole sheriff fell backwards head over heels down the hollow toward the river. He wuz screamin' and yellin' out! I took off in the fog after him, slidin' down the hill actin' lack I meant to save him." He paused, looking pleased with himself.

"Well, what happened?" Webster asked anxiously.

"Down the hill in some bushes that ole sheriff wuz knocked out cold! I grabbed up a big rock and whacked him hard on his head to make sure he be gone! I look for his gun but couldn't find it 'cause the damn chains hold me back. Then I hear other mens yellin' and callin' out his name comin' down the hollow in the fog. I grabbed up the big rock I hit him wif and throwed it in the river! Then I jumped in the river and swum 'cross to the other side. Them mens ain't see'd me 'cause of the fog!"

"Did they come looking for you?" Webster asked.

"No. They wuz huntin' in the fog for that ole sheriff, and they plum forgits 'bout me. So, I crawl lack a snake in that fog. By the time it wuz burnt off, I wuz way up in these hills. I wait 'til night and got a big rock and beat on that chain all night. It wuz jest 'fore day when that chain snapped open." With a proud look, Noah added, "I skeedaddled!"

"Skeedaddled up here," Webster said.

"No. First, I run through the thicket 'til I come to them caves up in the bluffs and hid in one. I wuz watchin' the railroad for two days until I see'd two mens ridin' up that way, and I knowed I best git away from there. So, I lit out up here."

It had been four days since Noah had come to the cabin, and Webster was thoroughly enjoying his company. In a short time he had learned to like Noah. But on the fifth day of Noah's stay, Webster knew he had to leave the hills, but he just couldn't go without saying good-bye to Tai.

Webster slipped out of the cabin and hurried through the hollow to the meadow hoping Tai would be there. When he reached the meadow, she wasn't there. He decided to chance going up to Euraw.

Just as Webster was nearing the houses, he spied Skelly waving to a big man on a horse who was riding toward him. When the man reached Skelly, he jumped down off the horse and greeted him with a big bear hug. After the greeting, the two men walked toward the houses.

Webster grew apprehensive after seeing Skelly. Perhaps it wasn't a good idea for him to go into Euraw, looking for Tai. He walked back toward the creek, but before he reached it, he heard some footsteps coming fast. Fearing it might be Skelly with the big man, Webster ducked into the reeds.

Peeking out through the reeds, Webster saw Tai come into view. She was hurrying and was out of breath.

Webster stood up and called to her. Looking frightened, Tai beckoned for him to get down. Not knowing if something was wrong, Webster dropped to his knees in the grass, and Tai squatted down to him. "Tom Biggers is at our house and he's hunting for you!" she told him.

"Hunting for me? Why?" Webster asked.

"I heard Tom Biggers tell Skelly that he was looking for a prisoner who might be hiding up here. Skelly told Tom Biggers a man was hiding over in the hollow! You'd better get away from here!" Tai said in a frightened voice. "If Tom Biggers finds you and you resist him, he'll shoot you!"

"Tai," Webster replied anxiously, "I'm not an escaped prisoner. I am not who that man is looking for."

"Then what are you doing up here?" Tai asked.

"I came up here on a different matter."

"What matter?" Tai insisted.

"Look," Webster said, "I've never been in trouble with the law, and I sure as hell haven't been on the chain-gang. Is your brother a bounty hunter?"

"I don't know," Tai replied solemnly. "Tom Biggers is not my real brother, but my ma raised him. He's cruel and can be dangerous. I once saw him knife a man, and if it hadn't been for Skelly he'd have killed that man." She looked at Webster and said, "If you're not that man, then come with me to the house and tell Skelly and Tom Biggers."

"I just can't," Webster answered. "I wish I could."

Tai stared at him for a moment, then replied, "You and I have nothing more to talk about since I'm not to be trusted."

When Webster tried to take her into his arms, she struggled out of his grasp and slapped him across the face. "You stay away from me! You're probably that criminal!"

Tai then ran off up the path toward the houses.

Webster didn't pursue her even though he could have called her back and told her the truth about her brother, but couldn't bring himself to do so.

Webster knew who Tom Biggers was after and knew he'd surely find the cabin and Noah. He couldn't let that happen. He had to get to Noah before the bounty hunter did.

Webster raced along the creek bank until he reached the woods and the secret path he'd made for himself.

Noah was lying on the bed half-asleep when Webster burst into the cabin. Out of breath he blurted out, "We've got to get away from here! Bounty hunter coming!"

Noah sprang up off the bed. "Where?" he shouted and grabbed the gun.

"He's over in Euraw and coming this way." As he said this, Webster quickly began gathering his things and stuffing them into the burlap sack.

"I bet them lyin', lowdown black Indians put him on my trail. Them is no-good folks!" Noah shouted and ran outside, holding the gun. He looked anxiously toward the creek.

When Webster had finished gathering his things, he rushed outside to the pen where he kept Amos' mule. In haste, he bridled and saddled Ben, led him out of the pen, and tied the sack onto the mule's back.

With Webster leading Ben, and Noah keeping close watch behind with the gun, the two men crossed over the creek and began climbing the steep side of the hill. They kept close to the dense bushes, hoping not to be spotted. It took some time before they finally reached the hill's crest.

Sweating and out of breath, Webster stopped to give Ben a rest because he believed they were far enough away from the cabin.

As they sat resting, Noah, who was looking back to where they had come, cried, "Look!" and pointed down toward the hollow. A cloud of thick, black smoke trailed skyward. The bounty hunter had found the cabin.

North Is a Big Place

"Where are you going now?" Webster asked Noah, who sat rubbing his left leg.

"North," he answered.

"Why not come with me to Smyrna?" Webster asked. "I'll hide you."

Noah kept on rubbing his leg for a few more minutes, then he said, "I better not go to Smyrna. That'll be the next place that ole bounty hunter will look, 'cause that's where black folks live. Right now, he still up in them mountains lookin' for me. So, I'll trick 'em. I'll backtrack, jest lack a sly fox, when a passel of hounds be on his trail."

"You mean you're going back to the railroad?" Webster questioned.

Noah nodded his head. "You be right. I'm goin' back up to that steep grade, hide in the bushes 'til that long freight train, ole Number 40, come huffin' up, and jest as soon as that ole cowcatcher go by, I'll hop on and ride him down the hill to Virginia!" He laughed. "North, heah I come!"

When Webster started down toward the valley, Noah stopped him. "We go this way," Noah said, and pointed toward the steep ridges that towered over the valley.

"But that's not the short route down," Webster said. "Going that way will take hours."

"It's the way I be going," Noah replied. "If there be other bounty hunters, they be waitin' for me in the valley. I'll fool 'em and sneak down the hard way."

"What if there aren't any other bounty hunters?" Webster said. "That means we'll be doing all this hard work for nothing."

"You go your way," Noah replied, "and I go my way. You ain't got to come with me. You ain't owed me nothin'." He started off toward the ridges.

Webster hesitated for a moment, then followed him.

The two climbed up a steep ridge, and as they neared the top, a blizzard of fog from a gray cloud swept down and met them. At the top of the ridge, the land descended to the valley and the railroad tracks could clearly be seen.

"Winter be settin' in soon," Noah remarked as he stood looking down at the tracks and wiping the fog from his face. "I be gettin' north jest in time."

"Winter's already set in up north," Webster remarked. "It's no time for a stranger to be going there."

"You be worried 'bout me, boy?" Noah questioned Webster. "You thank I can't look after myself?"

"I didn't say that. I'm just saying what is," was Webster's answer.

After climbing over the treacherous ridge, they came into the valley that was still thick with weeds the early frost hadn't killed off yet. As they waded down through the weeds that came up to their arms, Ben, the mule, decided he'd go no further. He quickly began munching and soon had made a wide swath through the weeds where he feasted. It was as if he'd not eaten in months, and no amount of coaxing from Webster could get him to leave his banquet.

"Guess we stop heah," Noah announced. "That ole mule ain't goin' nowheres 'til he fill his belly."

Webster looked at the winding road that led to Smyrna. "We should have taken the easy route," he remarked. "Climbing that steep ridge and coming all this long way just wore old Ben out. I hope he can make it back to Smyrna."

"Aw, quit fussin'" Noah replied. "That ole mule still got steam. Jest let him rest awhile and he be ready to go."

Noah stretched, then laid down on the ground and beckoned for Webster to do the same. When Webster stretched out on the grass, Noah began talking. "This place put me in the mind of the time that ole bull got after me."

"How so?" Webster asked.

"I got a real sore leg then, jest lack I got now." Noah began stretching his leg back and forth.

"A bull hurt your leg?" Webster inquired.

"He sho' did," Noah replied. "You see, I got this cravin' for eggs, so I'd go to this ole farmer's henhouse and git me a few. One day that ole man wuz layin' for me. The minute he see'd me sneak in the henhouse, he fired a handful of raw eggs at me. Wham! Them eggs slammed into my face, and then the ole man went for his Betsy!"

"Betsy?" Webster asked.

"He gun." Noah answered, surprised that Webster didn't know that a shotgun was called a Betsy. "I run zigzagging to his pasture, jumped the fence and—"

"Did he shoot you in the leg?" an anxious Webster interrupted.

"Naw. He fingers be too stiff. Couldn't pull the trigger," Noah explained. He paused for a moment then said, "If that ole man ain't had stiff fingers, I wouldn't be heah now tellin' you this story."

"What happened?"

"I wuz wipin' them egg yokes out of my eyes in the pasture. I ain't see'd him 'til I hears a snort! I look up and see'd this big ole rascal movin' his head from side to side. . . ."

"'Was it a bull?" Webster interrupted Noah again.

"Yeah, that wuz him. His tongue wuz lolled out and big gobs of slobber dripped outta the side of he mouth. That bull paw the ground, grunted, and gave a big fart and come for me! Next thang I knowed I wuz on his horns!" Noah grabbed hold of his leg and cried, "My left leg be hooked!"

Before Webster could interrupt him again, Noah quickly added, "I knowed right where to kick that bull, in his bollix!"

When Webster seemed confused at the word "bollix," Noah explained. "That big ole thang that hang down twixt his legs. That ole bull leap up on he hindlegs, bellowed, and slung his head up! I went flyin' over the fence in some bushes! I jump up and run holdin' my leg. I heer'd that ole man laffin' his head off!"

It was all Webster could do to keep a straight face. He wanted to laugh, but he wasn't sure how Noah would react to his laughing at his being hurt. So he asked a civil question. "Were you hurt from the hooking?"

"It burnt lack hell! But I smoke me some rabbit tobacco and soon I didn't feel a thang."

Webster knew about the herb, rabbit tobacco, because Bessie often made a tea from it and gave it to women who had given birth. She once told him that it relieved childbirth pains. She also told him that she kept the tea ingredients a secret. When he questioned her why she didn't tell the women what they were drinking, she replied that too much of the tea made them crave it, and that wasn't good for them.

"I sho' wish I had me some rabbit tobacco now," Noah remarked, and then to Webster's surprise, he sprung up, pushed his hat to a rakish angle, and danced a jig. "Ole rabbit tobacco put the gitty-up in your legs jest lack this!" Noah said, and stopped dancing. He shook his leg back and forth several times, and laughed. "Jest thankin' 'bout rabbit tobacco made me feel better."

"Must be some powerful stuff," Webster commented as Noah walked around testing his sore leg. "Your leg feel better?"

"Sho' do," Noah said and flopped back down on the ground.

It wasn't until early evening that the men started off again. Noah led the way down toward the bluffs. He had come this way when he escaped from the work gang, and it wasn't long before the bluffs loomed in the distance.

These were the same pockmarked bluffs where Webster had found a cave and escaped through it when two men who were after him set the briar patch afire where he was hiding. He'd never forget that incident.

When Webster told Bessie about his escape through the cave, she told him he'd been on sacred ground. Those limestone caves were used by runaway slaves who hid there until the abolitionists smuggled them onto supply boats that often docked at Scroggs Island on the Nebo River. Many times these boats sailed back up the river with slaves hidden among their cargo.

Bessie also told Webster that because the caves were like catacombs, any slave hoping to escape had to memorize what passage to take that opened out to the river. Once a slavecatcher went into the caves after a slave and never came out. And after that, slavecatchers around Cowpens never ventured into those caves again.

Soon, the winding railroad track that made its way up from the valley floor along the Nebo were in full view. The track cut through the red bluffs and up a steep grade toward a massive gray cement wall that surrounded Fort Belton, which stood guard overlooking the river below. Just before the tracks reached the top of the grade, there was a switch where railroad tracks had been laid across a trestle to Scroggs Island, where the old mental hospital was built. The asylum was now abandoned and the trestle had fallen into disrepair. It too, like the hospital, was rotting away and was closed because it had become too dangerous to use.

Although Noah and Webster were well concealed in a pine grove, they had a good view of the tracks. Noah said this was where he would wait. He pointed out to Webster the steepest point on the railroad tracks. Trains had to crawl up the grade, and it took little effort to jump on one. At the top of the grade, the trains picked up speed as they rolled down on the other side of the hill and on into Virginia.

"Yep, I wuz workin' right up there," Noah told Webster as he gazed up toward the crest of the hill. "Up there wuz where I got away!"

When Noah saw Webster tying Ben to a tree, he was puzzled. "Ain't you goin' on to Smyrna?"

"Thought I'd stick around and see you off," Webster replied. But that wasn't the real reason Webster stayed. He wanted to find out more about this colorful man because of what Amos had told him that Enoch had said. Could he be the Noah Amos mentioned? He wanted to find out.

Noah looked suspiciously at Webster, who started a conversation because he needed time to do his prying. 'Whatever happened to that old farmer whose bull hooked you?" he asked.

Noah began laughing heartily, slapping his leg, and between spurts of laughter, he told Webster the story. "I got even with the ole bastard! I wait in the bushes 'til I see'd him goin' in his outhouse. I knowed he was shitting 'cause he be in there some time. So, I sneak up and push his shit-house over with him in it!"

Noah fell to his knees laughing. He laughed and laughed! Then he stopped a moment and added, "I got away from there fast, 'cause that ole man had a shell wif my name on it!" And he began laughing again.

Finally, when Noah had ceased laughing, he said to Webster, "Tell me 'bout your liddle gal. You lay her?"

Webster shook his head.

"How you know you lack her?" Noah questioned. "That be lack gittin' a pig in a poke."

When Webster didn't respond, Noah went on. "Me? I lacks big wimmins! There be more to 'em! I ain't goin' for no bag o' bones. When I git north, the first big woman I meet, I'm goin' grab her and hang on lack a snappin' turtle! When that ole turtle bite, he hang on 'til you burn the rascal off!" Webster smiled, because he had heard that story about how strong a snapping turtle was when it bit you.

Noah talking about women was just the opening that Webster needed. This conversation would allow him to explore the snippets Amos had told him. Although Webster never once believed Amos' story that his mother was white and his father black, he wanted to disprove it. That way, when he got back to Smyrna, he could tell Amos to forget about what Enoch was saying. "You ever lay a white woman?"

Noah stopped chuckling and stared at Webster. "White woman? Why you ask me that, boy?"

"No reason," Webster quickly denied his intent. "Say, if you weren't in such a hurry I could get them chains off your legs." He smiled and said, "It's going to be hard laying a woman with chains on your legs."

Noah thought for a moment. "You know how to cut iron?"

"No, but my friend Amos knows."

The name Amos struck a chord with Noah. "Amos . . . Amos . . . I once knowed a man called Amos." He shook his head slowly. "That be a long time. I wuz jest a youn' man."

"Where did you know Amos?" Webster urged.

Noah ran his hand over his unshaven face and thought for a moment. "Now, let me see."

Believing that Noah needed help, Webster helped him on by explaining some information about Amos. "He was a slave on the Margrace Plantation."

"Yeah," Noah said, his eyes brightened, "that be it. When I wuz there, I ain't see'd much of him 'cause he worked in the big house." He frowned as if remembering something distasteful about the slaves who worked in the house. "Them folks in the big house wuz stuck up. Thought they wuz better then us field hands." He thought some more, then added. "Yeah, I 'member him, but that Amos must be dead now."

"No," Webster said. "Amos is living in Smyrna making shoes."

"Well, ain't that somethin'!" Noah said. "He still livin'!"

"If you'll come with me to Smyrna," Webster insisted, "he'd be glad to beat them irons off your legs."

"No," Noah replied. "I be losin' time."

"Amos works fast," Webster said.

"No," Noah said, and walked off into the bushes to pee.

Webster had thought that if he could get Noah to Smyrna, he could confront Enoch and clear up this matter, but realized that Noah wasn't going to budge from what he had set out to do.

When Noah returned, Webster asked him another question. "Did you know a man named Enoch who lived on the Margrace Plantation when you were there?"

Flashes of anger shot into Noah's eyes. "That sonofabitch!" he cried. "He'd sell his soul for a piece of sweet bread! I hated the bastard! I come near drownin' him in the river. If it hadn't been for Nicodemus he be gone!" He banged his fist in his hand.

Webster was surprised at Noah's anger. In all the time that they had been together, he hadn't seen him so angry, not even when he told him about the bounty hunter.

What was it about Enoch that caused Noah to get so angry?

Webster waited until Noah had calmed down before asking him about Nicodemus.

"I ain't lacked him that much," Noah said. "He call himself a black Injun and thought he be better than me. But in my eyes, he be a slave too. He could lie lack a dawg!"

"How's that?" Webster asked.

Noah stopped talking for a few minutes as if he were remembering something. Then he turned and gazed at Webster. "I thank Nicodemus be doin' funny stuff at night with ole Brute. You know why I thanks that? Nicodemus set on his ass whilst the other men worked and ole Brute ain't never give him no floggin'! The stinkin' bastard!"

"Did other white women visit Margrace?" Webster asked.

Noah seemed surprised at the question but answered, "A few on Sunday. One gal who wuz always visitin' wuz loose. She slip outta the big house at night and come to our quarters."

"What did she want?" Webster asked.

"She want a man to lay her."

"You lay her?"

Noah drew back. "Me? Well . . . jest one time." He frowned. "I ain't lack it. Didn't give me no kick."

"What about Au Bignon's daughter, did you lay her too?"

At first, Noah was speechless, and it took him a moment to get his voice. "You askin' me if I laid Dolly? You must be plumb crazy! If I did, I'd sho' keep it a secret! Au Bignon would have shot me on sight!" He paused. "Why you askin' me 'bout layin' white wimmins?"

"Amos thinks a white woman is my ma."

"Ain't . . . ain't . . . ," Noah sputtered, "ain't your ma be in Smyrna?"

"I'm talking about my blood mother," Webster said.

Shaking his head vigorously, Noah said, "Dolly can't be your ma. You ain't nothin' lack that gal. She wuz a mean bitch!"

"It was just a rumor," Webster said.

Noah thought for a few minutes, then asked, "This Amos say who be your pappy?"

It was hard for Webster to answer Noah's question but finally responded, "He said he heard the name was . . . er . . . was Noah."

Noah leaned toward him, "Wuz what?"

"Was Noah," Webster blurted out.

"Did I heah you right? Did you say 'Noah'?"

Webster nodded.

"Whoa," the stunned Noah said. "You thankin' I be your pa?"

Webster shrugged and walked over to the tree where Ben was tied and leaned against it. He wasn't sure what to think now. He'd heard his father was a white man, perhaps his name was Noah.

"So, this be why you be hangin' 'round me?" Noah called to him.

When Webster didn't answer, Noah came over to him. "Look at me, Webster. I got big, thick lips and nappy hair. Why, you ain't favorin' me at all. Didn't you tell me you wuz white and Injun?"

"I did," Webster answered and looked away from Noah. "Look, it was only a rumor. Forget I told you."

Webster had doubted the story, but when Noah showed up he began to think that there might be some truth to it. He did have that name and had been a slave at Margrace. But why should he believe Amos' story and not Bessie's, his mother? She had told Tessa when she first brought him home that his mother was an Indian and his father a white man.

Noah, acting disgruntled, had walked off a way and sat down by himself. Every now and then he glanced over at the silent Webster leaning against the tree Then he stood up and came back to the tree. "The way you be standin' 'ginst that tree put me in the mind of Nicodemus. He wuz always crowin' 'bout layin' wimmins, both white and black. He could be your pa, 'cause he jest up and left Margrace."

Feeling antsy at Noah's story, Webster retorted, "Noah, you don't have to make up a pa for me. And besides, how could a slave just up and leave a slave plantation? Where would he go?"

341

"I ain't said he wuz your pappy. I jest said you put me in the mind of the bastard!" Noah broke off a nearby twig and held it in his mouth between his teeth. "I ain't cared where the sonofabitch go!"

After awhile Noah said, "Why you be lookin' for your folks? I thought your mammy and pappy be livin' in Smyrna?"

"They do," Webster answered. "My folks in Smyrna aren't my real mother and father."

"They raise you up?"

Webster nodded.

Noah gave Webster the once over and remarked, "From the way you be lookin', they did good by you. You need to stick with the folks that brung you up, wiped your ass, stuck bread in your mouth, and took care you when you be sick. They be your real folks. *Ain't no need huntin' for grass in the wind.*"

"It's just that I thought I was part Indian and wanted to know for sure," Webster said. "I have a right to know who I really am."

"You be huntin' up Injuns?" Noah said. "It be a good thang you ain't found 'em! Injuns kept a passel of slaves jest lack the white folks. Bastards!" He retorted angrily.

"Slavery is over," Webster said.

"Slavery ain't never over if you wuz a slave," Noah said emphatically.

As they waited for dark, Webster explained to Noah why he had come to the hills and it was not to look up the Indians. "I was looking for the man who cheated me out of some money."

"Listen, boy," Noah said earnestly, as if he hadn't heard Webster's explanation and railed on about Webster wanting to be Indian. "You is now the same person you wuz yistiddy, last night, and night 'fore that. You'll be you, t'morrow, the next day, and on and on 'til you die. Huntin' down Injun blood ain't goin' change who you is. You is you!"

Webster smiled at Noah's convoluted philosophy. He knew that Noah was trying to tell him that what he was seeking wasn't worth his effort. He'd already been molded into a man and finding out his heritage now wouldn't change him.

"You goin' keep that name the gal give you?" Noah later asked.

"I might," Webster said.

"Two-Hawks?" Noah repeated cynically. "Why the hell you want to be called after some nasty ole birds?"

"It's only a name, Noah," Webster informed him.

"It be ugly," Noah snapped, and stretched out on the ground, pulled his cap down over his eyes, and waited.

Noah had explained to Webster that he meant to hop on Number 40, the big freight train from Cowpens, when it came up the tracks on its way to Virginia. Number 40 was huge and formidable looking, satin black, standing sixteen feet high, and weighing nearly a hundred tons. Old 40 ate fuel like a starved beast, and it took ten hours of stoking its boiler before there was enough steam to get 40 moving. When 40 did get going, it could pull sixty loaded boxcars. Because the freight was always loaded, it took a long time for it to climb the steep grade through the bluffs.

"Come dawn," Noah boasted, "I be leavin' these parts for good. And soon I be sleepin' on feather ticks with my woman in my arms." He laughed and looked over at the solemn-faced Webster, who was stretched out next to him. "When you goin' light out for home?"

"Soon as I see you hop your freight," Webster said.

Noah reached over and patted Webster's arm. "You ain't got to stay. I be fine."

"It's too late for me to head home now," Webster told him. "From here, we're a couple of hours away from Smyrna. It'll be too dark to travel. If we had taken the short route, I'd have been home a long time ago." Webster looked over at Noah and teased, "but you had the gun."

Then Noah handed the gun to Webster. "Tell you what, boy, when you git though wif your learnin', you come on up north and look me up."

"North is a big place," Webster reminded him.

"You be right," Noah agreed, "but you kin find me. I be makin' a big splash!"

An Unexpected Happening

Rataree had become psychotic. He was obsessed with the idea that he had been falsely imprisoned and he meant to get justice. In his mind, he had now abandoned all of his original plans for the Raiders but one: that of destroying Fort Belton.

When Rataree first solicited the outcasts Eli Bean, Jinxie Red, Tom Biggers, and Brute to join forces with him, they believed that they'd soon be rich by robbing the Cowpens bank and plundering the citizens of Smyrna. Destroying Fort Belton, however, didn't set well with two of the men, Jinxie Red and Tom Biggers. But they went along with Rataree and decided that, after the bank robbery, they'd take off for parts unknown.

Eli Bean was the first to get away from Rataree. He had been dispatched to the valley to spy on the Cowpens bank and the people in Smyrna. He had sent a message to Rataree in a pair of boots that some men in Smyrna had learned about the Raiders' plans. These men had secretly armed themselves and meant to take the Raiders down when they rode into their settlement.

Rataree put his plans on hold and waited for more information from Eli, but it never came. Eli had moved in with Manny White, an old

Confederate soldier, and soon the two became lovers and they left the valley for good. Eli's last message to Rataree informing him that he had quit had been intercepted by Webster.

It was from Mary Lou, his cousin Elliott's wife, that Rataree learned of Eli's desertion. One day, she exposed her breasts to him and when he scolded her for being brazen and behaving like a lowlife, she told him about Eli.

"What's the matter, ole man?" she taunted him as she buttoned up her blouse. "You waitin' for Eli to come back? Well, you best forgit about him. He done run off with another lover."

Rataree grew so furious at what Mary Lou had told him that he left his cousin's house and took up quarters in the old abandoned hospital on Scroggs Island. Now, whenever the Raiders met with him, they had to row a boat across the Nebo River to Scroggs Island because the railroad trestle that connected Scroggs Island to the mainland had fallen into disrepair and was too dangerous to ride a horse across.

From Scroggs Island, Fort Belton could clearly be seen, and being so close to the fort made Jinxie Red nervous. He still remembered that it was from Fort Belton that he had escaped during the Civil War and had became a war deserter.

Leaving his horse tied to a tree on the shore of the Nebo and rowing across the river in a leaky boat didn't set well with Tom Biggers. Even though he was a powerful swimmer, he knew places in that river where a tremendous undertow could suck a man under in a matter of minutes.

Brute was the only Raider who didn't grumble about Rataree. He didn't mind taking orders from him because he looked upon Rataree as a hero who had helped the Confederacy with money in its hour of need; if there had been more brave white men in Cowpens like Rataree, he'd still have his job as an overseer on a slave plantation instead of living as an outcast.

The week before Webster and Noah had come to the bluffs overlooking the Nebo, Rataree had sent Brute to fetch Jinxie Red and Tom Biggers to the Island.

Brute knew exactly where to find Tom Biggers, at Roy's Saloon in Mush Creek. Tom Biggers loved whiskey and spent most of his time at this rundown saloon, drinking whiskey and carousing with loose women.

Brute hated going to Mush Creek. To him, all the scum of the world hung out in Mush Creek. There were former slaves, drunken Indians, homeless folks, wounded war veterans, thieves, thugs, and of course, the prostitutes.

The summons from Rataree thoroughly annoyed Tom Biggers. Not only was he engaged in his favorite pastimes—drinking and making love—but he also was making plans to go after an escaped convict. He had seen a poster describing the man and the offering of a reward. Tom Biggers meant to bring Noah in and collect the hundred-dollar reward.

Because of Brute's insistence, Tom Biggers decided to put bounty hunting on hold and go find out what Rataree was planning to do. Tom and Brute rode back to the Nebo, tied up their horses, shoved the boat in the water, and started rowing for Scroggs Island.

Rataree, who had come down to the riverbank, was pacing back and forth. When he spotted the boat coming across the river, he strode closer to the riverbank's edge and, standing tall with legs agape, his wide-brimmed felt hat shading his cold eyes and brooding countenance, he waited in silence.

Jinxie Red, who had come to the island earlier, waited with Rataree.

It wasn't until Brute had hauled the boat up on shore that Rataree finally spoke in an accusing voice. "You've kept me waiting."

Brute threw up his hands in despair. "It was Tom Biggers," he explained. "He didn't want to come. Said he had something else to do."

"Like what?" Rataree snapped.

"Like going after that escaped convict up in the hills," Tom Biggers retorted.

"I haven't given you permission to go bounty hunting!" Rataree thundered.

Anger flashed in Tom Biggers' eyes. He hated being yelled at. "Listen, bastard, who the hell do you think you are hollering at? I'll kick your bony ass!"

Brute reacted to Tom Biggers' words as if he'd been shot. He jumped in front of his face and yelled, "Don't you threaten Mr. Rataree, nigger!"

Being called a nigger was like a knife cutting into Tom Biggers' heart. No one ever called him a nigger and lived to tell it. He was a black Indian! Angrily, he jerked off his hunting knife that had been hanging on his belt, grabbed Brute, and held the knife to his throat. Through clenched teeth, he said, "I'm going to gut you like a pig, white trash!"

Jinxie Red, who had been standing at Rataree's side, raised his gun and aimed it at the two men.

"Shoot him!" the enraged Rataree screamed. "Shoot the nigger!"

Brute's eyes had bulged out as Tom Biggers choked him. He was gasping, sputtering, and fighting for air, trying to tell Jinxie Red not to shoot because he'd hit him.

"Turn Brute loose!" Jinxie Red shouted. "I've got an itchy trigger finger, nigger!"

Realizing that he was outnumbered, Tom Biggers, in a split second, flung Brute head over heels to the ground, raced to the river, and leaped in.

Jinxie Red chased after him and fired his gun, but it missed the mark because Tom Biggers had disappeared under the water.

On the riverbank, Jinxie Red, Brute, and Rataree watched anxiously for Tom Biggers to surface, but there was no sign of him. Believing that Tom Biggers had drowned, the three men walked up to the old hospital.

Tom Biggers had not drowned. He had dived deep and come up in the middle of the river. Being a powerful swimmer, in a short time he had reached the other shore. Soaking wet, he quickly retrieved his saddled horse and headed over the hills to Euraw, the black Indian settlement.

Back at the hospital, Jinxie Red and Brute thought that this meeting was to be about robbing the Cowpens bank, and secretly they were glad to be rid of the hotheaded Tom Biggers. There would be more money for them.

Rataree told Jinxie Red he was to ride to the railhead in Cowpens, wait until he saw a chance to break into the railroad storage hut, steal some dynamite sticks, and bring them back to him. He cautioned Jinxie Red that stealing the dynamite wouldn't be easy because the hut would be well-guarded and anyone trying to get into it would be shot. Jinxie Red replied that there wasn't a place built that he couldn't break in.

"Just give me a few days," he replied cockily. "I'll be back with enough dynamite to blow up Fort Belton!"

Jinxie Red had said that in jest, not knowing that this was exactly what Rataree was planning to do.

"When you get the dynamite," Rataree told him, "bring it back here at night."

Jinxie Red became concerned. "You want me to ride my hoss over that ole trestle with dynamite at night? That would be a sure death!"

"No." Rataree replied. "I don't want you bringing dynamite to this island. Just signal me when you get back with—"

"With what?" Jinxie asked.

"With a lighted lantern," Rataree told him.

Jinxie Red had been gone for three days before Webster and Noah had come to the bluffs waiting for the freight train. That night, as they lay sleeping, Noah was awakened by the sound of a galloping horse. Believing it might be the bounty hunter, he sprung up and listened as the sound came closer and closer.

He awakened Webster. "Somebody comin'," he whispered. "I bet it be that ole bounty hunter."

"You sure?" Webster replied.

"Who else be ridin' out here at night?"

The two crawled on their bellies until they came to a rocky ledge that was part of an outcropping on the bluffs. Just below them, they could see the river and a horse that had stopped near a couple of small trees. A man climbed off the horse and tied it to a tree. Then he lit a lantern, walked over to river's edge, and began waving it back and forth.

"What the hell he be doin'?" Noah whispered to Webster.

"Looks like he's signaling someone."

"Ain't no folks 'round heah."

"Maybe someone's over on Scroggs Island."

"Ain't nothin' over there but rattlesnakes," Noah said. "You be crazy to stay over there."

"Let's get a little closer," Webster whispered.

"Where?" Noah whispered back.

"Down there in them brambles behind that big rock."

The men crept down from the rocky ledge ever so cautiously and crawled behind a large gray rock. From there, the man standing on the riverbank could be clearly seen.

Soon, there was a sound of lapping water, and in the pale moonlight, Noah and Webster saw a small row boat with two men in it. One man paddled the boat up to the shore. Then a tall man climbed out of it and walked deliberately over to the man with the lantern.

When the heavy-set man who was paddling the boat pulled the boat ashore, Noah whispered with astonishment, "I can't believe my eyes! That be ole Brute!"

"Brute?" Webster whispered back.

"Yeah, that be him! He wuz the overseer at Margrace Plantation. Last I heah of him he be a bounty-hunter. I thought the sonofabitch be shot by now!"

The tall man was Rataree and the rider was Jinxie Red. They talked for a moment, then Jinxie Red went to his horse and carefully took off his saddle bag and came back to Rataree, who opened the bag and looked in.

Suddenly, he became enraged at what was in the bag. He threw up his hands, looked heavenward as if he were praying, and began stamping his feet like a baby having a temper tantrum. His coattail was flying in the air and he yelled at Jinxie Red who had jumped back from him. "Five sticks are not enough! I mean to blow that fort to kingdom come!"

"Whoa!" Jinxie Red yelled back. "I didn't steal that dynamite to blow up Fort Belton. I thought you wanted it to get inside the bank!"

"Who's giving the orders in this army? The general or the private?"

"You're talking crazy," Jinxie shouted. "We're not in the army!"

"Hey, hey, Mr. Rataree," Brute said anxiously trying to calm him down. "He'll get more for Fort Belton. Let's blow the bank first."

Rataree whirled around and faced Brute. "Are you against your general?"

Before Brute could answer, Jinxie Red yelled, "We blow up Fort Belton, we'll ruin the railroad too! Then we got soldiers and the railroad folks after us!"

Rataree turned away, strode over to the boat, pushed it into the water, and climbed in.

"What the hell do you want me to do with this dynamite?" Jinxie Red yelled to him. "We still going to use it?"

"I'll make my decision at dawn," Rataree snapped. He beckoned for Brute to get in the boat.

Jinxie Red watched for a few minutes as Brute rowed out onto the river with Rataree sitting erect at the front of the boat. "Damn crazy fool," he yelled. "I'm not carryin' this stuff around!" He took the sack, walked the several yards to the old trestle, slid down the slope near the bottom of it, and hid the sack. After that, he mounted his horse and rode off.

"The sonofabitches goin' blow up Fort Belton!" Noah roared.

"Yep, that's what they are planning to do," Webster concurred. "But that's foolish. A stick of dynamite won't put a dent in that cement wall."

"Yeah, but with all that noise, this place be crawlin' wif folks! I'm goin' git that dynamite."

"Dynamite is dangerous," Webster cautioned. "You ought to leave it where it is."

"But them bastards kin blow up the tracks 'fore the freight gits heah!" Noah replied. "What is I gwine do then?"

Webster knew Noah was right. If these men set off that dynamite before the freight came, he'd never get away.

Since Noah was determined to go get the dynamite, Webster said he was going with him.

"I ain't wantin' you hurt 'cause of me," Noah told Webster. "You jest stay put."

Webster didn't listen. He followed Noah down the slope to the bottom of the trestle where a rusting girder stood. Inside a clump of overgrown bushes, they found a brown burlap sack. Carefully and cautiously, Noah lifted up the sack and set it gently on the ground. Breathing heavily, he waited a few minutes before looking in.

Slowly, he reached into the sack and took out five sticks of dynamite wrapped together with twine and tied to a very long safety fuse.

"Whew!" Noah said, looking at the package. "This be the first time I had that stuff in my hands. Give me goose bumps! Guess we kin throw it in the river."

"No, wait," Webster said. "That dynamite can kill two birds with one stone."

"What you be talkin' 'bout, boy?"

"Well, we can set off that dynamite under the old bridge just before dawn when Brute will be coming back across the river. The loud noise will bring the soldiers down here, and when they see Brute, the bounty hunter, they'll think he blew up the trestle and arrest him. Then you'll be rid of him. You can hop your freight and get away."

Noah chuckled. "I be goin' north and ole Brute be goin' to jail! You is real smart, Webster!"

Carefully, Noah carried the bundle to an old girder and waded in the shallow water, holding the dynamite up over his head so it wouldn't get wet. He placed the bundle in a niche of the girder. Then cautiously and slowly he maneuvered the long fuse through several niches, then waded back to the shore making sure the long fuse stayed above the water.

"We've got to get that fuse up there," Webster told Noah and pointed to some rocks up near the top of the grade.

"It ain't goin' stretch up there," Noah said, shaking his head.

"It will," the confident Webster replied and he took hold of the fuse and walked up the grade to the rocks. Noah followed.

"Now," Webster told Noah, "just as soon as the freight's engine gets up here, you hop on a boxcar. I'll wait until the boxcar passes, then I'll light the fuse and run like hell to where I left Ben."

"I ain't sho' 'bout that," the worried Noah replied. "I ain't wantin' you to git in trouble 'cause of me. Jail ain't a good place to be."

"I won't be getting into trouble," Webster assured Noah. "I'll be long gone before the soldiers get here."

It took some time before Webster could convince Noah to let him do it. When he finally agreed, the two sat down to wait.

It was near dawn when a sharp sound pierced the silent sky. It was the cry of Number 40. The great freight was blowing its whistle as it began huffing and puffing up the grade. But there was another sound on the wind, the sound of water breaking against a boat.

"Get up to the top of the grade," Webster yelled to Noah over the din of the freight's sound as it came closer and closer.

"But . . ."

"I'll take care of the dynamite!" When Noah hesitated, Webster commanded. "Go!"

Before the massive engine thundered to the crest of the grade, Noah ran half-bent alongside the tracks, through knee-deep pepper grass and stink weeds, as the chains slammed mercilessly against his sore ankles and grit from the iron wheels sprayed into his eyes and ears.

When the first boxcar that had a ladder came by, Noah grabbed onto it, swung up, and climbed hastily up to the top. His heart was pounding as he laid flat on his belly for a few minutes, hoping not to be observed. When he felt it safe, he inched his way along the boxcar top until he came to where two cars were joined and climbed down between them. He had seen that one boxcar door was slightly ajar as it passed, and he needed to get inside that car.

Wedged in between the cars amidst black smoke, rattling noises, and grit, Noah stretched his legs wide over to where he barely got one foot inside the cracked door. Then with all his strength, he shoved the sliding door back.

Just as Noah swung over to the opened door, a tremendous roar shook the train violently and the bales of cotton that were stacked on one side of the boxcar tumbled down like toy blocks. It was a good thing that Noah hadn't entered the car because he would have been crushed by the falling cotton bales. Instead, he gripped the sides of the door. Then the freight jerked forward, and Noah fell inside against a six-hundred-pound cotton bale. The freight picked up speed and rolled down the other side of the bluffs on its way to the Virginia state line.

Webster had waited until he spotted Noah climbing atop the boxcar before he lit the fuse. Then with trembling hand, he struck a match, lit the fuse, and took off toward the rocky ledge like a frightened deer being chased by a pack of wolves. Never in all his life had he run this fast.

The boat was nearing the shore when a terrible, monstrous, growling sound bellowed in the stillness. Rusting steel, dust, and debris spewed into the sky, and then a tremendous crashing of timber fell into the Nebo River as a huge orange fireball leaped skyward, its red flames licked the old rotting railway ties, setting them afire.

The mighty blast knocked Rataree and Brute up out of the boat and sent them flying in the air until they splashed down into the cold water, where they were quickly engulfed in thick, acrid smoke that billowed up from the burning bridge.

Struggling mightily in the dark turbulent water, filled with floating splinters of railroad ties, uprooted bushes, tree branches, leaves, and other trash, Brute and Rataree made it ashore where they lay gasping for air.

Within minutes of the explosion, the soldiers at Fort Belton were quickly mobilized and on their way to the trestle to find out what had caused such a blast. Near what was left of the trestle, they found the weakened Rataree and Brute drenched and bruised, lying on the shore exhausted. They were taken back to the fort for questioning.

Jinxie Red, who had been on his way to meet Rataree and Brute, heard the blast and surmised that something had gone badly wrong. He turned his horse around and headed up into the hills because he didn't want to get captured again by the military.

Noah's heart was pounding and hot tears rolled down his face as he sat squeezed between two bales of cotton in the boxcar. He had never cried in all his adult life, and he had suffered so much. So, why was he crying? Was it for joy—joy that at long last he was fulfilling a dream, a dream to go north?

As Noah sat weeping, he silently said good-bye to Webster and was suddenly engulfed in sadness. Deep down, he wished Webster was his son. In the short time since he had met Webster, he had known happiness and contentment. Saying good-bye to him was like tearing out his heart.

By the time the soldiers from Fort Belton reached the trestle, Webster had made it back to where he had left Amos' mule, and he and Ben were well on their way to Smyrna.

Margrace Revisited

Trembling with fright, Webster hurried down from the hills toward Smyrna. The realization of helping a convict escape by blowing up a trestle grew vivid in his mind, and from time to time, he glanced back expecting to see a hoard of soldiers galloping after him. He had to escape.

Then another thought caused him even greater fright. What if the men in the boat had been killed in the blast? This was a terrible crime, and a murder conviction in North Carolina meant death by hanging.

Because Webster was feeling sheer terror, he hadn't thought about losing Noah. His only thought was getting away, so he kept to the shadows of the trees and pushed the old mule to his limits. He was only a few miles from Smyrna when Ben stopped, refusing to go further. Webster dismounted, pulling off the saddle and the burlap sack so Ben could rest.

All the time Webster sat there hiding in the quiet autumn woods, the smallest crackle of a falling twig gave him cause to spring up and look about.

A lot had happened to Webster while he was in the hills. For the first time in his young life, he had felt vibrant and alive, eager to taste life. He had known fear and felt anger, contentment, and disappointment. But most importantly, he had learned that the things you seek in life are often found where you began.

The longer Webster sat in the woods, the more he reflected on his journey. He remembered Noah. The times they had spent together had been some of the happiest hours of his life. Webster wanted to hop on that freight train and go with Noah because he liked him immensely.

Noah, however, decided differently. Instead of asking Webster to go north with him, he told him to go back home. Webster tried to understand why Noah told him to go home. Perhaps it was because Webster had tried to squeeze into Noah's life, and Noah wasn't having it. Noah was a free spirit and wanted no attachments, and it had been selfish of Webster wanting to intrude.

Sitting there in the woods, Webster decided not to tell anyone about Noah. His chance meeting with Noah would stay his secret.

While Webster was away, Bessie had become ill with the dreaded influenza, Her friend Tessa was taking care of her. Tessa came every morning to cook Bessie's breakfast and clean her house. Although Tessa loved Bessie, she grumbled mightily about having to take care of her because Enoch never helped out and Webster was traipsing around in the hills while his mother lay sick.

On the third morning of Bessie's illness, Tessa hurried up the path through the woods to her house. She knew Bessie liked her breakfast early and she was late. As Tessa approached the house, she passed the old shed where Enoch kept his horse. To her surprise, the old horse was standing patiently at his stall's door. This was unusual, because no matter how drunk Enoch got, he always put his horse in the stall at night.

Seeing the horse alarmed Tessa. She thought Enoch too had come down with the dreaded flu and had felt too sick to put his animal in his stall. Enoch was the last person in the world Tessa wanted to care for. That would be too much.

Tessa rushed into the house and on to the bedroom, expecting to find Enoch lying in bed beside Bessie. He was not there. Because Bessie was sleeping, Tessa tiptoed to Webster's room and looked in. His bed was undisturbed. Just looking at Webster's bed angered her. He ought to be home taking care of his sick mother, she thought. Because he was gone and old lazy Enoch wouldn't cook, she had to climb out of her bed every morning and come over to care for Bessie.

In the kitchen, Tessa quietly went about cooking Bessie's breakfast. But her thoughts turned to Enoch. Where was he? Why hadn't he put his horse in the stall?

After the biscuits had baked and the coffee perked, Tessa fried two pieces of fatback and scrambled three eggs in the grease. She put the eggs, fatback, and four hot buttered biscuits on a big plate, and poured two cups of strong black coffee. She then put all the food on a tray and carried it to Bessie's bedroom.

Tessa set the tray down on a nearby table, went to the window, and raised the shade so that the sunlight could come in. Then she tapped Bessie gently on her shoulder.

"Wake up and eat your breakfast."

Bessie rolled over on her back and yawned. "I ain't sure I can eat," she said weakly.

"You feelin' better, ain't you?" Tessa asked.

"Yeah, I'm feelin' a lot better."

"Then you got to eat so you can keep on feelin' better," Tessa replied. "Now you just raise yourself up. I want to plump up your pillows. You can get to your food better if you be settin' up."

It took Bessie a few minutes to pull herself up by holding onto her iron bed's headboard. After she had done this, Tessa plumped up her big feather pillows and pushed them against her back. She set the tray of food across Bessie's lap.

Surveying the food, Bessie said, "Why you bring me two cups of coffee? One's goin' get cold."

"Poured one for myself," Tessa explained. "I was late and had no time to make my own coffee. When you're ready for your second cup, I'll git it from the stove." Tessa sat down in a chair near the bed and took a sip of the hot coffee. "Whew!" she said, and blew in the cup to cool the coffee. "Where's Enoch?"

A worried look came over Bessie's face, and she looked toward the hallway. "Ain't he in Webster's bed?"

"No," Tessa replied. "I don't think he come home last night."

Bessie lifted a forkful of scrambled eggs and put it in her mouth and chewed deliberately. "That ain't lack Enoch," she said after swallowing the food. "No matter what, Enoch always set his shoes under my bed. Guess I best go look for him."

"You'll do no such thing!" Tessa cried. "You stay right there in bed and git yourself well." She frowned. "Webster ought to be here instead of runnin' off up in them hills! What's he doing up there anyway?"

Bessie coughed slightly. "Amos ain't said. Just said Webster be coming home soon."

Tessa leaned closer to Bessie. "How come Amos know what Webster be doing? Why didn't Webster tell you that himself?"

Bessie waved her hand weakly at Tessa. "I ain't wantin' to git into that now. I'll take that up with Webster when he git home."

Tessa drank some more of the coffee as Bessie continued eating. Since Bessie seemed to be enjoying her breakfast, Tessa thought this was a good time to ask again about Mrs. Au Bignon.

Bessie had told Tessa in confidence that Mrs. Au Bignon had sent for her to come see her in the hospital at Cowpens the week before. Soon after Bessie's visit to the hospital, Mrs. Au Bignon died.

Tessa wondered why a rich white woman like Mrs. Au Bignon, who had inherited Margrace Plantation, wanted to see Bessie. She didn't know Bessie. Why didn't she send for Enoch? Although Margrace Plantation had been sold eighteen years ago, Mrs. Au Bignon would have remembered Enoch. She had once owned him and she had freed him.

When Tessa had inquired of Bessie about her trip to the hospital, she'd been evasive, saying she didn't want to talk about it. But the curious Tessa wasn't about to be put off. She was determined to find out about Bessie's secret visit.

Tessa cleared her throat and said, "You know what I believe? I believe you picked up this ole flu bug when you went to see Mrs. Au Bignon."

Bessie, who was chewing on a piece of fatback, waited until she had swallowed it before responding to Tessa. "Why you say that?"

"She died, didn't she?"

"Tessa," Bessie explained. "Mrs. Au Bignon was in the hospital, and she ain't died from flu."

"Well, what did she die of?" Tessa asked.

"It had somethin' to do with her cripple leg. Whatever caused her leg to be lame come back."

Not convinced, Tessa said, "I ain't never heah of a cripple leg killin' you."

"She be old, Tessa," Bessie snapped. "Anything can kill an old person."

Tessa waited until Bessie had eaten all her food and then asked if she wanted more coffee.

"I ain't never goin' refuse coffee," Bessie said with a smile.

Tessa went to the kitchen and brought Bessie another cup of the strong black coffee. "You never did tell me why that old woman wanted to see you."

Bessie waved her hand at Tessa. "I'm too weak to talk about that now. Look, I want you to tell Amos to go look for Enoch. Tell him I'm real worried."

Tessa knew that Bessie meant not to talk about her visit with Mrs. Au Bignon at this time, so she took the dirty dishes to the kitchen, washed and dried them, and stacked them inside a cabinet. By the time she'd done this, Bessie had gone to sleep. So, since Tessa couldn't ask any more questions, she reluctantly went to Caleb's store to find Amos. If it were left up to her, Enoch would stay lost.

Amos was sitting in a chair on the store's porch eating. Tessa walked up to the porch and sat down on its steps. "I'm plumb tuckered out," she said to Amos. Then she looked over at Amos' plate of fried chicken and biscuits. "What you eatin'?"

Amos smiled. "What it look lack?"

"Fried chicken?"

"That's what it be, good ole fried chicken."

Tessa fully expected Amos to offer her a piece of chicken. After all, he had six pieces on his plate. He didn't.

"Enoch lookin' after Bessie now?" Amos ventured to say between bites.

"He ain't there," Tessa retorted. "Didn't come home last night. Bessie want you to go look for him."

Amos primped up his mouth. "I ain't doin' no sech thang. How I know that Enoch ain't settin' up somewheres with his woman?" He chuckled. "I go pokin' my nose in where I ain't' spose to, and Enoch won't be lackin' that."

"Amos, you shet up and listen," Tessa shot back. "When I come over to Bessie's this mornin', I see'd Enoch's ole hoss standin' outside that ole shed where he keeps him. That hoss ain't had no saddle on. Bessie told me, no matter what Enoch be doin', he always come home at night. Now, she's too sick to go lookin' for him. You got to do it."

Amos frowned at Tessa. "Why don't you do it?"

Annoyed that Amos hadn't offered her a piece of his chicken, Tessa jumped up off the steps and wagged her finger in his face. "You talk lack a fool! He's your friend, not mine! I'll just go back and tell Bessie you won't go!" She started off in a huff.

"Hey, wait," Amos called. "No need to bother Bessie. I'll go."

After Amos finished his last piece of chicken, he took his plate back into the store and came out onto the porch again, mumbling to himself. He wasn't sure where he'd look. Lately, Enoch had been real secretive about his comings and goings, because he'd found a new woman and didn't want Amos to know.

Amos walked out to the middle of the road and stood trying to decide which direction he'd go when he saw the outline of a mule and a rider coming in the distance. Amos gazed for a minute, then rushed up the road toward the rider. It was Webster.

Webster stopped the mule, jumped down to the ground, and greeted Amos with a bear hug.

Laughing and slapping Webster on his back, Amos managed to say, "Boy, you is a sight for sore eyes!"

"I guess you thought you'd never see ole Ben again," Webster teased as they walked back to the store.

"Naw," Amos replied confidently.

As they came closer to the store, Amos said, "I wuz jest goin' to look for Enoch."

Webster stopped walking. "Something happen to Enoch?"

"Don't know," Amos replied. "Your maw done took to her bed and . . ."

"Ma's sick?" Webster interrupted. "What's the matter with her?"

"She come down with the flu. Ain't nothin' to be worried 'bout. Tessa be takin' care of her."

"I'll put Ben in his stall and get on home to her," Webster said.

"Naw, that ain't what your maw be wantin'," Amos told him. "She be wantin' us to go find Enoch. He ain't come home last night. Tessa saw his hoss outside his stall, so your maw thanks somethin' happened to Enoch."

"Just because Tessa saw Enoch's horse doesn't mean something happened to him," Webster said.

"Hoss ain't got no saddle on," Amos explained.

Webster's face contorted into an angry frown. "Aw hell, Amos, Enoch knows how to get home! I'm not going to look for him! I'm going home to see my sick ma!"

Amos knew that Webster didn't like Enoch. But since Bessie wanted him to look for Enoch, he meant to have Webster come with him.

"Now, you listen to me, boy," Amos cautioned. "Stop actin' lack a hothead! Your maw be sick whilst you is up in them hills. She ain't see'd you then. It ain't goin' hurt for her to wait a little longer. If we don't look for Enoch, your maw will get up outta her sickbed and go look for him, and we can't stop her."

Webster glanced downward. He felt ashamed of himself for behaving this way to Amos, but he was out of sorts. What had happened back in the hills still loomed in his mind. This had been an unbelievable night for him, and it was going to take time for him to get over the ordeal.

"We go find your pa," Amos said and grabbed hold of Ben's bridle, led him around the back to a shed and into his stall. When he took off Ben's bridle the old mule snorted and playfully kicked up his heels, glad to be home again! He too had been through hell.

"I thank I know where Enoch is," Amos told Webster as they walked down a path through the woods. "He over in Black Bottom."

Black Bottom was a cluster of old ramshackle houses set in a grove of scrub pines on the other side of the creek that flowed in the woods behind Smyrna. It had been a thriving red-light district during the time when Sadie had her saloon there. After Sadie's Saloon was forced to close, she and her girls moved to Mush Creek. Black Bottom then fell on hard times, and only a few destitute prostitutes still conducted their business there in secret. A man looking for a good time could still buy corn whiskey and a woman for a few hours.

To visit Sadie's brothel in Mush Creek cost big money now. Since Enoch was always strapped for cash, he'd sneak over to Black Bottom at night. There, he'd drink and carouse with women until the wee hours of the morning. Then, in a drunken stupor, he'd get on his old horse and whip and curse the animal to go fast to get home before Bessie woke up in the morning. The poor beast took terrible abuse from Enoch.

When Amos and Webster reached the creek to cross over to Black Bottom, they stopped short. Down in the creek, lying face down in the shallow water, was Enoch. Amos' voice trembled as he pointed to him. "Hoss throwed him!" he said anxiously. "We best git down to him and help him back to the house."

Webster, who was still feeling queasy about the dynamite blast, said, "Aw, just call to him. That'll get him up."

Amos frowned. "If he kin git up, he be up. We got to brang him up."

Webster wasn't listening to Amos. He walked closer to the riverbank, cupped his hands to his mouth, and yelled, "Get the hell out of that water, Enoch!"

When Enoch didn't respond, Amos scrambled down the creek embankment to him. Small ripples of water flowed over the faded overalls Enoch was wearing. His battered old straw hat and one of his plowshoes he had been wearing was missing. Upon a dead tree branch that hung over the creek dangled his horse's saddle. Underneath the saddle, there was a swath of muddy earth that had broken loose from the embankment where the horse must have slid down into the water.

"Enoch fell off-a his hoss and knocked hisself out," Amos called up to Webster, who was still standing on the creek bank. "You git on down heah and help me!"

Reluctantly, Webster scrambled down into the creek. Amos motioned for him to get Enoch's feet. Webster waded in the chilly water over to Enoch and took hold of his feet, then Amos took hold of his shoulders.

As they lifted him up, water and pebbles poured from his soaked over-alls. Carefully, they turned him over and Webster saw Enoch's face. He was barely recognizable! His bruised face was puffed up around his big swollen eyelids. A huge knot protruded from his forehead and one tooth dangled from the side of his lips. His hair was matted down with bits of leaves. From his ripped-open shirt, Webster saw scratches and bruises from his neck down into his chest.

Suddenly, pieces of men's faces blown to bits from the dynamite blast flashed into Webster's mind! He cringed in terror, dropping Enoch's feet. "They're dead!" Webster screamed.

"Is you crazy, boy?" Amos yelled. "Enoch ain't dead! Enoch's drunk! Git back hold of them feets!"

"Dead! Dead! Dead!" Webster screamed again and again.

Amos didn't know that Webster was hallucinating about the men in the boat. He thought Webster was referring to Enoch. Squinting his eyes from the bright rays of the sun, Amos saw Enoch's twisted bruised face and believed he was dead. He yelled in horror and dropped the head.

Enoch's body fell back into the creek with a thud as Amos slipped on a wet rock and fell backwards. Amos clawed at the creek bed trying to get up. Again and again he tried to stand up, but each time he slipped on the wet rocks.

While Amos was trying to right himself, Webster, who was screaming hysterically in the cold water, came to his senses and stopped. It was then that he heard a faint sound. Shaking violently, he waded over to Enoch's head and heard a low guttural moan coming from him.

Webster looked back and saw Amos struggling in the water trying to stand up. One of his arms was stretched up toward the sky as if he were praying, and with his other arm Amos tried to get his balance. "Poor Enoch! Poor Enoch!" he kept saying over and over.

When Amos finally managed to stand up, he came over to Webster, weeping copiously and shaking his head mournfully, as he looked down at Enoch. "This be a ter'ble way for Enoch to go! He musta broke his neck when he fell. I never thought, Enoch, you would go this way!"

"Enoch's not dead," Webster said solemnly.

Looking startled, Amos sputtered, "He . . . you . . . he . . . ?"

"He's not dead," Webster repeated.

"How . . . how you know he ain't dead? He look dead."

Webster pointed to Enoch's moving lips as he moaned again. The sound was barely audible.

"Git hold of his feets," Amos quickly commanded. "I'll take his head. We got to git Enoch home and in his warm bed!"

With as much speed as they could muster in the slippery creek bed, the two men lifted Enoch up out of the water and, struggling to keep their footing on the eroding creek bank, they made their way up the embankment. There they rushed with Enoch back up the path, through the woods, to his house.

By the time they reached the house, Enoch's moaning and groaning was louder and he was moving his head from side to side. Without stopping to open the kitchen door, Amos kicked it open with his foot, and he and Webster rushed headlong through the kitchen.

"We put him in your bed," Amos told Webster.

When Webster looked as if he were questioning Amos' decision, he explained, "We can't lay Enoch in the bed with your sick maw."

They went into Webster's room and quickly laid Enoch on the bed and stripped off his water-soaked overalls and his shirt. When Webster jerked off the one plowshoe, Enoch gave a loud moan.

Enoch's legs and feet had turned purplish. Upon seeing this, Amos announced, "Snakebites!" He rushed over to a trunk in Webster's room where Bessie kept her extra quilts stacked. He grabbed two quilts and covered Enoch from head to toe.

"Git Caleb!" he barked to Webster.

Caleb was called upon to administer medicine whenever a person or an animal became sick or injured in Smyrna. Dr. Baker was the only doctor in Cowpens who would treat black people and Cowpens was ten miles away. When Dr. Baker was busy with his patients in Cowpens, he refused to make the trip to Smyrna.

Smyrna didn't have a doctor or a hospital. Cowpens' General was the nearest hospital, and it had set aside just five beds in its basement for black people. These beds were seldom empty. The people in Smyrna had come to rely on Caleb, who had spent a year in a medical college when he was a young man.

Just as Webster ran to his bedroom door, Bessie was standing there holding onto the threshold to steady herself. She had been awakened by all the commotion in Webster's bedroom and came to find out what was going on. When she saw Amos covering up Enoch, she rushed pass Webster to the bed and collapsed in a faint.

It was all Webster could do to keep her from crashing onto Enoch. As he held onto his mother, Webster became frightened that his mother may have suffered a stroke. With Amos' help, they got Bessie back to her bed. Webster began slapping her on the cheeks trying to revive her.

Suddenly, Bessie came to and cried. "Enoch's gone and left me!" Then she began weeping hysterically.

Webster put his arms around her. "Ma," he said softly, "stop crying! Enoch's not dead. He just hurt himself."

It took a few minutes for Bessie to stop crying. When she did, she remarked that she thought she had lost Enoch. "Thank God you come home in time, Webster, to help save Enoch! Go git Reverend Bates so we can have a prayer meeting!"

As Webster left Bessie's room, Amos reminded him to get Caleb and forget about Reverend Bates. He could come later. Right now, Enoch needed medicine, not prayer.

As Webster ran up the road to Caleb's store, he was acutely aware that things at home had not changed. Here was his poor ma sick in bed, probably from being overworked, and Enoch still getting drunk. Enoch caused his mother so much pain! He didn't like Enoch before he went up to the hills, and he still didn't like him now that he was back.

Webster remembered how when he was a little boy he prayed every night that God would kill Enoch. After Enoch didn't die, he stopped believing in God because God didn't answer his prayers.

When he told Bessie about his prayers, she said, "God don't work like that. God wants you and Enoch to love one another. God ain't in the business of smiting down folks just 'cause you want it. What you thank God is anyway?"

At the store, Webster told Caleb that Enoch had been badly hurt and he needed to come right away. The old man quickly got his black bag and put some bottles and bandages in it, and hurried off with Webster.

Amos explained to Caleb when he arrived that, at first, he thought Enoch had broken his neck, but when he saw the condition of his legs he believed Enoch had been bitten by a rattlesnake.

After Caleb had examined Enoch, he determined that he had not been bitten by a rattlesnake and his neck was not broken. His legs, however, had been badly bruised, and his ankles were sprained from the fall.

"Heat some water," Caleb told Webster. "Amos, go cut me two thin splints of wood."

When the water was hot, Webster brought it to Caleb, who dabbed first at Enoch's face with a washrag until he had cleaned all the debris off. He also cleaned out his nose and his ears. Enoch gasped loudly when Caleb yanked out his dangling tooth with a pair of pliers. Then he took a tin can of smelly salve from his black bag and gently rubbed some on the bruises and scratches on Enoch's face, neck, and chest. Next, he washed Enoch's legs with the hot water. Then he poured some whiskey into a bottle of his special mixture, shook the bottle vigorously, and saturated Enoch's swollen legs and feet with it.

When Amos came with the splints, Caleb bound the splints to Enoch's legs to keep them straight.

The last thing Caleb tried to do was to give Enoch a spoonful of his medicine. Every time the medicine touched Enoch's lips, he shook his head from side to side causing it to spill. Becoming exasperated, Caleb had Amos hold open Enoch's mouth, and he forced a spoonful of his medicine into it. Enoch gagged, but Amos wouldn't let him spit out the medicine.

"Bathe him and put a nightshirt on him," Caleb told Amos as he was leaving. "I'll come back tomorrow and take a look at his legs."

"When's Enoch gone be talking'?" Amos asked anxiously.

Caleb chuckled. "He'll be calling for his breakfast in the morning. The medicine I gave him will settle his stomach and make him eat like a horse. It's a good thing Enoch's a drinking man. That whiskey kept him from catching pneumonia while being out in the elements."

"When's he goin' be up and 'bout?" Amos asked.

"In a week or two," Caleb replied, "but he'll have to use a stick for awhile."

For the next week, Webster cared for Bessie and Enoch with the help of Tessa, who came over in the mornings, cooked the breakfast, and gave Bessie her bath. Tessa positively refused to do anything for Enoch. She said if he wasn't such a womanizer he wouldn't be in the fix he was in. It was left up to Webster to look after Enoch.

One morning after Webster had brought Enoch his breakfast, Enoch told Webster to go to Mush Creek and bring Jonny Bluebaby to the house.

Jonny Bluebaby had come to Mush Creek a few years before, and soon men in Smyrna were whispering that Jonny Bluebaby had a tonic that increased men's virility. One bottle was all a man needed to take, and he'd feel like a young man in his prime.

Even though he knew what Enoch wanted, Webster still asked, "Why you want to see Jonny Bluebaby?"

Enoch looked to the door to see where Tessa was, then glanced down at a bulge between his legs that was sticking up under his nightshirt. In a near whisper he said, "I be needin' lots of help when I git outta this bed."

A wave of disdain swept over Webster. He knew Enoch was up to his old self again, wanting a loose woman. "What kind of help?" he said in a loud voice.

"You got a big mouth, boy," Enoch snapped. "You just do as I say."

"The hell I will," Webster replied and snatched up the tray that had empty dishes on it from Enoch's breakfast and stalked out of his room.

"Bastard," he mumbled when he reached the kitchen. Here he was taking care of Enoch and all he could think of was having sex with some woman.

After Webster had washed the breakfast dishes, he told Bessie he was going to Caleb's store to buy a box of salt. He didn't need salt. He just wanted to get out of the house to cool off.

After purchasing the salt, Webster went downstairs to Amos' quarters.

"How's the sick?" Amos inquired when he saw Webster descending the stairs.

"Ma's better."

"Ain't you got somebody else sick at home?"

"You mean the sonofabitch, Enoch?"

"Hey," Amos said, "wait a minute. Why you callin' your pa a sono-fabitch?"

"Cause that's what he is," Webster replied matter-of-factly. "You know what Enoch is thinking about? Not about Ma getting well, but about him being with a woman!"

A sly smile curled up at the corners of Amos' mouth. "What so bad 'bout him wantin' to be with your ma?" he asked. "They be husband and wife."

"He's not wanting to be with Ma, Amos, and you know it. He wants a loose woman and needs Jonny Bluebaby's tonic. Bastard! I hope he takes that tonic and it blows him up like a watermelon!"

Amos dissolved into laughter. "Ole Enoch gittin' ready, and he ain't even walkin' good!"

"'Cause he's a sonofabitch!" Webster repeated.

"Aw, stop being so mad," Amos said. "Enoch ain't all bad. You and me ain't got a right to judge Enoch. You see, ole Mother Nature done give Enoch a lot of natures. Ain't nothin' he kin do 'bout it. Jest look on his good side."

Amos paused for a moment to put a piece of chewing tobacco in his mouth. After he had chewed on the tobacco for a few minutes, he asked, "What did Mrs. Au Bignon want with your ma?"

Surprised, Webster answered, "Mrs. Au Bignon?"

"Yeah," Amos responded. "She used to own Margrace, but I heah she went to live in Cowpens. She sent her buggy the other week for your ma so she could come see her."

Webster said his mother hadn't told him about seeing Mrs. Au Bignon. As a matter of fact, his mother had never spoken about Mrs. Au Bignon. How did Amos know his mother had seen this woman? Amos quickly told him that Tessa had mentioned it to him, but he didn't want Webster telling Bessie because he didn't want to get Tessa in trouble. He just thought Bessie may have told Webster about her visit.

"Ma's been too sick to talk about things," Webster said. "When she's well, she'll tell me if she wants to."

When Webster returned home from the store, he found Bessie on her knees at her bedside praying. He waited until she had finished praying and then entered her room.

Bessie had climbed back into her bed and, upon seeing Webster, she patted on the bed. "Come set down heah," she told him. "I want to talk to you."

When Webster had sat down, Bessie began, "I'm glad you came home. I was beginnin' to thank you wouldn't come back."

"Ma, you know better than that," Webster replied.

"Well, you did come back and I thank God for that." Bessie was silent for a few minutes, then added, "I been prayin' and askin' God to show me what to do. And today, the Word is clear: Seek the truth and it will set you free! It's time I set you free."

Webster knew his mother was a religious woman and often quoted the Bible, but this sounded ominous to him. Was his mother going to tell him she was going to die? If so, he didn't want to hear it. He reached over and took her by the hand. "Ma, you're still weak and talking will eat up your strength."

"I'm strong now and gittin' stronger every day," Bessie responded. "God done took care of that ole flu bug. No, I got to tell you now what's been on my mind for eighteen years. That's a long time to carry around a big burden."

Webster tried to dissuade her from talking but couldn't. She would have her say.

"You been wantin' to know since you was a little boy who your folks wuz." When Webster tried to deny it, Bessie said, "Now, I knowed for a long time you been sneakin' 'round askin' questions."

"I found out," Webster finally admitted. "Ozell told me a long time ago."

"Ozell told you what I told Tessa."

"Ain't that the truth?" Webster asked.

Bessie hesitated for a few minutes, then replied, "Well, part of that be true and part of that is a lie." She paused. "Go over there to the trunk and get me that brown envelope I put in there."

Webster found the brown envelope and brought it back to Bessie.

Bessie began running her fingers up and down the envelope as if she was undecided about revealing its content. "I started to tear up this envelope," she said. "God told me not to." She sighed deeply and looked lovingly at Webster. "You been livin' in a make-believe bubble, a bubble I blew. Now, I got to bust that bubble."

"Ma," Webster protested, "I don't know what you're talking about, and I don't want to know."

"You got to know," Bessie insisted. "You're a man now, eighteen years old, and if you keep on livin' in that bubble, your life ain't going be nothin' but lies."

Seeing it was useless to stop his mother from telling him what was on her mind, Webster shrugged and said, "All right, Ma, tell me." He knew when Bessie wanted to do something, nothing stopped her.

Then to Webster's surprise, Bessie abruptly changed the conversation. "Now that you've made some money from that job," she said, "I want you to git on to Philadelphia to school, like you promised."

"I mean to do that, but I haven't saved enough," Webster replied. "But you were talking about something else, Ma."

"Yes, I was," Bessie replied thoughtfully. "While you wuz gone, I went out to Cowpens."

"Why did you go there?" Webster asked her.

"Mrs. Au Bignon was in the hospital and she sent for me."

When Bessie saw that Webster looked puzzled, she explained. "Mrs. Au Bignon was that rich white woman who owned Margrace. The plantation where your pa and Amos lived."

"Yes, Ma. I know about that slave plantation," Webster reminded her.

"Oh, Margrace is such a beautiful place!" Bessie said. "A big white mansion filled with fine furniture! And all around it there is grass, flowers, and blooming trees! Why there's a duck pond on the grounds and a whole lot of other buildings all painted white. Margrace just takes my breath away!"

Sounding a bit impatient, Webster said, "Ma, I know where Margrace is and I know how beautiful it is."

"How you know that?"

"When I was little, me and Ozell used to sneak up there and play in the woods behind the grounds. Now, will you go on with your story?"

"Oh yes, I was tellin' you how I got this envelope. Mrs. Au Bignon was real sick, and dying. She wanted me to have this envelope."

Believing his mother to be stalling, Webster wanted to speed things up. All this procrastinating was causing Webster to become tense. "What's in the envelope?"

"Something you need to see," Bessie answered.

She handed the envelope to Webster, who just stared at it. He was afraid to find out what was in it. Whatever it was, it had to be bad news. Why else was his mother taking so long to give it to him? Bessie motioned for him to open the envelope. He did and pulled out a letter. With his voice quivering, Webster asked, "You want me to read this?" Bessie nodded her head. Webster's hand trembled as he unfolded a handwritten letter in spidery writing. He couldn't imagine what the letter revealed. Fearing the worst, he read the letter in silence.

"Dear Webster,

"I am dying, and before I go, I must write you this letter. I cannot keep this secret any longer. Bessie tells me she named you Webster. That's a real strong name. I have thought about you every day since you were born. My deep regret is that I was not able to see you grow up. Once I saw you with Bessie in Cowpens. What a beautiful child you were! I wanted to rush over and take you in my arms, but I dared not do that! Why did I want to hug and kiss you? You see, dear boy, you are my grandson! You are an Au Bignon! One of the finest families in the state!

"Let me explain why this is true. Dolly, my only child, was your mother. I couldn't keep you because your father was a black man, and, as you know, the mingling of the races is absolutely forbidden by law! I cannot justify these cruel laws, but that is the way it is here in North Carolina.

"I found you a loving mother, Bessie. And from what she tells me you've turned out to be a fine young man! Perhaps, you are wondering who your father was? Dolly, my only child, your mother, never revealed that to me. She took that secret to her grave.

"Now, Dolly, and my husband Karl, your grandfather, are both dead and I will be joining them soon. Before I meet my Maker, I want to right the wrong that was done to you because your father was a black man. Bessie tells me you want to go to college, so I am giving you a large sum of money for you to do that.

"I bought back my beloved Margrace, the home where I was born, that has been in my family for four generations. It's where I grew up and lived so happily. Now, I am passing Margrace to you and your loving

372

mother, Bessie. I am giving Margrace and all my money to you because you are my rightful heir and to Bessie for loving and caring for my grandson all these years without any compensation from me. God bless you both. Mary Eliza Calhoun Au Bignon."

Webster slowly put the letter back in the brown envelope and laid it on the bed next to Bessie, who waited anxiously for him to say something. His throat was so tight that he could only manage to say, "I'll give it back."

"You'll do no such thing," Bessie said, and reminded him that Margrace was now his inheritance and he had to keep it.

Webster couldn't stand any more talk. He felt he was going to explode. He rushed out of Bessie's room, through the kitchen, and out into the backyard and ran behind the shed where Enoch kept his horse. He fell down on the ground numb from what he had learned. He felt stunned and angry, angry at the rich, powerful Au Bignons who had lived in splendor as a poor black midwife struggled week after week, year after year, trying to keep bread on the table for their black grandson!

What kind of people would discard a child, their flesh and blood, because of the color of his skin? They never once lifted a finger to help Bessie feed and clothe him, and they had millions. And now that Mrs. Au Bignon was dying, she wanted to square herself with God by giving him her money because she'd have no further use for it.

"I hope she burns in hell!" Webster said aloud. "I hope that whole damn Au Bignon family burns in hell!"

Bessie wasn't surprised at Webster's reaction. For eighteen years, he believed his mother was a poor Indian girl, and now he had learned the truth. His mother was a rich white woman. The shock of it all must have been overwhelming! It had caused him to want to give back his inheritance.

But she wasn't going to give back Margrace, nor would she let Webster give back the money to Mrs. Au Bignons' greedy lawyers!

As Bessie lay there waiting for Webster to return, she reminisced about the day she met these lawyers in Mrs. Au Bignon's hospital room. She had heard them arguing with Mrs. Au Bignon, trying to convince her not to give Webster his rightful inheritance!

No, Bessie thought, she'd keep Margrace for the people of Smyrna in memory of the slaves who had toiled year after year with bent backs and gnarled hands on that plantation under conditions too harsh to describe. These men and women were pushed to their limits by Brute, Karl Au Bignon's cruel overseer, as they planted, cultivated, and harvested the crops that earned millions for the Au Bignons.

The vast plantation of Margrace was a constant reminder to the people of Smyrna of things past. It remained a symbol of slavery and injustices done to the men and women who had lived, worked, and died there. How ironic that this vestige of slavery was being passed on to a black woman, a former slave.

Bessie decided as she lay there that Margrace's buildings would be made into a hospital for the sick and a college so that the young people of Smyrna could be educated and have a better chance at life. The land would be offered as farms to black people who had been displaced and made homeless after the Civil War.

Bessie closed her eyes and remembered the night Enoch had told her that Mrs. Au Bignon had promised him freedom to marry her if they would take care of a baby. The baby's father was black and the mother white, and that's all she told them.

In addition to Enoch's freedom, Mrs. Au Bignon promised them a small sum of money to buy some land and build a house in Smyrna. To get these offers, they had to swear never to tell who gave them the baby. If they did, there'd be consequences!

Bessie, who loved Enoch and wanted him for her husband, agreed to take the baby. So, on an August night, she went with Enoch to the Margrace mansion.

Mrs. Au Bignon was sitting alone on the darkened veranda holding a baby. When she heard Bessie and Enoch coming, she rushed from the veranda and met them. She quickly thrust the baby in Bessie's arms and handed Enoch an envelope.

"The papers of manumission are in the envelope," she told Enoch, "and enough money to buy you a house. You're not to ever come back to Margrace, nor speak of this," she warned. "If you do, my husband will have some men pay you a night visit."

Fearing that Au Bignon would take away his freedom, Enoch and Bessie swore never to tell anyone the truth about the baby. Bessie concocted the story about Webster's mother being an Indian girl and his father being a white man and told that to her friend, Tessa.

Bessie didn't need to know who the baby's parents were, because she had fallen in love with him at first sight and was thankful to Mrs. Au Bignon for giving her the two things she loved dearly, the man she loved and a baby she would love.

Her hardships in bringing up Webster had been worth it, and she had no regrets. Each day she thanked God for Enoch and Webster, for without them her life would have been empty indeed.

And after that clandestine meeting that night, eighteen years ago, Bessie never once thought that one day she'd be a rich woman, owner of Margrace!

Then Bessie's thoughts wandered off to Smyrna and its very beginning. Smyrna had come about because Mary Pettigrew, a Christian white woman, believed slavery was wrong in the eyes of God and, after her husband's death, she manumitted his slaves Bessie, Tessa, Nate, Scully, and Ben. Not only did Mary manumit Will Pettigrew's slaves, but she also made his plantation a free settlement for black people.

Bessie and Tessa named Smyrna for the slave woman who freed herself from Will Pettigrew. This black woman refused to give up her identity and her humanity by not allowing a white slaveholder to change her name. Since the settlement's beginnings, many people had made sacrifices for it to grow and to become a safe haven for black people. It, however, still needed help.

Webster had been sitting behind the shed for hours trying to come to grips with what he had read. The more he thought about the letter, the angrier he became. How could racial heritage become so important that a mother would give away her own child? He felt deeply betrayed by his birth mother and from the mother who raised him.

He felt betrayed because he had been led to believe his mother was Indian and his father a white man. Now, his world had been turned upside down. The real truth was out, and it was hard for him to cope with it. In his mind, he blamed Enoch and Bessie for not telling him. Didn't they realize how important it was for him to know who he was?

Webster had been sitting behind the shed for several hours. His thoughts turned to Noah. Already he was missing him. Then he remembered some words Noah told him about what a family meant. "Real folks be the ones who love you and brang you up. Lookin' for somebody else is lack grass in the wind."

There was little doubt in Webster's mind that Bessie loved him and had worked hard to bring him up. Perhaps it was time for him to forget about who his folks were and acknowledge his real parents, Bessie and Enoch, and in the words of Noah, "Stop searchin' for grass in the wind."

Sitting behind the shed, Webster decided he'd take his inheritance and use some of the money to go on to college, as Bessie so desperately wanted him to do.

It was near midnight when Webster came to the sleeping Bessie's bed. He leaned down and gave her a big kiss.

Bessie opened her eyes and saw Webster's smiling face looking down at her. "Ma," he said softly, "I hope my real pa's name is Noah."

Puzzled, Bessie quizzed, "Noah?"

Webster wanted so much to tell Bessie about his chance meeting with Noah. But it was better left untold, so he just smiled and said, "It's a good name."

"Yeah," Bessie agreed, "Noah's in the Bible."

Glossary

1. rootworker: one who uses special roots to cast spells
2. paddyroller: slave catcher
3. jumpin' the broom: getting married
4. jackleg preacher: a pretend preacher
5. black Indians: one whose heritage is Indian and black
6. raise the hymn: giving the key in which to sing
7. fire-eater: people in the South who wanted to go to war
8. bootleg whiskey: illegally made whiskey
9. creesy greens: wild plants similar to turnip greens
10. Blanche K. Bruce: black U.S. senator from Mississippi (1875–1881)